W9-CFQ-120

A Song
to Die For

BY MIKE BLAKELY
from Tom Doherty Associates

Comanche Dawn

Come Sundown

Dead Reckoning

The Last Chance

Moon Medicine

Shortgrass Song

The Snowy Range Gang

Spanish Blood

Summer of Pearls

Too Long at the Dance

Vendetta Gold

What Are the Chances
(with Kenny Rogers)

A Song to Die For

MIKE BLAKELY

A Tom Doherty Associates Book

New York

A SONG TO DIE FOR

A Forge Book
Published by Tom Doherty Associates, LLC
175 Fifth Avenue
New York, NY 10010

www.tor-forge.com

Forge® is a registered trademark of Tom Doherty Associates, LLC.

The Library of Congress Cataloging-in-Publication Data is available upon request.

ISBN 978-0-7653-2751-2 (hardcover)
ISBN 978-1-4299-4489-2 (e-book)

Forge books may be purchased for educational, business, or promotional use. For information on bulk purchases, please contact the Macmillan Corporate and Premium Sales Department at 1-800-221-7945, extension 5442, or write to specialmarkets@macmillan.com.

First Edition: November 2014

Printed in the United States of America

0 9 8 7 6 5 4 3 2 1

Dedicated to the memory of
two great American songwriters:

Floyd Tillman (1914–2003)

and

Steven Fromholz (1945–2014)

Acknowledgments

For sharing their stories of the music business and the honky-tonk trail, I am indebted to Floyd Tillman and Steven Fromholz, and to the coauthors of two of my previous books, Willie Nelson and Kenny Rogers. Special thanks to Alex Harvey for his keen insight on songwriting.

For the detailed accounts from his career as a twentieth-century Texas Ranger, I express my gratitude to Joaquin Jackson.

I also owe a debt to several friends who served in Vietnam and who recounted their personal wartime experiences. In particular, I thank cowboy, soldier, rancher, teacher, and coach Wayne Neely for allowing me to fictionalize many details from his real-life Vietnam service.

A Song to Die For

CHAPTER

1:10 A.M.

Creed Mason shut the guitar case on his Fender Stratocaster and secured the latches. Feeling the sweat-drenched satin plastered to his skin, he unbuttoned the flashy purple shirt, took it off, and reached for the stack of clean white towels placed there for band members.

Backstage smelled of stale beer and sweat, whiskey and perfume, smoke from store-bought cigarettes and hand-rolled joints. He could still hear the hum of the crowd filing out of the Armadillo World Headquarters, the hottest music venue in Austin, Texas. Laughter erupted among the musicians backstage, punctuated by profanity, the clinking of bottles, the squeals of starstruck women, and someone banging on an acoustic guitar.

He toweled off and reached for the spare denim shirt he had brought along with him, but before he could put it on, he heard her voice behind him.

"Damn, Creed, what happened to you there?" A well-known, oft-used Austin groupie, she called herself Shine.

He winced a little at the intrusion of her cool fingers touching the scar on his lower back. He pulled the shirt on before she could see the much-worse exit-wound scar in front. "Shot in 'Nam," he said, buttoning up the shirt as he turned to face her.

"Oh . . ." She stared glassy-eyed, beautiful even if she was wasted. "Great show tonight." She smiled, long blond hair falling all over her tie-dyed tank top.

"Thanks, Shine." He was relieved to see Willie approaching. "Excuse me. Gotta get paid." He grabbed the brim of his felt Silver Belly Stetson and slapped it onto his head with familiarity, simultaneously raking his brown hair back behind his ears. The hat fit so well that he could scarcely feel it on his head. An East Texas version of the cowboy hat, he had seen its like worn by cattlemen, farmers, loggers, and deputy sheriffs when he was growing up in the Piney Woods near the Louisiana border. He side-stepped Shine to greet the night's headliner.

Willie, a respected Texas songwriter, had turned his back on Nashville and had taken Austin by storm lately. He had called and asked Creed to sit in with him tonight on the Armadillo World Headquarters stage. He handed over a wad of bills. "Wish it was more. You played my ass off."

Creed chuckled. "I appreciate the gig, Willie. Call me anytime."

"When you goin' back to Nashville?" Willie handed him a smoking joint.

Creed pretended to take a polite drag and handed it back. "Don't know. Feel like I've been blackballed there."

Willie's laughter came out in smoke. "Join the club. Hey, come on back to the bus later."

Creed held up the folding money Willie had just handed to him. "Thanks, but you just staked me to a poker game south of town. I better get down there if I want in on the action."

"Wish I could go with you, but I'm too damn popular here." He flashed a smile. "Good luck, Creed."

Someone pulled Willie aside, and Creed grabbed his guitar case handle.

Good luck, he thought. He could sure use some of that. He was overdue, in fact. Maybe, just maybe—starting with the great gig tonight—his luck was going to change.

Creed was respected among the Austin musicians as a true talent, and as a guy who had had his brush with the big time, having taken a hit record to number eight on the country music charts. That was eight years ago, and a lot had happened since. Mostly hard luck.

Born William Mason, the eldest son in a large family, he had demonstrated precocious skills with musical instruments as early as the age of five. His father, an East Texas logger and guitar picker, had encouraged him. Later, his father would be quoted in the *Music City News*, saying, "Bill—or Creed as y'all call him—was so good that none of his younger brothers or sisters would even try to play a musical instrument. They just couldn't keep up with him."

Young Bill Mason started his first band in the eighth grade. By the time he was in high school, he was performing at dances most Friday and Saturday nights. Playing for a high school prom at a nearby town, Bill

Mason met a strikingly gorgeous senior named Jo Ann Houston. She asked if she could sing a song with the band. The song she chose was, of course, "Crazy," the Patsy Cline hit.

"You know how many chick singers it takes to sing 'Crazy'?" he had asked her.

"No, how many?" she had replied.

"Apparently every damn one of 'em."

Jo Ann Houston had placed her hands on her hips and smirked at the young band leader. "Just give me the microphone, hotshot," she said in her Piney Woods twang, "because you ain't never heard nobody sing 'Crazy' like me. Not even Patsy."

Taking the stage, Jo Ann did not disappoint Bill Mason, or the audience. After that night, she became the guest girl singer for the band, and took to the honky-tonks and dance halls as if she had been born performing. One night, coming home from a gig, she asked Bill to pull the car over on a dirt road in the woods. She didn't have to coax much to lure him into the backseat.

After that, Bill began to work in more songs for her to sing, including some duets for the two of them to sing together. They found that they had a natural charisma onstage. Mostly it was Jo Ann putting on a show, and Bill following her lead, but he liked the way she drew attention to his guitar picking. They evolved from a band that played background music for dancers, to a stage show that fans liked to watch as much as listen to. Jo Ann was definitely an eyeful onstage, and dressed the part—scantily— employing all of her assets to her best advantage. They changed the name of the act to Mason-Houston, and left for Nashville soon after they both graduated from high school, though the rest of the band members refused to go.

The competition in Music City stunned Bill, but he learned quickly from some great guitarists, and became recognized as a raw talent, especially in tandem with Jo Ann. He found employment fixing diesels, having worked summers at his uncle's diesel shop. Jo Ann tended bar. Barely able to pay the rent and buy groceries, they were nonetheless ambitious and confident. Lovemaking in the tiny apartment was raucous and almost as frequent as their nightly rehearsals.

In Nashville, Bill met some great songwriters, including a fellow Texan named Willie—the guy who had written that Patsy Cline hit "Crazy." Inspired, Bill began to write songs and came up with an upbeat duet for himself and Jo Ann called "Written in the Dust." They made a demo and shopped it around town to the artists-and-repertoire executives at the major recording labels. The year was 1966, the top act in country music was Buck Owens and the Buckaroos, and there were some two dozen record labels in town. Just three weeks after cutting the demo for "Written in the Dust," after a high-energy showcase in a Printer's Alley nightclub, one of the A&R execs they had met approached Bill and Jo Ann.

"I had to make sure your live show stood up to the demo," he said. "I like what I see here. I want you two in my office at nine o'clock tomorrow morning to sign a development deal."

Bill and Jo Ann signed hastily, before they could even think about securing representation from lawyers or agents. Years later, Bill would hear rumors that Jo Ann had cinched the deal the same way she had secured her place in Bill's band in East Texas—in the A&R guy's backseat, down a dirt road outside of Nashville. There would be a lot of rumors like that about Jo Ann.

The label chose the rest of the songs for the first album and rushed the LP into production. "Written in the Dust" was slated as the single, much to Bill's gratification. Publicity photos were shot, promo material written by marketing staffers, tour dates booked. A week before the street date for the release of the single, A&R invited Bill and Jo Ann to the label office to see their new album cover.

"Wow," Bill said, truly impressed by the cover photo. "Jo Ann, you look killer, baby."

"You got a *thang* goin' on, too, hotshot." She always called him "hotshot."

Bill stared at the cover a little longer, now taking in the only two words of text: "Dixie Creed."

"I don't get the title," he said. "We didn't cut a song called 'Dixie Creed.' And where's 'Mason-Houston' gonna go?"

The A&R exec flashed a straight-toothed smile. "It's self-titled. The new name for the act is Dixie Creed. We changed your name to Creed Mason, and Jo Ann's name to Dixie Houston."

"Whoa, now," Bill argued. "My folks named me William Mason. Not *Creed*. Who names a kid Creed?"

"Be realistic," the suit said. "How are we going to market Bill and Jo Ann? We're letting you keep your last names."

"Well, what if we don't go along with it?"

The A&R man grabbed a stack of publicity photos and flipped them out across his desk like a card dealer. "Then we scrap your project and put your marketing budget into one of these acts instead. Your choice."

Bill looked at Jo Ann, who had stayed out of the argument. "What do you think, Jo Ann?"

She had shrugged. "Call me *Dixie . . . Creed.*"

On the road, promoting the album at small venues and country radio stations, Dixie began carrying a stash of marijuana whenever she could acquire the stuff from fans. Creed didn't mind. He had smoked the weed before and considered it pretty harmless. He even enjoyed it in moderation. Dixie liked it a lot more, but it never seemed to affect her performances, nor did the whiskey they typically started slamming with the onset of every show.

"Written in the Dust" began to climb on the charts, and Dixie Creed got an invitation to open a big show for none other than Buck Owens. The opener went well and led to a string of tour dates with Buck and the Buckaroos. Their album sales soared. The first pressing quickly sold through, and another twenty thousand were packaged and shipped to distributors nationwide. "Written in the Dust" peaked at number eight—not a bad start for a new band. The label started clambering for more material and a second album before Dixie Creed even got in off the road.

Reality waited back at their Nashville apartment. Creed found a stack of bills he couldn't pay, and a draft notice from Uncle Sam. His number had come up. He was to report to boot camp in three weeks.

Dixie threw a fit, as if it were his fault for getting drafted. "Why did you even register, you dipshit!"

"It's the law, and I ain't no draft dodger."

"You dumb-ass!" she wailed, pulling at her hair and raking dirty dishes off the kitchen counter like some insane woman.

The night before he left for basic training, Creed snuggled with her in bed, after making love to her for the last time. "I've been thinkin'," he said. "Maybe we should get married. If I get killed over there, you'll have benefits for life."

"Shut up," she said. "I ain't marryin' you. If you come back with your arms and legs blowed off, I don't want to have to wipe your ass." She cackled loudly as if her laughter could compensate for her lack of tact.

"Jesus, Jo Ann . . ."

"It's Dixie, damn it. Hey, I's just kiddin.' You'll be fine. Come home a war hero and we'll go right back into the studio."

Willie's bass player slapped Creed on the shoulder, and his thoughts returned to backstage at the Armadillo. The bassist gave him a thumbs-up sign, and Creed shot a cocky smile back. Just for a moment, he thought he smelled Dixie's perfume. It was as if she had just been standing there. But no . . . That part of his life was over . . .

CHAPTER

1:15 A.M.

Headlights appeared in her rearview mirror, and her fear surged again. It had come and gone in waves since she left Las Vegas, sixteen hours ago, headed for a sorority sister's place in Austin. Her speedometer hovered around eighty miles per hour, the engine and transmission of the Corvette singing a discordant harmony. Whoever that was gaining on her from behind had to be doing ninety-five.

Was it a cop, or was it *him*? The Fuzzbuster radar detector on her dashboard remained silent, suggesting a civilian vehicle on her tail. Maybe it was just another Texas cowboy driving way too fast in a pickup truck, headed home from a Friday-night rodeo or a wild spree at some dance hall. She hoped against hope that might be the case. She prayed the headlights did not belong to Franco.

Her mind seemed to whir like the tires on Highway 71, thinking about the terrifying turn her life had taken in the last couple days. Rosabella Martini was twenty-five years old. Born and raised in Las Vegas, Nevada, her mother had died of heart disease when she was only six. She grew up surrounded by lavish opulence, thanks to her father, successful restaurateur, Rob Martini, whose swank eateries fared well through the booming fifties and sixties in Vegas. Rosabella knew very well that she was a spoiled only child—a daddy's girl. She had boasted about it to her friends in high school, where she became the student council president, head cheerleader, and an all-state flautist.

When she turned eighteen, she began to worry about the possibility of inheriting her mother's heart condition. Her father dropped the bombshell as gently as he could. Rosa had been adopted. The blood that ran through her veins was Italian blood, he assured her, but it was not Martini family blood. Her mother had been too frail to carry a pregnancy to term, so her parents had adopted her from an agency.

"Not even I know who your birth mother was," her father had told her. "But she must have been a beauty, because, look at you. You're the most beautiful girl in the whole world."

It explained a lot. Her uncle Paulo, known as "Papa Martini," and his son, Franco, who was Rosa's adoptive cousin, ten years older than her, had never made more than halfhearted attempts to accept her as family. Franco had always remained especially cold toward her.

At her high school graduation party, Franco had told her, "So, I hear you're going to the University of Texas."

"Yeah," she replied, shocked that he was talking to her at all.

"When you get your degree, why don't you just stay in Texas. You're not one of the family and you never will be, so don't try."

That was her mistake. She had tried. She should have taken Franco's advice.

Rosa had returned to Las Vegas to work for her father after her graduation from UT-Austin in 1972. With her degree in interior design, she began remodeling and decorating her father's four restaurants, even winning a design award at the flagship business—Il Ristorante Martini—for the Tuscan motif she created. A month later, her father died in his sleep of a massive stroke. Rosa's grief, confusion, and emptiness led her to her uncle Paulo for solace.

But Papa Martini proved a poor comforter. His embraces were stiff, and brief. Her cousin Franco was even colder. They only wanted to talk about the restaurants her father had left her. "You don't know the food trade," Papa Martini insisted. "I'll pay you a fair market price. You can put the money into your little design studio."

"What do you want with dirty dishes?" Franco had added. "Freakin' doped-up waiters, crooked health inspectors. Stick with your ruffled pillows, Rosa."

Her whole life, Rosa had laughed off rumors that Papa Martini was some kind of Las Vegas mob boss, and that all the Martinis were mafiosi. "Why, because we're Italian?" she had often scoffed to her high school friends. True, Papa Martini tended toward seedier business ventures than her father's restaurants, including nightclubs, casinos, and even a topless joint or two. True, there had been charges pressed by jealous competitors, but no indictments, except for Franco's aggravated assault arrest. That matter was dropped when the plaintiff mysteriously disappeared.

"Chickenshit didn't have the guts to face me in court," Franco had said.

Of course, the rumor was that Franco had bumped the plaintiff off, but Rosa only rolled her eyes at that kind of talk. Yes, he carried a pistol, but only for protection as he often moved large sums of cash. Franco acted like a tough guy, but he was nothing more than his father's ramrod who sternly oversaw his many business concerns. For that reason, Rosa knew that Franco would do a better job at running her late father's restaurants than she could. And she could use the cash from the sale to upgrade her interior design studio. She decided to take her uncle up on the offer to sell out.

On Thursday—a day and a half ago—Rosa drove to Papa Martini's mansion unannounced to surprise him and Franco with her decision to sell. As she rounded the corner to the entry gate, she saw her uncle's Land Rover barreling away toward Rancho Drive. The choice of vehicle probably meant her uncle was going out to the ranch, for the roads were rough out on the piece of land her father and uncle had bought as a getaway years ago. She tried to catch up to the Land Rover, but got caught at a traffic light.

Rosa knew the code to the entry gate at her uncle's house, so she turned around and let herself into the complex. She saw Franco's Shelby GT parked in front of the house, so she used her key to enter.

"Hello? Franco?" She heard no reply. She checked her uncle's office. On a whim, she pressed the play button on his Code-A-Phone telephone recorder. There was one message, from Franco:

"Pop. I got the tree from the nursery. I'll meet you out there."

Rosa knew that "out there" meant the ranch. Her uncle Paulo had a penchant for planting trees around the ranch house. It was an hour's drive, but she had nothing better to do, and she was anxious to move forward with the sale of her late father's restaurants.

She drove back to her father's house, a few miles away on West Tropicana, left her Corvette there, and fired up the Jeep Wrangler, the vehicle she and her father always took to the ranch. Rosa hadn't been "out there" in months, and she missed the place. A ranch in name only, it consisted of a thousand acres of desert dirt and scrub rising to a pine-forested slope in the Spring Mountains, bordering the Humboldt-Toiyabe National Forest.

Her father had often taken her there as a little girl, and she had enjoyed hiking and horseback riding for miles in the national forest, and swimming in the pool her uncle had built in the yard. She thought the trip there, in her father's Jeep, would do her good.

On the way to the ranch, she began to get giddy, thinking what fun it was going to be to surprise her uncle, and her cousin Franco. The sale of the restaurants had begun to make her feel closer to them, standoffish as they were. She had even begun to believe she could win them over, and finally get them to accept her as family. She had no one else. No steady boyfriend, though she dated often enough. She had even lost touch with her high school friends and her sorority sisters from UT.

The sun was low in the sky as she eased up to the last ridge in the dirt road that led to the ranch house. The ridge would give her a view of the house and surrounding outbuildings from a couple hundred yards away. Suspecting her uncle and cousin might be lounging poolside this time of day, she decided to stop the Jeep and get out with her father's hunting binoculars to check out the scene from afar. She didn't want them to spot her from the pool, spoiling her surprise. Killing the motor of the Jeep, she felt the mountain quietude wash over her, and she was glad she had come. Gravel crunched under her sneakers as she walked up the road with the binoculars. She peeked over the ridge. She saw no one. Good. She might be able to coast up to the house undetected and surprise them.

Lifting the optics to her eyes, she saw that the diesel backhoe had been pulled out of the barn, and a hole had been dug in the backyard. Franco's four-wheel-drive Ford pickup was backed up to the hole, and a pine tree with a large root ball waited on the tailgate. Rosa smiled as she lowered the binoculars. Her uncle had nurtured a couple dozen saplings over the years. A man who liked to plant trees had to have a heart, she thought.

Just then, she heard the corrugated tin door fly open on the toolshed, and saw three men walk out of the dark interior of the little ramshackle building. The first man staggered as he stepped into the light. Rosa recognized the man. One of her uncle's top men, the manager of his largest casino: The Castilian. His name was Bert something-or-other. She knew him by his permanent limp, from an auto accident, she had been told. Bert couldn't bend his right knee, so his gait was easy to recognize, even as he stumbled out of the shed. Drunk already, this time of day? She shook her head and smirked, then raised the binoculars for a closer look.

Papa Martini and Franco followed close behind Bert. Franco was wiping his hands on a rag. As she focused the lenses, Rosa got a better look at Bert, and her breath caught in her throat. Blood covered his face and his shirt. Had he fallen? Was he that drunk? She thought she had better get to the house quick and help the men doctor Bert's injuries. But something urged her to watch a moment longer.

Papa Martini grabbed Bert's arm to guide him. But instead of going to the house, he led Bert to the edge of the hole that had been dug for the planting of the tree. The two men stopped there, and her uncle stepped aside. Franco came up behind Bert. He threw the rag he had been using to wipe his hands into the hole. Then he reached into the front of his trousers and pulled out his pistol. He put it to the back of Bert's head.

Bert's head jerked forward, spray flying from the exit wound in his forehead. By the time the crack of the gunshot reached Rosa, Bert had already buckled and fallen into the hole. She dropped the binoculars, her breath shuttering into her lungs. She placed both hands over her mouth to keep that breath from screaming out. She collapsed onto her hands and knees on the gravel road, partly from weakness, and partly because she didn't want them to spot her. One of the lenses from the binoculars had shattered, the pieces scattered on the gravel.

She lost track of time, trying to make sense of everything—the things she had heard and denied, the naive fool she had been, and what she had just witnessed. She heard the diesel engine of the backhoe start up, and peeked over the ridge again. The tree had been lowered into place on top of Bert's body, and Papa Martini was using the machine to fill in the hole around it with dirt. Franco was using a garden hose to spray the inside of the toolshed.

The diesel engine died, though there was dirt left to spread. The first wave of fear hit Rosa like an electrical shock. Had she been spotted? She froze, afraid to move, or even to breathe. Franco was rolling the garden hose. In the dry mountain air, sound carried easily. She heard her uncle shout:

"Hey, Franco! Take some rib eyes out of the freezer, will you?"

Franco waved. "Sure, Pop."

Shakily, Rosa grabbed the binoculars, backed away, and returned to the Jeep. She waited to hear the diesel tractor start back up before she cranked her motor.

Back in the city, Rosa retrieved her Corvette from her father's house, and went home to her own place. Then paranoia overwhelmed her, so she checked herself into a hotel downtown, using a fake name. She showered and wept, trembled and paced the floor. Finally, she slept. When she woke on Friday morning, she was no longer a Martini. She remembered that her father had gone to the ranch to plant trees in the past. When this was over, she was going to find her real mother and live happily ever after. Right now, she had no one.

Rosa had once dated a cop. Nice guy, good-looking, very athletic, but boring. She called him. "Jake? This is Rosa. Rosa . . . *Martini*." She had to spit the surname out, for it felt dirty in her mouth, like dust from the desert. "I need to talk to you at the police station."

Lieutenant Jake Harbaugh came to work early to meet Rosa in his office at 7:30 a.m. He smiled and hugged her. She broke from his embrace, and refused to make small talk with him. "I'm here to report a crime. I witnessed a murder." To her own amazement, she told the story methodically, coherently, and unemotionally. It was like listening to a TV documentary narrated by her own voice. When she was finished, she focused on Jake's face. He looked pale.

"Who else have you told?" he asked.

"No one."

"Good." Jake let out a great sigh and got up from his desk. "I've got to find my supervisor. Wait here, Rosa." He walked out of the office.

She sat there, feeling somewhat purged of the guilt and filth she knew she didn't deserve to suffer in the first place. She wondered about the witness protection program. She wondered why her real mother had given her up for adoption. She felt utterly alone and devoid of identity. After waiting a few minutes, Rosa stood and paced around Jake's office, which was adorned with all sorts of manly trophies: A mounted bighorn sheep head with glass eyes staring at nothing. A rainbow trout in perpetual rigor mortis on a pine board. Then there were the bronzed sports trophies for golf, basketball, baseball . . .

A team photo caught her eye. She was drawn to it as if it were a window out of her own little hell. Stepping closer, she saw about twenty guys in rugby uniforms. Jake was on the back row with the bigger men. A face leapt out at her from the front row of players. It was Franco. He was looking right at her, and smiling. He was holding the corner of a banner. One of Papa Martini's casinos was the team sponsor.

That was seventeen hours ago, and she had been running ever since. She could not shake the feeling that she had been followed from the police station, though no one vehicle had stayed in sight behind her. As she sped ever onward toward Austin, she had stopped only to gas up, visit the ladies room, grab some junk food, and to use a phone booth outside a Jack in the Box in Albuquerque.

She had remembered a sorority sister named Celinda Morales. They had partied together at the sorority house, but otherwise were not close friends. That was good. There was no link for Franco to follow. Rosa recalled that Celinda had grown up in a tough neighborhood in San Antonio, and had lost a little brother to gang violence. Her undergraduate degree was in criminology, and she had stayed at UT to attend law school. Celinda's ultimate goal was to go home and prosecute gangsters—she talked about it all the time.

From the phone booth outside the fast-food joint, Rosa had called information for Celinda's number, and had jotted it down in ink on the Jack in the Box receipt, which was stapled to the top of the burger bag. She stuffed a few French fries in her mouth and called Celinda.

"I need your help," she said after the obligatory niceties. "I don't have time to tell you why on the phone."

Celinda had given Rosa directions to her apartment building on Riverside Drive, just off Congress Avenue in Austin.

Now Rosa was an hour away from Celinda's place, tired, and worried about the headlights in the rearview mirror. It couldn't be Franco. It just couldn't . . . She had come so far. She choked the fear down in her throat and waited, hopefully, for some cowboy to barrel past her on this lonely stretch of blacktop outside of nowhere.

CHAPTER

1:20 A.M.

Carrying his Strat, Creed made his way to the backstage door at Armadillo World Headquarters, a couple of the players patting him on the back along the way. Stepping outside, he heard Shine's voice behind him again:

"Hey, where you goin', Creed?"

He spoke over his shoulder, without making eye contact with her. "Nowhere."

The broad-reaching honesty of his reply hit him hard as he walked away. *Nowhere.* Maybe there was a song in the idea. "Nowhereville," or something like that. He felt he had been residing there for quite some time.

Shine persisted. "Can I go?"

He continued walking. "You don't want to go where I'm goin', Shine."

She let him get three steps farther away. "Hey, how many babies *did* you kill in Vietnam?"

Creed knew her scorn was driven by drugs, booze, and his rejection of her advances, but the words cut deep. "None," he answered. "Just one grown man."

As he trudged toward his van in the band parking area, his memories whirled back to a time before he knew what war was like. That had all been changed by a simple draft notice. *Change* was an understatement. *Turned upside down* was more like it.

Reporting for duty in 1967, Creed had found himself faced with an unexpected decision. He could choose to go into the U.S. Army as a draftee, and serve only two years, trusting the army to pick his military occupation, which would probably be that of a frontline grunt with an M16. Or he could enlist for three years, and choose his own Military Occupational Specialty.

Creed was proud to serve his country, but he didn't have a death wish and he wasn't mad at any little men in the Southeast Asian jungles. He couldn't shake the idea that the music business had something special waiting for him in his future, and he didn't care to miss it, six feet deep in a military graveyard.

He decided to enlist for three years. He looked over the M.O.S. choices and found heavy-equipment operator listed. This was an honorable way off the front lines, he thought. And if it turned out he was wrong about a glorious music career awaiting him, he could always find work back home operating heavy machinery. He liked big diesel machines already. His grandfather had big tractors on the farm. He had learned the basics of diesel mechanics at his uncle's shop, and at the garage where he worked for a time in Nashville. If he had to do something as crazy as go to war, this at least seemed like a logical way to do it.

After boot camp, he spent months training at Fort Leonard Wood in Missouri, learning how to push things around with big diesel cats and road graders. In army slang, he became a "heavy junk" operator.

He landed at Cam Rahn Bay on a commercial TWA flight. His airline trip to war struck him as odd for a boy raised with images of D-Day beach landings and paratrooper jumps in World War II flicks. With his first whiff of Southeast Asian air, he knew he was nowhere near Kansas anymore. The place smelled dank, damp, mildewed, and rotten. It took days to get accustomed to the strange odors.

Corporal William Mason's next set of orders sent him to a place called Chu Lai, for a booby trap and mine sweeping course. It was here that he discovered he would be using his bulldozer, as often as not, to explode enemy land mines. *Great.* The army bestowed upon him the lofty title of "combat engineer" and issued Creed orders for Fire Base Bronco south of Chu Lai.

When he arrived at Fire Base Bronco, also known as Duc Pho for the village located nearby, Creed could tell he was finally in the middle of the war. The soldiers stared weirdly here and the mood was somber. Morale consisted of the short-timers taunting him about the certainty of his impending death. They would sing a bastardized version of "Camp Town Races" to him and the other new recruits:

Oh, you'll go home in a body bag, doo-dah, doo-dah . . .

Bastards couldn't sing anyway.

His job at Fire Base Bronco would be to keep the roads clear to Chu Lai, which sometimes would mean driving a road grader through sniper-infested jungles. But when land mines were detected, which was often, he would be called in with a bulldozer. His sergeant explained:

"What you do is, you push just the right amount of dirt on top of the land mine, then you dig deep and push the whole pile hard enough to make the mine blow up inside the mound. I'll show you tomorrow. Sweet dreams, Mason."

After watching the sergeant blow up a couple of dirt piles, Creed was ordered to try his hand on the next enemy land mine located by sweepers.

He piled and pushed as the sergeant watched from a safe distance, feeling as if he had enemy sniper crosshairs on him all the while. Finally, he got the land mine to blow up. Though muffled deep inside the mound of dirt, the force of the blast rocked the dozer back and the explosion made his ears ring. The whole ordeal strained his nerves to the brink.

"Not bad for your first time," the sergeant said, having trotted close enough to shout over the diesel engine. "But you're too careful. I can do one in a third of the time it took you."

"I'm not in that big of a hurry to blow myself sky high, Sarge," Creed replied.

"You better get a hell of a lot more efficient, Mason, or you'll find yourself on point with some infantry outfit. The army gave you your M.O.S., and they can take it away."

After that, Creed got serious about the science of detonating land mines in record time, with just enough dank Asian earth piled on top of them to save himself from annihilation. Pushing the lethal ordnance around underground while keeping his M16 constantly within reach, Creed couldn't help but think: "Man, if the boys in the band could just see me now. They wouldn't believe this shit."

He and the other combat engineers built their own hooches and bunkers at Fire Base Bronco. His hooch didn't amount to much more than a shack slapped together with lumber, tin, and canvas with bunks inside. The bunker they constructed nearby was dug into the ground and surrounded with sand bags.

"You think we'll ever have to use this thing?" one of his bunk mates asked the sergeant while putting the last row of sand bags in place.

"Let me explain something to you morons," Sarge said. "Out here, we control the war by day. The Viet Cong control it by night. You better know your way into this bunker in the dark or you're dead meat. You'll see your first firefight soon enough."

Waiting for that first attack on his home base rubbed Creed's nerves raw, night after night. He thought maybe the sergeant had exaggerated the threat. After all, Fire Base Bronco was surrounded by barbed wire and trenches and protected by machine-gun placements. Would the VC really rush this place in the dark?

Creed wrote letters to Dixie for a while, but she never answered one. He had put in a collect phone call from Fort Leonard Wood, but Dixie had apparently changed her number.

In 'Nam, he didn't let on to any of his new military friends that he was Creed Mason from the country band Dixie Creed. There wasn't a guitar in camp that he knew of anyway. He was just plain ol' Bill Mason, from Texas, and that's the way he liked it. He didn't want any preferential treatment, and sensed that he might even be given the more dangerous jobs were he to flaunt his brush with stardom in front of his superiors. The army had a way of breaking everyone down to a common denominator.

One thing he did get good at was poker. There was plenty of roadwork to do on most days, and regular mechanical issues to deal with on the diesel machines, but long periods of boredom also dragged by, and poker was one way to pass the time. Creed had played with his dad and brothers back home, and now became a serious student of the game. Every hand of cards was like a song to Creed, and took his mind off the threats of impending death.

He was, in fact, sitting at a poker game in his hooch when his first firefight finally came. As they played cards, Creed and his friends were chuckling over the new kid, who had arrived today, dead drunk. The kid was now passed out on a bunk. As the laughter died down, Creed cocked his head at an odd whir he heard in the air.

An instant later, an enemy mortar exploded just outside the hooch, tossing Creed off the crate he had been using for a chair. He found a bunk on top of him.

"Take cover!" the sergeant screamed.

"Get in the bunker!" one of the short-timers yelled.

Creed scrambled out from under the bunk, grabbing a rifle from an overturned rack as he scurried to the bunker. Tracers, flares, and rockets lit up the sky like a rock-and-roll concert, but the music was all lethal gunfire and screaming death. As he piled into the bunker, he turned, as if ready to fight with the M16 he had grabbed.

"Give me that rifle!" the sergeant ordered.

Creed handed it over.

"The barrel's bent in the blast, Mason. This thing's useless. Just keep your head down." The sergeant threw the damaged weapon out of the bunker.

Creed's heart was pounding and his guts churned with a fear he had never known nor imagined. Then he heard the kid screaming back in the hooch. That drunken kid who had arrived today and passed out on a bunk had now awakened to a hellish firestorm and wouldn't know up from down in this strange place.

"I'll get him," Creed said. He took one step, but the sergeant grabbed him in a headlock and muscled him down. Looking back on it later, he would realize that he had failed to hear the whir of the next mortar round—the one that hit the hooch dead on and killed that kid on his first day at Fire Base Bronco.

The night dragged on, and Creed began to think he might actually be able to deal with his fear. It was intense, but there *was* a limit to it. A man could get just so scared, he thought. He stayed low and prayed from time to time, listening to the ordnance and small-arms fire being traded around the perimeter of the base. He thought about that kid screaming, about the sergeant having saved his life by preventing him from trying to retrieve the kid. He decided that getting drunk in a war zone was a very bad idea.

Finally, U.S. artillery zeroed in on the VC mortar camp and drove the enemy out of range by dawn. Fire Base Bronco lost three killed and seven wounded.

This was Verse One in Creed's personal ballad of death cheated. He would hear that kid screaming for a long, long time.

One morning, Creed jumped into a jeep to help the camp gunners set the M60 machine guns in place around the base. He got out of the jeep at the first placement and was walking behind one of the gunners toward the sandbagged site when another soldier called him back to help lug a crate full of 50-caliber rounds. Only seconds later, he found himself looking at his own blood in the dirt, just inches from his face. Stunned, he realized he had been knocked down by an explosion from behind and had busted his lip in the fall. The gunner carrying the M60 had stepped on a land mine placed the night before by VC encroachers. The gunner was dead. Had Creed turned back a second or two later, he probably would have been dead as well.

Verse two.

The days dragged on. There was a calendar in the hooch. He grew to hate that calendar. The pages did not turn fast enough to suit him.

Mounding a land mine one day, he misgauged the placement of the target. His blade hit the mine and exploded it. Shrapnel tore all thorough and around the bulldozer, instantly ricocheting around him like a swarm of bumble bees stirred from hell. The percussion stunned him.

He lifted his hands first, to make sure they were still there. He felt his face, finding it intact. He couldn't find a scratch anywhere on his body, but he was almost totally deafened by the ringing in his ears for three days.

Verse three. Would he run out of luck?

Ten months into his tour, Creed became one of those short-timers who had met him with empty stares upon his own arrival.

"Forty-five days and a wakeup!" he said to some newbie one morning at chow, bragging about the approaching end of this tour, knowing the recruit was staring at twelve months of war. That day, while working the road near the village of Duc Pho, Creed noticed some GIs gathered around the dirt-road entrance to the village. He realized they were taking pictures of something. He approached on his road grader and looked closer.

Heads. Severed human heads. Viet Cong fighters killed and decapitated by South Vietnamese loyalists, their heads then impaled on bamboo spikes. This was the most grisly thing he had ever cast his tortured eyes upon. The heads did not resemble any ghoulish props he had ever seen in a Hollywood movie. They were ghastlier—not cleanly sliced free, but sloppily chopped and hacked away, with flesh, veins, and windpipes dangling, bloodbathed, underneath.

"Oh, my God," he said to himself. "Those idiots are taking pictures. I'll spend the rest of my life trying to get that picture out of my head."

That night, somehow, VC combatants slipped past the guards and through the wire and attacked the base from within in a well-timed assault. It began with a fire grenade being dropped inside Creed's hooch through an open window. Flames leapt through the hooch and all hell broke loose. A couple of soldiers, engulfed in flames, ran screaming through the door only to be shot down by waiting enemy attackers. A couple of the other men seemed to get through the gunfire, but Creed wasn't sure.

What he was sure of was that he was the only one left alive in the burning hooch and he couldn't stay much longer. He had won a forty-five, Colt, semiautomatic, Model 1911 pistol from a master sergeant in a card game. He wore it most of the time, and had it strapped on now. He drew it from its holster and took a step toward the door. Bullets shattered the wooden doorframe and sprayed him with splinters, driving him back.

He smelled human flesh burning, heard staccato machine-gun fire outside. A face appeared in the window, followed by a rifle muzzle. In the light of the flames, Creed could clearly see that the face was Vietnamese. He locked eyes with the enemy, over the sights of his Colt. One shot made the face go away.

The hooch became so hot that he felt his skin was about to boil. It was as if he heard his own echo before he even screamed. Someone was yelling, and it was him. He tore out of the hooch with flames on his heels. The relative cool charged him with adrenaline that he felt roaring up his spine in an icy tingle. Muzzle blasts in the dark. He returned fire at full sprint, his eyes searching for some sort of cover under the flare-lit sky.

He ran and ran, finding no safe haven, yet somehow avoiding a spray of lead. The trench. He could only hope his own men held it. He got a glimpse of the man that shot him. The VC missed with the first couple shots, and Creed twisted to the right as he ran, firing his Colt at the enemy attacker. The bullet went into his lower back on the right side, tore through his guts, and still managed to strike his left forearm as well.

He toppled into the trench, breathless, crazed, afraid of death.

A soldier in the trench took one look at him and yelled, "Medic!"

Now Creed got strangely angry and pulled himself to his knees though his guts were roaring in pain. He peeked over the top of the trench, fired his .45 until it clicked, then felt himself slipping into shock.

"Medic!"

Verse four. Done.

The surgeons removed several feet of his intestines and sent him to Japan to begin a long recovery. The mangled and burned men he met there made him feel lucky and guilty all at once.

An army doctor, a major, showed him an X-ray of his shattered arm and jokingly said, "I hope you weren't a guitar player or something."

"Something," Creed replied.

The doctor leaned closer so no one else would hear. "Be thankful you got to keep that arm. On a busy day we would have taken it off. We had time to save it, but I can't promise you'll have the dexterity you once had."

Creed swallowed hard. "Thanks for not cuttin' it off, Doc," he managed to say.

"I'm sending you to Beach Army Hospital to recover from your gut wound. And they'll probably put some pins in your arm and set you up with some therapy for it."

Creed envisioned some swank facility by the ocean. "Where's Beach Army Hospital?"

"Mineral Wells. The garden spot of Texas."

Ah, Texas . . . Creed had never heard a word so sweet.

It turned out that Beach Army Hospital was nowhere near a beach. Mineral Wells, Texas, was just eighty miles south of the Oklahoma border, in fact. Six months after he landed there, Creed was up and around. He had eased back into his boot camp calisthenics and could do a hundred sit-ups, easy. He did his push-ups on his knuckles because he couldn't flatten his left palm out on the floor. The surgery on his left arm had somewhat improved his range of motion and dexterity, but he still couldn't bend his wrist enough to wrap it around a guitar neck.

Instead, he had purchased a Dobro in a Mineral Wells pawnshop. With the instrument on his thighs, strings up, his left hand could easily manipulate the steel bar on the strings over the neck. Still, he missed the control he had had with a fine electric guitar.

One day his surgeon, a Major Mark Fray, saw him playing the lap steel in the day room of the hospital. He walked near to listen.

"That's pretty good, Mason. Do you play a regular guitar, too?"

"I used to," Creed said. "I can't reach around the neck anymore. My wrist won't bend enough."

The doctor wrote something on a clipboard. "Do you play golf?"

Creed wondered about the leap in the conversation. "No, sir."

"My kid wants to play guitar. I'll teach you how to golf if you'll teach him how to play his six-string."

Creed couldn't find anything particularly wrong with the deal. "All right."

The next day he found himself on the driving range with a seven iron in his hands. Major Fray showed him how to grip the club and gave him a couple pointers on his swing. Within an hour, he found that he could actually hit a ball pretty straight. It felt good, even though the strain of the golf swing shot pains through his wounded left forearm.

"You're a natural, Mason. Even with that stiff wrist. I'll loan you that seven iron. I want you out here every day. Make it hurt a little. Work on your range of motion."

"Yes, sir."

"My kid will stop by the dayroom after school on Monday for his first lesson."

"Fair enough, Major. Thanks."

One day on the driving range, Creed reared back to hit the golf ball and felt a pop in his left arm in mid-swing, followed by a searing pain up his arm and down into his fingers. He dropped the club and looked at his hand, turning it this way and that. When the pain subsided, he compared his wounded wrist with his good, right one. He found that he could now bend the left one almost as far as the normal wrist.

There was a nip of autumn in the air, and it felt great after the long, hot, Texas summer. He was going to play guitar again. He had survived his tour in hell. Life wasn't over.

One day he heard a song by Dixie Houston on the radio. Judging by the production alone, he could tell that the label had invested a fortune in her. He wrote to her care of the label. No reply. He put in calls to his former producer. He left messages. No one returned them.

Creed Mason was honorably discharged from the army two months later with a purple heart, a pretty good golf swing, and a seething desire to play guitar on a stage again. He thought about Nashville, but didn't have the bus fare. Anyway, he knew he was not ready, as a picker, to return to Guitar Town just yet. He had heard about the live music scene down in Austin, three or four hours south. Might be a good place to get his chops back. He said good-bye to Major Fray, stepped out of Beach Army Hospital, hiked off the post, and stuck his thumb out in the air alongside the highway.

4
CHAPTER

1:22 A.M.

Highway 71 stretched out like a runway in front of her, and whoever that was behind her was taking advantage of the straightaway to gain some serious speed.

The Shelby GT passed inches from her door, cut in front of her, and blinded her with red brake lights. Rosa swerved and gunned the Chevy engine like a race car driver to regain her lead, but Franco's favorite car shot passed her again before she could get ahead. Out of nowhere she saw a reflector marking a blacktop turn to the left, so she skidded and fishtailed into the turn as Franco shot past it.

She made the left turn, then lined the Corvette into a screaming acceleration down the strange stretch of blacktop, her heart beating furiously in her chest. She startled a small herd of deer on the side of the road, and they bolted across the pavement behind her, causing Franco to slam on his brakes. That was lucky, she thought. This part of Texas was thickly populated by deer, and whitetail/auto collisions were common.

She sped on, and heard the engine rev as the pavement dipped away below her into a shallow creek bed. Bottoming out on shocks and springs, she kept her foot on the accelerator and rocketed up the other side of the creek on the narrow stretch of asphalt. She saw Franco's headlights behind her again, but now she was keeping her distance.

There was a chance to turn toward a town called Kingsland, but it came and went in a blink and Rosa found herself barreling past a sign that announced Sunset Shores, a lakeside development. She had to brake as the long, straight country blacktop gave way to curving residential streets, and Franco closed in from behind. Rosa switched her headlights off, downshifting when needed so her brake lights would not give her away. She had to rely on the moon, and the occasional porch light to guide her as there were no streetlights in this sleepy excuse for a town. From her college years, Rosa knew about the chain of lakes above Austin, impounded by several dams on the Colorado River. She sensed she had stumbled upon a road that would dead-end at one of those lakes.

Just as she saw Franco shoot by her last right turn in the rearview, a deer darted in front of her car and she had no choice but to brake to keep from hitting it. Before rounding a hairpin turn, she saw the Shelby's backup lights, and knew Franco would soon be back on her tail.

"Shit!" she blurted. This street followed the crooked lakeshore, she realized. Nothing to do but keep running and hoping, shifting and winding. She came to a fork, and bore to the right, sensing the lake on the left. She saw the "Dead End" sign too late, and found herself on a peninsula, heading for a parking lot adjacent to a marina and a boat ramp. Franco's headlights swept the terrain behind her, a quarter mile back.

Rosa pulled into a vacant parking spot near the boat ramp, using her emergency brake to stop, avoiding the red flash of taillights. She shut the engine off, grabbed the strap of her purse, and jumped out, cursing the dome light as she opened the door. Slamming the door, she ran, hearing the Shelby accelerate behind her. Looping the purse strap over her head and under one arm, she sprinted around a row of condominiums to find a beach and a lakeside bar. The neon "Open" sign switched off the moment she looked at it. She heard a boat motor start down the dock.

Running faster than she had ever run in her life, she came upon a man casting off lines as his boat idled. It was a classic wooden boat, about a twenty-footer, with the motor housing situated in the middle of the passenger area. "I need a ride across the lake!" she blurted, startling the man.

He stood straight and fell back in the seat behind the steering wheel as the boat rocked. His long hair blew across his face and he looked up at Rosa as if she were the answer to a prayer.

She glanced over her shoulder. "Please. Now!"

"Well, get in," he said, a slur tainting his words.

She dropped lightly into the watercraft. Peeking over the boardwalk, she saw Franco trotting along the beach toward the dock, looking for her. "Hurry!" she said.

The boatman eased his craft away from the end of the pier, toward the open lake. "It's a no-wake zone here, darlin'." She could smell his alcohol-tainted breath on the breeze.

"I like speed," she said. "It turns me on."

"Well . . ." The driver hit the throttle with such purpose that Rosa staggered back against the stern, the big-bore motor rumbling amidships. She saw him reach for a switch, illuminating the running lights.

"No lights," she said over the motor noise as she regained her balance. "It's more romantic."

The drunken boatman looked over his shoulder and grinned at her, reaching for the light switch again. Never had she dreamed of using her feminine wiles to manipulate a man in such a way, but she was desperate, and the man did not appear capable of much heroism on his own accord. He did not strike her as dangerous, and she knew she could handle him if he should get frisky. She hadn't taken ten years of karate lessons for nothing.

"Speed!" she demanded, afraid to look back. She felt something sting her hip as a bullet hole appeared in the windshield beside the driver's head.

"What the hell?" he shouted. Another bullet hit the dash, and the man seemed to sober up immediately. He pushed the throttle all the way forward and began swerving to avoid more gunfire, taking Rosa's feet out from under her again. As she clawed her way back into view, she saw Franco's silhouette at the end of the pier, and prayed she was now out of effective handgun range. The big motor under the cowling was roaring like the voice of an enraged dragon. She checked her left hip and felt slick blood.

"What the hell have you gotten me into?" the man demanded as they motored around a bend in the lakeshore, leaving Franco out of sight.

Even as she breathed a sigh of relief, a horrible thought struck Rosa. She had left Celinda's name and phone number on the Jack in the Box bag in her car. "You've got to get me to a phone quick!" she ordered.

The next thing she knew, Rosa was flipping over the motor housing, cartwheeling through the windshield, and flying through the air in front of the boat. It didn't even hurt. The motor was screaming, the prop having lifted above the drag of the water. As she hit the lake surface and skipped across it, she glimpsed the splintered V hull of the wooden boat descending on her, and knew this was the end. She knew, somehow, that she would soon meet her real mother. And she knew that she had beaten Franco out of the satisfaction of killing her the way he wanted to kill her, and planting her corpse under the weight of a root ball.

The steering wheel had slammed into his chest and thrown him back against the front of the motor housing. The boat was still speeding along, and water was gushing in from somewhere. He scrambled to the driver's seat, pulled the throttle back, and checked the steering. The boat responded, but the craft was taking on water fast.

He looked for the girl. She was nowhere in sight. He grabbed a flashlight and shone the beam all around the boat. Then, remembering the gunshots, he switched the light off. "Oh, God," he muttered, trying to calm his nerves. He had hit something, and the girl had flown out of the boat. Someone had shot at him. This was not his fault. The old Correct Craft was sinking. He had to get to the lake house.

Recognizing familiar shore lights, he regained his bearings, throttled up, and turned toward the lake house. By the time he pulled into the cove, the water was creeping up his shins and the motor was coughing inside its housing. In this high-dollar, lakeshore neighborhood, each home had its own boathouse, fronting the water the same way a garage would open to the street. He coasted in and hit reverse to stop. The motor sputtered and died before he even hit the kill switch. Now the boat began to sink fast, so he scrambled onto the boardwalk and watched it by the weird glow of the orange bug light inside the boathouse. Before it went under, he saw blood on the shattered windshield, next to a bullet hole.

The evidence sank from view, and he began to weep uncontrollably. He had left a stranger to drown on the lake—a pretty young girl. How could he explain that this was not his fault? All of the booze in his stomach suddenly wanted out. He collapsed and threw up over the edge of the landing, onto the water that now concealed the sunken boat. When he opened his eyes, he saw his reflection through his own vomit. He fell over on his side, pulled his knees to his chest, and blubbered as he had not done since he was a helpless baby.

5
CHAPTER

1:26 A.M.

Creed loaded his guitar into his Good Times Dodge van, crawled in behind the wheel, and left the parking lot. He motored down South Congress Avenue to Manchacha, the first little town south of Austin. He followed the directions he had memorized at the last poker game, eventually running out of pavement on a county road past the edge of town. Turning through an open gate with a red bandanna tied to it, he spotted a bunch of vehicles parked in a cow pasture next to an old wooden barn.

This was the place. He recognized some of the cars and pickups of the regular gambling cadre from previous poker games at other locations. This weekly game floated from one venue to another. You had to be at the last game to know where the next would take place, or know whom to ask.

As he approached a door on the side of the barn, a guard stopped him.

"Who are you?" the husky young bouncer asked.

"Just a poor wayfaring stranger."

Satisfied with the password, the guard opened the door. Inside, Creed saw that the barn, which looked like a ramshackle shell from the outside, had been converted to a fully-equipped saloon designed for gaming. A full bar stretched across one wall, manned by three bartenders. A dozen cocktail waitresses were dressed in high heels, hot pants, and halter tops, and it seemed that each had been handpicked for her ability to flatter such apparel. Creed went to the bar and ordered a shot of bourbon whiskey, neat. He leaned on the bar to look things over and get a feel for the joint.

One of the cocktail waitresses approached Creed, her shiny red lips smiling as her sparkling green eyes looked him over. She had her dark hair tied back in a ponytail that seemed alive. Creed knew her from previous games run by this same operation.

She glanced at the bartender. "Whiskey sour and a Long Island iced tea." She turned her smile on Creed again. "Did you have a show tonight, Creed?"

"I did, Gail." He gave her a warm smile. She was pretty in a wild sort of way. "I sat in with some guys at the Armadillo."

"I wish I could have gone. I love to watch you play."

"Maybe next time. If I had your phone number, I'd call you and let you know where I'm playing next."

The bartender placed the drinks on Gail's tray. "I'll make sure I give it to you before you leave tonight." She winked and turned away.

Creed felt a streak of overdue luck coming on. He saw the pit boss, Gordy, behind a caged-in counter converting cash to chips, so he took his gig money there to secure a stake.

"Hey, Gordy," he said, shoving his cash into the cage.

"Hay fever is more like it. I hate this barn." He sneezed as he counted chips, less the house fee. "Good luck, kid."

Creed saw a table with an empty chair that faced the door and would keep his back to the corner. He approached and asked if he could sit down. A couple of the players knew him.

"Howdy, Creed," said a rugged-looking rancher Creed knew from previous games. "Boys, he's all right for a Piney Woods peckerwood. I say we let him play."

The men nodded and Creed pulled up a chair. "What are we playing, Boss?" He congratulated himself for remembering that the rancher called himself "Boss."

"Dealer's choice. Winner deals." Boss was shuffling the cards. "How about seven card stud, jacks or better?"

"That's my favorite." Creed smiled.

Two and a half hours later, Creed's stack of chips had quadrupled and only two other men remained at his table—Boss and a stranger who called himself Joe. By this time, Creed had eased the grip of his cocked and locked forty-five automatic far enough out of the waistline of his jeans that he could draw it in a fraction of a second. He had sensed that someone at the table had been cheating since he sat down. Certain cards, long overdue to show their faces, did not do so until they benefited this guy, Joe. Now that all the players except for Boss and Joe had bowed out, broke,

Creed was certain that Joe was the cheater, for he had played with Boss often and believed him honest.

Joe was thirty-something, cocky, foul-mouthed, and ill-mannered. Right now, he had the biggest stack of chips on the table, and seemed bent on adding Creed's and Boss's chips to his stack as well. Creed was using the dipped brim of his Stetson to watch Joe's hands without Joe being able to see his eyes. He watched closely every time Joe touched his cards, and finally he saw it: While laughing at some irreverent quip he had thrown out as a distraction, Joe deftly pulled a card from his cuff and switched it for one that he had been dealt. The card he had rightfully been dealt simultaneously went into the cuff. A blink would have covered it, and it was the slick move of a true card mechanic, but Creed was sure of what he had seen.

His heart began to beat harder as he put his cards facedown on the table and reached for his gun grip. His index finger slipped behind the bend of the trigger guard and he began to draw the gun, sure of his decision to expose the card cheat.

The barn door flew open and a shotgun blast sent buckshot into the ceiling. A girl screamed and dropped a tray of drinks. "Nobody freakin' move!" yelled a man with a kid's Halloween mask over his face. "This is a robbery!" Two other armed men were coming in behind him, and Creed could see the young bouncer laid out on the ground outside the open door.

Creed stood and leveled his forty-five on the bandit leader as the robber lazily pumped another round into the chamber of his sawed-off twelve-gauge. Squeezing off a round, Creed hit the man in the chest, causing him to drop his weapon, knocking him back into his cohorts. One of the bandits got a round off that flew over the heads of the gamblers, but Creed was blasting splinters from the doorway with such relentless purpose that the thugs could only grab their fallen leader and drag him away.

With the first shotgun blast, Boss had hit the floor, but now he rolled over with a revolver in his hand and began shooting in the direction of the robbers under a vacant table. Now other handguns came out of other hidden places and continued to fire out through the door even after the bandits had disappeared.

"Hold your fire!" Creed shouted. "That boy's laid out on the ground out there." He peeked out of the doorway in time to see a pickup spray dust and gravel across the pasture. He checked the young bouncer for signs of life and found him breathing and moaning, a gash on his scalp. "They're gone," he said, slipping his weapon into the back of his jeans.

"How's the kid?"

"Just cold-cocked." He was looking at the floor where the bandit leader had fallen. The sawed-off pump was still lying there.

"You're pretty quick on the draw!" Boss said, getting up from the floor.

"No blood," Creed replied, sensing the relief in his own voice.

"Bullshit. You hit him square."

"Must have been wearing a flack jacket," Creed said. "Lucky for him. And me."

By this time men were filing out of the barn, for they all knew that much gunfire at three-thirty in the morning was likely to attract a visit from the law.

Gordy, the pit boss behind the iron bars, was hastily sacking up cash and chips. "Anybody with chips left can cash 'em in at the game next week. We'll be using the Jollyville location. Now, clear out. Everybody!"

Creed flipped the safety on the shotgun, put it down, and went to collect his chips. Joe was raking in the pot on the table.

"Whoa, now, stud," said Boss, slipping his snub-nosed thirty-eight back into his jacket pocket. "We haven't played out that hand yet."

Joe paused, flipped his cards over. "Three kings."

"Damn," Boss blurted.

As Joe reached for the chips again, Creed pinned his forearm to the table and pulled the card from Joe's cuff before he could even attempt to struggle free. He showed the five of diamonds to Boss.

"I believe you had a *pair* of kings," Creed growled. "This was the card you were dealt. I saw that third king come out of your sleeve."

"Son-of-a-bitch!" Boss snarled, reaching back into his pocket for this gun.

"Better not," Creed said. "The law could be halfway here from town by now. Better let him go."

Boss left his piece in his jacket, but kept his hand in his pocket. "You lucky little shit. If I ever see your sorry ass again . . ."

Creed flipped his cards over to reveal a pair of aces.

"I'm gettin' out of here," Joe said sheepishly, reaching for his stacked chips in front of his chair.

Boss stiff-armed him away from the table. "Don't even think about it. And I'd get clean out of Texas if I was you."

Joe fumed briefly, then trotted out of the barn.

"Let's go, gentlemen!" Gordy shouted.

"I'll split his chips with you," Creed said. "He was cheating both of us."

"No, you earned it, Creed. That was some real fast shootin'."

"Not really. I was already drawing on that asshole, Joe. The bandits just happened to bust in at the right time." Creed scraped his little fortune into his hat and headed for the door, where the pit boss waited impatiently.

Outside, he paused to shake Boss's hand. "Boss, you wouldn't happen to have a hundred on you, would you?" He offered him a red chip. "Just to get me through till next week?"

Boss chuckled and took the chip. He pulled a wad of folding money from his pocket and peeled off a hundred-dollar bill. "I'll see you in the near future or the far pasture."

"Thanks." He shook hands with the rancher and trotted toward his Dodge. Creed rounded his van to the driver's side, startled to see someone standing there. He quickly recognized Gail. She had her arm draped over the side mirror, and she held an open bottle of whiskey, half-full, propped on her hip like a rifle. "Don't forget my number," she said.

Creed glanced around. "Where's your car?"

"I rode with one of the other girls. She panicked and left without me, the bitch."

Creed was slipping the key into the door lock. "Well, looks like I better give you a ride home."

"My hero," she purred.

CHAPTER

He had the familiar dream; the one where he was holding the photograph in his hand. The dream was always the same, except for the face on the photo. This time, it bore the likeness of his adopted cousin, Rosabella. In the white fog of the dream, he studied Rosa's carefree smile, the curve of her cheek. Then he slowly slipped the photo into the shredder and watched it come out in ribbons that blew into a hole dug deep into the desert ground.

In the seat of his Shelby GT, Franco woke with a start to see the gunmetal blue of dawn creeping across his windshield. He felt a seething rage fuming down in the pit of his guts. He controlled it, but did not smother it. He used it, found motivation and purpose in it. He had been schooled by his father not to let anger get the better of him. He had learned, instead, to funnel it into purposeful violence—well-planned and executed deeds of brutality and, when necessary, murder. This was what Franco did for Papa Martini. He cleaned up messes. He shredded documents.

The shredding of Bert, for example, had gone exactly as planned—or so Franco had thought, unaware that Rosa had witnessed the shooting at the ranch. Bert had been a useful wise guy without a criminal record, well spoken and amiable, the perfect figurehead to install as the supposed manager of one of the family's casinos. Then Bert got too wise and started skimming off the top of the skim. He had been warned once before, years ago, and had the permanent limp to remind him of his transgressions. When Franco figured out that Bert was back to his old tricks, he had taken him for a drive to the ranch and worked him over in the toolshed until he was convinced that Bert was telling the truth about having acted alone in the embezzlement. Then he disposed of the problem under the root ball of a pine sapling.

The next morning, still out at the ranch, he had gotten the frantic phone call from Lieutenant Harbaugh, who told him Rosa was sitting in his office. As Franco quickly dressed to leave, the second call came in. Rosa had disappeared. Leaving the ranch house, Franco had spotted the Jeep tracks where she had turned around to flee after witnessing the killing of Bert. He had cursed her name all the way to the ranch gate. He had always known that spoiled, little adopted bitch was going to be trouble someday. She was not even Italian! She was the half-breed daughter of a Mexican hotel maid who had sold her for five hundred dollars to Uncle Rob because that sickly wife of his just had to have a kid.

Now Franco was stuck here in this parking lot in Texas, hoping someone might return for Rosa's car—maybe even Rosa herself. The Corvette was still parked where she had abandoned it. Positive that he remained inconspicuous and concealed, Franco had a good view of the Chevy from the position he had taken behind some small trees at the far corner of the parking lot. But he couldn't wait here forever.

He admitted to himself that he had botched the attempt to deal with Rosa. Taking those two low-percentage shots from the end of the pier had been foolish. He had used the silencer on the muzzle of his twenty-two, however, and was sure that no one had witnessed the gunfire, other than Rosa and the driver of the boat.

Still, Franco was worried. He hoped Rosa had been scared badly enough at the Las Vegas Police Department to prevent her from going to the cops here in Texas. He felt his teeth grind when he thought about that idiot, Lieutenant Jake Harbaugh, letting Rosa escape from his office in Vegas. The plan had worked well to use Harbaugh, who was on the Martini family payroll, to intercept any damaging intelligence Rosa might accidentally collect concerning the family business. It was Franco who had told Harbaugh where to go to meet Rosa. He had coached the big lummox on how to approach her, charm her, and seduce her.

That the moron had left the team rugby photo on display in his office was almost more than Franco could bear to think about, so he forced it out of his mind for now. At least Harbaugh had had enough sense to get on the dispatch radio and put a squad car on Rosa's tail as she fled the station, and had, himself, taken up the surveillance pursuit outside of town in his own car. Harbaugh had experience tailing suspects, and knew how to keep his distance so he wouldn't be spotted. He had done a surprisingly good job of keeping Rosa in sight until Franco could return from the ranch, fire up his Shelby, and haul ass to the east to catch up. The fact that Franco had to pull over every hour to call into Papa Martini's office for updates, phoned in hastily from Harbaugh during his chase, had slowed Franco down, and almost prevented him from catching up to Rosa before she got to Austin. It had become obvious after a while that she was heading back to her old college town.

Finally, after some fifteen hours of driving, Franco pulled within CB radio range where he could talk to Harbaugh on a seldom-used channel. The Martini family had caught on to the growing citizen's band radio craze, and had found it a useful way to communicate and coordinate, provided everyone knew the family radio code. Harbaugh knew the code.

"Hey, Snake, you got your ears on?" Franco asked, using Harbaugh's CB handle.

"Roger that." The reply was a raspy squawk.

"You got a twenty on your ex?"

"Roger. Not far ahead."

"Meet me at seventy-one and twenty-nine."

Franco had overtaken the exhausted lieutenant at a small town called Llano, at the intersection of the two highways he had mentioned on the radio. He saw Harbaugh's Malibu idling in a grocery store parking lot and pulled his driver's-side window up to the lieutenant's.

"Well?" Franco said, a scowl on his face.

"She's got about three minutes on you. Still heading east on seventy-one."

"You better hope I catch her, you stupid puke."

He spotted the Corvette's taillights on a lonely stretch of U.S. Highway 71 in the countryside. At that moment he thought he had her, but she had proven more adept behind the wheel than he had expected. The events that took place next were still confusing to Franco. Had Rosa planned to take that left turn to Sunset Shores? Had the man in the boat been waiting for her? Was it arranged, or just happenstance?

Either way, now Franco not only had to deal with Rosa, but whoever it was who had helped her escape in the boat. This was getting messier instead of cleaner, and that frustrated Franco. Frustration made him mad. Anger made him relentlessly, diabolically efficient. As he shifted and stretched in the car seat, he continued sorting through the late-night events in his mind.

He had seen Rosa jump into the boat. Running to the end of the pier, he had gotten a pretty good look at the boat by moonlight. It was a classic wooden vessel—perhaps a Chris Craft or a Correct Craft. He had seen plenty of that sort on Lake Tahoe, where vintage watercraft were in vogue, but in backwater Texas, that had to be an unusual boat in this day and age of cheap fiberglass and aluminum hulls. It should be easy to spot on this lake.

Thinking of the boat, he recalled the motor housing situated in the middle of the craft in such a way that passengers could walk around it. It had an old-fashioned flat glass windshield as opposed to the more modern, curved glass models. After taking those two ill-advised shots at the boat, Franco had stood, cursing, at the end of the pier as the boat cruised around a bend in the lakeshore. Refusing to give up, he had run back to his car, and sped away through the waterfront neighborhoods, trying to keep the boat in sight. Every quarter mile or so, he would kill the Shelby motor and listen for the growl of the marine engine. Once, between two lake houses, he saw the boat's wake silvered in the moonlight, pointing like an arrow out to the open water of the middle of the reservoir.

Then he had run out of neighborhood through which to pursue the craft. There were still big ranches along the lakeshore, separating the residential developments. Undaunted, he had sped back to U.S. Highway 71, where he had first caught up to Rosa, to find the next lake community on down the shoreline. Blue Cove, Horseshoe Bay, Marble Falls, Highland Haven, Granite Shoals, Kingsland . . . He had driven down to every boat ramp and marina he could find in his hasty search, in hopes that he might spot the old woody. But after spending hours circumnavigating Lake Lyndon B. Johnson, an impoundment on the Colorado River, Franco came full circle to Sunset Shores to find Rosa's car still there.

Using his shirttail to open her car door, wary of leaving fingerprints, he looked around the inside of the Corvette for leads. He found a name, Celinda, and a phone number scribbled on a receipt stapled to the top of a Jack in the Box bag. He yanked the receipt off the top of the bag to collect the phone number scrawled on it. This was his first lucky break since catching up to Rosa. He hoped this Celinda might lead him to Rosa, or the owner of the vintage woody that had whisked Rosa away. But he was also worried about how much this Celinda might know. How far had this thing mushroomed? He decided to conceal himself and watch Rosa's car until dawn, on the off chance that someone might come to collect it.

Now daybreak was upon him, birds were chirping in the branches, and

Franco knew he should get to a phone and report to his father. His failure was not going to be easy to explain. He dreaded making the call. He was stiff from sleeping briefly in the car, and hungry, having eaten little on the mad drive from Vegas. Fishing boats could be heard motoring out onto the lake, and people in the neighborhood were beginning to stir. An elderly fisherman was walking down to the pier with a tackle box in one hand, rod and reel in the other. The old-timer paused a moment to admire Rosa's cherry-red Vette. An early-morning jogger ran by. Franco began to get nervous about his Nevada license plates being noticed by someone, and decided to find a pay phone.

As he reached for the ignition, he heard a siren. A police car came barreling down to the boat ramp at the marina, killing the siren as it stopped, leaving its lights flashing. Franco slid lower in the seat. Seconds later, a sheriff's department pickup truck pulling a police boat appeared, and backed down to the boat ramp. He saw the old fisherman with the tackle box talking to the deputies as they launched the boat. The fisherman pointed at the Corvette. What the hell was going on?

Nosey residents and tourists began to filter out of the lakeside condos and nearby houses, no doubt all atwitter over the sirens in this sleepy lakeside burg. Franco decided to join them. He considered himself an expert at blending in, able to operate within any given circle of society, and even circles of sociopaths. He was still dressed in his casual ranch attire—a pair of jeans, hiking boots, and a short-sleeved button-up shirt—so he would fit in well enough with these Saturday-morning lake rats. He pulled a ball cap over his shaved head and put on some sunglasses.

Strolling casually down to the boat ramp, his hands in his pockets, he watched as the police boat motored away. Sidling up next to the retiree with the tackle box—the one who had pointed out the Vette to the cops—Franco said, "What the hell's going on?"

The old-timer was excited. "Some guys out fishin' on the lake found a body. A dead girl!"

Franco did not have to fake his surprise. "You're shittin' me."

"That's what I says to the deputy! I says, 'You're shittin' me!' The deputy says she was from Nevada. Had an ID on her. Says, 'You know anybody from Nevada around here?' I says, 'No, sir, but there's a red sports car right yonder with Nevada plates on it!'" He pointed to Rosa's car.

Franco looked, and this time he did fake his surprise. "I'll be damned. Wonder what happened to her?"

"Don't know. Shame, though."

"It's a damned shame." Franco turned and walked away, shaking his head, working hard to conceal his joy. Now the phone call to Papa was not going to be so dreadful. He could claim he shot Rosa fleeing in the boat, and for all he knew that was true, but he would have to admit to his father that he still had the boatman and this Celinda to follow up on. He wondered what the hell had happened out there last night.

Franco guessed that Celinda had expected to see Rosa some time last night. Probably a former college friend who still lived in Austin, or someone local whom Rosa had met while attending UT. He would have to get to Celinda before word of a dead Nevada girl on Lake L.B.J. hit the radio and TV news stations. And it was only a matter of time until someone connected the dead girl's last name with a reputed Las Vegas mob family.

Now Franco knew he really needed to get his Nevada plates out of the area without being spotted. As he walked back toward the Shelby, he looked over his shoulder. The commotion around the boat ramp provided the perfect distraction to cover his departure. The police boat motored slowly back toward the ramp, and everyone wanted to see the dead body, including Franco. He got into his car and waited in the parking lot as the boat docked.

The local cops had forgotten to bring anything resembling a body bag on the boat, so they just handed the corpse up to the gurney waiting on the dock where an E.M.T. covered it with a sheet. Franco saw enough long black hair and familiar clothing to know that was indeed the body of his late, adopted cousin, Rosa.

He started the Shelby and drove slowly out of the parking lot. Returning to Highway 71 without passing a single car, he turned toward Austin, minding the speed limit. He memorized Celinda's phone number and tore the Jack in the Box receipt into tiny bits that he threw like confetti out of the car window.

Finding a pay phone at a 7-Eleven on the outskirts of the capital city, he put the call in to his father, waking him up, remembering that Vegas was two time zones west.

"I fixed the problem, Pop." Always wary of phone taps, the Martinis forever had to dance around the facts.

"*The one from the ranch?*"

"Yes, sir."

"*Good. So, that's it?*"

"Uh . . . There might be some follow up . . . repairs."

"*Shit. How many?*"

"Two that I know of."

"*That you know of!*"

"I'm on it, Pop. I'll handle it."

Papa Martini sighed, which led to a long, hacking cough.

"Jesus, Pop, you need to cut back on the smokes."

"*Yeah, that's what my doctor tells me, too. Just handle the problem, Franco. You see what happens if you let termites go too long? You sure I don't need to call an exterminator?*"

"I can handle it!" Franco blurted, insulted at the insinuation. "It's not like I invited the termites into the house in the first place!"

"*Yeah, yeah. Good point. That was Rob. He never understood how to take care of his property.*"

"I'll call you when I'm finished."

"*Okay. Be careful,* capice?"

"Yeah, don't smoke so much, will you? Love you, Pop. *Ciao.*"

"*Ciao, bambino.*"

He chuckled a little at the comforting familiarity of his father's New York–Italian accent. Paulo Martini had come to Vegas by way of Havana, where he had learned to run casinos before Castro kicked the Americans out. He had lived in Nevada for thirty years, but would never shed that Brooklyn dialect. Franco, on the other hand, had grown up mostly in Las Vegas, and could turn the Yankee accent on and off to suit his purposes. In fact, he could affect a number of regional American speech patterns to meet his needs.

As he dialed Celinda's number by memory, he decided his news anchorman's generic voice would serve him best when he spoke to her.

After just one ring, the answer came. "*Hello?*" a woman's voice said, anxiously.

"This is agent Mark Dorsey from the F.B.I. I'm calling for Rosabella Martini. Is she there?"

There was a long pause. "*The F.B.I.? Is she in trouble?*"

"Is this Celinda?"

"*Yes. Is Rosa in trouble?*"

"Rosa left your name and number on my machine. I got the impression she would be staying with you in Austin. Is she there?"

"No. She didn't show up last night. What's this all about, Agent . . . ?"

"Dorsey. She didn't tell you?"

"No. She only said that she was in a bit of a fix and she needed a place to stay. She sounded scared."

"Look, Miss . . . I'm sorry, Rosa didn't leave me your last name.

"Morales."

"Miss Morales. I can explain what's going on, but it's not the kind of information I want to talk about over the phone. Do you mind if I come over? It won't take long."

"You're in Austin?"

"Just got in."

There was another long pause, then Celinda gave up her address and directions to her apartment, located not far from the intersection of Congress and Riverside. Franco left the phone booth and found the apartment complex within twenty minutes, but chose not to use the parking lot there. A few blocks away, he found an empty parking lot outside a club called Armadillo World Headquarters. What kind of stupid name was that? He left his Shelby there and walked to Celinda's apartment complex located on Town Lake. Nice complex. It had a swimming pool, and even a boat dock on the lake. He knocked on the door. It cracked open, then reached the end of the safety chain.

"Agent Dorsey?" she said.

"Yes. Miss Morales?"

"Can I see some ID, please?"

"Of course." Franco took his fake F.B.I. credentials from his hip pocket and held them up to the crack in the door. The badge and photo ID were excellent forgeries, produced by the finest craftsmen in the syndicate. The door closed, the chain rattled. The door opened wide to reveal a very pretty Hispanic woman, Rosa's age, with long black hair. She wore jeans and a T-shirt from the University of Texas. She was barefoot. Her toenails were painted. She turned into the apartment so he could follow her in. She was just as attractive walking away, shapely in an athletic way. He saw a pair of well-worn running shoes in the hallway, a diploma over a desk in the living room. The radio receiver was lit up on the stereo system, and a newsman was reciting the weather forecast for the day.

She turned back to face him. "Sorry I had to see some ID. You probably think I'm paranoid."

"I think you're smart. You gotta be, young girl living alone."

"Actually, I live here with my boyfriend, but he's gone on a canoe trip with his buddies. Five days down the Brazos."

Franco saw in the way that she rolled her eyes that she disapproved of such trips. He nodded at her, but he was listening to the radio newscaster as she turned into the kitchen.

"Coffee?" she asked, walking into the adjoining kitchen.

"*. . . Breaking news when we return. A disturbing discovery by fishermen on one of our Highland Lakes . . .*"

"Yes, please." Franco rushed for the stereo system and turned the big volume knob down on the receiver.

She brought two cups from the kitchen and sat at the dining table, looking a bit perplexed at the radio, having noticed that the volume had decreased.

"I turned that down," Franco said. "Sorry, I have hearing loss from the war. I can't separate sounds if there's too much noise. I hope you don't mind . . ."

Celinda shrugged. "No, that's fine. So, what's Rosa gotten herself into? Is she in trouble?"

Franco took the coffee. "Rosa's a good girl. She just got mixed up with the wrong guy."

"How wrong? Cream? Sugar?"

"Black's good. Rosa got swept off her feet by a guy in Vegas. I can't tell you his name, but he's the biggest heroin dealer from LA to Houston. I think she saw something she wasn't supposed to see. She's on the run from this guy. He's a bad dude."

"Oh, my God."

To Franco, she seemed sincerely shocked by all the information. That was good. She knew nothing, so she could have told no one anything.

"So, she reported something to the F.B.I.?"

"It's not quite that simple. I met Rosa at her father's restaurant a couple years ago. We dated a few times, but she couldn't deal with a cop's routine."

"Or lack thereof?"

Franco nodded, and continued with his made-up backstory. "A couple days ago, she left me a message on my home phone, saying she was hiding from her boyfriend, and didn't know who else to call. I was on a stakeout and didn't get the message until just a few hours ago. She said I could find her here. All she gave me was your first name and a phone number."

"Weird. Why me?"

"I gather you and Rosa went to school together?"

"Yes, but we weren't that close. I knew her from our sorority house. We partied a little together with the rest of the girls, but I have to admit I was surprised to hear from her. Maybe she picked me because of my criminology degree. I'm going to law school now."

"That's probably it. She needed a place to hide, and someone she could trust, but someone distant enough that she couldn't be traced here. Good choice." He sipped from his cup. "Mmmm. Good coffee."

"Thank you."

"So, when was the last time you heard from her?"

"She only called that one time. Yesterday. She said she was in New Mexico and needed a place to stay in Austin. She told me she'd be here in the middle of the night, but she never showed. What do you think happened?"

"There was a possible sighting of Rosa with a man in a boat last night on Lake L.B.J. Did she have a friend on the lake that you know of?"

"I honestly couldn't name one of Rosa's friends, unless it would be one of our sorority sisters. But I don't know any of her guy friends. I'm sorry I'm not of much help."

Franco took another sip of the coffee. It really did taste good after the long, tiring night. "You've been a big help, actually, Miss Morales." He stood up. "I have a feeling Rosa will check in with you this morning, so when she does, will you call me? I'll be staying at the Holiday Inn across the lake." Franco pointed, for he could see the hotel on the opposite lakeshore through the window.

"Sure," Celinda said. "I could almost shout at you from the window."

He laughed as he turned the radio volume back up, louder than it was before, then walked to the door. She got up and followed close behind him. "Oh, let me give you my card. It's got my office number on it."

Franco reached into his blazer and pulled his twenty-two from the shoulder holster. Celinda was holding her hand out for the card. He did it quick, so she wouldn't have time to be frightened. The silencer jutted past her hand, to her chest. He pulled the trigger twice. Both bullets must have gone right through her heart, because she buckled and fell like a marionette whose strings had been cut. The look of shock on her face faded in seconds, and he knew it was a clean kill.

It was a pity, really. He had enjoyed talking to her. This was Rosa's fault, not his.

He holstered his weapon and picked up the two shell casings that had flown against the wall to his right. He went back to the radio, and turned the volume down lower. He took a paper napkin from the table and wiped his fingerprints from the coffee cup and the radio knob, then the doorknob. He hadn't touched anything else. He was sure no one had seen him enter the apartment. Now, he could peek out through the window to make sure no one would see him leave. He turned the knob with the napkin, closed the door, and walked away.

Franco did not return to his car. He had spotted a sporting goods store nearby called Sports Nation. It was one of those franchise joints that were beginning to crop up across the country. There, he bought shorts, a jock strap, a jogging suit, a T-shirt, socks, and a new pair of running shoes. He paid in cash.

He took his bag of athletic gear to a hotel he saw across the lake, walking over the Congress Street bridge to get there. He checked into a room, showered, and sacked his old clothes up in the bag from the store. He put on the new running clothes and left the hotel. Finding a public trash bin on the street, he stuffed the old clothes in it. Before he recrossed the bridge to get to his car, he walked down under the bridge, where there was a jogging trail along Town Lake. He went to the lakeshore and stretched as if he were about to begin a run. When he was sure no one was watching, he dropped his murder weapon into the lake.

You couldn't be too careful these days. The evidence the cops were getting out of carpet fibers, hair samples, and tiny blood spots was amazing. Franco kept his head shaved for that reason. He had had all the carpet removed from his car. And he always ditched murder weapons and the clothes he wore after a hit.

With his mind free of those worries, he realized that he needed rest. Then he had to buy a wardrobe he could wear around town, as he had not had time to pack when leaving Nevada. Next, he had to find out who the guy with the classic woody boat was on Lake L.B.J. Oh, yeah, he thought as he approached his car in the parking lot. Got to get rid of those Nevada plates.

CHAPTER

Creed woke to the smell of Gail's stale perfume, and felt her arm draped over his bare chest. He opened his eyes, remembering that he had brought her home last night, stayed for a drink, and then just stayed. Remembering, he smiled, but didn't want to wake her. Best to sneak out if he could. Creed had consumed only half of his whiskey at the poker game, and less than half of the nightcap Gail had poured him. He felt pretty bright-eyed. She, on the other hand, had taken a few more drinks while serving at the gambling barn, and had finished both of her nightcaps. She was still out cold.

The shades were drawn, but Creed could see daylight around their edges. Typical night owl, Gail knew how to darken a room for sleeping all day. The purple glow of a lava light illuminated a clock on the nightstand: 9:45. Creed slipped out from under Gail's arm and crept into the bathroom for a long pee. Then he found his clothes, dressed, and stepped quietly out of the apartment door.

Gail lived in a garage apartment in a neighborhood north of the UT campus. The neighborhood was Sunday-morning quiet as Creed made his way down rickety wooden stairs. He got into his van, found his bearings, and soon was on his way down Guadalupe Street, known locally as "The Drag." He detoured into East Austin to Cisco's, an established Mexican restaurant with the best breakfast in town. Relishing his huevos rancheros with frijoles and potatoes, he thought about the gig last night, the growl of the Fender Twin amp, the appreciative crowd, and that one wrong note he wished he hadn't hit on the Strat. Then he thought about the poker game, the botched robbery, and Gail. He chuckled to himself, sitting alone there at his breakfast table, sipping his coffee. It wasn't every night a guy could play to a packed house at the Armadillo, survive a gun-fight, and get laid.

After breakfast, he headed for Lake Austin, where his houseboat waited in the marina. Turning down the drive to the boat slips, he saw some pretty college girls in bikinis piling into a ski boat with their boyfriends, getting a head start on their tans on this unseasonably warm day in early spring. Lucky guys, he thought. He wondered if he should have gone to college instead of Nashville. That would have kept him out of the war. He wondered if it was now too late for both—college or Music Row. How would a war vet be accepted on campus? But he didn't see himself in the corporate world, not even in the music business. Maybe it was time to go back to Nashville and start over in the clubs and studios. His guitar play-ing was back to ninety percent. But what were the chances of getting a second big break, this time without the charisma of Dixie driving the deal?

He parked in his reserved spot, grabbed his guitar, and strolled down the dock to the slip where his houseboat waited. It was home, and he liked it. That houseboat was the best purchase he had made when the record royalties were still rolling in from his one hit song, "Written in the Dust." He had paid cash for the boat, but he sometimes had trouble coming up with the slip rental and utilities nowadays. Between gambling and a few pickup guitar gigs, finances could get tight.

He stepped over the stern, unlocked the cabin door, and put his guitar in the corner. The light on his Code-A-Phone machine was blinking, so he pushed the button as he got undressed for a shower. A familiar voice spoke.

"*Hey, Creed, it's Willie. Good show last night. Hey, I got a hot tip for you. Luster Burnett is coming out of retirement. Yeah, the Luster Burnett. I rec-ommended you as a band leader. He wants to meet you. Monday at noon at his ranch on Nutty Brown Road. You'll know it's his place when you see the gate. It's Luster Burnett, amigo. Could be big if it works. Good luck.*"

Creed felt his jaw hanging open. He pushed the rewind button and lis-tened to the tape again. His heart began to thump, thinking of the oppor-tunity. Luster Burnett was the biggest thing to hit country music after Hank Williams died. His songs began dominating the charts shortly after Hank's death, filling the void, but with his own lyrical style, a sense of humor, and an authentic country voice that could move souls to laughter or tears. As a songwriter, he broke new ground in country-western music, bringing a poetic style to the down-home genre.

In Creed's first band, before Jo Ann—or Dixie, as she called herself
now—Creed had played every Luster Burnett hit to make the charts, and
even some obscure album tracks he liked. And he knew all the guitar in-
tros and solos—every riff and modulation. As a kid, he had listened to the
45s over and over, with the volume turned up loud so he could detect the
nuances of the techniques the studio guitarists had put on those old tunes.
If they hammered, he hammered. If they slid, he slid. Double-stops, pull-
aways, chicken-pickin', you name it . . . He learned to play every lick just
like the record.

Creed had also read up on Luster, and talked to people who had known
him in Nashville. The tragic facts were that, at the height of Luster's career, his wife had died in a car wreck, sliding off an icy road while Luster
was away on tour. Distraught, Luster had canceled all his appearances
and studio sessions. Everyone knew how much he had loved his wife, but
it was just a matter of time, they all thought, until Luster would return to
his booming career. His press conference held a year to the day after the
tragic wreck had shocked Music Row. Luster announced that he planned
to permanently retire, never to cut another side, or play another show.
The challenges were gone, he had said; the heart ripped out of his drive to
create.

Gossip hounds followed him for a while as he moved back to his native
Texas, taking up residence in his ranch house on Onion Creek outside of
Austin, where he had buried his wife. Like Creed, he was said to enjoy
gambling, and had recorded songs about gamblers and wild long-shot
bets, so he was supposedly spotted in Vegas or Atlantic City over the years.
He was seen in Texas honky-tonks and dance halls occasionally, listening
to good country bands, but he gradually changed his appearance, until no
one would know what to look for anymore even if they cared to look for
the great Luster Burnett at all. Other stars took his place, and curiosity
about him faded. His oldies still played on the radio, to which some deejay might remark, "That was the legendary Luster Burnett singing 'Chuck
Will's Widow.' Wonder whatever happened to him?"

It was as if he had died, and in fact some thought he was dead. Creed,
himself, wondered sometimes. How could he just quit? Would he ever
play even a farewell concert?

Now, as he stepped out of the tiny houseboat shower stall and grabbed
a towel, Creed had his answer. Luster Burnett was making a comeback
after fifteen years of silence. His mind was full of new questions. Why?

Why now? Did Luster still have it? Could he still put on a show? Was he washed up? A drunk or a drug addict? Could that golden voice still sing?

There was much to do before meeting Luster tomorrow, but right now he was so excited that he knew he had to go out to Nutty Brown Road and figure out what Willie had meant about Luster's ranch gate. He pulled on some jeans, a paisley shirt, a leather bomber jacket, and some well-worn cowboy boots. Leaving the houseboat, he trotted toward the van until he heard some psychedelic rock blaring from the marina office. He saw the marina owner's Yamaha 650 parked beside his van. On a whim, he stuck his head into the office door, coughed at the marijuana smoke, and shouted for Stew.

"Stew? You decent?"

Stew was a hippie who had inherited the marina from his grandfather. He wore his hair in blond dreadlocks, sported a year-round tan, and almost never wore shoes. The marina was a good little moneymaker for him, and he liked keeping it tolerably shipshape, so his life was complete, as long as he could score his weed. He was kicked back in a La-Z-Boy recliner, listening to some grinding rock.

"Creed! Killer show at the Armadillo last night, man!"

"I saw you on the front row."

"Yeah, I think you spit on me when you were singing harmonies, man!" He laughed for a good, long while.

"Can I borrow your bike this afternoon?"

"Go for it, dude. I ain't goin' anywhere today. I've got the Thirteenth Floor Elevators on the turntable, man, and I am rockin'!"

"I'll bring you some ribs from The Salt Lick." Creed grabbed the motorcycle helmet just inside the door and got out of there before he got swept up in more rambling conversation. The key was inside the helmet, as usual. He jumped on the Yamaha, kicked the engine over, and accelerated out of the parking lot, snugging the helmet strap under his chin. Seeing the gas gauge pegged left of empty, he coasted into a Texaco and put two dollars in the tank, almost filling it up.

Twenty minutes later, he had left Austin in his rearview and turned onto Nutty Brown Road in search of Luster Burnett's ranch gate. But what was it that he should be looking for, exactly? Maybe the initials "LB"? Willie had only said he'd know the place when he saw it. There were some fancy stone and wrought-iron estate entrances out here on this road, as if all the rich landowners were trying to outdo one another. He passed an attempt to re-create a Mexican-style hacienda gateway. Creed could only shake his head at the pretentious audacity of it all.

He continued his cruise. And then, as often happened, out of nowhere, some song lyrics began to emerge in his head, like a movie fading in on the screen, complete with a thumping blues/rock audio track.

> *I had two bald tires on my Harley*
> *Didn't have no job of any kind*
> *My gas gauge pegged left of empty*
> *I was too poor to pay no never-mind*
>
> *Then I saw you step out of your front door*
> *And I downshifted to the slower lane*
> *Your cowgirl boots and your cutoff jeans*
> *Made me hope my luck was gonna change . . .*

Like his current search down Nutty Brown Road, and his life in general for that matter, he wasn't sure where the song was going. All he knew was that he couldn't use "Yamaha" in a blues rocker, so he had changed it to "Harley." He shifted gears in time to the groove, but didn't try to force another verse. It would either ripen in time, or die on the vine. Hell, that in itself was a whole 'nother song.

Barreling down the country blacktop, he saw something oddly familiar flash by on his right. Downshifting into a U-turn, he swung around and motored back to the ranch gate he had just past. The gate was simple in contrast to the ostentatious entryways along this stretch of blacktop. It was just an inexpensive aluminum ranch gate you'd buy at the feed store if you made a living on a real, working ranch. Creed knew the manufacturer—Life-Time Gates. He had been schooled not to swing on a Lifetime gate at his grandfather's farm once.

"Get off that gate!" the old man had yelled. "This ain't no playground, and it ain't recess. Now get back to work and don't let me ever catch you swingin' on my gate again!"

This gate was the same type, with six horizontal aluminum bars spanning its length, evenly spaced from the ground up. But someone had made additions to this gate. There were iron discs, from an old disc plow, bolted here and there onto the six horizontal aluminum bars—dots placed on top of lines. To Creed, the horizontal gate members represented strings on a guitar, the plow discs were finger placements. That was a guitar chord, sure as one you might see represented in a book full of guitar chords. And not just any chord, either, but F sharp major. Luster Burnett liked to sing in F sharp, once claiming that the key most perfectly suited the range of his voice. It wasn't a common key in which to play, for most pickers. This had to be the place.

From the gate, the ranch looked like many another typical old-time spread in the Texas Hill Country. A line of scrubby cedar and mesquite trees stood guard behind the seven-strand barbed-wire fence. The mesquites were leafing out bright green this time of year, and an abundance of spring grass seemed available, as opposed to other overstocked ranches Creed had seen. Over the tops of the scrub brush, he could see the dome-like crowns of some sizable live oaks, and in the distance, between the live oak crowns, he recognized the tips of some bald cypresses reaching for the sky. Tall bald cypress trees like those had to mean permanent water—Onion Creek, one of the Austin area's most beautiful clear-water tributaries.

Excited to have solved the riddle and found the place, Creed toed the bike into gear, made a stop for ribs at The Salt Lick, and motored on back to his place on the lake. He spent the rest of the day on his houseboat, listening to his scratchy old Luster Burnett discs on the turntable, practicing the guitar parts on a Martin D-28 acoustic, remembering where the vocal harmony parts fell on each song. The parts came back to him easily out of some deeply ingrained place in his mind, long unused. His confidence high, he looked forward to meeting the great Luster Burnett.

CHAPTER

From the moment he saw her battered body in the morgue drawer, Texas Ranger Hooley Johnson was struck by an almost withering sadness. Corpses were part of the deal in law enforcement. He had grown accustomed to that long ago. But this wanton ruination of youth and life staggered him to the point that he didn't care for his job very much right now. For the first time in a long time, he thought he might actually vomit. Not from the broken human corpse or the autopsy incisions. Just from the sheer loss and waste of a life so young and filled with potential.

Doc Brewster, the Travis County medical examiner, was pointing out his findings from the autopsy: "She apparently was hurled through the glass windshield of a boat . . ." he was saying, clinically.

Hooley shook his head and sighed, tuning the good doctor out. This girl, Rosabella Martini, had long, black hair. He had seen her photos in the F.B.I. file faxed from Las Vegas. She could have been a fashion model, but it was hard to tell that in her current mangled state. He knew she was educated and accomplished. By all accounts she, and even her father, had taken little if any part in the organized crime ring her uncle ran. She had been a good girl. Her muscle tone told Hooley that she took care of herself; she respected her body. He looked away from her, then made himself look back again. If he was going to get to the bottom of her death, he was going to have to deal with this as an investigator. He would not have this chance to look over her fatal injuries again.

". . . so, she didn't drown," Brewster was saying. "As you can see, she was almost decapitated. The lacerations to the neck suggest a mechanical precision. My guess: a boat propeller at a high RPM."

"I read your report, Doc. Read between the lines for me."

Brewster, a stout little man with a thick shock of graying hair, took his glasses off and polished them with his white lab coat. "Usually in a case like this—dead body on the lake, young person, late at night—you'll find alcohol or drugs in the bloodstream. None here."

Hooley nodded. "All right. What else?"

"She wasn't sexually molested. That's not to say that somebody didn't have that in mind, but it didn't happen. She had her clothes on. Jeans, tennis shoes, T-shirt. I didn't find any bruises on her arms, her wrists, or anything else to suggest she was grabbed or manhandled. You know how it is, when some mean bastard grabs a girl."

Hooley nodded. "Her F.B.I. file said she had a black belt in karate. Any sign she used it?"

The doctor shook his head. "She had glass cuts on one knuckle, but no sign of any other abrasions."

"What was it about that glass?"

"Like I wrote in the report, it was plain old glass, not the shatterproof or tempered stuff you find on later models of boats or cars."

"What year did they start requiring that for manufacturers?"

Doc Brewster shrugged, cautiously. "You'd know that better than I would."

Hooley frowned and took his tally book out of his shirt pocket. He had learned to carry the notepad from his stepfather, a West Texas rancher from Loving County. Originally intended to keep an accurate count, or "tally," of cattle on the range, Hooley had found it handy for taking notes and writing reminders.

Flipping to the first open page, he wrote: "Call Glastron." Austin was headquarters for the Glastron Company, known nationwide as a manufacturer of pleasure boats. They would probably know what year the government began requiring manufacturers to install safer windshields.

He returned the tally book and the pencil to his shirt pocket. "How about the possible projectile wound?"

The examiner pointed to the victim's left hip. "It's just a flesh wound, but it looks for all the world like a bullet hole to me. Small caliber, probably a twenty-two. She was hit from behind. The exit wound is in front."

Hooley took his Stetson off and scratched his head. "That doesn't fit the scenario of a boating accident."

"It's troubling. Especially considering who she is. *Was*."

"Niece of a mob kingpin," the ranger said, mostly to himself. "There's no other explanation? Something else struck her?"

Doc Brewster shook his head. "I've seen a lot of bullet wounds."

Hooley nodded. "Did she chew gum?"

"Pardon?"

"You know . . . bubble gum, chewin' gum. Can you tell if she was a gum chewer?"

"Sorry, Hooley. I'm pretty sure she didn't dip snuff, but I can't tell if she liked to chew gum. Why?"

"In her car, there was a bag from one of them drive-through burger joints—the one where you talk to the clown."

"McDonald's?"

"No, the one that jumps out of the box."

"Jack in the Box?"

"That's it. The bag had a piece torn off of it, and I thought maybe she put her gum in it, but I didn't find any chewed gum in the car anywhere. So . . . Maybe she used that scrap of paper for something else. Maybe she wrote something down on it."

"You don't have much to go on with this one, do you?"

"Not yet," Hooley admitted. He slapped the hat back on his head as he looked down on Rosa's body one last time. He made her a silent promise, then said, "Close her up, Doc. She's gone anyway."

"Where do you even start?" the examiner asked.

The ranger tugged at his gun belt. "Well, Doc, I guess I'll go fishin'."

Brewster gave the ranger a slap on the shoulder. "Good luck."

As he walked to his pickup truck in the parking lot outside of the medical examiner's office, Hooley spotted the KVUE news van turning in off the street. He ducked behind a car and let the van drive by, assuming the reporters were probably searching for information on the dead girl. The press knew Hooley avoided cameras, but always provided colorful footage when cornered. He was an old-school, no-nonsense ranger, and used old Texas vernacular. That's just the way things came out when he spoke, but the press ate it up.

Satisfied that he had given the newshounds the slip, he hightailed it out of the parking lot. It helped that he drove his own Ford pickup more often than whatever vehicle D.P.S. was issuing to Rangers on any given year. The reporters had not caught on to that detail yet.

Two hours later, after having swung by his house in Liberty Hill to hook his bass boat trailer to the back of his pickup, Hooley found himself backing down the boat ramp where Rosa's car had been found. He floated the boat off the trailer, climbed aboard, started the outboard, and motored to the dock where he tied the boat to a cleat. Then he strolled back down the dock and got back in his Ford to pull the empty boat trailer out of the water. He parked in the adjacent lot, taking his gun belt off to leave locked in the truck.

Walking back to the dock, he saw a man and a small boy approaching, the boy wearing cheap, plastic, inflatable flotation devices around his upper arms. The boy was maybe five or six.

"Excuse me, sir," the man said, seeming unnecessarily nervous, "but are you Hooley Johnson, the Texas Ranger?"

Hooley paused, standing hip-cocked like a horse. "Yep."

The man offered his hand, so Hooley had to shake it. "I recognized you from the TV, when you were talking about that antiwar riot in Houston a couple of years ago."

Hooley nodded and looked at his boat.

"I don't want to keep you, but do you mind signing an autograph for my son? Jimmy, shake his hand, he's a Texas Ranger."

Hooley shook the tike's little hand and took the ballpoint pin and piece of paper from the dad.

"Are you here investigating that girl's death?"

Hooley looked over the top of his sunglasses at the dad. "What do *you* know about that?"

"Me? Nothin'. I just heard about it."

He handed the autograph back to the man. "You know those little arm floaters don't work. Do me a favor and get Jimmy a real life jacket. Don't use an adult one, either. They slip off. Get him a kid's life jacket."

"Oh, yes, sir. Okay. I didn't know they didn't work."

"Have a fine day." As he turned away, he heard little Jimmy ask:

"Is he a real Texas Ranger?"

"Yes, siree."

"He looks too old. What position does he play?"

"Not a baseball Ranger," the dad said, laughing.

Thankfully, they faded out of earshot about that time. Hooley found himself alone on the dock. His bass boat thumped against the pier, waiting for him to board, but he lingered for a bit there on the weathered wooden planks, getting a feel for the crime scene. He had stopped by briefly on Saturday, two days ago, when the call first came in for help from the Texas Rangers. He had been on his way to bust some cattle rustlers, so he had taken just enough time to look over Rosa's car before it was hauled off to the D.P.S. crime lab for processing.

Rosa's car had been abandoned in the parking lot, so it was reasonable to assume that she had boarded a boat here that had taken her out onto the lake, where her body had been found. The pier stood between the boat ramp and a sandy beach that stretched out in front of a little lakeside beer joint. Doc Brewster had found no alcohol in Rosa's bloodstream, but the presence of the bar, called The Crew's Inn, increased the possibility that she had boarded a boat with someone who had been drinking.

"What did you get yourself into, Rosa?" he asked, thinking about the bullet wound to her left hip. Maybe one guy had taken Rosa on a boat ride, making some other guy jealous. Maybe the jealous guy had shot at them as they cruised away. That might spook the boat driver into a high-speed getaway, leading to an accident that threw Rosa through the windshield. Hooley imagined where a shooter might have stood to take such a shot. He strolled down to the end of the pier, looking for shell casings, or whatever. He found nothing of import, but that didn't prove or disprove anything. A semiautomatic handgun might have ejected the shell casing into the water. Or, if the shooter had used a revolver, the empty brass shell wouldn't have been ejected at all.

He took out his tally book and wrote: "divers & metal detector." Then he waved a big hand at the lake, dismissing it as if fed up with it.

He walked back to his bass boat, got in, cast off, and throttled up the 140-horse Mercury to motor out past the end of the pier. He then killed the outboard and let the boat coast forward. He went to the swivel seat in the front of the boat and lowered the prop of his electric trolling motor into the water at the bow. He picked up his rod and reel, which already had a crank-bait tied onto the five-pound test monofilament line, and made a cast toward a boat dock at someone's lake house. The lure was a Hellbender—one of Hooley's favorites. He could feel it diving and wiggling underwater as he reeled it back in, bumping it off dock pilings and other submerged structures.

He could control the boat with the trolling motor, which he worked with foot pedals. He continued to cast as he looked the crime scene over from different angles. Suddenly—bang! He got a strike from a big bass.

He set the hook and began to fight the fish, working it close enough to grab within a couple minutes.

"Good one," he said to himself, smiling as he reached over the side of the boat to seize the lower jaw of the lunker and lift it aboard. Fried bass fillets would sure make a nice supper, but he wasn't sure he'd have time to mess with the cleaning and filleting of the fish, so he let it swim free. "You lucky bastard," he said.

He continued to fish his way out of the cove where The Crew's Inn did business. *The Crew's Inn,* he thought, as he fished farther away from the bar. *Clever. Good place to ask questions later.* "Y'all cruise in to The Crew's Inn," he said aloud, as if cutting a radio ad for the place.

Leaving the cove, the lake widened. He knew Rosa's body had been found floating somewhere in this wider part of the lake, but the sheriff's deputies had not thought to mark the exact spot with a float. These rural counties didn't see enough murders to warrant the training of full-time homicide detectives and sometimes investigations suffered because of it.

Rounding a bend to the left, he saw a small, weathered buoy sticking out of the water ahead, probably marking some hazard just under the surface of the water. He hoped so, because underwater structures made good bass habitat. Trolling and casting, he approached the buoy and found it bobbing over a large sunken tree—probably a big bald cypress that had washed down into the lake on some fence-lifter of a flood. The tree actually broke the surface of the water, but only by half an inch or so, making it a serious boating hazard. Hence the buoy.

"I'll bet there's a big ol' bass under that snag," he growled. Working the Hellbender low, he felt the hard strike of the fish and jerked back on the rod with gunfighter reflexes to set the hook. This one was even bigger than the first, judging by the fight in the fish. "Get out of there, you . . ." He held his rod trip high, trying to horse the wise old fish out from under the tree, but it dove deep, making the drag sing on the reel. Then the fish wrapped Hooley's line around a root or something and broke off.

"Goddamnit!" Hooley roared. "That was a two-dollar lure!"

Looking into the water, he realized he was close enough to the sunken deadfall to get a really good look at it now. He could tell from the huge trunk that it was indeed a cypress tree. There was a missing chunk knocked out of it just below the surface. Some boat, in spite of the marker buoy, must have slammed into the thing. The missing chunk indicated a hard hit at high speed. "Damn thing would have launched sky-high like a skippin' stone," he muttered.

Looking closer, he saw a piece of wood that didn't match the water-logged grain of the sunken cypress. It was just a splinter that had become lodged in the cypress wood, presumably left behind when some unlucky boater hit the tree. He got down on his belly on the front deck of the bass boat, reached into the water, and plucked the sample from the underwater hazard. "Wooden boat . . ." he muttered, remembering Doc Brewster's description of antique windshield glass.

For some reason, he thought about little Jimmy's inflatable water wings, then realized what his mind was trying to tell him. A lot of newer boats had flotation devices built in. You could blast a hole in them with a shotgun and they wouldn't sink. But an old wooden boat with a hole in it could easily take on water and sink under the weight of an inboard engine block. Maybe the boat that took Rosa for her last ride had sunk. But if so, how far had it gotten from the crime scene before sinking? It could be anywhere in Lake L.B.J., and the reservoir covered over six thousand acres.

Hooley stowed his fishing rod, and started the Mercury outboard again. Before motoring back to the boat ramp, he took out his tally book and wrote a note only he would understand: "Talk to the clown."

9
CHAPTER

Creed found the guitar-chord gate waiting open at Luster Burnett's Onion Creek Ranch. He pulled his van through, then put his foot on the brake to collect himself. Butterflies swarmed in his stomach. He took a couple deep breaths, nodded his head, then pulled forward on the gravel ranch road. Swinging around a curve, he saw the ranch gate disappear in the rearview mirror. As he drove on, the cedars and mesquites began to thin out, and he knew that had not happened by accident. Luster had left just enough brush along the paved road to provide a visual barrier for seclusion, and to make the ranch look like just another overgrown spread. But farther into the ranch, the cedars and mesquites had been cut down or uprooted, giving way to an open pasture dotted with mature live oaks, native pecan trees, and elms.

All this spoke to Creed. The other gentlemen's ranches along this stretch of back road had fancy gates, new board fences, and cleared pastures along the blacktop—like a bunch of beauty pageant girls screaming "look at me!" while they competed for attention from passersby. Luster, it seemed, just wanted to be left alone behind his veil, though his ranch was perhaps the real beauty among them all.

Continuing his slow drive, mindful of kicking up too much dust, Creed saw seven or eight well-muscled quarter horses behind a cross-fence. A windmill pumped a trickle of water out of a galvanized pipe, into a large stone water tank. The tail fin of the windmill was painted like the Texas flag. The gravel trace continued to wind gracefully among the native oaks, and then straightened through a manicured pecan orchard, the scores of trees standing in soldierly ranks. Coming out of the orchard, Creed saw the house—a rambling two-story limestone structure crowded with some of the biggest live oaks he had seen in Central

Texas. Behind the home, a row of tall bald cypress trees reached even higher than the metal roof, just leafing out with green shoots this time of year.

He shut the driver's-side door and listened to his boots crunch the gravel as he walked to the back of the van. He could hear water rushing, wind sighing through treetops, birds singing. The quietude was welcome, compared to the clamorous marina where he lived. He opened the back of the van and grabbed two guitar cases, one holding his electric Fender and the other his acoustic Martin D-28.

Passing through a nicely landscaped entryway, lush with leafy flora, Creed marched up to the door, put one case down, and pushed the electric doorbell. He heard it ring, then heard a voice shout:

"Come on in!"

Creed opened the door, carried his guitars in, and kicked the door shut behind him. "Mr. Burnett?"

"Creed?"

"Yes, sir."

"Be with you in a minute!" the voice said, apparently coming from a kitchen, where Creed could hear an ice tray crackling and cubes falling into glasses. "Make yourself comfortable!"

Creed put his guitars down and tried to shake off his nervousness. He looked around the living room. A large stone fireplace stood at one end, a huge cypress beam serving as a mantel. Overhead, a chandelier made of elk antlers hung from wrought-iron chains. A few obligatory whitetail deer heads and shoulder mounts jutted from the walls. The wall opposite the fireplace had eight gold records displayed in frames.

"You want some iced tea?"

"Yes, sir."

"Sweet or unsweet?"

"Plain is good. Unsweet." Creed felt drawn to the large bank of plate-glass windows facing the rear of the house. He strolled toward them and beheld the most dazzling view he could remember seeing anywhere. The backyard dropped away to the creek bottom, the gently sloping banks having been mowed all the way down to the stream's edge. There, rivulets of clear water snaked among the trunks of bald cypress trees so huge that five men clasping hands wouldn't reach all the way around one. Upstream, white water shimmered down a slanted rock slide and gushed into a perfect natural swimming hole.

"It's a little strong," Luster said, his voice nearer, "but the ice will melt and cut it like branch water in a jug of shine."

Creed turned and prepared to meet his country music idol for the first time. The legend came out of the kitchen, carrying two large glasses of tea. Creed's jaw dropped when he recognized the man's face—the same face he had seen across more than one poker table. "Boss?" he said, in disbelief.

Luster began laughing. "You ought to see the look on your face! You're starin' at me like a calf at a new gate."

"I'll be go-to-hell. All this time I wished I had met you, and turns out I already have."

"Well, you can't meet somebody too many times." He handed Creed the glass of tea and shook his hand. "Sit down."

Creed fell back onto the sofa, still shocked. But he had to admit he wasn't nervous anymore. He looked hard at Luster's face, trying to find some resemblance to the album cover photos he had seen years ago. Back in those days, Luster had been known for wearing sequined suits and rhinestone-studded guitar straps and hatbands. Clean-cut and clean-shaven, that younger Luster Burnett didn't bear much resemblance to the man sitting in the living room in his work clothes, with three days of beard stubble on his tanned face and a shaggy mop of hat-molded hair.

"I can't believe I never recognized you before, but I see it now."

"I was always good at going incognito. That's why I started wearin' all those fancy suits for all my publicity pictures and shows. Everybody got so used to seeing me that way, that I could dress in some old jeans and a work shirt, and nobody had a clue who I was." He smiled, ran his fingers through his hair. "Plus, twenty years of ranchin' tends to take the bloom off the rose, if you know what I mean."

Creed shook his head, and felt a smile stretch across his face. "I can't believe I'm sittin' here with Luster Burnett. If you had any idea how many times I've spun your records and learned those licks. Yesterday alone! I boned up as much as I could in one day's time."

"Relax, kid. You already got the job—if you want it. I know your background in Nashville, and I've been to some of your shows in Austin. I've even heard you play a couple of my old songs, and you nailed the guitar parts. You don't sing nothin' like me, but you got the guitar parts down."

"Nobody sings 'em like you," Creed allowed.

"Well, I hope you'll take the job, but it probably ain't exactly what you had in mind."

"What do you mean?"

"This comeback of mine is gonna be like startin' over from scratch. We're not gonna have any label support because I don't have a label behind me anymore. We're not gonna have a sound crew, a tour manager, a stage boss, any roadies or guitar techs. We're gonna lug our own amps, just like we did when we started out. I'm sure you started like that, too, right?"

Creed nodded. "Hell, yeah. I was the driver, the booking agent, the stage crew, the sound man, Jo Ann's bodyguard . . ."

"Jo Ann?" Luster said.

"Dixie. Dixie Houston. Her real name's Jo Ann."

Luster's eyes twinkled. "I saw her on the *Glen Campbell Good Time Hour*. Lord, have mercy! What was it like working with her? She's a looker, son, I'll tell you . . ."

"She's a handful, that's for sure. Not shy."

"She's a pistol, no doubt. Sings her ass off, too."

"We had a hell of a run. Then I got drafted." He didn't mention how Dixie refused to even see him after his return from Vietnam; how he suspected she had doctored the songwriters rights on "Written in the Dust," cutting him out of most of his duly earned royalties.

"Well, she's a big star now. And we're not. That's my point. Ain't gonna be no tour support. We're gonna have to do everything ourselves. This is a grassroots resurrection. I'm rising up from the grave, son."

"Do you plan to look for a deal in Nashville?"

"I already tried. Half the snot-nosed punks on Music Row said 'Luster Who?' The other half kissed my royal ass, but wouldn't give me a record deal. Hell, the mob has bought up the big labels and hired a bunch of coked-up college boys trying to force-feed country music to city folks. Gone are the days, Creed, when the pickers used to push a plow. Bunch of rejects from rock, pop, and folk; don't know a whip-poor-will from a washtub."

"Nashville's lost its way," Creed agreed. "This Texas scene is still authentic, though."

"Yes!" Luster said, lunging forward in his chair, sloshing his iced tea in his excitement. "It's regional, and therefore only marginally profitable, but it's the real deal. We can adopt this sound and grow it nationwide. That's the reason I didn't try to put the old band back together. Hell, half of them are in nursing homes, anyway. I want a bunch of young, hungry guys in the band; guys who understand this new sound. What do they call it? Progressive country?"

Creed smirked. "I don't know what to make of that term. I think we could use a little bit of *regressive* country these days. You do plan to do all your old stuff, right?"

"Oh, hell, yes. We've got to do the hits. But we've got to create a new sound. Something else. I just don't know exactly what *else* is yet. This ain't gonna be just some oldies band. I don't want my comeback to peak on Lawrence Welk. I want Johnny Carson."

"Heeeeere's Johnny," Creed answered, taking a long draw of the iced tea. "The sound will depend a lot on the pickers."

Luster nodded. "That's why I need to know right now: Are you in or out? You know the score. It ain't gonna be no trip down Easy Street. But if you're in, you're the band leader, and you need to help me pick the players."

"I'm in," Creed said. "There's not a doubt in my mind. I wouldn't miss this opportunity for anything."

"Good," Luster said, looking out through the front window, "because here they come."

Creed followed his gaze and saw a line of beat-up cars, vans, and pick-ups streaming out of the pecan orchard. "Auditions?"

"I sent the word out through some contacts I could trust for bass players, drummers, fiddlers, and pedal steel guitar players. I figured you and I would have the guitars covered."

"Release the hounds," Creed said, watching the hopeful musicians pile out of the run-down vehicles.

"Stick your head out there and tell 'em to wait around back till we call 'em in. I'll meet you in the studio, through this door." Luster pointed at the door beside the eight gold records.

"Before we get started, I better give them the same speech you gave me. Some of them may be expecting tour buses and fat per diems."

"Good idea. That'll cull some of the runts."

The doorbell was already ringing, so Creed went to the door and asked the musicians to walk around the house and wait on the back patio. Once they had gathered around back, he gave them the speech, and indeed several packed up and left. He went back into the house, collected his guitars, and entered the windowless studio adjacent to the living room. Luster was switching on amps and tapping on microphones to ensure they were on. Creed placed his cases on the floor and opened them.

"Let's see what you've got there," Luster said, looking over his shoulder. "Oh, a Martin D-twenty-eight."

"Yes, sir."

"Good guitar. Uh-oh," Luster said, sounding disappointed. "You brought a Strat? I figured you'd bring a Telecaster."

"If I had a Tellie that played like this Strat, I would have brought it in. This Strat is special. But if you want me to play a Tellie, I've got one in the van."

Luster looked at the guitar with a furrowed brow. "No, you play what feels right. Maybe this new sound of mine is gonna be more of a Strat thing, anyway."

"We'll figure it out, Boss. What do you want to do first?"

"You're the band leader."

"Let's start with the bass players."

"Put some bottom on it. Good call."

Creed went through the living room and out through the back door to the patio. "Hey, y'all," he said. "Listen up. I need anybody auditioning for bass guitar to wait in the living room. We'll call you in one at a time. The rest of y'all just make yourselves comfortable out here. This is gonna take a while. Smoke 'em if you got 'em."

Five bass players came into the living room and Creed picked one at random to invite into the studio. Luster picked up an acoustic Gibson guitar and prepared to sing one of his hits so the bass player could play along. With the first note Luster belted, Creed felt himself in the presence of a master vocalist, and it wasn't even showtime yet. Relieved that the legend could still sing, Creed played the lead parts on his Strat with all the soul he could muster.

He gave each bassist a verse and a chorus to get into the groove, and that was enough to know that none of them understood the style. It was just plain ol' country music, but you had to know how to put the note in the pocket.

"If you don't hear from us by tomorrow, you'll know we decided to go with somebody else," Creed told each of them.

"Are there any left?" Luster asked after the fourth one.

"Just one. I hope he can lay down a foundation."

"Yeah, that last guy couldn't lay a ten-dollar whore."

The last hopeful carried in his case without a word and began to open the latches. He was taller than Creed, and lean. He had a roofer's tan.

Creed could see by the pale flesh around his hairline that he had just gotten a haircut, maybe for this audition, to look more country and less hippie. His dark brown hair was combed down with a little dab of Brylcreem.
He wore motorcycle cop shades, though the studio was not brightly lit.

"This is Luster Burnett," Creed said.

"I figured that," the man said, without looking up. "Who are you?"

"Name's Creed Mason."

The man nodded and strapped his bass guitar over his shoulder. "They
call me Tump. Tump Taylor." Only now did he venture across the studio
to shake Luster's hand. Walking back to the bass amp, he paused to shake
Creed's hand. "Creed Mason, huh? 'Written in the Dust.'"

"Right. You got a particular Luster Burnett song you want to audition to?"

Tump shrugged. "One of them F-sharp tunes, I guess." Tump plugged
his guitar chord into the bass rig, hit a few notes, and adjusted the amp
settings to his liking.

"Dear John Note," Luster suggested.

Tump nodded.

Luster sang the a cappella intro and Tump stabbed the downbeat for
the first bass note. Halfway into the first verse, one side of Tump's mouth
drew up in a wry smile, as if playing the bass was the only thing that even
remotely gave him any happiness. His head bobbed to the meter and his
fingers walked up and down the frets as smoothly as pistons.

Finishing the song, Creed nodded. "Good."

"Damn good," Luster added.

"I want to play that," Tump said, pointing at a stand-up bass leaning in
the corner.

They decided on a bluegrass number Luster had written called 'Chuck
Will's Widow,' Tump beating a sure rhythm, every note precise on the fret-
less neck of the acoustic bass fiddle.

"I've heard enough," Luster said.

Creed nodded his agreement. "You want to stay and play so we can
audition the drummers?"

"I got nothin' else to do."

The drummers proved more painful. After the third one was dismissed,
Tump shook his head and groaned. "Holy shit, that was bad."

"Sounded like he was buildin' a house back there," Creed opined.

"Sounded like a gunfight at a poker game to me," Luster added, shooting a glance at Creed.

The door from the living room opened, and a young Chicano kid stepped in. "I gotta be next," he said in a south-of-the-border accent, tapping his wrist, even though he wore no watch. "I gotta be at work in forty-five minutes, man."

"Where do you work, son?" Luster asked.

"I've been bussing tables at Matt's El Rancho. I just got to town last week, man. Metro. Metro Valenzuela." He shook hands with the three older men.

"Where are you from, Metro?" Creed asked.

"The Valley, man. Harlingen." He took the liberty of sitting on the drummer's stool. He picked up some sticks, tested the kick drum and high-hat pedals.

"Are you old enough to know any of my tunes?" Luster asked, suspiciously.

"Shit, yeah, man. My great-grandpa had all your records. He was a gringo."

Luster laughed. "Great-grandpa! All right, let's see what you've got."

They chose a song Luster had written about a Mexican border town. Metro swung his sticks into the complex rumba beat flawlessly, somehow ringing the cymbals and thumping the cowbell with the butt end of his stick along with all the snare and tom shots.

"That's a radical tune, man," Metro said at the end of the song. "It's a song about Mexico, but it has a Cuban beat."

Luster was staring at the young drummer, looking a bit perplexed. "You know, on the record, we added the cowbell and the cymbals on two other separate tracks."

Metro threw his hands in the air, as if he had just discovered a prank played at his expense. "No wonder it was so hard to learn. I thought I sucked, man."

"He's the one," Tump said, jutting his thumb Metro's way. "This is the kid."

"Well, we have a few more waiting to audition," Creed cautioned.

Tump took his bass off and leaned it against the amp. "Hey, the kid sounds like a damn octopus playing the kit back there. If you don't hire him, I ain't playin' in this band."

"We've got four more drummers out there. I can't just tell them to go home."

Tump walked to the living room door, opened it, and said, "We've found our drummer. The rest of y'all can go home." He slammed the door, turned to Creed, and said, "I can."

Creed knew the bass player was right about the drummer's talent, but he already found his leadership being tested by Tump. Still, he was grateful not to have to sit through the rest of the percussionists. "You two can go home," he said to Tump and Metro. "Rehearsal here tomorrow?" He looked at Luster.

Luster nodded. "Noon."

"Be back at noon tomorrow," Creed said, looking at the bassist, then the drummer.

"Thanks, dudes," Metro said, hurrying out with a big smile on his face.

Creed walked up close to Tump and spoke low as Tump put his instrument in its case."

"Mr. Burnett hired me to run this band," Creed said. "I'm open to all suggestions. But from here on out, Mr. Burnett and I make the decisions."

The dark glasses turned on Creed, the eyes behind them presumably sizing up the band leader. "Whatever. I'm just the bass player for the opening act."

Creed nodded. "See you tomorrow."

10
CHAPTER

After Tump left, Luster put his guitar on an instrument stand and began methodically cracking his knuckles. "It's beer-thirty, Creed."

"I hear that."

They walked through the depopulated living room and went to the refrigerator in the kitchen. Luster grabbed two Schlitz beers and handed one to Creed. "Go for the gusto," he said.

"Don't mind if I do," he replied, though he had figured Luster for a Lone Star man.

"We're halfway there."

Creed looked out the kitchen window at the ragtag gathering of musicians on the back patio, smoking cigarettes and laughing. He saw an attractive black woman with a huge teased-out Afro come around the corner, having just showed up. She had charmed one of the other musicians into carrying her bulky cases around back. "I think I see our steel player," he said.

Luster stepped to the window. "Which one?"

"The chick."

Luster stared. "The colored gal? I never knew a woman to play pedal steel, much less a colored gal."

"She's good. Name's Lindsay Lockett."

Luster chugged about half the beer. "A good-lookin' gal in the band? Could be trouble."

Creed chuckled. "I reckon I ought to know that as well as anybody. Lindsay's a piece of cake, compared to Dixie. A bit of a prima donna, but I can manage her."

Luster shrugged. "We already got the Meskin kid. Might as well have a colored gal, too. Hell, why not? The world's changin'. Even I'm tired of white cracker country, and I *am* a white cracker."

"I'm an East Texas peckerwood, myself."

Luster laughed. "I'm gonna let you stay in the band anyway. Call her in." He grabbed another beer from the fridge.

Luster was on his fourth beer by the time Lindsay Lockett got her steel set up and tuned. She seemed to have no concept of the time she was taking, and no idea that anyone might be waiting on her. When she finally got ready, she looked up, and almost seemed surprised to see Luster and Creed in the studio with her. She had not even spoken to Luster yet.

Creed made the introductions: "Lindsay Lockett, this is Luster Burnett."

"I prefer LockETTE." As she spoke, she held up her index finger, the silver finger pick pointing upward as if to punctuate the emphasis on the last syllable of her name. "The way you would say BurNETTE." Again, the spangled fingertip gave visual reference to the accent on the last syllable, spoken in a lush southern-black dialect.

Luster threw his beer can into the trash. "You can call me Luster. Can I call you Lindsay?"

"Oh. Okay, Luster." She smiled. Her teeth were perfect, like the rest of her ebony doll face. Her Afro possessed a glimmering quality. She wore false eyelashes and ruby red eye shadow that matched the glimmering shade of lipstick on her full lips.

"Unless you'd rather I call you LindSAY, and you can call me LuSTAIR."

Lindsay put her silver finger pick alongside her chin, and rolled her eyes toward the ceiling, as if considering the proposal. Then she began to laugh. "Oh, Luster, you are a cutup, I can see that right now." Again she laughed, a surprisingly harsh cackle considering her petite frame.

Luster smiled. "Where are you from, Lindsay?"

"I'm a refugee from Mississippi."

"How long have you been in Austin?"

"Almost ten years."

"Ten years? You look like a teenager."

"Thank you!" She beamed. "I'm thirty-four years old, Luster. Good genes. Clean livin'."

Creed called a tune with a steel guitar pickup riff, and Lindsay played it so perfectly that Creed could almost hear the scratches pop on the old seventy-eight. After a couple more tunes, Creed and Luster were both sold.

"All right, rehearsals start tomorrow . . ."

Creed cut Luster off there and added, "At eleven a.m., sharp."

When Lindsay finally got her steel guitar torn down, and packed up, and got Creed to carry it to her car for her—a 1963 Chevy Impala with a trunk big enough for four steel guitars—Creed found Luster in the kitchen, opening another beer.

"You ready?" Luster said, handing him the beer.

"Born ready." Creed took the ice-cold can.

"I sent the rest of the steel players packin'."

"I noticed the stampede."

"You know any of those fiddlers out there?"

"Can't say that I do."

"I guess we'll just have to wade through 'em like swamp water."

"Which one do you want to start with?"

"Eenie-meanie-miney-mo."

The fifth fiddler to audition walked into the studio looking very nervous. He called himself "Trusty" Joe Crooke, and he resembled something out of a Roy Rogers look-alike contest, except that he wore his hair in long, drab-brown locks reaching halfway down his back. His shirt was a Western pearl-snap affair with gaudy roping around the pockets and yoke. He also wore a cowboy hat and boots and a silk scarf tied around his neck.

After the obligatory introductions, he started chattering like a machine gun: "I sure hope I get this job, because I'm probably gonna get fired. I've been playing in a cowboy band at a dude ranch in Bandera for seven years, and I've never missed a show, not even once, but I'm missing one right now. I thought I'd be done here by now. Anyway, maybe it's time I quit, because I'm sick of playing the same twelve songs, three shows a day, six days a week. I want to see some blacktop. I sure hope I get this job."

"Step one: relax," Luster said. "You want a beer?"

"No, thanks. I don't drink till after the show."

Creed picked a Luster Burnett hit that leaned heavy on the fiddle and let Trusty Joe kick it off.

After the song, Luster sighed and looked earnestly at the fiddler. "That sounded just like the original except for one thing," he said. "Your tone is better. You're almost too good. Almost."

"It's this fiddle," Joe said, apologetically. "It's a hundred and fifty-two years old. I can play a cheaper fiddle if you want me to."

"It's not the fiddle," Creed said. "It's you. I think Mr. Burnett was giving you a compliment."

"Oh. Sorry. I mean, thanks. God, I'm so nervous I feel like I'm gonna puke."

"Take it easy, Joe. You're doing fine. Is that a mandolin in your other case?"

"Yes, sir."

"Bust it out, and let's do some bluegrass," Luster suggested.

They played a Burnett original called "Bolt from the Blue"—a song that gave Trusty Joe ample opportunity to show off his mandolin licks. Creed watched the picker's right hand as he frolicked through his half of the lead break like wind through a clothesline, thinking that he needed to adapt some of that style to his own guitar playing. The pick action was as clean as any he had ever seen among the A-list Nashville cats.

Trusty Joe looked up at Creed and Luster as if he feared a scolding when the song was done.

"That's some of the smoothest flat-pickin' I've seen in years," Luster said, reading Creed's mind.

"The key to mandolin is all in the right hand," Trusty replied, nervously. "Like the fiddle—all in the bow."

Luster looked at Creed. "You satisfied?"

"And then some."

Luster switched his guitar amp off. "You can tell that cowboy band to kiss your trusty ass, Joe. You got the job. Rehearsals tomorrow at noon."

"Oh, my God!" Trusty blurted. He buckled, catching his weight with his left knee and his right hand on the floor of the studio. "Oh, thank you, God!" he said, an actual sob escaping from his chest. Then he began to cry real tears, which quickly transmogrified into a blubbering torrent.

Creed and Luster looked at each other as if the new car they had just driven off the lot had lost a wheel.

"Are you all right, big 'un?" Creed asked.

Trusty held a hand up and nodded, wiping his cheeks on his shoulders, trying to compose himself. "Yeah. I'm just so happy!" Another gush of tears poured forth.

"Let me give you a tip," Luster said. "Cry equals sad. Laugh equals happy."

"I'm sorry," the fiddler said, pulling himself upright by sheer will. "I'm just real emotional right now, that's all. I prayed for this gig. Prayed and prayed."

Creed was growing increasingly disgusted with Trusty's outburst. "Well, quit blubberin', or you're gonna piss God off."

"I'm already pissed off," Luster said. He chuckled to himself then raised his eyes to the ceiling. "Forgive me, Lord," he said, under his breath. "Just a little joke."

Suddenly, Trusty began to heave like a dog about to cough up a bad piece of meat. He burst out through the living room. Creed followed, watching Trusty scramble out the back door, past the three remaining fiddlers on the patio. There, he leaned against the trunk of a large pecan tree and puked on the rhododendrons.

Trusty turned on the astonished hopefuls waiting to audition. "I got the job!" he announced.

Creed shook his head. Well, at least he wouldn't have to tell them to go home. They were already picking up their cases.

CHAPTER

Hooley pulled up to the plastic, clownlike dummy situated over the menu alongside the drive-through lane at the Jack in the Box. The cracking voice of some adolescent kid blared from the speaker:

"Welcome to Jack in the Box. May I take your order?"

"Cheeseburger and a Coke."

"Would you like fries with that?"

Hooley figured he'd joke with the kid a little. "You got calf fries?"

There was a pause. "Sir?"

"Mountain Oysters!"

"Uh . . . Sir?"

Disappointed, he could tell the boy had neither a sense of humor, nor an understanding of what calf fries even were. "Never mind. No fries."

"Okay, drive up to the window."

He stopped at the sliding glass portal to what he considered a greasy hell. There, he paid an overweight kid who gave him his change and a drink sealed in a waxed paper cup with a plastic lid. The kid then shut the window on him. Hooley waited. He tasted the drink. Coca-Cola. He hated Coca-Cola. According to Hooley's West Texas upbringing, the word *coke* was synonymous with "soda pop" or "soft drink" or whatever people said in other parts of the country when they referred to a store-bought carbonated drink. To Hooley, there were several kinds of cokes from which to choose. His favorite was Dr Pepper, but he could easily settle for an R.C. Cola or even a Grape Nehi.

The kid opened the window and handed Hooley a paper bag without so much as a thank-you before he spoke to someone behind him in line:

"Welcome to Jack in the Box. May I take your order?"

The window slid shut.

Hooley looked the bag over. The kid, or somebody in there, had stapled a receipt to the top of the bag. The receipt named the location of the business, and the date. He sure wished he had that piece of evidence from Rosa's burger bag. He knocked on the window, and the kid opened it, making eye contact for the first time, a perplexed look on his face.

"You need something else? People are waiting behind you."

"You didn't ask me what kind of coke I wanted. What if I wanted a Dr Pepper?"

"You asked for a Coke," the kid replied, his facial features bunching into such an extreme sneer that his pinched brows drove a droplet of sweat down his nose like a flash flood down a mountain slope.

"Do you sell Dr Pepper or not?"

"We have Coke, Seven-Up, and root beer. You asked for a Coke."

Hooley sighed. "You always staple a receipt to the bag?"

The kid screwed his face into a look of confusion. "Yeah . . ."

"Why?"

He shrugged. "That's just the way we do it."

A horn honked from behind.

"So it's company policy, at all these greasy little joints?"

"Sir, there's people waiting, and your boat's taking up a lot of room. Nobody can even order behind you."

Hooley flashed his Texas Ranger badge and ID. "Hooley Johnson, Texas Rangers. Where's corporate headquarters for Jack in the Box?"

"I don't know," the kid said, looking nervous.

"Get the manager."

After some scuffling around inside, and more horn honking, which Hooley ignored, a middle-aged, sweaty man ventured up to the window. "What's the problem here?" he demanded.

Hooley flashed the badge again. "Where's corporate headquarters for Jack in the Box?"

"San Diego," the manager said, his tone of voice suggesting that Hooley must have been some kind of ignorant idiot if he didn't know that.

Hooley looked at window boy as he put his truck in gear. "Kid, you're surrounded by food all day long in that place. You need to get out of there and get some exercise. I'd look for another line of work if I was you."

As the kid and the manager looked at him as if he were a sideshow freak, he pulled aside in the parking lot to look the bag over. He smelled the burger, but the odor of a recently caught fish on his hands overwhelmed it, so he left it in the bag. He took the lid and the plastic straw off the cup and drank a few gulps of the cold Coca-Cola. He didn't care much for the taste, but it felt good going down. He briefly thought about adding a splash from his whiskey flask in the glove box.

A Ford Pinto pulled up next to him and honked. Hooley rolled down his window.

"Hey, asshole," said the driver, a lanky, bushy-haired, redheaded youth wearing a karate uniform. "You're not the only one in line, you know. It's supposed to be fast food."

"What do you plan to do about it?" Hooley asked.

"Maybe I'll open a can of whoop-ass, grandpa."

Hooley stepped out of his truck with his hand on his service weapon and his badge leading the way into the open passenger window of the Pinto to give the youth a good look. "Listen here, Kato, you're interfering with a police investigation and you just committed a verbal assault against an officer of the law. You want to rethink your attitude?"

The driver's eyes bulged, and his mouth dropped open. "Sorry, man. I saw the boat, and thought you were some redneck."

"I *am* some redneck. You're lucky I don't have time to haul your ass to jail. You'd be real popular there in those pajamas. Now, get the hell out of here."

Later, in the men's room of the Department of Public Safety headquarters in Austin, Hooley tried his best to wash the smell of largemouth bass off his hands. Always mindful of tainting evidence, he aimed to be scrubbed like a surgeon before he touched the items collected from Rosa's car. The case was fresh enough that the evidence was still in the office Hooley used at D.P.S., awaiting cataloging and storage.

Entering the office, he hung his felt Resistol on the hat rack, and gazed briefly at the items spread out on the Formica top of the folding table against the wall. His eyes fell on the Jack in the Box bag. That piece torn off the top had intrigued him from the get-go. Often, missing pieces of evidence tended to drive an investigation, and Hooley sensed that might be the case here. His eyes drifted to the ballpoint pen found in Rosa's car. Somebody in the lab had tagged it:

"Solid gold Cross ballpoint ink pen."

If Rosa had written something on the bag, she would have used that pen, for it was the only writing implement found in the Corvette. "There's a month's salary for me," he grumbled, looking at the gold pen.

Hooley thought of the person Rosa had by all accounts been before the trouble befell her: a beautiful and talented young designer who appreciated stylish things like the Vette, the gold Cross pen, the Calvin Klein jeans she had been wearing when she died. The Jack in the Box meal seemed completely out of character, and reaffirmed that she must have been in an awful hurry that day as she fled Las Vegas. He had her figured for more of a health food nut under normal circumstances.

From his shirt pocket, Hooley took the pencil he usually sharpened with his pocketknife and stuck it into the electric pencil sharpener on his desk to get a machine-smooth lead tip. Carefully picking up the fast-food bag, he examined the top edge of the paper sack, comparing it mentally to the one he had purchased earlier and left in his truck. There was no staple on the bag, and no receipt had been found in the car. Hooley reasoned that the receipt had been torn off, taking the staple and part of the bag with it.

Carefully flattening the bag on his desk, he imagined how Rosa might have written something on the receipt with her pen, hopefully while it was still stapled to the bag. He formed an image in his head: Rosa, in a hurry, had stopped to get a burger and use the ladies room at a Jack in the Box somewhere between Las Vegas and Lake L.B.J. Spotting a phone booth, she had taken her burger into the booth to wolf it down while she made a call or two. She may have written down a phone number, an address, or directions.

So, just under the place on the bag where the receipt and the staple had been presumably torn off, Hooley used the side of the lead point of his pencil to lightly color the paper bag, hoping to reveal a trail traced by the pressure of Rosa's ballpoint as it pressed through the receipt and left an indentation in the paper bag below. His big hand held the pencil gently, like an artist with a paintbrush. He feathered it across the paper, just dusting the bag with graphite from the side of the sharpened tip.

His eyes widened as a faint set of markings began to emerge, reminding him of a whitetail deer stepping out of a fog bank. The message was incomplete, but started with a capital C followed by a blank area, an *l, i, n,* another blank, and an *a.*

The first thing that popped into his head was *Carolina,* but *a, r, o* wouldn't have fit into the small blank space between the C and the *l.*

"Celinda?" he asked, speaking to Rosa.

He continued to brush the paper bag with broad strokes of the pencil lead, causing a few numbers to emerge below what was presumably a name. The first three digits seemed to be "512," the area code for Austin and a wide expanse of Central and South Texas. After that, only three or four digits were legible, but the second set of three looked as if it could be an Austin exchange: "444." Two possible numbers came up in the last set of four, but the other two were too faint. The curve of one could have been a six, a five, or a zero.

Hooley started a long sigh that ended in a growl. "You couldn't bear down a little harder?"

He sat down and looked at his watch. It was almost 4:30. Only 2:30 in San Diego. Reaching for the phone, he called information and, after a few attempts, tracked down a woman at the Jack in the Box headquarters who seemed smart and interested enough to help a detective with an investigation.

"I need the address and phone number of every Jack in the Box between Las Vegas, Nevada, and Austin, Texas. I need to know if there's a phone booth at any of those places, and if there is, I need to know what the number of the phone is in the phone booth."

"I have no way of knowing what the phone booth numbers would be," the lady said.

Hooley rolled his eyes impatiently, but tried to remain polite. "Ask the managers at your burger joints to get those numbers. The number's usually printed on the rotary dial."

The lady said she'd try to help.

Next, he called Glastron Boats, across town, and asked for his friend Bobby, who had specially designed Hooley's bass boat for him. He explained what he needed to know about the old-fashioned glass windshield that had apparently sliced Rosa's body as she flew through it.

"That's a tough one, Hooley. Those safer kinds of glass have been around a long time. You know, the laminated stuff and the tempered stuff. Different manufacturers started using them at different times, though. Most even before the government mandated it. So it's hard to say what year you're looking at, but it's probably going to be an antique boat, unless some do-it-yourselfer slapped a piece of glass into a windshield on a newer boat."

"Thanks for nothin', Bobby. Hey, how's the fishin' on Lake Austin? I caught an eight-pounder on L.B.J. this morning . . ."

They talked angling for a while before they hung up. Hooley got out a map and looked at the route Rosa would have taken between Las Vegas and Austin. Most of it was desert interstate. There couldn't be too many talk-to-the-clown burger joints between here and there. What was taking that gal at corporate headquarters so long?

Finally, the fax machine kicked into gear and spit out a surprisingly useful list of company franchises located along Rosa's probable route, and the phone booth numbers for the ones that had phone booths nearby. Hooley had already thought about when Rosa might have gotten hungry enough to stop and order a burger. Probably mid-afternoon, which would have put her near Albuquerque. The list from corporate headquarters included a franchise in Albuquerque with a phone booth outside.

Hooley wrote the phone booth number and the date in question onto a scrap of paper and walked down the hallway to his favorite Department of Public Safety secretary, a black woman in her forties, named Lucille. Lucille liked getting involved with Hooley's investigations to break the monotony of her clerical work, so he often threw chores her way.

"Lucille, I swear you look younger every day," he said, approaching her desk.

She looked at him over the tops of her glasses, her fingers continuing to type as she spoke. "Uh-huh. What do you want this time, Captain Johnson?" She yanked the page from the typewriter, put it facedown on a stack of pages, and fed a new sheet of paper into the machine.

"Well, there is one little thing. I need a record of all calls made from this number on that date." He handed her his slip of paper. "It's an Albuquerque phone booth."

"What are you looking for?" she asked, hungry for intrigue.

"I'm hoping to find a call made from that phone to somebody in Austin, possibly named Celinda. I don't have a last name yet. And, Lucille, darlin', I know you're busy, but I could sure use it pronto."

"Public phone booth? Shouldn't be a problem. Is this for that girl they found dead on the lake?"

"Yeah. Have you lost weight?"

"You've already got me hooked, Hooley, don't push it."

"I'm serious, you look thinner."

Lucille smiled. "Well, I *am* taking Jazzercise."

Walking back to his office, a question nagged at him. If Rosa had called someone named Celinda, why hadn't this Celinda come forward by now?

Rosa's death had been front-page news for two days, and had been fea-
tured on all three local TV news channels, too. The fact that the mysterious Celinda had not emerged yet troubled him. It suggested that she
might be somehow involved, scared, in danger, or worse. Then again, she
might simply be out of town. There could be any number of explanations.
There was no certainty yet that Rosa had even called the number she had
written down. Maybe the name wasn't even Celinda, but Hooley couldn't
concoct anything else that fit, given the letters on the burger bag. Maybe it
was some weird business name, and not a given name at all. Maybe it was a
town name, or some kind of shorthand only Rosa would be able to explain.

He found himself walking through that familiar cloud—the one that
descended on every new investigation. It would give him glimpses of information occasionally, but refused to let him see the whole picture. It
was frustrating and invigorating all at once, and it drove his imagination
to concoct dozens of whirling scenarios, each of which had to be stood up
to logic, motive, and common sense.

When he came out of the cloud, he was standing in his office. He
grabbed the greater Austin area phone book and checked the businesses
that started with C. No matches. Scenario eliminated. Back to Celinda.

In his office, Hooley had a book, updated annually, that cross-referenced
phone numbers with names. You could look up a number and find the
name of the individual or business that corresponded to that number.
He didn't have Celinda's complete number, but he could guess the area
code and three-digit exchange. There were going to be multiple possibilities for the last four digits.

He got the book out and identified the block of numbers that would
include the fragmented combination he had lifted from the fast-food bag.
There were hundreds of numbers in the block. He was hoping he could
scan through the names, which of course came in no particular order,
and eventually find a Celinda.

He had been combing through the names and numbers for several minutes, when the phone rang. He picked up the receiver.

"Johnson."

"Gettin' anywhere?" It was the familiar voice of Doc Brewster, the
county medical examiner.

"Spinnin' my wheels. Hopin' for some traction. You got anything?"

"Just an observation."

Hooley marked his spot in the number book, threw his red pen down, leaned back in his chair, and rubbed his eyes. "Enlighten me."

"No one has contacted my office to claim the body of Rosabella Martini yet."

"You're sure her next of kin have been notified?"

"My secretary left a message for her uncle, Paul Martini."

"It's been less then forty-eight hours. Is that unusual?"

"Not for dead drifters or prostitutes. But for a society gal? Strikes me as odd."

"Tell you what. Why don't we just wait it out for now and see how long it takes for this little oversight to dawn on the grieving Uncle Paul."

"I guess we can wait a little longer. But sooner or later . . ."

"Let's give it a day."

"All right, Hooley. See ya'."

The Ranger leaned back into the tedious task of searching the names and numbers. The task had already become second nature—a chore his subconscious mind could sort through as his conscious thoughts whirled about the cloud of scenarios that loomed over and around him. Then, suddenly, a name shouted at him from the page. Celinda Morales. He double-checked the Jack sack to confirm the number. Bingo!

His phone rang. Hoping for a call from Lucille, down the hall, he answered it. Instead, it was the department's public relations agent. The media were clamoring for a press conference.

"Tell the goddamn vultures they're gonna have to wait!" He slammed the phone down, then picked it right back up and dialed the number for Celinda Morales. He heard a recording of a pleasant female voice, with a touch of a Mexican-American accent:

"Hi, you've reached Celinda. Sorry I'm not here to answer this call . . ."

Hooley thought about leaving a message, but decided against it. He wrote the name and phone number on a piece of paper to give to Lucille. On another scrap, he copied Celinda Morales's address on Riverside Drive. He sprang from his chair, grabbed his hat, and headed out. He stopped at Lucille's desk to give her the new information.

"This is the match I'm looking for. If you hear from the phone company, have dispatch radio me."

He was almost to the address on Riverside when the call came over the radio: "Unit Thirteen, come in."

"Roger, this is Thirteen," Hooley said into his mic.

"Yeah, Thirteen, you have a match on the name and number you requested. A positive ID from your phone booth."

"Ten-four." So, Rosa *had* called Celinda. He immediately thirsted for details that he couldn't ask about over the radio. No telling who might be listening on police scanners all over town, including those press vultures. Some of them probably already knew that he was "Unit Thirteen." Still, obvious questions begged his attention. How many calls? What time? What was the duration of each call?

Celinda Morales's address led him to an apartment building on Town Lake. He stepped into the business offices on the ground floor and flashed his credentials to a receptionist. "Do you have a Celinda Morales living here?"

"Yes, sir," the slightly plump, attractive young blond woman said, staring out through oversized lenses.

"Apartment number . . ."

She glanced at his side arm in the holster, then flipped through a card file on her desk. "She's in two-oh-five."

"Can you describe her for me?"

"She's real pretty. About twenty-five, I guess. She's Spanish . . . Well, I mean, her name's Morales, so you probably . . ."

By "Spanish," Hooley knew she meant Mexican-American. He had heard Celinda's accent on the answering machine. She wasn't from Spain. Sounded like a San Antonio girl to him, and he was good at placing Texans by their dialects.

"What does she do?"

"I think she goes to UT. She always has her books with her when she comes in with the check."

"Boyfriend?"

"Yeah. He lives with her. I hear he's a lawyer. I don't know his name.."

The cloud was lifting, affording glimpses of places still veiled in a lingering fog. "I'll need to use your phone, darlin'."

The receptionist shoved the phone toward Hooley. He dialed Lucille's number and extension.

"*D.P.S.*" Lucille said.

"Lucille, this is Captain Johnson."

"Hooley. The call was made from the phone booth in Albuquerque at three seventeen in the afternoon. It lasted a minute and forty-two seconds."

"Just one call?"

"No. Right before the call to Austin, there was a call to directory assistance. Information."

"Thanks." He hung up. "I'm gonna go up and knock on Celinda's door. Do you have a master key?"

She nodded.

"Why don't you grab it and come with me."

"Is someone in trouble?" the receptionist asked.

"I hope not."

Together, they left the office and headed for the nearest staircase. Hooley remained silent, thinking: Rosa was on a first-name basis with Celinda, but didn't have her number memorized. She had had to call information. So they were friends, but not that close. They were about the same age. College acquaintances? He knew Rosa had graduated from UT just a couple of years ago.

When they got to the door, Hooley knocked on it. No answer. He knocked again, louder. He could hear something inside. A radio? He knocked again, still louder. Nothing. He turned to the receptionist.

"Here's the deal, darlin'. I don't have a search warrant. But this girl, Celinda, may be in trouble. You're the manager here, so you have the right to open the front door. If you do that, I can look in, but I can't enter, unless I see evidence of a crime. Are you okay with that? I just want to see what I can see from the doorway. I'm worried about Celinda."

The wild-eyed receptionist nodded, seemingly caught up in more excitement than she usually encountered in her job.

Hooley pulled his bandanna from his left hip pocket and handed it to the blonde. "Use this to turn the doorknob. I don't want your prints on top of anybody else's."

She put the key in the lock, turned it, and opened the door, using the bandanna.

With the first glimpse of the body on the floor, the screaming started. Hooley rushed in to check for a pulse, but the body was already cold and stiff. The shrilling continued—a spine-twisting siren of a scream. He went back to the door and shook the blonde by her shoulders.

"Hush! Hush, now! Get ahold of yourself."

The girl quit screaming, mostly because she had run out of breath.

"You okay now?"

She nodded, but didn't really look okay.

"Gather your senses, go downstairs, and call the Austin Police. Tell them what we found, and tell them there's a Texas Ranger already on the scene."

The girl trotted off. Hooley hoped she wouldn't fall down the stairs. He picked up his bandanna from where she had dropped it. Some guy looked out of a nearby doorway.

He flashed his badge. "Everything's under control, sir. Sorry for the disturbance."

He turned back to the body, feeling that devastating sorrow from Rosa's morgue drawer seep back into his heart. Celinda looked as if she had reclined on the floor for a nap. Long black hair spread across the beige shag carpet. It was Rosa all over again, and he had arrived too late to stop it.

CHAPTER

The song ended four different times, Metro Valenzuela putting the last of the finales on it with a completely unnecessary tom-tom roll and a kick drum blast. Frustrated, Creed took a deep breath to calm himself.

"The outro is exactly like the intro," he said. "We all end together on the last downbeat. Or, we're *supposed* to. We need to clean that up."

"It's just the third pass," Luster said. "We're gettin' there."

The door to the studio opened, and Lindsay's perfect Afro floated into the room like a shiny black bubble. "Sorry I'm a little late," she said. "Can somebody come help me carry my stuff in?"

Tump put his bass on a guitar stand. "Go help her, kid," he said to Metro.

Metro sighed and slammed his sticks down on the snare. "I carry my own stuff," he muttered as he trudged to the door.

"I'll help," Trusty Joe said. "I don't mind."

Luster spoke low to Creed. "I thought we told her eleven o'clock. It's almost one."

"I'll talk to her." He racked his Strat and stepped over to the turntable. "Let's listen a few more times while Lindsay sets up her stuff."

"I think we know the song by now," Tump said.

"All right, we know the song. Now let's listen to the arrangement. Listen to the dynamics. The breaks should be clean. Seems like everybody wants to fill them up with something that's not on the record."

"I like to be spontaneous. Does it have to be exactly like the record?"

"Yes," Luster said. "People expect it. They hear a song on the radio, they want to hear it the same way live."

Tump reached for the smokes in his shirt pocket. "I'll listen from the backyard."

Metro and Trusty Joe came in with Lindsay's gear and she began slowly setting up her steel guitar, pausing to listen to her parts on the record. The rest of the band wandered out to the backyard with Tump. When the song had played through, Creed approached Lindsay.

"We need everybody here at the same time, Lindsay. I hope you don't plan on making a habit of showing up late."

"I don't believe in habits," she dodged. "Or vices."

"I told you rehearsal was at eleven. It's almost one."

She looked him in the eyes with a cool stare. "Everybody else said rehearsal was at noon."

"Well, Luster and I wanted to work with you on some leads before the rest of the guys showed up." He realized he was explaining himself to her, instead of the other way around. "Anyway, if you thought it was noon, you're still almost an hour late."

"I had to drop my sister's kid off at day care. Family is the most important thing, Mr. Creed, don't you agree?"

Creed sighed. "Just try a little harder, Lindsay. That's all I'm sayin'."

"Be a doll and move that amp over for me, Mr. Creed. And put that record back on, too. I *love* this song." She flashed a perfect smile at Luster.

When the band came in, Creed smelled marijuana smoke following Metro into the studio. Trusty Joe looked a little glassy-eyed, too. He made the band listen to the record twice more, talking them through the rough spots. When they played it, Lindsay got every lick perfectly in place on the steel, yet the bass, drums, and fiddle were still noodling around.

Three hours later, Creed finally got the band to nail the song like the studio cut. "Good!" he announced. "Now, if everybody will just remember that, we've got exactly one song in our repertoire. What's next, Luster?"

"Short rehearsal today, boys and girls. I gotta go see a man about a bus. Let's meet back here tomorrow at two o'clock. Lindsay, that'll be ten thirty a.m. for you."

Lindsay cackled. "Oh, Luster, you are a pistol!"

"There's cold beer in the icebox if anybody wants one," Luster announced.

Only Creed and Trusty Joe went with Luster to the kitchen for a beer, and Trusty Joe took his away with him for the drive.

"What do you think so far?" Creed asked, pulling the top on a beer can in the kitchen.

"It'll come together. They're all good players. They'll make a band someday."

"Maybe we need a deadline. Do we have any gigs lined up?"

Luster waved the suggestion aside. "I can get gigs. Right now, I want to see about getting us a tour bus. You and Dixie ever have a bus?"

Creed nodded. "Our last little tour across the South we used a bus. Man, I thought I had arrived."

"We had three buses for the band toward the end. That's rollin' in style. Spoiled me. I know we can't afford one, but I think I can sweet-talk one out of the son of an old friend of mine. He rents tour buses to bands." Luster looked at his watch. "I better skedaddle on over there. It's across town."

"Mind if I ride with you?"

"Hell, no. Let's grab a couple for the road."

They grabbed a six-pack of Schlitz beers, sank into the plush seats of Luster's Cadillac, and left the ranch. On the drive toward Austin, Creed resumed his campaign. "Anyway, like I was saying back at the house, if we had a gig—say, two weeks from now—maybe the band would get a little more serious about rehearsals."

"All right, Creed, I'll line something up."

"Are you nervous about it?"

"About what?"

"You know . . . Being onstage again, and with a new band, at that."

"Why should I be nervous? I'm Luster Burnett. I know what I'm doin'. I hired you to be nervous for me."

Creed nodded. "It's workin'."

They turned onto Ben White Boulevard, passing old farmhouses now crowded by an expanding city.

"I've been wondering . . ." Creed said.

"Yeah?" Luster shot a glance toward the passenger seat.

"I've got this song I've been writing. I wonder if you'd help me with it. I mean, if you like where it's going."

"I don't co-write."

Disappointed, Creed stared out through the windshield, but couldn't let it alone. "Why not?"

"Did Rembrandt co-paint?"

Rejected, Creed did not reply.

They drove past Bergstrom Air Force Base, and Creed watched a huge Sikorsky helicopter lift from the tarmac. His mind shot back to Vietnam, where the "Super Jolly Green Giant" gunships had rumbled the whole sky with rotor wash and fifty-caliber machine-gun fire.

"So, what do you call it?"

Creed came warping back to the present time and place, safe in the Cadillac, except for the fact that Luster was at that moment running a red light. Realizing Luster was asking about the song, he said, "'Fair Thee Well.'"

"Sing me a little."

Creed shifted in his seat, wishing for a guitar. "It's like an old Irish toast. It would be a good song to end a show with, or put on the last track of an LP."

"Don't sell it to me, just sing it."

"It starts on the chorus."

Luster shot a glance at him that said, *just sing the damn song*.

"Okay, Boss. I'm just gonna sing the parts I've got so far."

"Yeah, good idea. Don't sing the parts that don't exist yet."

"Okay, here goes . . ." Creed patted out a rhythm with his palm on his thigh.

> *"Fair Thee Well*
> *May your good times never end*
> *May you always find a friend*
> *At every crossroads and bend*
> *And may the sun*
> *Shine warm upon your trail*
> *Blah, blah, blah, blah, blah, blah blah*
> *Fair Thee Well."*

He risked a glance at Luster and found his head tilted like a dog trying make sense of some unknown strain.

"How do you like it so far?" Creed said.

"I've heard worse at the Opry."

"So, you'll write it with me?"

"I told you I don't co-write. But finish it, and maybe we'll work it into the act. Gonna need some new tunes."

Luster slammed on the brakes, almost missing his turn into the bus yard. Three shiny Prevost buses waited in the lot, but each had the name of a band spelled out above the windshield: ZZ Top; The Allman Brothers; Pure Prairie League.

"Looks like those are all taken," Luster said. "Hopefully, Junior will have another available by the time we start touring."

"Junior?"

"You're fixin' to meet him. He's the son of one of my former guitar players who wised up and got into the bus business instead of the band business. He made a killin' before he kicked the bucket and left the business to Junior."

They left the Caddy and walked across the crushed gravel drive toward the office. Creed noticed a fourth bus—an old Silver Eagle—squatting on flat tires under a shade tree at the edge of the lot, its chrome bereft of sheen.

Entering the office he found a man about his own age on the phone, shouting at someone about parts that hadn't come in. Creed saw a worn army field jacket hanging on a coatrack with sergeant's stripes on the sleeve and a patch indicating service in the 101st Airborne Division. Looking up from the phone call, the man recognized Luster, and his eyes brightened. He yelled, "Just send the parts!" into the phone and slammed it down.

After playfully cussing each other out and shaking hands, Luster made introductions. "Junior, this is Creed Mason. Creed, Junior."

"You're Creed, of Dixie Creed."

"'Fraid so," Creed admitted.

"I dig your song, man. 'Written in the Dust.' Cool tune."

Creed nodded modestly, always uncomfortable with the approbation. "Thanks."

"Junior, what've you got for me?" Luster began.

"What do mean?"

"We've got a nationwide tour planned. I'm making a comeback."

"You're shittin' me?" Junior grinned. "That's great! When?"

"Two weeks."

The grin dropped from Junior's face. "Two weeks? I'm booked months in advance, Luster. I've got five buses out on the road right now."

"I'll take one of those," Luster said, pointing out the window at the three in the parking lot.

"Those are all contracted out to major label bands, Luster."

"Aw, hell, contracts are made to be broken, aren't they?"

Junior shook his head in fear. "They got mean Jew lawyers, Luster. They'd crucify me."

"What about that old Silver Eagle under the live oak tree?" Creed asked.

Junior scoffed. "That thing hasn't run since Christ was a corporal."

"Or before you were a sergeant?" Creed said, jutting his thumb at the field jacket.

"What do you know about that?" Junior asked, testing.

"I was an E-five combat engineer. Fire Base Bronco."

Junior nodded. "Airborne. All over the goddamn place."

"I imagine."

"Well, seriously, Creed, that thing hasn't run since I took over the business from daddy. I don't even know what all's wrong with it. Nobody wants to rent those old, narrow, ninety-six-inch Model Ones anymore, anyway. All the bands insist on a hundred and ten inches in width nowadays."

"Will you supply the parts if I fix it?" Creed asked.

"You can do that?" Luster asked, shooting a surprised look at Creed.

Creed nodded. "I was a diesel mechanic before I got my major label deal. And I usually had to fix my own heavy junk in 'Nam."

Junior shrugged. "You get it runnin' and y'all can tour your happy asses off in it. I'll buy the parts, and you can use anything you need in the shop."

"Let's take a look," Creed said to Luster.

The phone rang, Junior answered it, and resumed his shouting match with the parts people on the other end of the line.

Leaving the office, Luster and Creed strolled toward the bus, Luster shaking his head at the dilapidated Silver Eagle.

"You sure you can fix that thing?"

"No . . . I'm not sure at all. But it's worth a try. Under one condition."

"What's that?"

"You co-write 'Fair Thee Well' with me."

"What did I tell you about Rembrandt?"

"Actually, he did co-paint. He had these protégés who would do the backgrounds and maybe the clothes people were wearing, then Rembrandt would do the important stuff like the people's faces—put the finishing touches on the final project." Creed wasn't at all sure that was completely accurate, but he had successfully bluffed Luster at poker games before.

Luster shook his head. "You know when to play a hole card, Creed, I'll give you that." He turned and walked toward his El Dorado.

"Where are you going?"

"To get the beer and a guitar. You get to work on the bus."

"So you'll write the song with me?"

"You frame it up. It'll do the trim work."

CHAPTER

Hooley took a sip of coffee gone cold, frowned, and dumped the rest of the cup into his kitchen sink. He headed for the back door, grabbing his Resistol from the deer antler hat rack without breaking stride. His shoulders slumped under the subconscious weight of the two recent deaths until he saw the sun rising east of Liberty Hill. He took a moment to admire the orange rays streaking through the live oak branches. As he turned back to lock the door, the phone rang in his den.

Thinking it might be some reporter, he considered not even answering it, but gave in to his curiosity and went back inside.

"Johnson," he said, picking up the receiver.

"Mornin', Hooley," said the voice at the other end. "This is Dolph."

Surprised, Hooley looked at his Rolex wristwatch, then felt odd when he realized the time piece had been a gift from the man at the other end of the phone line. "Mornin', Governor. You're up and at 'em early."

"Got to stay one step ahead of the screw worm, Hooley. How's Glenda?"

"Just fine since she divorced my sorry ass three years ago."

There was a pause. "Oh. Sorry to hear that. It's been a while, huh? Listen, Hooley, what the heck is going on with these killings?"

"I'm headed out to try to make sense of it right now, but I've also got a cattle rustling operation and a dope smuggling case to mop up, too."

"Put all that on the back burner. You can turn the stove around after you solve these killings. Two young girls. One from a reputed mob family. I don't like the looks of it."

"Well, the view wasn't any better from the morgue, Governor."

"Hooley . . . We've been friends since we were kids. Worked cattle and hunted deer together. So, don't blow up, okay?"

"Don't light my fuse and I won't."

"I had to call the F.B.I. I *had* to, Hooley, it's a jurisdictional matter."

"Relax, Dolph. You saved me the dime. I was gonna call them myself this morning."

A sigh of relief wafted through the receiver. "They're going to send an agent from the Las Vegas office. I want you to pick him up at the airport at one o'clock. The name's, uh . . . Doolittle."

"Perfect," Hooley groaned.

"And Hooley . . . Try to avoid the press, will you? I don't want this turning into a circus like that riot down in Houston."

"You know what they say. One circus, one ranger."

The governor chuckled. "Thanks, Captain."

Hooley left the house and headed for Austin and the registrar's office at the University of Texas. He asked for copies of the files for Celinda Morales and Rosabella Martini. While he waited, he got out his tally book and pencil. On the first blank page of the tablet, he wrote:

> 10:00—*boat ramp*
> 11:00—*morgue*
> 12:00—*lunch*
> 1:00—*airport*

As he sat in an uncomfortable wooden chair and waited, he watched people come and go at the UT registrar's counter. Pasty-skinned professors . . . college kids that looked hardly older than twelve . . . administrators moving mysterious stacks of paper. Finally, the secretary brought his copies, handing them to him somewhat fearfully. Hooley realized he was a dinosaur to these people.

He strolled to the Texas Union Building, observing the long-hairs and the short-hairs, skinny-legged girls in miniskirts and hot pants, perky breasts bouncing bra-free under gauzy shirts. An ROTC kid strutted by in full uniform. Bet he was glad the war was over. He glanced up at the tower from which that nutcase had shot all those people back in 'sixty-six.

At the Texas Union Building, he bought a cinnamon roll and a cup of coffee and sat down to peruse the school records. Rosa's file suggested she was all about art, architecture, and design. Celinda was business, criminology, and pre-law. They didn't seem to have much in common, except a shared address. The Kappa Delta Sorority house located just off campus at the corner of Nueces and 24th.

He exited the Texas Union Building and left the campus when he walked west across Guadalupe Street. Another couple of blocks brought him to Nueces Street where he found the Kappa Delta House—a handsome structure with Greek columns out front and ivy growing up one wall. He rapped on the door, using a large brass knocker.

A girl in skimpy pajamas answered. Hooley flashed his badge. "Captain Johnson, Texas Rangers."

The teenager's eyes just about popped out of her head. "Is this a raid?"

"Take it easy, sweetheart, your stash is safe. I need some information on a couple of former residents here."

The realization clicked with the freshman. "The two dead girls! My roommate told me they had lived here. I didn't believe her."

"I'd like to talk to your roommate. Or anybody who knew either of the girls."

The youngster turned and yelled back into the room. "Man in the house! He's a cop!" She ushered Hooley through a door, into the front parlor. He sat on a sofa and waited. You'd have thought the house was on fire from the sounds of feet running around upstairs. A couple of girls carrying stacks of books appeared in the doorway to the parlor and leered in at Hooley as they passed by on the way to their classes. More curious girls peeked in, some giggling ridiculously as they ran off.

Hooley felt like a freak in a carnival.

Finally, two girls in jeans and T-shirts came in. One was a blonde, the other a redhead.

The redhead spoke first. "Is some psycho killing Kappa Delta girls?"

"Yes," Hooley said, immediately regretting the quick answer. What if she talked to the press? "Well, I mean . . . Any cold-blooded murderer is a psycho in my book. I don't know if the deaths are related yet. One of them may have been just a boating accident. That's why I'm here—to figure it all out. Did you two know the girls?"

The blonde sat down. "I did." She seemed a little stunned, though she had to have known about Rosa for days. Sometimes the reality took a while to sink in. "What do you need to know to catch the psycho?"

Hooley studied the blonde. Classic Texas beauty. West Texas drawl. Oil money, he guessed. "Did Rosa and Celinda know each other?"

"Yeah, but . . . Well, all the girls in the house know each other."

"But were they close friends?"

"Not so much. Not that I ever noticed, anyway. But there's a bond among sisters. If somebody needs help . . ."

"Tell me what you remember about them. Their personalities."

The blonde smiled. "Celinda was all business. Three-point-nine. She took eighteen and twenty-one-hour loads every semester. Summer school, too. She wanted to be a prosecutor."

"And Rosabella?"

"She just called herself Rosa. She was very artsy and creative. Always sketching and doodling little designs. More of a society girl. A little spoiled by her daddy, maybe. Different boyfriend every week."

"And Celinda? Boyfriend?"

The blonde shook her head. "She didn't have time. But I saw her on campus a couple weeks ago. She's going to law school. *Was* . . . going to law school." The stunned look crept back over her face. "She told me she had a boyfriend. A lawyer. Do you think he . . . ?"

Hooley shook his head. "He seems to check out okay. He was on a trip with some buddies when Celinda was killed."

The redheaded girl began to sob, and walked out of the room. The blonde could only shrug.

"Your name is . . ." Hooley said, flipping open the tally book.

"Amanda Lynn Rogers."

"If you think of anything else . . ." He handed her his card. "Off the record, Amanda . . . Did Rosa take drugs?"

"No way. Well, she may have smoked a joint or two, but she wasn't one of those cokeheads or pill-poppers or anything. She liked her cocktails, but only on the weekend. No, she was a pretty straitlaced girl."

Too bad her laces got tangled, Hooley thought. Too bad.

At 10:09, he pulled up to the familiar boat ramp on Lake L.B.J. The divers contracted by the Texas Department of Public Safety were peeling off their wet suits and stowing their scuba tanks in the back of a pickup truck with a camper shell on it. Hooley introduced himself to the leader of the dive team, an athletic sort, pushing thirty, who had ex-military written all over him, probably Navy SEAL, maybe Air Force Pararescue.

"Duke Bible," the diver said, shaking Hooley's hand.

"Find anything?"

"Visibility was poor. It was slow going. We didn't find anything useful out by that submerged cypress snag, other than a few shards of glass. Bagged 'em up for you." He jutted his thumb at a cardboard box in the back of the truck that presumably held the scant evidence. "There was a bunch of other crap down there that I didn't bother collecting."

"Like what?" Hooley said.

"An old tire. A cinder block with some broken trotline tied to it."

The ranger nodded. "Typical fishermen stuff."

"Exactly."

"Where did you find the pieces of glass?"

"The sketch in my report will show you exactly where, but generally, it seems to support your theory that a boat may have left this dock at high speed, hit the snag, and thrown the victim through the windshield just beyond the snag."

Hooley glanced at his Rolex. "Find anything around the docks?"

Bible grabbed a towel and polished the glass on his diving mask. "A history of the beer bottling industry, rusty pocket knives, fishing weights, about ten dollars in change, and . . ." He carefully set his mask aside and reached into the cardboard box. ". . . two shell casings." He lifted a plastic sandwich baggie into view, containing the brass shells.

Hooley removed his sunglasses as he took the baggie. "Twenty-two caliber," he muttered. "They don't look like they've been in the lake very long."

"Not more than a few days. They were on top of the muck."

"Good work, Duke. Where'd you find 'em?"

"End of the pier. A little bon voyage salute?"

"Hell of a send-off, huh?" Ranger Johnson collected the evidence and turned back toward his truck. As he walked toward the parking lot, he happened to see that The Crew's Inn had opened for business. Maybe he and F.B.I. Agent Doolittle should have an off-duty beer there this evening. Hell, why not?

He found Doc Brewster in the morgue at 11:17.

"We've got to stop meeting like this," Brewster said, no humor in his voice as he slid the drawer open to reveal the lifeless body of Celinda Morales. "I wanted to be a small-town doctor until this job came up. Days like this, I wish I was delivering babies."

Hooley could only nod his understanding. "What did you find?"

"Two twenty-two-caliber bullets through the heart. Instant death. The bullets were still in her body. They're being cataloged as evidence. She had powder burns on her clothing and flesh. The muzzle must have been pressed right up against her chest." He made a pistol of his index finger and thumb and pressed it against his own chest as a visual aide. "The shooter angled slightly down. No signs of a struggle."

"Sounds like a professional hit."

"Nothing like the death of the other girl. If that was a hit, it was botched. This one was textbook." Brewster habitually removed his glasses to polish them on his lab coat. "You think the same killer was responsible?"

Hooley nodded as he slowly shoved the drawer closed. "The girls knew each other. Lived in the same sorority house at UT."

"But what about the different MO?"

"Good question. In Rosa's case, she was on the run from her killer. She knew she was in trouble. On her way to Austin, she stopped and called her friend Celinda. Phone records all but prove that. I'm not sure what happened on the lake yet, but I'm sure it wasn't an accident. After murdering Rosa, her killer found out she had made a phone call to Celinda, and decided to make sure Celinda would never talk about that phone call. Celinda never saw it coming, so the hit came off clean. The weapon was a twenty-two with Celinda. The divers found two twenty-two casings at the boat dock near where Rosa died."

Doc Brewster gestured toward the door and began to walk that way. "But there were no casings found in Celinda's apartment."

"Right. Either the killer picked them up, or he used a different twenty-two. Maybe a revolver."

They walked out of the cold morgue, into the hallway. "Two young women. So, who's next?"

"I've got the same gut feelin' eatin' at me, Doc. I ain't gonna sleep good till I catch this trigger-happy son-of-a-bitch."

Hooley went to Matt's El Rancho for lunch, and ordered up a plate of beef enchiladas. He couldn't finish the whole order. Matt, the restaurant owner and a former prizefighter of some renown, stopped by Hooley's table to shoot the breeze and seemed insulted that Hooley had not eaten his whole meal.

"It ain't the food, Matt. I just got through looking at a dead body this morning."

"Good way to get down to your fighting weight. I never thought about that one."

Hooley got Matt to tell some boxing stories to take his mind off the case for a while, then he glanced at his watch and realized he needed to haul ass to the airport and meet the F.B.I. agent who was flying in to assist with the case. This Special Agent Doolittle probably thought he was flying in to take over, but Hooley wasn't about to let that happen.

He got to Austin-Mueller Airport at the stroke of one o'clock. He parked and strolled inside to find that the flight from Vegas had arrived. Apparently, more than one flight had just arrived because it looked as if somebody had opened a gate and released all humanity on him. He stood at the entrance to the terminal, the only way out, figuring any fed worth his salt would be able to spot a six-foot-four Ranger wearing a Resistol and a sidearm.

Several of the disembarking passengers took note of him. He had been on TV in connection with several different high-profile cases in the last few years. He had to admit that he didn't mind the celebrity. He just didn't feel worthy of it right now. One young man approached him and asked if he was "that Ranger."

"I reckon I am. One of 'em anyway."

"Saw you on the tube."

He saw a young black man approaching him next. A businessman, he guessed, dressed in a sharp black suit, carrying luggage.

"Are you Captain Johnson?" the young black man asked.

"Yes, I am," he replied, impressed that this one actually knew his name.

"Special Agent Mel Doolittle, F.B.I." The sharp-dressed agent extended his hand.

Hooley just stared, dumbfounded.

"Oh . . ." said Special Agent Doolittle. "I see they forgot to mention the pigmentation situation." He smiled, as if amused by Hooley's surprise.

Hooley stared at the young black man's hand, extended toward him, the palm slightly turned up, waiting. Doolittle remained patient; his hand never wavering, demanding attention. Finally Hooley grasped the man's hand, found the handshake firm and confident.

"Captain Hooley Johnson. Texas Rangers." He nodded his Resistol toward the exit. "This way."

Special Agent Mel Doolittle fell in beside the ranger. "Where'd you get a name like Hooley?"

"Short for Julio." He looked over Doolittle's bags: a suitcase, a briefcase, and some kind of black leather case about the size of a cinder block.

"I see." They covered several long strides. "Where'd you get a name like Julio?"

"My mother named me after my father," he growled, "but I never knew that sorry son-of-a-bitch."

"Julio? Was your father Mexican-American?" the agent said in a small-talk sort of voice.

Inquisitive runt, Hooley thought. "That's an insult to Mexican people everywhere. He was white trash. I was raised by my grandfather. My mother's father. He was a good man."

"Already we've got something in common. I'm very close to my grand-father, and I never knew my father, either."

Hooley led the way to the parking lot. "Might be the last thing we have in common, but it's something, I guess." He regretted his surly tone, and tried to soften it. "So, your daddy run off, too?"

"No, he was a cop in Chicago. Killed in the line of duty when I was still in diapers."

Hooley led the way toward the truck in the parking lot. "Mel. Short for Melvin?"

"No, my parents named me after Melenik the First, king of Ethiopia, son of Solomon and Sheba."

Hooley jutted his thumb at the bed of the truck, and Doolittle threw his suitcase in. "Hop in, your majesty."

As Hooley started the truck, Special Agent Mel Doolittle jumped in the passenger side with his briefcase and the leather-covered cinder block. He slammed the door so hard that Hooley flinched. Hooley lightly pulled his door closed. He glanced and saw Doolittle looking for seat belts, but they were all lost down the crack of the bench seat.

"I'll want to see both crime scenes," Agent Doolittle announced. "Then you can take me to D.P.S. headquarters and show me what kind of evidence you've got."

Hooley jammed the truck into reverse gear, but left his foot on the clutch. "Slow down, hot rod. You just landed and you're on my stompin' grounds now. Of course I'll take you to the crime scenes. On the way, you can tell me what *you* know that I *don't* know."

"Of course," Doolittle said, opening his brief case. "Fair enough."

Hooley backed out of the parking space as Doolittle began.

"Let's start with the late Rob Martini, brother of mob boss Paulo 'Papa' Martini."

"Rosa's father?"

"Yes, Rosabella's father."

"Her friends called her Rosa. So, what do you have on Rob Martini?"

"Compared to Paulo, he was pretty clean. He ran a few nice restaurants. He died in his sleep a couple years ago of a stroke. No telling what kind of information he took to his grave. Rosabella, a.k.a. 'Rosa,' Martini was adopted. The rumor in the family was that her parents bought her from an illegal immigrant, a Mexican hotel maid, but they always told Rosa she had come from Italy."

Hooley was turning right onto Airport Boulevard. "But she knew she was adopted?"

"She found out, but apparently never knew she was non-Italian. Rosa was clean. Her father shielded her from the organized crime side of the family."

Hooley heard himself sigh with relief. He wanted her to have been a good girl. "And then what happened? Did she get crossways with the family somehow?"

"That's what I came here to find out. At this point, it's all speculation."

"Don't hold out on me, Mel. I can speculate with the best of 'em."

The young F.B.I. agent let out a sigh of frustration. "I'd prefer you refer to me as Special Agent Doolittle at this point, Captain Johnson."

Hooley shrugged as he merged onto southbound I-35 and stomped on the foot-feed. "Suit yourself, but if some shooter's about to blow your head off, it would be a lot easier for me to just holler, 'Mel!' "

Doolittle winced as Hooley swerved into traffic, garnering horn blasts and finger salutes from other drivers. "Okay . . . *Hooley* . . . I see your point. Here's the speculation: We have reports from the Las Vegas Police that Rosa visited the police station less than twenty-four hours before her death. We're trying to get video from some surveillance cameras, but the police are stalling."

"Stalling?"

"Rosa used to date a local cop. A Lieutenant Jake Harbaugh. Maybe the locals are protecting him. We don't know yet."

"This Hairball dirty?"

"*Harbaugh.* We don't know. He's been spotted with Franco Martini a couple of times."

"Franco? Now, who the hell is Franco?"

"Rosa's cousin. Adopted cousin, that is."

Hooley visualized the branches of the Martini family tree: "Rosa's adopted father's brother's son?"

"You got it. Franco is Papa Martini's son, right-hand man, and reputed muscle, suspected of several mob hits."

"With a twenty-two pistol?"

"That's his usual MO. He likes a semiauto with a silencer."

As Hooley sped down the freeway, weaving in and out of traffic, Mel Doolittle continued to brief him on Franco's rumored hits until he crossed the Colorado River, which was also Town Lake, and exited onto Riverside Drive.

"I guess you know what my next question is," Hooley said, testing the agent.

"Where was Franco when Rosa died?"

"And Celinda."

"We don't know. We try to keep Franco under almost constant surveillance, but he and Papa Martini had gone off to the mountain retreat that they call 'the ranch,' and we don't have any way to watch them there without blowing our cover."

"So he has no alibi."

"I'm sure he'll claim he was at the ranch, but we can't verify that."

Hooley noticed that Mel was opening the leather case shaped like a cinder block. "Just out of curiosity, what does Franco drive?"

"He has a hell of a car collection. His favorite seems to be his Shelby GT."

"No shit? I met Carol Shelby. Hell of a guy."

Mel opened the lid on the leather case. "Carol Shelby?"

"The designer of the Shelby GT. Race car driver. Carol Shelby. You never heard of him?"

Mel shook his head and pulled a telephone receiver out of the leather box, attached by a spiraled cord. "I don't follow automobile racing."

"You into basketball? How about that Lew Alcinder? What does he call himself now?"

"Kareem something? I don't know; I don't have time for basketball. Too many games to watch." Mel was pushing buttons inside the leather case, and listening to the telephone receiver.

"Football?"

"No, I'm a track and field man. I barely missed the cut for the Olympic Decathlon when I was in college at Delaware State." He thumped the telephone receiver on the dashboard and listened to it again.

"Easy on my dashboard, hot rod. What the hell is that thing you've got there?"

"The latest thing we're testing," Mel said. "It's a portable telephone."

"What are you trying to get it to do?"

"I'm trying to call the Vegas field office. Let them know I arrived."

Hooley grabbed his radio mic. "This is Thirteen."

"*Go ahead, Thirteen.*"

"Agent Doolittle is in town. Please advise his home office."

"*Roger, Thirteen.*"

"Portable phone, huh? Kind of like a two-way radio?" Hooley turned into the parking lot of Celinda's apartment complex. "This is crime scene number two. Celinda Morales."

Chagrined, Mel stuffed the cord and receiver back into the leather box. Like Hooley, he got out of the truck. Unlike Hooley, who lightly pushed his truck door closed, Mel slammed the passenger door with a loud metallic thud.

Hooley stopped in front of the truck and turned to the young F.B.I. agent. "Mel, you want to do me a favor? I mean, as a track and field man, and all?"

"Sure, Hooley. Name it."

"Next time you slam that door, just back off and take a good run at it. Now, come on and let's get this over with. I'm sure they want to rent this apartment out again as soon as possible."

14
CHAPTER

Creed strolled around the carcass of the forty-foot-long Silver Eagle bus, wondering what he had gotten himself into now. The three-axle configuration told him this was an 01 Model, built in Germany. It was nicknamed The Silver Eagle for its nickel-plated siding, though this one had a tree sap patina to it. The U.S. company, Continental Trailways, had contracted the construction of this model of bus in Europe, but had given the engine contract to the Detroit Diesel Company. Creed had helped repair more than a couple of Silver Eagles in his uncle's diesel shop working summers there, as his uncle held a regional maintenance deal with Continental Trailways. A precious few of these old buses had been converted to entertainers' coaches.

Kicking back the weeds around the wheels, he found all the tires flat. He walked around back and opened the engine cowling. There was a Detroit Diesel engine, sure enough. He wondered if it was blown.

He circumnavigated the bus and wound up at the front where he muscled the door open on the right side and stepped in. He nodded, finding the interior in remarkably good shape. He walked back through the sitting area and peeked into a couple of bunks. It would take some cleaning and patching here and there, but he didn't see any water damage or rats' nests. The diesel engine and drive train were his primary worries.

Walking back up to the driver's seat, he looked at the old registration sticker on the inside of the windshield. He could barely make out the year model: 1961. He frowned, for he knew what this meant on a Model 01 Silver Eagle: four-speed manual transmission and manual steering. This thing was going to be a bear to drive on long hauls. He noticed a key sticking out of the ignition. He wondered. He sat down in the driver's seat. Slowly, he reached for the key.

"Those batteries are deader than Buddy Holly," Junior said, stepping into the door unexpectedly. "Help yourself to whatever you need in the shop. Batteries, parts, tires, tools, whatever. If you get this thing runnin', you can have a job here after your music career craps out."

"Thanks," Creed said, smirking.

Junior shook his head and went back to work.

Still sitting in the driver's seat, Creed tested the pedals. The clutch felt good. The brake and accelerator seemed normal. He grabbed the stick shift jutting up from the floorboard and went to jam it into first.

"Uh-oh," he muttered. The stick flopped around like a handle in a butter churn. Something between the shift knob and the transmission had gone bad.

He bailed out of the bus and tried to figure out where to start. He decided his first task would be to replace the dead batteries and attempt to crank the engine. He found a toolbox in the shop and went to work removing the old batteries. He then lugged two new batteries out to the bus and connected them.

Back in the driver's seat, he turned the key one notch and saw, somewhat to his surprise, that the gauges on the dashboard sprang to life. Maybe the wiring was not completely shot, as he had feared. Rodents liked to chew on wiring insulation, causing short circuits, but there were a number of semiwild house cats living around the bus yard, so maybe they had kept the mouse population in check.

Creed saw that the fuel gauge showed empty. The inside of that empty tank was probably corroded by now, he thought. He would probably have to flush the tank out with solvent before he filled it with diesel.

His hand was still on the key. He decided to try cranking the motor briefly, just to see if it would turn over. He turned the key clockwise, slowly, as if cracking a safe. He heard the starter catch the flywheel and move the internal organs inside the motor block. He turned the key back off and risked a smile on one side of his mouth. The motor wasn't frozen. With some new fuel and fluids, it might actually run.

His mind now drifted back to that lazy stick shift. He figured he'd better check that out next. Borrowing a flashlight from the shop, he dropped to the ground, rolled onto his back, and began to shimmy under the front of the bus. With all the tires flat, he didn't enjoy much crawl space, but he scooted as best he could, brushing aside dead leaves and spiderwebs as he made his way. The clothes he had worn to rehearsal were not the best for greasy mechanic work, but he wanted this heap up and running as soon as possible, and he had no way to go home and change, anyway, having left his van at Luster's ranch.

Creed found the bottom of the stick shift lever and quickly saw that the bolt at the bottom of the gearshift had sheered off from thousands of gear changes. He crawled out from under the bus and went to the shop, grabbing an assortment of bolts that might fit, and nuts and lock washers to hold them in place.

Back under the bus once again, he began testing the parts to see which would work best. The linkage was hard to reach and the bolt would be difficult to work back into place, but he knew he could make it work. While struggling to get the linkage hooked back up, he heard the purr of Luster's El Dorado, its tires crunching gravel. The door slammed with that precision *choonk* of a Cadillac.

"I figured you'd have it runnin' by now," Luster prodded, for he could see Creed's boots sticking out from under the bus.

From his own perspective, Creed could see Luster's well-worn ranching boots in the crack of daylight that shone under the bus. The country music legend had duct tape wrapped around one toe to keep the sole from flapping.

"I don't think we'll be taking any bus rides today," Creed admitted.

"This is good practice for you."

"What do you mean?"

"When things go wrong, the band leader is the guy who always gets thrown under the bus."

Luster opened a folding lawn chair. Creed saw its aluminum frame settle into the gravel. Beside it, a Coleman cooler dropped into view, presumably full of iced beer. As if to answer that question, Luster rolled a cold one up under the bus.

"Thanks," Creed said, pulling the tab on the can of Pearl. "I thought you were a Schlitz man."

"It was on sale."

Lying on his back, Creed poured a swig into the corner of his mouth and managed to get the new bolt to slip into the linkage with his left hand. Now if he could just get the lock washer and the nut on, he would be in business. Luster sat in the lawn chair, and then Creed heard the strum of a fine acoustic guitar—a Gibson, judging from the fat bottom end. Luster began to sing:

"Fair thee well . . . May your good times never end . . ."

To Creed's surprise, Luster sang the whole chorus, never missing a word or a note, though he had only heard the tune once, an hour ago, in the car. Creed felt chills run up his back at the sound of that gold-record voice singing something he had written. At least he hoped they were chills, and not black widow spiders or fire ants.

"Must be a catchy song," Creed suggested.

"My ears have a photographic memory."

"Sounds like a hit song when you sing it."

"Son, the Preamble to the Constitution would sound like a hit song if I sang it." He laughed to soften the arrogance of the comment.

"Maybe you should record it."

"Maybe I will, if this song don't pan out."

"I'm hoping this one will pan out," Creed said. "Here's an idea for the first verse." In the same key, Creed sang, *"May your fires warm your hearth and home in winter, may your garden bloom with flowers in the spring . . ."*

"Hold on, Hoss," Luster said, interrupting. "Let's have a little talk first. We're giving birth to a song. It's not something you take lightly. Now, you've got a good chorus started, with a pretty strong hook-line—a familiar phrase. A good hook-line is rule number one. But here's the deal: The first line of the song has got to be better than the hook-line. That's rule number two. And the first verse has got to be solid, but the second verse has got to be better than the first verse. That's rule number three. Then there's rule number four: Everything in the song—every word, every phrase—has got to tie into the hook-line."

"That's a lot of rules."

"Wait till you hear rule number five."

"There's more?"

"Rule number five is that when you start writing, you throw all the rules out the window. Don't think about it. Just let it flow."

"I thought that's what I was doing," Creed mumbled.

"Kid, how many chart hits have you written?"

"Well, let me think," Creed replied. "That would be a total of . . . uh . . . one."

"If you want to write some more, you should pay heed to the master. Now listen, I'm serious about this, no matter how crazy it sounds. You've got to know what the rules are, and use 'em, while ignoring the rules all at the same time."

An empty beer can hit the gravel beside the lawn chair and the cooler. Creed could hear Luster plunging his fist into the ice for another can.

"I hear you, Boss. I'm listening. So . . . Where do we start?"

"We finish the chorus. You know that line where you wrote 'blah, blah, blah, blah, blah . . .'"

"Well, I didn't actually write that, I just . . ."

"How's this: *May a fair wind fill your sail, fare thee well . . .*"

Creed finally got the nut to thread on the bolt, the muscles in his left arm burning from reaching awkwardly upward for several minutes. "I like that. That fits right in." He dropped his arm to the gravel to rest his muscles before tightening the nut on the bolt.

"Good," Luster said. "Now what was that line you had for a first verse?" He rolled another beer under the bus for Creed though Creed still had half of the previous one left.

"What I said a while ago: *May your fires warm your hearth and home in winter; may your garden bloom with flowers in the spring . . .*"

"I see where you're going," Luster said. "Okay . . ." He strummed and hummed as Creed laboriously tightened the nut on the tempered-steel bolt. After a minute or so, Luster began to sing: "*May your fires warm your hearth and home in winter; may your garden bloom with flowers in the spring; May your hills know the shady trees of summer; that in autumn rain down gold and crimson leaves . . .*"

"That's beautiful," Creed said. "It's not an exact rhyme—*spring* and *leaves*—but it's pretty close."

Luster gulped. "Close enough. Don't nitpick. Now, what's the first line of the second verse?"

"I was thinking something like . . ."

"Don't think. Just blurt it out."

"*May your heart lead you down the path you follow . . .*"

"That ain't bad, Hoss. Are you writing this down?"

"I'm under a bus, Boss."

"You ought to write under a bus more often. That's pretty good. Let me get some paper."

Creed finished his first beer, the cold brew running down his cheek as he struggled to drink it lying flat on his back without much room to lift his head. He opened his second can, and went back to tightening the linkage bolt.

"I found a grocery sack in the trunk," Luster said, returning. "There's nothing I like writing on better than a grocery sack, except maybe a Big Chief tablet or a paper placemat at some diner. Not a cocktail napkin, though. All these stories you hear about writing some hit on a cocktail napkin . . . That's bull. You can't write shit on those things. They're too small, and they rip too easy."

Creed heard a whittling sound, and saw pencil shavings fluttering to the ground. Faintly, he heard the pencil point scribbling on the grocery sack. He could tell by a certain resonance that Luster was using the back of the guitar as a makeshift lap desk on which to write. Creed, himself, had often used the same method to scribble lyrics.

"How about this, Creed? *May your heart lead you down the path you follow; May your trail soon and often cross my own?*"

"I like it."

"Pipe down, I ain't done: *And in the end; When your wandering days are over; May the road you travel safely lead you home . . . And fair thee well.* Back to the chorus."

"That's good. Damn good."

"Why do you think they call me Luster?"

"Sing the whole thing, Boss."

Luster stumbled through the freshly penned co-write with just enough of a flow to give a fair rendering of the new composition. Creed listened on his back under the bus, his heart swelling to hear the voice of his hero singing something they had just written together. By the end of the tune, he was lost in daydreams about performing the song for huge crowds of admiring fans.

"You still alive under there?" Luster asked.

"Yeah." He realized that he had finished tightening the linkage bolt, snugging the nut down on the lock washer.

"Well, do you hate it, or like it?"

"I think I like the hell out of it."

"Me, too. But we'll let it set for now and see if it stands up tomorrow. Might be the dumbest dirge in history for all we know. You can't tell when you're in love with the creativity of it all." He put the guitar down and picked up his beer can. "What's the diagnosis down there, doc?"

Creed shimmied out from under the Silver Eagle, stood and dusted himself off, then climbed into the bus. He sat in the driver's seat, stomped on the clutch, and tested the gearshift. It seemed jammed, but he didn't want to force it.

"What are you doing?" Luster asked, peeking inside.

"Trying to get the gears to shift."

"Jiggle it a little in the middle, it'll go."

Creed grinned. "Write that down." He took Luster's advice, jiggling the shift knob. The gearshift fell magically into place. He ran through all four forward gears and reverse. "Feels like we have a transmission, Boss. We need to get some new tires on this thing and flush that fuel tank out. We'll put some fresh diesel in it and some new oil in the motor and crank it. Then we can figure out what else it needs. I think I might actually be able to fix this behemoth."

Feeling a sudden need to relieve himself after having consumed four beers between Luster's ranch and here, he turned and marched toward the back of the bus.

Luster followed him. "I was afraid you might say that. How are we going to explain this thing? We'll have to claim we chose it on purpose in a fit of nostalgia or something."

Once around the back of the bus, out of sight of the highway, Creed unbuttoned his Levi jeans to relieve the pressure of four beers in his bladder. Angling away, for some semblance of privacy, Luster followed Creed's example. It was a little awkward, but they both knew that two guys in the same band were going to have to learn to urinate together at some point.

"You know," Creed said. "In my wildest dreams, I never thought I'd be pissin' shoulder-to-shoulder with Luster Burnett."

"If this is your wildest dream, you need to set your sights a little higher."

"I'll take that to heart," Creed promised, buttoning up. "I've been wondering . . ."

"You sure wonder a lot, Hoss." Luster began the stroll back to the other side of the bus.

"Why now?"

At the front of the Silver Eagle, Luster sat in the lawn chair and gestured to the cooler for Creed to sit. "The comeback? After all these years?"

"Yeah."

Luster sighed. "You know I quit when my wife died."

"That's what I'd always heard."

"I didn't have the drive anymore. My Virginia, God rest her soul, she just loved that ranch on Onion Creek. As addictive as that honky-tonk trail can be—and you know it is—the best times of my life were with her, there on the ranch, when I was off the road. I buried her there. Then, when it came time to hit the road again, I just couldn't do it. I couldn't leave her." Luster snapped his finger and pointed at the cooler.

Creed jumped up, opened the lid, and reached in for two more Pearls. "And now? What's changed?"

"I don't want to lose her all over again."

Creed gulped the Pearl, feeling the buzz of several beers now. "What do you mean?"

"I had this business manager. Buster Tull. One of my oldest pals from back home. Luster and Buster. We made quite a pair. He played drums in my first band, but he wasn't very good, so he became my business manager. He was good at that. Real good. He looked after my money. He made my money make money. When Virginia died, and I retired to the ranch, Buster stayed in Nashville and pitched my songs on a commission basis. He kept my songs making money, year after year, cut after cut."

"Sure. I've heard dozens of covers of your tunes over the years. None as good as yours."

"You can't beat an original Luster Burnett cut, son. It just can't be done. But those covers kept the mailbox money coming in, and I was grateful for every one of them. I thought I was set for life."

"What changed?"

"I came home from a poker game about dawn, a few weeks ago. I had lost a few thousand, but I didn't care. Hell I didn't need the money. So I thought. I had been in a slump for a while, to tell you the truth, and I had some gambling markers out there, from here to Louisiana. But everybody knows I'm always good for my markers. I always pay up when the royalty checks come in.

"So, I crawl into bed about dawn, and the phone rings. It's my lawyer. He says, 'Luster are you sitting down?' I said, 'I'm in bed.' He said, 'Get out of bed and sit down.' So I did. Then he proceeded to tell me that my old pal and business manager, Buster Tull, had blowed his brains out with a twelve-gauge shotgun."

"Oh, shit," Creed said.

"That's what I said. My lawyer goes on to tell me the reason. Buster had been raking off the top for years. Decades. He'd been stealing from me. Worse yet, he did my taxes for me, too, and he'd been lying to the I.R.S. about my income. Well, he got called up for an audit, and knew the shit was about to hit the fan. I guess he couldn't face me, or live with himself, so he put the muzzle of that old scatter gun in his mouth and . . ."

Creed gulped more beer. "How bad is it?"

"Pretty bad. He's still dead." Luster laughed and turned his beer can upside down over his mouth.

"No, I mean . . ."

"I know what you mean. It's pretty bad. I owe about fifty grand in gambling debts here and there. But that's chicken feed compared to what I owe Uncle Sugar. I'm in for about seventeen million with the Infernal Revenue Service."

The sum hit Creed like an anvil. Seventeen million? With no major label deal. No distribution. No tour support. No radio. How in the hell did Luster expect to earn back that kind of money? "Whoa" was all he could think of to say.

"They want to take my ranch, even though it ain't worth seventeen million. I can't let them do that, Creed. My wife is buried there. That would be like taking my Virginia all over again, and I won't have that."

"How much time do we have before they take the ranch?"

"You don't even want to know, son."

Creed looked into the face of his hero. He seemed relaxed, even amused. "How do you do it? How do you deal with it? You don't even seem worried."

"That's the funny thing. I'm eatin' this shit up. You remember that old hungry feeling you had when you went to Nashville the first time, without a job, a deal, or a dollar in your pocket?"

"Sure."

"Well, I've got the hunger again. Never thought I would. Once I got over the shock of what Buster had done, it just hit me. I got off my ass, picked up a guitar, and started singing. Felt good. Then I went to Nashville and those snot-nosed sons-of-bitches told me I couldn't make a comeback. That just fueled the hunger. The hell I can't make a comeback. I'm Luster by-God Burnett! I'm gonna take the world by storm all over again!" Luster guzzled a beer, crushed a can, then tossed it over his shoulder.

"Damn right!" Creed slammed his beer, too.

"But you know what worries me, Creed? I mean, do you know what *really* worries me?"

Creed shook his head.

"Not a cotton-pickin' thing!" Luster blurted. He laughed and motioned for another brew. "If I can't out-bluff some piss-ant bureaucrats arrogant enough to think they can tax music, I don't deserve to be called Luster." He looked over his shoulder, as if a revenuer might be standing there. "Tax this, you son-of-a-bitch!"

Luster strummed an open chord, and with his golden voice, began to sing:

> *"Fair thee well*
> *May your good times never end*
> *May you always find a friend*
> *At every crossroads and bend . . ."*

Creed sat on the cooler, staring at his country music hero as he smoothed out the bumps in the infant song. "Damn, that was pretty," he said. "I can't believe I just wrote a song with Luster Burnett. *The* Luster Burnett."

"Yeah, well, you know the deal. Get your ass back under the bus."

CHAPTER

Hooley woke to the sound of the truck door opening, his hand reaching instinctively for the grip of the autoloader holstered at his hip.

"Take it easy, Hooley," Mel Doolittle said in the dark. "It's just me, Mel."

Hooley had dozed off in the seat of his truck in the parking lot, waiting for Mel to come back from The Crew's Inn.

"Have a nice nap?" Mel said.

"Lovely. You get anywhere?" Hooley rubbed his face and sat up in the seat.

Mel got in and politely clicked the passenger door closed as he sighed in resignation. "Have these people *ever* seen a black man before?"

"I tried to tell you." He pushed at the ache in his lower back.

"The owner gave me an application for a dishwashing job!"

"You should have took it. Good undercover cover."

"I graduated summa cum laude from Delaware State," Mel said, defensively.

"Well, you're Leroy-come-lately around here. Did you get *anything*?"

"I followed the plan. I posed as a fisherman. Nobody would give me the time of day. I asked around about the girl who had died on the lake. They all clammed up tight. The owner told me I'd better stop harassing the customers, or he'd throw me out."

"Don't take it personal. Nobody around here wants to talk to a colored Yankee about a dead mob girl. Besides, you look like a cop."

"They didn't make me. I'm sure of that."

"Uh huh."

"Anyway, it wasn't a total loss. I witnessed the owner—his name's Patrick Palmer—I witnessed him selling beer to minors. They looked like they were about fifteen. And he let a couple of customers walk out with their drinks."

"I saw 'em, too. They got in their car and drove off with their beers."

"That's a liquor violation in Texas, isn't it?"

"Yep. Maybe that'll give us a little leverage." He reached over and nudged Mel's shoulder roughly with his fist. "Good job, Special Agent Doolittle. You got more than I thought you would in that white cracker bar. So, is your ol' pal Patrick shuttin' the place down for the night?"

"I was the last one to leave. He still wouldn't talk to me, even after everyone else had gone. But I overheard him in conversation say that he lived in the condos next door."

Hooley saw the light go out in the back of the bar. Patrick Palmer stepped out and locked the door. "My turn," he said to Mel. "Wait here."

Hooley quietly stepped out of the truck and shut the door. He walked toward the bar as the owner turned to trudge toward the condominiums.

"Mr. Palmer!" he shouted.

Palmer wheeled. "Who's that?"

"Captain Hooley Johnson, Texas Rangers."

"Now what," Palmer whined.

"I thought you could use some advice."

Palmer's shoulders slumped, weary of all the unwanted attention. "Advice? On what?"

"How to keep your liquor license." Hooley walked up close to the bedraggled entrepreneur and stopped in front of him.

"Why are you people harassing me?" Palmer said. "I run a quiet little lakeside bar. I ain't askin' for trouble."

"Selling to minors? Letting drinks walk off the premises?"

"Yeah, I'm a real menace to society, Captain. You gonna bust me, or what?"

"I'm here to help you, Mr. Palmer. I can keep these other law dogs off your back."

"Yeah? In exchange for what?"

"Information. I need to know what happened that night."

"I already told the other cops everything I know, which is *nothin'*. You know, if you'd coordinate with the sheriff's office and the F.B.I., you'd know all this already."

"F.B.I.?" How had Doolittle allowed himself to be pegged as a fed, Hooley wondered.

"Yes, there was an agent here."

"Colored?"

"No, not the one tonight. That kid had cop written all over him, but I didn't figure him for F.B.I."

Puzzled now, Hooley pressed. "If not tonight, when?"

"Last night. Some agent nabbed me on the way home. Right about here, just like you. Flashed a badge, but I forgot his name."

"What did he look like?"

"About five-ten, burly. White guy."

"And he said he was F.B.I.?"

"Bigger than shit. He was wearing an F.B.I. cap."

Hooley pretended to remember. "Oh, yeah. That would be Special Agent what's-his-name. By the way, the colored kid was F.B.I., too. He's sitting in my truck right now. He's got one of those new portable spy telephones, and he's just dying to call you in for liquor violations and ruin your life. He's a little pissed that you pegged him for a dishwasher. But if you'll help me, I can keep him off your ass."

Palmer bowed his head in surrender. "I don't know who gave that girl a ride. I didn't see anything."

"But . . ."

"But . . . A guy had been hanging around the bar, maybe twice a week, for a couple of weeks. He would boat to the dock, and come in for a couple of drinks. I never got his name. But I haven't seen him since the girl died."

"Describe him."

"White guy. Tall. Maybe six-two or -three. Long hair. Brown, or dark brown, or maybe black, I don't know. I never had reason to notice the details, you know what I mean?"

"What was he like in the bar?"

Palmer shrugged. "He hit on some girls. They all shot him down. He'd play the jukebox a lot."

"What kind of music?"

"Country. The old classic stuff. He played this one Luster Burnett song over and over. 'Like an Old Coyote.' You know, the one where he howls like a coyote. Drove everybody crazy with that song."

"That's a good song," Hooley argued.

"Not ten times a night."

"What did his boat look like?"

"I never saw it. But I seem to recall it sounded like an inboard. A big-block

Chevy or some such thing. I can't testify to any of this, you know. I don't want to get mixed up in this mob shit."

"You're not in any danger from the mob," Hooley groaned.

"There's been two victims already!" Palmer hissed.

"They were both five-foot-four and gorgeous. If you start growing tits, worry." He thought of saying something about already having grown a vagina, but he thought better of it.

"You're sure. They're not after me, are they?"

"Why would they be? You don't know shit, and you haven't told me shit, right? Go on home, Mr. Palmer. Thanks for nothin'."

Palmer sighed and turned away.

Returning to his truck, Hooley found Mel anxious for information. "The guy made you for a cop, all right."

"Did you get anything?"

"Hell, yeah. We have an earwitness. We're looking for an inboard, big-bore motor."

"Earwitness," Mel said, derisively. "Anything else?"

"Only a description of a possible suspect: white, tall, long hair. Likes county music, girls, and beer."

"And owns a boat with a big-bore inboard motor?"

Hooley nodded. "Sounds like it."

"That's it?"

"That's more than you got, sumo-come-loudly. Sounds like a fat . . ."

"Don't say it," Mel warned. "I got the image."

Hooley chuckled a little. "That is funny though, ain't it?"

"Racial stereotypes are never funny."

He swore Mel was holding back a grin. "Sumo-come-loudly. You know, like one of them Jap *rasslers* . . ."

"I know what a sumo is!" Mel said, letting a chortle escape, in spite of himself. "God Almighty, you are one relentless redneck, Captain Johnson!"

Hooley enjoyed a short chuckle. "There is one more thing. I need you to level with me here, Mel. Are you the only fed assigned to this case?"

"The only *special agent*? Yes."

"You're sure?"

"Yeah, why?"

Hooley told him what Palmer had said.

"That sounds like a description of Franco!" Mel blurted.

"Rosa's cousin, Franco Martini?"

Mel nodded. "He's been known to impersonate officers before. He's good at it, too. He probably has as much information as we do, and he's a day ahead of us."

Hooley's mood darkened to think that he had been standing on the footsteps of that girl-killing mob punk, the trail just twenty-four hours old. He reached for the ignition and started the truck. "That cockroach is on my stompin' grounds now. And like you said, Mel. I am one relentless redneck."

16
CHAPTER

When Creed got the early-morning call from Luster to come in three hours early for rehearsal, he envisioned a protracted songwriting session. Instead, he found a quarter horse saddled and waiting for him.

"You ride, don't you?" Luster asked.

"It's been ten years or so, but I used to ride on my grandfather's farm."

"Well, any kid in the world could ride ol' Baldy there, so just hang on. He knows what to do. I need you to help me round up some cows."

After climbing into the saddle, and settling in astraddle of Baldy, Creed wondered why he didn't ride a horse every time he came here. As they began their ride, he remembered an old saying his grandfather often repeated:

"The outside of a horse is good for the inside of a man."

The steady gait of the gelding, the mild spring weather, and the morning sun made him feel honored that Luster had enlisted his help. The cool breeze seemed to carry away his worries with the band, his memories of Vietnam, and the hurt he had suffered at the hands of Dixie and her record label.

"Let's kick 'em up to a trot," Luster suggested. He didn't have all day.

Creed trotted past the first bluebonnet blossoms he had seen this spring, dancing at the bottom of a south-facing slope. The steady trot reminded him again of his grandfather, who claimed that all real cowboy songs were set to the cadence of horse hooves. The rhythm of the trot bolstered the claim as he found himself humming the melody of "The Old Chisolm Trail."

> On a ten-dollar horse and forty-dollar saddle
> I wound up chasin' them longhorn cattle
> Come a ti-yi yippee-yippie yay yippie-yay . . .

Riding up onto a crest that afforded a long view, Luster pointed out the herd of cattle below, grazing along the back fence line of his ranch. Judging from the distance they had covered, Creed estimated the ranch at five thousand acres or so. He considered it rude to ask a man how many acres he owned, so he had never inquired. It seemed tantamount to asking someone how much money he had in the bank.

They rode slowly to the right side of the herd of black Angus beeves. The size of the herd also helped Creed judge the size of the ranch, as he knew each cow needed about twenty acres to survive in this part of Texas. Baldy indeed knew the roundup routine. He swung around the herd and began pushing it toward the front of the ranch, where the working pens were located. It turned out that the cattle also knew more or less what to do. Though a young heifer or steer tried to break ranks every now and then, the older cows had been herded to the pens before and knew the futility of resistance. Creed and Luster also used the barbed-wire fences to keep the cattle bunched together and moving. Creed knew he lacked the skills of a true cowboy, but he indulged himself by humming a couple of Sons of the Pioneers classics as he rode drag on Baldy.

After an hour of pushing the herd, the old cows led the rest of the bovines into the pens where Luster shut the gate on them. "That's my kind of cowboying," he said, dismounting his horse. "You don't think I'd risk getting these guitar-playing fingers tangled in a rope, do you?" He wiggled his ten fingers in the air.

"No, sir. I've seen more than one old cowhand with a missing digit or two. I didn't know you had this big of a herd."

"I have cattle because I have a ranch," Luster said, shrugging. "Keeps my ag exemption current."

Creed knew from working his grandfather's farm that the state exempted agricultural lands from school property taxes. "What are you gonna do with the cattle now that we've got 'em penned?"

"I'm sellin' 'em to keep the I.R.S. off my ass for a while."

"What about your ag exemption?"

"I play poker with the county tax assessor. He owes me. He'll look the other way until I'm back in the black."

After dismounting and tying the horses at the stables, Luster invited Creed to take a look at his barn.

"All right," Creed said, shrugging. He had seen a barn or two, and wondered why Luster's warranted a tour. Walking up to the building, he judged the barn to be a hundred years old, or older, though well preserved, and perhaps even renovated by Luster.

Throwing open the two large wooden barn doors and flipping a handy circuit breaker to illuminate the interior with electric lights, Luster gestured grandiloquently toward a full stage, complete with stage lighting and large sound system speakers. Though the old structure still smelled of hay, it had been totally converted to a performance venue, with a concrete dance floor in front of the stage, wooden tables and chairs around the other three sides of the slab.

"Holy crap," Creed said, impressed with the setup. "This is great. Have you ever used this place?"

"Not yet. I've been waiting for inspiration. I didn't know it was going to come in the form of poverty. You think you can run this PA system?"

Creed nodded, grinning. "I can figure it out."

"I want to rehearse in here, today. Get the band used to a stage."

"Good idea."

"I called the band and told them to come in early." He looked out through the open barn doors. I believe that's Trusty Joe driving down through the pecan orchard right now."

As the band members showed up, one by one, Creed tinkered with the mixing board, the equalizer, the effects, and the amps, gradually getting the PA system tuned into the building. Meanwhile, Luster lifted and propped open hinged windows, letting the fresh spring air and sunlight into the barn.

Within an hour, all the band members were onstage except for Lindsay, who was just pulling up in her Impala. Half an hour later, rehearsal commenced.

The beautiful Texas springtime weather seemed to inspire the band. Apparently, they had all been listening and practicing at home, for they played smoothly through half a dozen tunes as if they had absorbed the old studio tracks from the grooves in the vinyl. They took a short smoke break, then learned four more songs, rounding out a pretty respectable repertoire of ten classic Luster Burnett tunes.

"That's a full hour set," Creed said.

"Hell, I can stretch it to two hours with a little bullshit between songs," Luster boasted.

Creed racked his guitar. "I think we're ready for a gig."

"I've got one booked."

The band perked up, wanting to know when, where, and for whom.

"We're playing at a public auction," Luster explained. "And we'll also be auditioning the band for a government organization."

"Huh?" Tump grunted.

"*Quando?* When?" Metro demanded, just happy to have a gig.

"About two hours from now. That looks like the auctioneer pulling up outside right now."

"The auction's here?" Creed said. "Today?"

"What does it pay?" Tump asked, propping the stand-up bass against an old barn pole.

"*Does* it pay?" Lindsay added, suspiciously.

"It'll pay," Luster said, reassuringly, stepping down from the stage. "I don't know how much, but it'll pay more than you expected to go home with when you pulled into the front gate for a rehearsal."

"What was that about the government organization we're auditioning for?" Trusty Joe said.

Luster stopped and turned back to the band. "Oh, that. That would be the Infernal Revenue Service. I owe them a little money. If we put on a good show, they might let us go out on the road and earn it back. If not, this band is finished. No pressure. Creed, you better get the band up to speed with what's going on in the life and times of the great Luster Burnett." Luster strolled out to greet the auctioneer.

Creed, who was as shocked over the developments as anyone, found four band members glaring at him.

"I didn't even bring my show clothes!" Lindsay said, her lips pursed in anger.

"You look like a cover girl," Creed assured her.

"I haven't filed since 'sixty-nine," Trusty Joe hissed. "The last guy I want to play for is a tax collector!"

"They're after Luster, not you. Trust me, your tax debt is chicken feed compared to his." Creed frowned at Trusty Joe's reaction, the fiddler's eyes searching for some kind of escape route, or maybe a place to puke.

Tump lit up a cigarette. "Was he serious about the audition? It's a make or break deal?"

"We just had a great rehearsal. We'll do fine. Anyway, what does a tax man know about country music? All he wants to know is whether or not Luster can still sing. And face it, the man can still sing his ass off."

"I'm going to run home and change," Lindsay said, getting up from her steel guitar.

"No!" Creed ordered. "You don't have time. Besides, you're in a barn."

"It ain't no Studio 54," Lindsay allowed, scowling at the cobwebs in the rafters.

"Let's just take a smoke break, and relax. Grab a beer. Luster put the cooler backstage. Think of it as a paid rehearsal." He stepped off the stage as Trusty Joe bolted for the back, holding his fist over his mouth.

Stepping outside, Creed saw an eighteen-wheel livestock rig coming for a load of cattle, the trailer taking a whipping from pecan branches as it barreled through the orchard. He shook his head, wondering if touring with Luster would always be this unpredictable; wondering if there was even going to be a tour with Luster after today. He noticed a white sedan following the Mac truck, the unmarked car getting a proper dusting from the big rig.

"Hey, Creed!" Luster shouted. "Bring the horses and push the cows into the chute! Get Trusty Joe to help you. He's a cowboy."

Creed mounted Baldy and led Luster's horse as Luster guided the driver of the Mac truck back to the loading chute. A man in a suit got out of the white sedan with a briefcase. Creed figured him for the taxman. More vehicles were pulling up to the barn and the pens now. He found Trusty Joe behind the barn and told him to mount up.

"How do I get on?" Trusty Joe said.

Creed dismounted. "You better ride this one. I'll ride Luster's horse." He showed Trusty Joe which foot to put in the stirrup and helped him get astride Ol' Baldy."

"I thought you were in a cowboy band."

"You didn't have to be a real cowboy. Man, if the guys at the Broken B could see me now!"

Creed mounted Luster's bay, which pranced under him with much more vigor than Baldy, but still responded well to the reins. Together they rode to the pens, where Luster was opening a gate to let them in, the auctioneer standing beside him.

"Is the PA still hot?" Luster asked. "The auctioneer wants to check the mic."

"It's hot. Tell him I can dump the reverb for him if it's too wet."

"All right, y'all load those cows!"

As Creed and Trusty Joe pushed cattle to one side of the pen, and into the funnel of the loading chute, Creed watched more cars and trucks pulling up to the auction site. Another livestock tractor-trailer rig was rattling up to the pens. He couldn't help but notice one car going against the flow, leaving the ranch: Lindsay's Impala. "Aw, shit," he groaned.

"Yee-ha!" Trusty Joe yelled, apparently having the time of his life on the back of Ol' Baldy.

Having loaded the cattle, Creed went back to the barn and adjusted the mic for the auctioneer. Though a professional who knew how to work a mic, the auctioneer still didn't have the vocal projection skills of a Luster Burnett, and needed to be cranked up to be heard. Luster was gallivanting around with the supposed taxman. Lindsay was gone. Trusty Joe was taking a joy ride around the property on Baldy. Tump and Metro were off somewhere, smoking God-knows-what.

The auctioneer began the proceedings, working the crowd like an old pro with a couple of jokes, then rattling off his machine-gun pricing banter for the first item up for bids, a seventy-horse John Deere tractor.

Luster broke the hypnotic trance that the auctioneer had cast over Creed: "Hey, Creed, meet Sid. Sid . . . uh . . ."

"Sid Larue," said the man in the gray suit and the fat blue tie. "I'm a big, big country music fan. Man, I *begged* for this assignment. Got my own country band back home. We play your hit, 'Written in the Dust.'"

"Oh, great . . ." Creed said, trying to force a smile.

"Sid's gonna do his best to help me out of this little bind my late manager got me into," Luster said, slapping the tax hound on the back.

"We all are," Creed said.

"Hey, listen! That old tractor just went for two grand!"

Larue smirked. "That's the first drop in a very big bucket. This auction money will help me hold off the vultures upstairs for a while, but what I'm interested in is the band. When do you guys play?"

"Right after the auction," Luster said.

Larue looked at his wristwatch and frowned. "I don't have that much time. Can you play now?"

"Now? Sure!" Luster said.

"Uh, how about if we get the auctioneer to take a midway break," Creed suggested, thinking of Lindsay's trip home for a wardrobe change. "He just got warmed up."

Larue looked at his watch again. He shrugged. "Okay. Mr. Burnett, show me around the house and the grounds. I'll get my camera."

Larue headed for his car, and Creed grabbed Luster by the sleeve.

"Stall," he said. "Lindsay went home to change."

"She what?" Luster rolled his eyes. "I knew a girl in the band was trouble!"

"Remember what worries you, though? I mean, what *really* worries you?"

Luster's glare softened, and he smiled. "Thanks for reminding me. Not a cotton pickin' thing." He joined the taxman, put his hand around Larue's shoulder, and began showing him the grounds with the old Luster Burnett charm.

An hour later, Luster could stall no more. Larue demanded to hear the band. Lindsay still had not returned. The auctioneer called for an intermission, and introduced the great Luster Burnett. A crowd of a couple hundred auction attendees managed a smattering of applause and turned curiously toward the stage.

Luster addressed the crowd as if he were back at the Grand Ol' Opry: "Ladies and gentlemen, the rumors of my death have been greatly exaggerated!" He waited for the ripple of laughter to pass. "Seriously, I want to thank you all for turning out on such a beautiful spring day to help me celebrate the first day of my comeback in the music business . . ."

"What are we gonna kick with?" Tump said in a stage whisper.

"Lindsay's not back, so we'll let Trusty kick it with 'Dear John Note.'"

"I gotta kick it?" Trusty Joe complained. "I'm shakin' like a leaf."

Creed looked out through the barn door and saw Ol' Baldy at the hitching rail. "Just imagine you're back in the saddle on Ol' Baldy," he suggested. "Fix your eyes on him, and just do it. Metro will click the tempo for you."

Trusty Joe took a deep breath. Looking as if he might burst into tears at any moment, he said, "This one's for you, Baldy!"

Tump and Metro looked at each other, concern mixed with disgust.

". . . so we're going to kick off our worldwide tour right here and right now," Luster said, "with one of my old standards. I'm sure you'll recognize this one! Kick it, boys!"

As Metro clicked his sticks together, Creed saw Lindsay's Chevy winding through the pecan orchard. A teary-eyed Trusty Joe Crooke, his gaze fixed on Baldy, stroked off a perfect pickup riff with his fiddle bow, and the rest of the band, sans steel guitar, fell into the intro like a machine.

Luster turned to Creed, his wild eyes betraying his fake smile. "I thought we were going to kick with 'Old Coyote.'"

Creed faked his own smile back. "Lindsay's not here, Boss. Trusty had to kick it. We'll play the intro again." He palmed his guitar pick and made a circle in the air with his trigger finger, signaling the band to repeat the intro so Luster could get his head around the right song.

"How about this band!" Luster said, stalling. The crowd clapped dutifully. Then came time for the singer to sing, and that godlike voice pierced the dusty barnyard air, rattled the rafters with deep baritone vibes, and melded the silly gawks of onlookers into expressions of astonishment. Not satisfied to simply strum, Luster windmilled his guitar with a flailing right arm, threw his head back, and without any vocal warm-up, other than the first verse, belted out that note in the chorus that soared an octave and a half above the verse.

And now Creed knew. Luster had been holding back in rehearsal. Creed only *thought* he had heard the legend sing. He had been saving that edge for an audience—his first in fifteen years. He smiled through the chills that shot up and down his spine. He glanced at the players in the band, and found them as wide-eyed as he felt. Even Tump's eyes, behind those ever-present shades, had pushed his brows into peaks of surprise. Lindsay, in her flashy show clothes, her Afro teased out to the size of a beach ball, was scrambling to get onstage to be a part of this. She had the showbiz sense to slip around behind the stage and wait for the end of the song, at which point she took her seat behind the steel, her silver finger picks already in place on the tips of her long, talented digits.

Creed knew this was no time to scold Lindsay, so he flashed her a smile and mouthed the title of the next song—"Like an Old Coyote"—which she deciphered like a lip reader. As the applause for the first song finally dwindled away, Lindsay kicked the next tune with a perfect mysterious waver in the pedal steel.

Now Creed had a chance to search the audience for Sid Larue. He found the taxman standing in front of the stage and watched him as Luster added his solid gold vocal to the smooth foundation the band had laid out. He saw Larue singing along, mouthing every lyric, all misty-eyed, and Creed began to think that this multimillion-dollar comeback might just have a chance after all.

The rest of the set only escalated, the band members getting loose and beginning to relax toward the end. Creed himself stepped up and hung his toes over the edge of the stage during one lead break on the Strat, garnering a spontaneous ovation from the crowd in the middle of the song.

Every soul on the premises had gravitated into the barn. Even the truck drivers. A few husband-and-wife couples who had come to bid on ranch equipment had found a vacant corner of the dance floor upon which to two-step.

Finally, the set ended, Luster introduced the band members to the audience. Amid a roar of cheers and applause from an audience that had come for bargains rather than music, Luster threw kisses out to the ladies in the crowd and announced the resumption of the auction.

Almost giddy, Creed was looking forward to cracking a beer open backstage with the band, when he heard the taxman's voice: "One more! Come on, you guys! One more song!"

"We don't know any more goddamnit songs," Metro said.

Tump shushed him.

"You know what they say, Sid," Luster beamed, "always leave 'em wantin' more!"

"Oh, come on!" Sid insisted. "You've almost got me sold. What's one more song? What do you say, folks? One more?"

The satisfied crowd raised an obligatory encore ovation.

"Play something new!" Sid ordered. "Don't you have anything new?"

Creed felt the panic coming on . . .

"As a matter of fact," Luster began, "I found Creed under the bus the other day, writing a song. Sounded like he needed help so I finished it for him."

Creed turned to Tump. "Play the doghouse."

Tump racked his bass guitar and reached for the standup bass.

Creed turned to Metro. "Let Luster start it a cappella. I'll tell you when to come in. Don't overdo it." He stepped closer to Tump. "Key of Charlie. I'll call the chords out to you."

Tump nodded.

Creed shook his head at Lindsay and Trusty Joe so they would lay out until they learned the progression. He heard Luster finishing his introduction to the song:

". . . So we'll leave you with this, folks. Thanks for being such a wonderful audience. The best I've had in fifteen years!"

Luster strummed an open C chord and began to sing:

"*Fair thee well . . .*"

As the chorus gave way to the first verse, Creed counted four beats to

Metro, who instinctively came in with a sparse kick and high hat combo as Tump struck the note indicated by Creed's guitar chord. Perfect, so far.

"... *May your hills know the shady trees of summer; that in autumn rain down gold and crimson leaves . . .*"

It was almost a plea to Sid Larue, who was looking on in judgment, chin in hand. Winding up the first verse and a repeat of the chorus, Luster turned to Trusty Joe, who mimicked the singer's melody on the violin, note for note, then looked toward Creed, who looked toward Lindsay, who took the second half of the solo, her pedal steel swelling and quavering in a perfect compliment to the band.

These are really good musicians, Creed was thinking. They've never heard this song before and they're laying it down like a roofer with a nail gun.

" ... *And in the end; when your wandering days are over; may the road you travel safely lead you home . . .*"

The last chorus was easy. But how would Luster end the song? They hadn't had time to arrange the tune yet.

Luster signaled for the band to break, and he invented a tag:

" ... *May a fair wind fill your sail; may your good luck never fail . . .*"

That note soared two octaves above the melody, Creed thought. He was in the presence of the master. He saw Luster take the mic from the stand and wander toward Trusty Joe.

"... *May the sun shine on your trail; and fair thee well . . .*" Luster looked at Trusty and whispered: "Play something Irish."

Picking up the tempo of the song, Trusty followed the chord progression of the chorus, stroking out a melody that sounded vaguely like the TV ad for Irish Spring bath soap. The rest of the band joined in for a few bars until Creed found a place to end, directing the band through a turnaround to wrap up the tune.

"Stick around for the rest of the auction, folks!" Luster said. He turned to Creed. "Well, now we know the song stands up a day later."

Creed grinned and nodded.

Sid Larue stepped up to the edge of the stage. "That was great. World class, Luster."

"Thanks, Sid."

"There's only so much I can do for you, but I'll try my damnedest to buy you some time."

"That's all I can ask. Thanks."

Sid looked at his watch, glanced his good-byes to the band, and headed out of the barn. He stopped, turned. "You're going to send the auction money in, right?"

"You're damn skippy, I am."

Larue left.

Luster turned to face the players. "Right after I pay my band a grand."

"Cool, *jefe*!" said Metro. "That's two bills a man."

"Or a woman," Lindsay scolded.

"No, I mean a grand *apiece*," Luster said. "I don't lowball good pickers." He handed his mic to the auctioneer, amid great joy on the stage.

"I'm so happy, I could vomit!" said Trusty Joe, breaking into tears.

CHAPTER

Hooley drew a deep breath of cool, damp lake air and held his lure at arm's length so he could see to tie the line on. Pushing forty-five, his eyes had begun playing tricks on him lately, but he had yet to go to Walgreen's for a pair of those reading glasses. He noticed the reddish glow from the corner of his eye, and looked east to see the sun rising over Lake L.B.J., the ripples of the tiny waves catching the orange hue. He knew it would only last for seconds.

"Ain't that a thing of beauty?" he said, looking toward the back of the bass boat, where he found Special Agent Doolittle fiddling around with his spy phone. "Hey, city boy! Look around you."

Mel glanced at his surrounds. "Yeah, it's rustic," Mel said. He went back to fooling with the phone. He was wearing one of Hooley's denim jackets in an attempt to make him look more like a fisherman than a cop. The sleeves were too long, so he had rolled the cuffs.

"Put that damn thing away and grab that fishing pole." He cast his lure into the rising sun.

"I'm trying to leave a message with my partner, Samantha, at head-quarters."

"Samantha!" Hooley railed. "There's female feds?"

"A few. Don't you guys have women in the Texas Rangers?"

"Ha! That'll be the day. It's called the Rangers, not the Rangerettes."

Mel looked up from his phone. "But there's African-American Rangers, right?"

"There's plenty of colored state troopers. A lot of good ones. Good officers."

"But not in the Rangers?"

"No. No colored boys in the Rangers."

Mel sighed. "Hooley, would you mind saying African American?"

Hooley glared. "Huh? I said colored. What's wrong with that?"

"Let's start with the *boy* part. When was the last time somebody called you a white boy?"

"When I was about eleven."

"That's my point. A man doesn't want to be called a boy."

Having retrieved the lure, Hooley cast again. "Okay, there ain't no colored *men* on the Rangers."

"Thank you. Now, about that *colored* part. I never understood a white man calling a black man *colored*."

"Why the hell not? You're colored. Black."

"Exactly. A black man is born black, stays black, and he dies black."

"Yeah . . ." Hooley flipped a sidearm cast toward some weeds sticking out of the water near the shore.

"A white man turns red when he's mad, blue when he's cold, green when he's hung over . . . and you guys call *us* colored?"

Hooley ceased reeling the lure to absorb what Special Agent Doolittle was getting at. He saw the images in his head. Red, blue, green . . . A smile stretched across his face, and he began to laugh. "Well, goddamn, Mel, if you ain't right about that! I've seen some technicolored white son-of-a-bitches in my time!" He doubled over and listened to his own laughter echo across the water. "All right, from now on it's African-American gentlemen. How's that?"

"Thank you," Mel said, smiling. He picked up the fishing pole and made a heave with it, slamming the lure down on the surface of the water a mere three feet from the boat.

"Ha! You look a little *green* with that pole, Mel! This ain't lacrosse, it's fishin'. Just flip it out there with your wrist, son!"

"Do I look like your son?" Mel made a better cast.

"That's more like it, young African-American gentleman, who is no kin to me whatsoever." Hooley shot a wry grin toward Mel just in time to see his rod bend. "Set the hook! Reel, Mel! That's a whopper!" He grabbed the net. "Hold the rod tip up! Straight up! That's it!"

The bass broke the surface of the water and danced on its tail in front of the ascending amber orb of the sun.

"Wow!" Mel cried. "Oh, my God!"

"Reel him in close. Don't let him under the boat, he'll cut the line on the prop! That's it! Closer . . ." He made a swoop with the net and scooped up the writhing lunker. "Woo-ha!" he cried, happier than if he had caught the fish himself. "That bastard'll go seven pounds, maybe eight!"

"Holy mother!" Mel said, wide-eyed. "That's the first fish I ever caught in my whole life! That was a rush!"

"I told you it was gonna be good fishin' this morning! Throw another one out there. Let's catch enough for supper, then we'll cruise the lake for evidence."

Hooley caught three fish, and Mel one more, though none was as big as Mel's first catch. After throwing the last bass in the live well, Hooley pulled up the trolling motor, fired up the outboard, and showed Mel where the boat carrying Rosa had presumably hit the submerged tree in the cove.

"I found a piece of wood, looked like from a wooden boat, stuck in that tree and took it to headquarters for analysis. Found out yesterday it was mahogany."

"So we're looking for a Chris Craft, or some similar boat."

Hooley nodded. "Maybe a Correct Craft or a StanCraft. They're all similar."

"Who registers boats in Texas?"

"That would be the Parks and Wildlife Department."

"Surely they list the type of boat, or the make and model."

"I've already got my assistant, Lucille, on it. It's gonna be a long list, but maybe something in there will help us."

Mel nodded. "So, which way did the boat go from here?"

"Pure guesswork. It was apparently headed out of this cove and on to some other part of the lake. It's not the biggest lake in Texas, but there's a lot of shoreline, and a dozen communities and little lakeside developments. For all we know, the boat could have been pulled out of the water at some boat ramp."

"What's your hunch?" Mel asked.

"I'm wary of hunches."

"I agree. We still have to follow all the leads, not just the hunch. Still . . . What's your hunch?"

"My hunch is the boat sank. Antique wooden boat, no emergency flotation, heavy inboard motor. But, if it sank, that's bad for us. It'll be hard to find underwater."

"Yeah, this isn't Lake Tahoe," Mel added. "You can see fifty feet deep there. In this muddy water, you can't see two feet."

"So what do you recommend we do, Special Agent Doolittle?"

"Ask the public for tips? Information on a classic wooden boat on or near Lake L.B.J.? Possibly a damaged boat?"

Hooley smirked and shrugged one shoulder. "Worth a try. But this thing has already been publicized as a mob hit. That tends to scare witnesses off. Let's cruise, and get a feel for this lake. Maybe we'll talk to some folks on some docks or somethin'."

Mel nodded, and the outboard roared itself into a grinding scream as the fishing boat went skipping across the glassy surface on this almost windless morn. They sped past miles of undeveloped lakeshore, Hooley pointing out herds of deer and flocks of wild turkeys to Mel.

Reaching Blue Cove, the first of the lakeside communities, they checked at boat ramps, resorts, lakeside neighborhoods. They found nothing of use to them in their investigation.

"Is this lake always this dead?" Mel asked as the outboard slowed to an idle. They were entering the no-wake zone of a cove along Horseshoe Bay, a swank development featuring brick and rock homes spaced rather close together on the lakeshore, each with its own dock or boathouse, some of which were actually enclosed with garage doors. Though the day had turned out sunny and warm, they saw no one on or near the water.

"It's a weekday, and we're between seasons. The snowbirds have gone home, and the natives ain't quite ready to work on their sunburns."

"Snowbirds?"

"Yankees. The rich retirees who can't handle the cold winters up north anymore, so they come down here to winter. They migrate down here in flocks."

"And the natives?"

"Water-skiers, fishermen, campers, college kids. And these rich people who own these fancy lake houses. They come to L.B.J. from all over the state. Folks from West Texas will drive six hours to find some water to cool off in. Houston's only four hours to the east. Folks there come to escape the humidity, the fire ants, and the mosquitoes."

"Seems like a pretty popular part of Texas."

"Suits me. But it's gettin' *too* popular in my opinion."

Mel pointed forward as the boat rounded a bend in the narrow channel. "Hey, there's a guy on a dock up there."

Hooley looked ahead and saw an elderly man standing on his private pier, slowly cranking a fishing reel. The man was wearing Bermuda shorts that revealed pasty white stick-figure legs, a golf shirt, and a Houston Astros ball cap.

Hooley cut the motor as they drifted by. "Catchin' anything?" he said, trying to muster some casual cheer.

"Not with that Mercury chuggin' along through here."

"Sorry about that. Hey, you know anybody around here who has an old antique woody? Maybe a Chris Craft, or something like that?"

"Who wants to know?" The old man squinted. "Hey, wait a minute. You're that Ranger. I saw you on TV."

"Captain Hooley Johnson."

"Who's this?" the old man said, pointing at Mel. "A suspect or something?"

Mel shook his head in disbelief of the redneck-ness of this place.

"No, this is my sumo-come-loudly partner, Special Agent Mel Doolittle, Federal Bureau of Investigation."

"The F.B.I.?"

"You catch on quick."

"The boat may have been damaged," Mel said.

"Or not," Hooley added. "Have you seen a boat like that around here?"

The man reeled in his fishing lure. "This is about that dead mob princess, isn't it?"

"Is that what they're calling her on TV now?" Hooley said.

"I don't know anything about any of that. This is the first time I've even been to the lake since last August." He began backing away from the water.

"You live in Houston?"

"What's that to you?" the old man said.

"Nothin'," Hooley replied. "I just noticed your ball cap, that's all."

"I don't know anything about any of it. Now listen, you two get out of here. I don't want you casting up into my boat and tearing the upholstery."

"What?" Hooley said.

"You dumb shitheads. You're not going to catch anything today, anyway. The wind is wrong."

"Well, you're fishing, too," Mel said, beginning to chuckle at the grumpy old fart.

"You're probably Republicans, too."

"Listen here, now," Hooley growled, "you can call me a shithead, but don't go callin' me a Republican!"

"I'm late for my tee time!" the retiree snapped as he stormed away.

"Nice talking to you," Mel groaned, unable to disguise the sarcasm in his voice. He turned to Hooley. "People *are* nervous."

Hooley nodded. "That ol' boy may have been a little *too* nervous. But . . . That's just a hunch."

Later in the evening, Hooley grilled the bass fillets over a charcoal fire in the backyard of his house on the outskirts of Liberty Hill while Mel studied a map of Lake L.B.J. spread across the kitchen table. Mel had just asked a question Hooley thought he heard correctly over the sizzle of the fillets on the hot grill.

He yelled into the open back door of the house: "If you're asking about that channel where we talked to the nervous old fart, I'd say it was a twenty-minute boat ride to The Crew's Inn. Stir those taters on the stove, will you?" He forked the slightly blackened fillets onto a plate and walked inside.

Mel was at the stove, poking at a skillet with a wooden spoon. "Seems reasonable our antique boat owner might make the trip from there to the bar for a beer."

Hooley raked the map aside and placed the platter of fish on the table. "Those spuds done?"

"I guess," Mel said. "They smell good."

"Bring 'em." Hooley grabbed a loaf of store-bought bread in a plastic bag. "If I knew how to make hush puppies, I would. We'll have to settle for plain ol' white bread. He noticed the brand name of the bread: Rainbow.

"Look here, Mel. *White* bread. *Rainbow.*"

Mel scraped the potatoes and onions, grilled in butter, onto the two plates waiting at the table. "Supports my theory, doesn't it?"

"Ha!" Hooley used a bottle opener to pry the caps off two Lone Star long necks. "Dig in!"

They began shaking salt and pepper everywhere, and devouring the bass fillets and potatoes. Hooley opened a jar of pickled jalapeños and grabbed one with his fingers. "You want one?" he asked.

"No, thank you," Mel said.

"You don't have a hair on your ass."

Mel looked insulted, and spoke through a mouthful of his dinner: "Okay, give me one, then. Hell, give me two!"

Hooley used his fingers to drop two whole peppers on Mel's plate. As if to show the way, he bit off about a quarter of his own jalapeño. Mel followed his example. Hooley waited. Mel began to squirm. His eyes began to tear up.

"Ha!" Hooley reached for his cold beer, again showing the way. As Mel guzzled, Hooley handed him a slice of white bread. "This helps. You hollerin' calf rope?"

"Huh?" Mel said, tears running down his cheeks as he stuffed bread past his teeth.

"Hollerin' uncle?"

"What?" He sucked in air, then reached for the beer bottle again.

"Are you *givin' in*?" He took another bite from his own jalapeño and chased it with a fork full of potatoes and grilled fish.

"Hell, no, I'm not giving in, uncle calf rope, or whatever!" He wiped a tear away and took another bite of the little green torpedo that seemed to have exploded in a ball of fire inside his mouth.

The phone rang. Laughing, Hooley got up to answer it. "Hello . . . Oh, howdy, Dolph . . . We've got some leads, some things to follow up on . . . Agent Doolittle? Yes, sir, I've been treating him with the *warmest* of hospitality. He's right here, you want to talk to him? Okay . . ." He held out the phone to Mel, his palm over the mouthpiece. "Try not to harelip the governor."

Panting for cool air, Mel got up and reached for the receiver. "The governor? Of Texas?"

Hooley smirked. "No, of Rhode Island. Of course, Texas! Governor Briscoe."

Mel took the phone. "Good evening, Governor Briscoe. This is an honor." About then it was plain to Hooley that Mel realized he had forgotten to grab his beer. Wild-eyed, he ran to the end of the curled telephone line, but couldn't make it stretch far enough to reach the beer bottle and keep his ear to the governor at the same time. Desperately, he snapped his fingers at Hooley, and pointed at the Lone Star. "Yes, sir, we're concerned that the owner of that boat may be in danger if the killer gets to him before we do."

Hooley slowly fetched the bottle and had a few seconds of fun holding it just beyond Mel's grasp before finally handing it to him.

"Yes, sir, we're treating it as a possible double homicide." He guzzled beer so fast that it poured out of the side of his mouth. Wiping his cheek on his sleeve, he panted in relief. "Yes, sir, a waste of two young lives . . ."

He took another swig. "I agree, Governor . . ." He looked at Hooley. "It leaves a bad taste in my mouth, too."

Hooley felt such a peal of laughter coming on that he had to leave the kitchen lest Dolph should hear him guffawing over the phone.

Franco found out about the place in the classified ads of the local weekly newspaper under "Houses for Rent." The front page of the same newspaper featured a sketchy story about a young woman from Nevada who had lost her life on Lake L.B.J. last Saturday night or early Sunday morning. He read the article, only to see if the small-town newspaper hacks might have stumbled onto something he needed to know, which of course they hadn't. His main purpose in purchasing the paper was to find a place to stay while he was looking for the schmuck who had given his late, adopted cousin her last boat ride. He found just that in the classifieds. The ad boasted lakefront houses for rent to tourists and fishermen, by the day or year-round.

The place he chose could scarcely have been more perfect for his purposes. Located on the same cove where he had fired his parting shots at Rosa, within view of The Crew's Inn, it came fully furnished and included its own fishing boat and dock on the lake. He had made the arrangements on the phone, paying with a credit card featuring a fake name and a Wisconsin address. He didn't have to meet the owner of the place, or any employees of the property management company that handled the rental, so no one got a look at him. They left the key in the mailbox for him.

The place wasn't cheap, but Franco gladly rented it for three weeks, hoping this chapter in his clandestine career would be closed by then. He had gotten settled in a couple days ago, hiding his Shelby GT with Nevada plates in the garage after dark. This morning, the rental car company left a sedan in the driveway, so he could drive around freely, casing the lakeside neighborhoods, looking for that classic wooden boat. He had also jogged up and down just about every street in Sunset Shores, turning up no evidence of the woody.

From the second story of his rental house, he could also watch the boat ramp beside The Crew's Inn through the sliding glass door that opened out onto the deck. This morning, while drinking his coffee, he spotted two guys—clearly cops—launching a boat. A tall, older white guy and a young, athletic black guy. Only the law would throw such an unlikely pair together here in the middle of redneck Texas.

Watching through his binoculars, Franco thought he recognized the black kid as a fed from the Las Vegas office, an underling fresh out of the academy, named Doolittle. He figured the white guy for a sheriff, a deputy, or maybe even a Texas Ranger. He wore a cowboy hat. The two were posing as fishermen. Franco had to give them some credit. They did actually catch some fish. Then they looked over the underwater boating hazard that had led to Rosa's timely demise, and headed on out to the open part of the lake.

Later, when the news van from KXAN-TV in Austin showed up, Franco knew without a doubt the two fishermen were really cops. They returned before sunset to find the reporter and the cameraman waiting on them. The tall cowboy granted them a brief interview, before the two cops trailered their boat and left. Franco looked forward to seeing that interview tonight on TV. The rental house included a tall antenna that could pick up all three Austin stations, though the picture was a bit fuzzy.

This was what Franco had been waiting for. Now that the authorities had looked around on the lake, it was his turn. He hadn't wanted to stumble on to any lawmen while he was out there, especially one like Doolittle, who might recognize him. It was indeed a good thing he had waited them out. Now he was ready to launch his rented boat, first thing in the morning, and do some snooping around, looking for that antique wooden vessel with the inboard motor. It was probably damaged, and might even have sunk. He wondered if the two odd-couple cops had found it already.

The thought made him nervous. What if they found the guy who owned the boat and got him to talk? What if the guy could identify him as the shooter on the dock? Imagine making that call to Papa. *Hey, Pop, we're screwed.* The thought made him shudder. He couldn't see the case sticking in court on one guy's testimony, but sometimes when one guy talked, everybody started cutting deals and talking. Franco was not afraid of jail time. The syndicate had a strong organization on the inside. But the idea of wasting all those years in prison did not appeal to him. He *had* to find the schmuck first, and make sure the poor slob would never, ever utter so much as a syllable about what had happened that night.

The phone rang, startling him, even though he had been expecting a call. "Yeah," he said, picking up the phone.

"*Yo, Franco. This is Jake. Jake Harbaugh.*"

"Where are you calling from?"

"*A phone booth. It's safe.*"

"Don't ever say my name on the phone, you stupid shit!"

"*Sorry, Franco. I mean . . . Sorry . . . I forgot.*"

"Yeah, you forget a lot, don't you? Did you forget to take the rugby photo off your freakin' office wall?"

"*It's gone now.*"

"Too late."

"*The damage has been contained. She's gone, right? Every record of her being in my office or at the station has been destroyed. The surveillance videos have been erased. Nobody here is gonna talk. Everybody knows the score.*"

"Your score is zero with me, you stupid puke. You better pray I don't get busted over this."

"*I've been busting my balls to make everything right. It's all okay here now. I talked to your pop today. He told me to call you at this number, so I'm calling. What more can I do for you?*"

"You can blow your freakin' brains out, and save me the trouble."

"*Come on, Franco. Seriously. Let me know what I can do.*"

"Don't say my name! Jesus, you're dumb."

"*Sorry. I'm just . . . Okay . . . What can I do?*"

Franco growled and looked out over the lake, its surface glittering under the moon now. "What do you know about fishing?"

"*What kind of fishing?*"

"I don't know! Catching stupid fish! I'm on a lake in Texas."

"*You after bass or catfish?*"

"It doesn't matter, idiot. Do you know how to catch the bastards?"

"*Yeah, sure.*"

"All right, drive your ass to Lake L.B.J., west of Austin. Leave now. Call me when you get close."

"*Oh, man, I can't just get off work, just like that, you know.*"

"Hey, stupid. You got two choices. Get your ass down here, or bend over and kiss your ass good-bye."

Harbaugh sighed heavily into the phone. "*All right, I'll be there.*"

"One of Pop's boys will drop off a briefcase for you to bring with you. Some shit I need."

"All right, I'll bring it."

Franco hung the phone up and cracked his knuckles. He walked down the stairs and went to the garage. The washing machine was kicking into the spin cycle as he entered the garage. Inside the closed garage, he opened the trunk of the Shelby and took stock of what he had to work with. He had a .22 with a silencer, like the one he had discarded in the lake in Austin. He also had a .32, a .45, and a .357. All were semiautomatics. He lay them out on a workbench in the garage and checked the action of each. He inventoried his ammunition for each weapon. He had enough rounds for a protracted siege.

Next, he looked over his cache of fake ID's, falsified police credentials, and credit cards. He chose a new credit card and put it into his wallet. He took the credit card he had been using the past few days out of his wallet and placed it on the workbench, beside the ammunition. He counted his cash: a couple grand and some change.

The washing machine quit whirring and rumbling, so he took the clothes he had bought yesterday out of the washer and put them into the dryer—some jeans and shirts, boxers and socks. He was determined to wash the "new" out of them before he wore them. He went back into the kitchen and poured himself a glass of some mediocre California merlot—all he could procure at the liquor store outside of Austin. He yearned for some decent Tuscan grape. He went to the living room, sat in a Naugahyde La-Z-Boy recliner, and thought about the problem at hand.

What had he left undone? What else should he be doing? A thought had begun to creep through his mind. Why sit here and wait for the cops to find something? That was driving him crazy. There had to be something else he could do. He thought of a tactic he had used many times before. Give the cops something else to think about. A false lead. The morons were always easily confused and led astray. Even the smart cops.

He knew one way to do it in this case. It was almost unthinkable, even for Franco, but he knew how to take the heat off the family. What if . . . He shook his head, smiling, and took another sip of merlot. Just thinking, hypothetically . . . What if another young sorority babe should get whacked? Just pick one, at random—one who had no connection with Rosa or Celinda. That would throw a wrench into the investigation. The press would eat it up. Some stalker, some nutcase, was killing sorority bitches. It had nothing to do with Rosa's reputed crime family. Hell, the prime suspect would be the guy who owned the antique boat!

Franco chuckled a little. He shook his head. No . . . He couldn't . . . That was just too outrageous.

He decided to wait for Harbaugh to arrive and follow the plan he had already made with Papa Martini. That one made more sense. The irony of the situation struck him. How could a guy like Harbaugh, who knew so little, know too much? One thing Franco knew for sure. He had never heard a corpse sing.

19
CHAPTER

Creed had flushed the fuel tank out with some solvent, and siphoned it dry. Now he was finishing the task of filling it with 130 gallons of diesel, which he had to hand-pump from 55-gallon drums. Next, he managed to jack up the rear axles, one at a time, high enough to get new tires on. The boys in Junior's shop were having a slow day, so they installed the new rubber on the rims for him, and balanced them all.

While all this work was going on, a shop heater had been blowing hot air on the engine block. Creed hoped the warm metal would help fire the slow-burning diesel fuel. He had learned long ago that sometimes you had to baby these old clunkers to get them to start, especially after sitting for a while.

"You fixin' to crank this thing?" Junior asked, taking a break from his office chores.

"I hope."

"Combat engineer, huh? Good luck."

Creed was really hoping to get this thing running before this afternoon's rehearsal, so he would have some encouraging news to report to Luster and the band.

As he wiped the bulk of the grease from his hands onto a shop rag, he noticed Luster barreling up to the bus yard in his Ford pickup. The Cadillac was gone—sold at auction. Somehow the F-100 Ranger suited him better, anyway. Luster parked beside the bus and turned off the Ford's motor, but left the door open and the music blaring from the dashboard speaker. It was one of his old classic tunes, "Oh, Delilah."

Creed thought it odd that Luster would drive around listening to himself. He knew the man was jokingly egotistical, but this seemed a little much. Maybe he was trying to refresh his memory on some nuance of the vocal.

"You're just in time for the test-fire," Creed announced, as Luster walked up.

"Good! We're gonna need the bus tonight. We got a gig."

"Tonight? I don't know, Boss. Even if it starts, it's still a mess inside."

"Aw, it'll start. And I left a note on the rehearsal stage in the barn, telling the band that if they want to ride in style to the gig tonight, they'd better get their asses over here and clean up the bus you've been busting your butt to fix for 'em."

Creed was thinking he needed to go home to the boathouse, shower, get dressed, and change strings on his Strat. Then, he'd still have to go to the rehearsal barn to load up amps. "Where's the gig?" He hoped it wasn't a hundred miles away. He was beginning to learn that you never knew with Luster.

"You know Bud's Place, out west of town?"

"Yeah, sure. Played there a couple of times," Creed said, the image of the good old-fashioned honky-tonk beer joint coming to mind. Not the best PA in the world, but he could make it work.

"Well, I called Bud and told him the band needed a practice gig. He canceled whatever band he had scheduled tonight, and told us to come on."

"All right." He stuffed the grease rag in his pocket. "Kind of short notice. Wish we had done some publicity."

Luster laughed. "Don't you think I thought of that? Listen . . ." He jutted his thumb over his shoulder, toward his own song blaring from the open door of the Ford.

Creed shrugged. "You got an eight-track player in there?"

"Hell, no! That's KVET, the Tom Denny show. Bud's fixin' to go live on the air."

"Holy crap," Creed said. KVET was the hottest country radio station in Central Texas. Tom Denny was the drive-time deejay, and the most-listened-to radio personality in town. He was a bigger local celebrity than that gorgeous blonde who did the weather on channel seven. Creed heard the song fade, then recognized Tom Denny's distinctive voice:

"Folks, that's a classic from Luster Burnett, and have I got a news flash for you. After more than fifteen years of obscurity, the great Luster Burnett is coming out of retirement, and he's playing a show tonight in our own backyard. To tell us more about it, I've got Bud Frazier right here on the phone, live from Bud's Place on Seventy-One West."

"Am I on? Tom? Are we live?"

"Yeah, Bud, you are live on the air, so watch your language!"

"They're gonna be swamped," Creed said, a grin stretching across one side of his jaw. "I hope Bud called for another truckload of beer."

"Shh!" Luster hissed.

". . . and he's got a hell of a—I mean, heck of a band together with some of the best pickers in Texas, and therefore the world . . ."

Creed heard his own name along with the others in the band, impressed that Luster had seen fit to get all the band members' names mentioned. "Do you know how valuable this airtime is?" Creed asked. "I mean, if you had to buy an ad?"

"Listen!" Luster ordered.

" . . . so come on out early to get a seat. I don't know when the hell they're gonna, I mean, the heck they're gonna start, but it ought to be the show of the year!"

"Folks, that was Bud Frazier of Bud's Place, live on the phone, and you heard it right here first. The legendary Luster Burnett is coming out of retirement tonight! Now, if I'm not mistaken, the guitar player, Creed Mason, is the same Creed from the one-hit-wonder band called Dixie Creed that launched the career of superstar Dixie Houston. So, let's listen to Dixie's latest number one smash hit, right here on KVET, ninety-nine point nine!"

Creed heard Dixie's familiar twang, and felt the grin melt from his face. "Turn it off, Boss."

Luster trotted to the Ford and turned the key. "I hear you. The only music I want to listen to right now is diesel music." He grabbed two beers out of a cooler in the back of the truck. "Fire that puppy up, Creed!"

Creed shut down the shop heater blowing on the engine block and walked to the front of the bus to turn the key and crank the starter. "Cross your fingers, Boss."

"Just crank it, son!"

Creed turned the key and listened to the starter chirp, way in the back, behind the rear axles. It cranked long enough for him to think of Dixie cruising down the road in her brand-new Prevost, a host of buses and eighteen-wheelers chasing her down the highway to her next sold-out concert. Then, before he had time to worry over it, the old diesel sputtered, popped, turned over, and began rumbling.

"Voilà, maestro!" Luster roared in his country twang. He began laughing, and tossed one of the cans to Creed.

Creed caught the Buckhorn Beer—it must have been on sale—and pulled the tab on the can. He guzzled about half the brew to wash the thoughts of Dixie out of his head, and began looking forward to the gig tonight. As he dragged his sleeve across his mouth, and breathed in an aromatic cloud of black diesel smoke, he saw Lindsay's Impala driving into the bus yard, Metro hanging out of the back window. Tump had a gangling elbow stuck out of the front passenger side, and that had to be Trusty Joe in the backseat behind Lindsay.

Luster let down the tailgate of his pickup to reveal an assortment of cleaning supplies he had thrown into the bed of the Ford: water hoses, buckets, brushes; bottles of Windex, Endust, Pine-O-Pine; brooms, cleaning rags, paper towels . . .

The band got out of the Chevy and gawked at the bus for a while. It probably wasn't what they had expected, Creed thought.

Suddenly Trusty Joe leaned over, hands on his knees, and panted. "Man, I need to ride in the front next time, Tump. I get carsick in the back."

"Not unless you call shotgun first," Tump replied.

Lindsay gently patted the fiddler on the back. "You can ride bitch, beside me, Joe-Joe."

Metro was the first to comment on the bus: "Cool, man!" He grabbed the water hose out of the bed of the Ford and dragged it toward a spigot sticking out of the side of the shop.

"A little elbow grease, and this thing will shine up like a Roll-Royce!" Luster declared, reaching into the Igloo cooler for another Buckhorn Beer.

Trusty Joe, shaking off his nausea, grabbed a large bucket and squirted in some liquid soap from a plastic squeeze bottle. "Hey, Luster, can I give Baldy a bath tomorrow?"

"Sure. Maybe he'll kick some sense into your head."

Tump flicked a cigarette butt into the gravel driveway and found a spray nozzle in the back of the truck. "Hey, kid!" he yelled at Metro. "Screw this on." He tossed the nozzle to the drummer who caught it over his shoulder, like a football player going long.

Lindsay was still shaking her head. She grabbed a broom, the Windex, and some paper towels from the truck, giving Luster a stern look. "This is the only time you will *ever* see Lind-SAY Lock-ETTE doing windows. You have an hour and a half of my time before I have to go home and start putting on my makeup." With her cleaning supplies in hand, she sauntered toward the open door of the bus.

"Good work, Creed," Luster said. "You know I'm an optimist, but I had my doubts about this battleship."

"Channel your optimism toward the transmission," Creed said. "We haven't put it in gear yet."

"All right, gather around here," Luster ordered. "Lindsay, get off the bus! We're having a band meeting!"

The band members gathered in a circle like a huddle for a six-man football team.

"I don't care if you think Christ was a conman," Luster said. "We're going to say a prayer for this bus, and I want you all to mean it! Now, bow your heads!"

"I don't bow my head," Tump said. "I lift my face to the heavens. The spirits have no respect for a man who cowers."

"Suit yourself," Luster replied.

"I'm agnostic," Trusty Joe said.

"You're going to Hell," Lindsay warned.

"There is no Hell," Trusty groaned.

"This ain't a theological debate!" Luster shouted. "What would it hurt to pray for a bus?"

"Okay, I'll fake it," Trusty said.

Luster closed his eyes. "Lord, you've cursed me with a band, and blessed me with a bus. Now, we pray in the name of all the saints and holy relics and guardian angels, please grant us a transmission! Amen!"

"Amen!" Lindsay sang.

"Is it ah-men, or ay-men?" Trusty Joe quizzed.

Luster sighed. "Creed, put this thing in gear before Trusty pisses God off again."

Creed stepped on the bus, sat down, and stepped on the clutch pedal.

"Remember to jiggle it a little in the middle!"

Creed nodded, and added his own silent prayer. He wiggled the gearshift lever and felt it slip into first as he heard a clunk in the rear of the bus. He made a mental note to adjust the clutch linkage. It seemed a little loose. Gradually, he let out on the pedal and revved the motor, and the old Silver Eagle began to roll!

Creed heard applause and hallelujahs from outside as he eased across the parking lot. He motored out onto the side street and shifted into second. Again, the gearbox clunked, but shifted. He rushed into the third gear, then fourth, just to make sure they all worked, then made the block back to the bus yard.

By the time he returned, Junior had joined the band in a Buckhorn Beer toast. Creed shut the bus down and jumped out to join the celebration. Even Tump saw fit to pat him on the back. Lindsay gave him a marvelous hug and Metro forced some kind of barrio handshake on him.

"This is a dream come true," said Trusty Joe, fighting back a sob. "I'm gonna see some blacktop through the windshield of a Silver Eagle! First Baldy, and now this!" He began to cry.

Luster shoved a beer at him. "Drink that and shut up. Any more blubberin', and you're fired. Pukin' is optional."

CHAPTER

As the sun set down a two-lane stretch of U.S. 71, a clean, vintage bus—gears grinding—pulled into the entrance of Bud's Place, trailing a cloud of black smoke. An assortment of pickup trucks, cars, and motorcycles already filled half of the parking lot. The band began to load into the back door as Luster and Creed stepped in to look things over.

Bud Frazier, a big man with a big smile, busy tending his own bar, spoke up as he poured a beer from a tap. "That's him! That's Luster Burnett!"

Luster soon found himself swamped with admirers, so much so that they stormed the stage, seeking autographs.

Creed was trying to get his amp in place onstage amid the fans. He grabbed Luster by the sleeve and spoke into his ear. "Boss, if you'll go up front, we can get the gear set up while you sign autographs," he suggested. "Don't let 'em wear you out, though. Go hide in the bus if you have to."

Luster grinned. "I've been hiding long enough, son." He turned to the fans. "Folks, I am here to declare that the legendary Luster Burnett is *back*!"

A cheer burst from the small crowd.

"Come on, now, get off the stage so my band can set up, and I'll sign some of these albums y'all brought with you. That'll make 'em worth a nickel more in the garage sale."

As Luster cleared the crowd, Creed shook hands with a sound engineer named Tony and began explaining what the band would need. "If you don't mind, I'll set the PA with you," Creed said, trying to avoid stepping too heavily on Tony's toes.

"It's all yours, man," said Tony, a toddy of some kind in his hand.

After almost an hour of stumbling over one another, four band members had drums and amps set up, each staking a claim to a portion of the stage. Lindsay arrived in her Impala, dolled up like Black Barbie.

"I'm going to need some more room here, Metro, honey," she purred.

"*No problema.*" Metro began moving his entire kit over toward Creed's amp to make room for Lindsay's.

"We missed you on the bus," Tump said.

"I wasn't sure that thing was gonna make it," Lindsay admitted.

Creed was running mic chords to the stands. "Oh, ye of little faith," he said.

"I got faith galore," she replied. "In this band, you got to have faith."

Creed smirked and nodded his agreement. "Let's get some mic checks. Trusty?" He trotted to the mixer board, located at the side of the dance floor.

Trusty, looking rather nervous and green, tapped on his mic, then spoke into it. "Check, two, check, two, check, one, two, three, check, check, check . . ."

Creed found Tony turning knobs on the wrong channel. "He's channel five," Creed said, pointing to the strip of masking tape that ran along the bottom of the control console, where he had written Trusty's name under his channel.

"Oh. That's Trusty? I thought the drummer was Trusty."

"No, that's Metro."

"Don't y'all have any normal names in this band?"

"Not a one," Creed admitted, worrying about Tony cranking knobs.

Trusty Joe was still stuttering, "Check, two, check, one, two, check, check, check . . ."

Creed equalized the vocal toward the closest thing he could find to a sweet spot, considering the PA and the room. "Okay, that's good," he said, cutting Trusty off in mid-check.

"Can I have more monitor?" Trusty Joe asked.

"Sure." Creed pretended to adjust the monitor, though he actually did not turn the knob at all for fear of causing feedback onstage. "How's that?"

"Check, two, check, two. Perfect."

"Lindsay?"

Lindsay sang her mic check: a stirring a cappella verse of "He Ain't Heavy, He's My Brother" by the Hollies. Creed went back to the stage and talked Tony through the settings for his own mic and Luster's. Then he got the band to try an intro to a song, begging Tump to turn his bass amp down.

"I guess that's the nearest thing to a sound check we're gonna get," Creed lamented. "Let's go to the bus for a band meeting."

"Band meeting?" Tump complained.

"This is our first public gig," Creed reminded him. "I want us all to start out on the same page."

Tump sighed, and probably rolled his eyes behind his shades. "Let me smoke a coffin nail first, then I'll be there."

"Me, too," Lindsay said, putting a Virginia Slim to her lips. "You got a light, Tump, baby?"

He pointed to the back door with a nod of his head.

"I need some fresh air," Trusty Joe blurted, charging outside.

Creed pushed his way through fans to extricate Luster from the crowd that had gathered around him. "We need you in the bus, Boss."

Still, it took a good ten minutes to move Luster from the bar to the bus, as every fan there had a story and a handshake for him. Boarding the old coach, Creed shut the door and found the band waiting in complete silence. Luster must have noticed, too.

"Which one of us were y'all talkin' about?" Luster said, knowingly. "Anybody want a beer?" He opened the refrigerator.

"That thing doesn't work yet," Creed said.

"Damn. That's the most important thing."

"I carried the Igloo in." He pointed to the cooler, which Tump was using as an ottoman.

Luster brushed Tump's long legs aside and began passing out beers.

Lindsay took one. "Tump, baby, can you open this for me. I just put on these nails."

Luster looked at Metro. "How old are you?"

"I'm old enough." Metro reached out his hand.

"In Mexico, maybe."

"I'll take it," Tump said, handing Lindsay the beer he had opened for her. Taking the next can from Luster, he handed it to Metro behind Luster's back.

"Let's pace ourselves on the drinkin'," Creed warned, putting on his band leader's hat. "We can get drunk as a bunch of hoot owls after the gig. Just play like we do in rehearsal, all right? Play the songs like the records we've all heard for years. Remember, these folks came to hear Luster sing, so let him sing. No noodlin'. Don't step on any lyrics."

The musicians nodded their agreement.

"Well, let's go do it," Creed said.

"Oh, I forgot to tell you," Luster said.

Now what? Creed was thinking. "Yeah, Boss?"

"I want you to open for me."

"Huh?"

"Play that hit song of yours, 'Written in the Dust.'"

"We didn't rehearse it."

"Oh, hell, it's a hit. Everybody knows that song."

Creed looked at Tump. "Do you know it?"

Tump sighed. "I've played it a thousand times, in a dozen cover bands."

"Metro?"

"I think I've heard it."

"I'll talk him through it," Tump said.

Before Creed could even ask, Lindsay said, "I can sing Dixie's part. I've heard it a million times on the radio."

"There ain't no fiddle part," Creed said, apologetically, looking at Trusty.

"Thank God. I've got enough to worry about. This is not easy for me, you know."

"Let's just go do it," Creed allowed.

As the band filed out of the bus, Luster held Creed back.

"Yeah, Boss?"

"Are you carryin'?"

Creed lifted his shirttail to reveal the grip of his forty-five automatic sticking out of the front of his Levis. "I'll put it in my guitar case once we're onstage."

Luster pulled the snub-nosed revolver from the top of his boot and tossed it nonchalantly onto the table in the bus. "You're in charge of security."

Creed nodded, and they left the Silver Eagle for the smoky bar.

21
CHAPTER

Creed felt the good, solid weight of the Stratocaster on his right shoulder as he looked out through the cigarette smoke at the reckless mix of humanity in Bud's Place.

"Ladies and gentlemen," Lindsay said, even before Creed was ready to start the show. "I would like to introduce the opening act."

The crowd groaned in disapproval.

"Don't worry," the pedal steel player continued, "we're only going to play one song before the great Luster Burnett takes the stage." She gestured to her right, her silver finger picks shooting sparks Creed's way . . . "This is Creed Mason, formerly of the band Dixie Creed, here to play the smash hit song that he wrote, called 'Written in the Dust'!"

Creed switched to autopilot and cranked out the familiar guitar riff that he himself had invented to kick off the song. Not just any song, but a by-God, top-ten, country charter that *everybody* in the place had heard on the radio.

Before he knew it, the band was into the groove, though Metro was rushing a bit, and Tump was hollering directions to him. Now Creed looked out at the crowd, and even as he sang the lyrics he had written years before, the wave of panic struck him . . .

> *"There were eighteen dirt road miles or more;*
> *Between your place and my front door;*
> *And when the weather got dry, that dust would cover my beat-up*
> *Ford . . ."*

For now he looked at Lindsay, realizing too late that she was about to sing the part Dixie used to sing . . . Lindsay . . . whose skin was darker than

Creed's—or Dixie's—was about to answer his opening to a crowd that was about fifty percent redneck . . .

The crowd at Bud's Place—not the fake urban-cowboy wannabes, but the real snuff-dippin', tobacco-chewin', cedar-choppin', cow-punchin', shit-kickin', beer-guzzlin', goat-ropin', pistol-packin', truck-drivin', cousin-courtin' white-trash yahoos from the sticks out west of town.

This in itself was not a problem.

But, Creed realized, Lindsay was about to sing Dixie's part. Oh, shit . . . Why hadn't he thought of this on the bus? He rolled his eyes toward Lindsay, and found her smiling fearlessly, holding a chord on the steel with her left hand as she adjusted the mic with her right.

"I remember so well, that first sweet night," she began, lending her sweet, mellow vocals to the part Dixie used to growl out to the audience's delight, *"I said please stay and you said all right . . ."*

The redneck element of this crowd didn't seem delighted, though the rest of the audience, made up of country music fans from Austin, was whole-hog enraptured by the surprise opener. Lindsay plowed through the tune with undaunted professionalism and the band ended to a rousing round of whistles, hoots, and applause.

As Creed tuned his guitar, he saw one particularly burly, pig-eyed redneck push his way to the stage. Through the applause, and appreciative hollers of the crowd, Creed heard very clearly what the hateful son-of-a-bitch said:

"Hey, boy, you some kind of nigger-lover?"

Creed felt the ire boil up from his guts as he reached for the strap to undo it from the Strat. He had piled off more than one stage to whip some ass, usually when some drunk got too fresh with Dixie, back in the old days. But before he could get the strap undone, he heard Lindsay's unflappable voice:

"Ladies and gentlemen, welcome to the stage, our host, Mr. Bud Frazier!"

Bud, no small man himself, stepped between Creed and the big redneck. "Take it easy, Creed. I'll handle it."

Creed, still seething with anger, grabbed Bud's hand and pulled him up onto the stage.

"Folks, look at this band!" Bud said. "It's America, ain't it? And now, let me introduce to you a fine American. The man you've all come here to see. The great, the legendary, the one and only . . . Luster Burnett!" Bud stepped off the stage and dragged the offensive redneck away with him.

As Lindsay kicked the first song on the set list, she smiled at Creed and said, "Don't let them get to you, Creed, honey."

Creed nodded as Luster stepped onto the stage. The band had to repeat the intro three times as the legend strapped on his guitar, shook hands, and waved. Finally, his overpowering, dulcet voice rang out, stunning the crowd almost instantly into awed silence, filling every cobwebbed corner of the room. That voice somehow rattled windowpanes and settled nerves; eased tension and tingled spines, pierced eardrums and erased pain. Even Creed felt his anger slipping away, and it wasn't easy to let it go, after it had gotten a good hold on him.

Yes, Luster was living up to his legend, but the band seemed scattered. Tump and Metro felt out of sync, the two of them constantly speeding up and slowing down, trying unsuccessfully to lock in together. Trusty Joe's bow was scratchy and reticent. Even Lindsay got lost in the nebulous shapelessness of what was supposed to be a song, so unsure of the tempo that she began fading her volume pedal out in the vicinity of the down beat so that she didn't have to commit to it.

The crowd couldn't have cared less about the band. They were in the presence of greatness, in the form of Luster Burnett.

After the first song, Trusty Joe made the mistake of hollering "I need more monitor!" to Tony, the soundman.

Creed cringed. As he suspected might happen, Tony turned the wrong knob and cranked up Luster's monitor, instead of Trusty's. Luster didn't even like monitors, preferring to hear his voice in the main speakers, bouncing off the walls, as opposed to the speakers pointing back at the band. He had such confidence in his voice that he had no need for the reassurance of the monitor at his feet, blaring back at him.

But Tony had already cranked the wrong monitor up, causing Luster's microphone to feed back if he got too close to it. But Luster was a pro. Though he must have been frustrated, he just backed away from the mic and compensated with sheer vocal power. He could almost outblare the guitar amps with that amazing vocal instrument of his.

"Turn down!" Creed said to Tump and Trusty. Lindsay had already assessed the problem and backed off with her volume pedal. "Metro, back off!"

After the tune, Luster turned to Creed, an almost evil grin on his face.

"The soundman keeps screwin' with the PA," Creed said apologetically.

"That's the reason I don't carry a gun onstage with me, because I'd shoot the sons-of-bitches if I did. Just point your guitar strings at the audience, Hoss, and smile. I'll handle the soundman."

Creed nodded, as Luster turned back to the still-applauding crowd. "Folks, how about a big round of applause for our soundman, Tony!" he said, gesturing toward the mixer board. "Tony's been working his ass off for us tonight. Let's see that ass, Tony! See! Damn near worked off! Tony, step over to the bar because I want to buy you a drink. Bud, for God's sake, come over here to the mixer board and spell poor Tony. Give him a break, you slave-driver!"

Bud took the hint, assuming control of the mixing console. As the band kicked off the next song, Creed tried to make himself relax. He looked at the crowd and faked a smile, as Luster had requested. He noticed some guy wearing a sling on his arm, glaring at him. The guy wouldn't stop staring, and he looked pissed off. Creed's mind whirred as he played. He thought about the guy he had shot at the poker game a week ago—the guy wearing the flack jacket. He thought about the forty-five, just out of reach in his guitar case. The guy in the sling had two buddies with him. All of them looked pissed. He was pretty sure they were the robbers from the poker game.

Aw, shit, Creed thought. Well, this wasn't such a bad way to go. Shot while giggin' with a legend. He glared back at the guy, his fake smile turning to something of a leer. He wasn't going to be intimidated at his own gig: not by some punk, wannabe gangster.

A couple of songs later, the band still locked out of anything akin to a vibe, Creed noticed another familiar face in the crowd. It was the I.R.S. agent, Sid Larue. He was pushing his way through to the stage, causing the hardscrabble rednecks to spill their beers, oblivious to the fact that they needed little more of an excuse to give him a good thrashing.

"Play 'Chuck Will's Widow,'" Larue demanded.

"Already played that one, Sid," Luster said, off-mic.

"Then play that one about the pawnshop."

"We will. We're saving that one for later."

Sid looked at his watch. "I don't have all night. Got an early morning."

Luster sighed. "Sid, what are you drinking?"

"I'm not. I told you, I have an early morning."

"Sid, you're in a shit-kickin' honky-tonk. You have to drink to get the whole experience. Go over to the bar and order something. I'm buying." Before Sid could complain, Luster put the mic back to his lips. "Folks big round of applause for a fellow country music picker, Sid Larue, down here from Missouri. Sid, let me buy you a beer. Bud, take Sid to the bar, will you? Give him the V.I.P. treatment."

Luster looked at Creed, as if imparting wisdom. "There's power in a microphone. Use it! Let's play 'Dear John Note.' Kick it."

The lack of groove in the band continued to hurt. To make matters worse, Creed noticed that a TV cameraman and a reporter had slipped into Bud's Place to record some of the show. They didn't stay long. He figured they were trying to get back to the station to air their scoop on the ten o'clock news.

Eventually, Creed decided to take Luster's advice to heart. He looked at the audience, and smiled. He avoided looking at Sid Larue, and at the three thugs who were still glaring at him. Instead, he found a girl in the crowd upon whom to focus his attention.

She was dancing like a hippy chick, eyes closed, swaying, arms waving above her head. She was dressed in a business suit, as if she had come straight here from some office job. She looked like a very sexy librarian. Maybe she was a lawyer or something, he thought. Anyway, she was really groovin' on this song, and that bolstered Creed's confidence. When the song was over, her eyes opened as she applauded, hopping up and down like an excited little cheerleader. She happened to lock eyes with Creed for a moment, and she smiled at him. But then her eyes were back on Luster, who was working the crowd with the power of his mic.

Creed kept his eyes on the sexy librarian the rest of the night, and things went better, but far from good. The only real bright spot was Luster, himself, whose jokes and stories never failed to entertain. And, of course, the voice . . . It was as if he had actually gotten better since he quit, all those years ago. Yes, Creed thought. His voice actually sounded *better* than the old records. More maturity. Deeper lows, stronger highs. And . . . yes, more soul. The recorded vocals had always had a real country heart to them. But now they somehow possessed an abiding sense of loss and gratitude, all rolled together. He sang with a need to impart something even beyond his brilliantly simple lyrics and the word images that had become part of American culture.

Luster was not remotely intimidated by his own legend. He *knew* he was better now, and he wasn't afraid to flaunt that fact.

22
CHAPTER

Finally, the last encore behind them, Luster bid farewell to his fans and began shaking hands with drunks. Creed racked his guitar and slipped his forty-five into the front of his pants. He looked for the three thugs, but couldn't find them, which made him nervous. He looked for the sexy librarian, too. She was waiting to meet Luster, but not having much luck getting close to him through the crowd.

Luster continued to talk to fans while the band tore down and packed up. Creed kept one hand on his amp and one on the grip of his pistol as he took his first load to the bus, slipping his gear into the baggage compartment. He almost expected to encounter the poker game robbers, but they failed to materialize.

Later, the stage cleared, he saw Luster finally turn away from the remaining fans to face the band members, who were standing around on the stage. He noticed the sexy librarian lawyer had failed to work her way up to Luster, and looked disappointed. He thought he might go talk to her, arrange an introduction to the legend. Luster changed that plan.

He turned around and scowled at the band. "I want everybody on the bus. *Now!*"

"Uh-oh," Tump said.

"Uh-huh," Lindsay agreed.

On the bus, Luster guzzled a beer to calm himself. Then he began:

"The only reason they didn't hate this band," he said, pausing to swig the last of the beer, "is because they *loved* me. Y'all played like hammered shit!" He collected himself again, grabbed another beer.

"Now, you're all good pickers, but you didn't live up to your potential. You forgot that you were a band. Metro, you rushed all night long. Tump, you had that damn electric bass turned up to *stun*. Lindsay, no matter how bad the band is playing, you've got to commit! Trusty, you don't need more monitor, you need to play fewer notes. Creed, you didn't miss a lick, but you didn't put out ten percent of the soul I know you've got!"

"I didn't rush," Metro said, followed by a grunt brought forth by Tump's elbow.

Luster continued his rant: "You all played fine at the auction on the ranch. But throw a few distractions at you, and you fall to pieces! What do you think it's gonna be like out there on the road? Shits and giggles? When we play a venue, we've got to storm it and take it by force, if necessary. It starts with you two," he said, turning his attention to Tump and Metro. "If you two can't lock in together, the rest of the band is lost in the dark. We need a foundation. You two need to go get drunk together, or something."

"I don't drink," Tump said.

"And I'll tell you somethin' else . . ." Luster continued. A knock on the bus door interrupted him. "Aw, shit, it's probably that I.R.S. vulture. Creed, start this thing up and get us out of here."

"Did we get paid?"

"Yes, I got it in my pocket. A whopping fifty dollars a man."

"Or woman," Lindsay said.

The knocking at the door came again.

"Start the bus, Creed!"

"All right, Boss," Creed said, his morale low. This was all his fault. He was the band leader. He hadn't prepared his troops. He sat down in the driver's seat and turned the ignition. Nothing. "Something must have come loose," he said, sheepishly. "I'll have to go look at it."

"Shit!" Luster said. "All right, the rest of you go have a beer or something, and I'll talk to the vulture."

Creed just wanted off the bus. He hopped out of the driver's seat and bolted for the door. Expecting to find Larue, he flung the bus door open and found, instead, the sexy dancing lawyer librarian.

"Oh, hi," he stuttered.

"Hi," she purred. "I'm sorry, I didn't mean to . . ."

The rest of the band filed out past them. Tump grunted a surprised "humph," sound. Lindsay went "hmmm," as if in mild disapproval.

"I didn't mean to disturb the band. I just wanted to know if I could buy an album. "I love the new song: 'Fair Thee Well.'"

That was good news. "Yeah. Uh, unfortunately, we don't have any albums."

"Huh?" she said, downright shocked.

"I know."

"No eight tracks, even?"

"We haven't, uh . . ." he shrugged. "This is our second gig." He stuck out his hand. "My name's Creed," he said, feeling lame.

"Oh, I know who you are." She smiled, shook his hand with a warm, firm grip. "I'm Kathy."

"I've got to fix the bus," he said apologetically. "Would you like to meet Luster?"

Her eyes and mouth flew open. "Oh, my God. I would *love* to meet Luster Burnett!"

"I saw you waiting in line, inside. Come on, I'll introduce you." He nodded his head toward the inside of the bus, and she followed him in. "Boss, I've got a real pleasant surprise for you. That wasn't Larue knocking on the door. This is Kathy . . ." He found Luster digging around in the beer cooler, grinding the ice cubes against the plastic of the Igloo.

"Kathy Music," she said, excitedly.

Luster reached deep. "What's that?"

"Music?" Creed said. "Really?"

"It's German. I have no musical talent whatsoever, if you're wondering."

"You dance nice."

She smiled.

About then, Luster looked up, his eye brightening. "Well, hello there. Beer?"

"Sure!" she said, perky as ever.

Creed left them, stepped outside, and trudged to the back of the bus. Visually, he swept the customer parking lot, empty now, except for one car—a Carmen Ghia that he had to assume belonged to one Kathy Music. He ceased to worry about the three thugs who had been eyeballing him. Maybe he was just paranoid. He couldn't be sure those were the guys from the holdup. But he was reminded that there was a poker game tomorrow night at the Jollyville location. He wondered if Luster was going.

Crawling up under the engine cowling, he used his cigarette lighter to look things over, but his mind was on the crappy gig, the ass-chewing from Luster, and that beautiful babe on the bus right now. Kathy Music. He wouldn't forget that name. Wow, she was better looking up close, which wasn't always the way things worked out on the honky-tonk circuit.

Without having to think about it too hard, his eyes found the problem. The battery cable had shaken off the ground post of the battery. He shoved it back on, made a mental note to tighten it tomorrow. Latching the engine cover, he thought about stepping back onto the bus, but felt he didn't deserve to right now. He thought he'd give Luster a little space with the beautiful fan. That would give him a chance to step into the bar and check himself over in the bathroom mirror. He hoped she wouldn't slip away too soon, but he didn't want to sniff too desperately around her, either.

"You can play it cool with the best of 'em, kid," he said to himself.

Entering the building, he saw the band members sulking at the bar, sipping brews Bud had given them. It was late and the last customers had left. The bartenders were cleaning the place up. The local station was on the TV above the bar. It was running a commercial for the new Ford Pinto. What a stupid-looking ride that was, he thought. There was an open seat at the bar, so Creed took it, feeling he should say something to the band, but he didn't know what that might be. He had Tump and Metro to his right; Lindsay and Trusty to his left.

"Maybe I should quit," Trusty was saying. "I'm holding the band back."

"Maybe we should all quit," Lindsay replied. "I don't appreciate being spoken to that way by someone who thinks he's so perfect."

"He *was* perfect," Creed said. "And we were far from it. Nobody quit, okay? It was just one bad night. It'll get better."

Trusty hung his head, his lower lip jutting. He took a long pull of his beer. Lindsay pouted.

"Hey, Creed!" Bud said, coming out of the kitchen. "You want a beer?"

"Yeah. Thanks, Bud."

"Great show!"

Creed scoffed. "What gig did you go to?"

Bud waved his big, thick hand at him. "It was great. The people loved it."

The Ford commercial ended and the local news came back on. This time of night, they reran the ten o'clock news for night owls. They were airing some story about a car wreck that reminded Creed of the gig. He turned his attention to the discussion going on with Metro and Tump.

"But I don't rush!" Metro complained. "I'm a human metronome!"

"You were leanin' forward," Tump assured him.

"What does that mean?"

"You're thinking of the beat like a thin line on a piece of paper."

"I am? I thought I was just playing the drums."

"The beat's not a thin line," Tump continued. "Expand it, in your mind. Think of it as a pocket. You're leaning forward, hitting the front edge of the pocket. I want you to lean back. Hit the back edge of the pocket. That's where you'll find my bass note. Man, you do that, and we'll lock into a groove like waves on a beach. Like an old Indian motorbike, broke in by the miles."

Creed kept his mouth shut. That was good advice, and more poetically expressed than he would have expected, coming from the typically taciturn Tump. The news anchor switched from his somber car-wreck voice to his cheerful, happy-story voice:

"*Country music legend, Luster Burnett, came out of retirement with a surprise concert tonight at Bud's Place, west of town on Highway seventy-one . . .*"

"Hey, that's us!" Metro blurted, watching the video of the gig.

"Oh, my God," Linsday groaned. "He was right. We sound like crap."

"*Caca*," Metro agreed.

"Listen to Luster, though," Creed said. "Even on those cheesy TV set speakers. That's a million-dollar voice."

"Better be a seventeen-million-dollar voice," Tump said.

Trusty Joe began to sob. "I played so many notes. Why did I do that? So many, many notes."

"*. . . sources say the entertainment icon has fallen upon difficult financial times, and is planning a comeback tour. Judy . . .*"

The shot on the screen switched to the incredibly attractive, bright-eyed blond news gal who had driven the ratings up on the station.

"*We've been following the story of a young Nevada woman, Rosabella Martini, who was killed on Lake L.B.J. last week. A K-eye news team tracked down Texas Ranger Captain Hooley Johnson earlier today for a comment.*"

Creed watched the shot change to a boat ramp, somewhere on one of the area lakes. The ranger captain looked vaguely familiar to him as sort of a celebrity lawman.

"*We're looking for a fancy, vintage, wooden boat. Maybe a Chris-Craft or something like it. Maybe damaged. If anybody's seen anything like that on or around Lake L.B.J., we'd like to know about it.*"

Before the Ranger could turn away, the reporter got in another question:

"Is there any connection between Miss Martini's death and the murder of Celinda Morales, who died the same day?"

"Miss Martini's death has not been ruled a homicide. Miss Morales was possibly an acquaintance of Miss Martini through their sorority, but so far there's no connection in the two unfortunate deaths."

Odd, Creed thought. At the end of the shot, he caught a glimpse of the ranger carrying a stringer of fish as he turned away. The blond bombshell anchorwoman was back on the screen in the studio now:

"The Texas Rangers are cooperating with the F.B.I. in the increasingly bizarre case. And, speaking of Texas Rangers, Roger has a report from spring training camp when we return."

Smooth segue, Creed thought, wincing.

"Bud!" Tump yelled. "Turn that goddamn thing off and bring me a beer!"

Without even looking, Bud reached back and thudded a big ham against the power button while simultaneously filling a beer mug for Tump.

"I thought you didn't drink," Metro said.

"I had quit, but if Luster thinks us gittin' drunk together will make us a tighter rhythm section, I'm willing to make that sacrifice."

Creed wasn't sure he liked that development, but he wasn't Tump's keeper. As he grabbed his beer mug, he faintly heard a singsong voice, audible now that the television was off. It came from outside, and though he had only heard her speak a few words, Creed knew it was Miss Music's voice:

"Thank you so much, Mr. Burnett. I mean . . . Luster." She giggled. "You won't regret it!"

The Carman Ghia cranked and purred, rather like Kathy herself. *Regret it? Regret what?* What had Luster done now? Before Creed could ponder the possibilities, Trusty Joe bolted from his bar stool and ran for the back door, barely making it outside before a ghastly, guttural, retching sound invaded the smoky silence of the after-hours beer joint.

Metro and Tump burst into laughter.

"Lovely," Lindsay said, pushing her mug away. "Bud, I'm not much of a beer woman. Can you make me a Tequila Sunrise?"

"Sure, darlin'."

"All right, Tump, let's get drunk!" Metro said, clicking his mug against Tump's. "Hey, is Tump your real name?"

"It's a nickname. And you're fixin' to find out why." He lifted the beer mug to his lips and somehow miraculously poured it down his throat in a matter of two or three seconds.

Creed groaned.

CHAPTER

With the first ring, Creed began wondering where he was. He opened one eye and recognized the familiar interior of his houseboat, broad daylight streaming in through the cabin windows. He was home. That was good. His head hurt. Bad.

The phone rang a second time. Sitting up, he began remembering last night: the crappy gig at Bud's Place, drinking with the band after hours. Bud had begun to pour free shots of tequila. After that, the memories became spotty. Not good.

Third ring. Creed reached for the phone. "Yellow," he said, his voice a croak.

"Sorry to wake you." It was Luster.

"That's all right. I had to get up to answer the phone, anyway. What's up, Boss?"

"Be at the ranch about five this evening. No rehearsal tonight. We're having a band meeting. Make sure everybody's there, all right, Hoss?"

Creed rubbed his aching head. "All right. Uh . . . hey, Luster. Did we leave the bus . . ."

Luster chuckled. "I drove it home to the ranch. You don't remember? Lindsay gave the rest of y'all a ride in her car. She was the only sober one."

"It's coming back to me," Creed lied.

"See you at five."

He hung up the phone and thought about lying back down, but he had to pee, and the thought of a hot shower beckoned. He got up, finding himself naked. Well, at least he had been sober enough to get undressed before he hit the rack last night. As he turned toward the tiny shower stall, he thought he saw something move under the covers of his bed. It startled him. He glanced around and found clothing strewn everywhere, not all of it his own.

Stepping quietly toward the bed, he pulled back the sheets to reveal an Afro that led to Lindsay's peaceful, lovely face. Her eyes opened, her head turned to look at him.

Creed suddenly looked like a Mickey Mouse watch at six thirty. She smiled.

"No need to cover up now, Creed, baby. I saw you in all your glory last night."

Creed backed into the shower stall. All he could think of to say was, "Mornin'." He took a quick shower, knowing that he had to step out and say something to her. Something like, last night shouldn't have happened. He stepped out with a towel wrapped around him, one hand covering the scar of his war wound. He found Lindsay dressed and waiting, pushing her Afro into place. She beat him to the rhetoric he had just rehearsed in his head.

"You realize, Creed, baby, that last night was a mistake. I had a couple drinks when I got here, and I let my guard down. We should just pretend it never happened."

Creed shrugged as if a little disappointed, though he was eminently relieved at her attitude. "I guess you're right. I mean, but . . . I was okay, right? I mean . . . You had a good time?"

She smiled wickedly at the realization. "You don't remember, do you? Oh, that's really too bad for you for two reasons."

"Two reasons?"

"Number one, because it was fantastic. Number two, because it will never happen again. So I guess you'll just never know how good it really was. Poor baby . . . Now, hurry up and get dressed before *they* wake up." She jutted her thumb out of the window toward the stern.

He took a step closer to the window to find the rest of the band sprawled across the deck. Trusty Joe's head was actually hanging over the edge. "Oh. I guess I forgot about them, too."

Lindsay shook her head. "Get dressed. I'll give you a ride back to your van at the bus yard."

"Right. Oh, that was Luster on the phone. Band meeting at four o'clock."

"I could hear his million-dollar voice, Creed, honey. He said *five*."

Creed grinned at her. "So he did." He shrugged sheepishly.

"I'm gonna sneak past the aftermath. Meet you in the car." She winked and left.

Pulling up to Luster's ranch house at five, the boys in the band riding with him in the Good Times van, Creed was surprised, and a little confused, to find a certain Carmen Ghia parked next to the bus and Luster's pickup. Kathy Music was here. He liked that idea. But hey, she wasn't one of those girls who went for older guys, was she? You don't think Luster . . . He decided not to jump to conclusions, and not to look too interested just yet.

The second perplexing vehicle in the drive was the government-issued sedan that one Sid Larue drove. What the hell was going on?

The band members slowly unfolded from the van, still nursing hangovers. Trusty Joe veered toward the stables. "I'm gonna check on Baldy," he mumbled.

Creed, Metro, and Tump ambled slowly toward the house.

"Where's Lindsay?" Tump asked, looking around for her Impala.

"Runnin' late, as usual," Creed replied.

"What happened to her last night?" Tump said.

"She went home. Y'all about ready for some hair of the dog?" Creed suggested, changing the subject.

"Couldn't make me feel much worse," Tump admitted.

"What does that mean?" Metro asked. "Hair of the dog?"

"Kid, you got a lot to learn," Tump said. "Come on. I'll explain it to you."

Creed smelled the aroma of barbecue on the wind, and suggested they walk around back to the pit. They found Luster, Sid, and Kathy Music conversing over Texas Pride beers while Luster flipped steaks on the grill. Luster greeted the band members like old friends, showed them the beer cooler.

"Ain't it a beautiful afternoon?" he said, obviously in high spirits.

Creed smiled strangely at Kathy, grateful that he was wearing shades to cover his bloodshot eyes. "Pleasant surprise to find you here."

"I'll explain when everybody arrives," she said. "Let's see, we're waiting on Lindsay and . . . Trusty Joe?"

About that time, Trusty Joe rode by, bareback, on Ol' Baldy, the two of them loping along the creek bank as if they had done so every day for years.

"Just Lindsay. As usual."

He sat down across from Kathy and Sid at the backyard picnic table. He couldn't help noticing that Tump and Metro went straight to the beer cooler, Tump still explaining the hair of the dog comment.

"So, the dog bites you," Metro was saying, "and you get some hair off that dog, and put it on the bite? Sounds like something my *abuela* would do. She's a *curandera*."

Tump pulled the tab on his beer. "It's just a saying, kid. It has nothing to do with an actual dog. It means that if you're hung over, you drink whatever it was that ... Oh, never mind. I guess your grandma knows best."

An hour later, Creed's hangover and attitude having improved, Lindsay finally arrived. Luster found a bottle of wine and poured her a glass. Creed still had not had much time to talk to Kathy. Sid Larue had pulled her aside to go over some paperwork—ledger books and other sundry notes. It looked as if Kathy had been recruited to help with the Luster Burnett comeback in some capacity, and it was clear that Larue was agreeable to that development. Creed caught a few words of their conversation, and decided that Kathy was neither a librarian nor a lawyer, but an accountant.

As twilight fell, Luster rang a triangular iron dinner bell and ordered his guests to sit at the picnic table. He served steaks, baked potatoes, salad, and cornbread. As the diners carved meat and began to eat, the conversation predictably evaporated.

"Sure got quiet," Luster commented.

Trusty Joe swallowed. "Not to me. I hear all kinds of noises in my head. Horns honking and people screaming, guns shooting, music, dogs barking ..." He shoved another bite of rare steak into his mouth.

Tump patted him on the shoulder. "That explains a lot."

After dinner, Kathy uncovered a buttermilk pie she had brought with her. Creed took a bite. "Wow," he said. "Did you make this?"

Kathy shrugged modestly. "Yeah, it's easy."

"This reminds me of my grandma's buttermilk pie."

"Thank you!" she sang.

Luster found some whiskey in the house, and dumped more beer and ice into the cooler. To Creed, the band meeting seemed to have turned into nothing more than a dinner-and-drinking party. Still, after the morale-busting gig last night, and the ass chewing on the bus, he saw no harm. Maybe this was Luster's way of smoothing things over.

Luster sat at the end of the picnic table—silent for a change—seemingly amused by the conversations of the band members as they continued to knock back the beers, tossing the cans into a pile to be picked up later. Like Luster, Creed listened to the conversation stray all over the place, a vehicle out of control in a big, muddy pasture. Somehow, Trusty Joe and Tump got onto some nasty limericks they had learned.

"I know one," Metro said. "My name is Pancho. I live on the rancho. I make-ee five dollars a day. I go to see Lucy. She geeve me some pooh-see. And take-ee my five dollars away."

"That's not really even a limerick," Trusty Joe said.

"Not only that," Lindsay complained, "it's racist. Why would you disparage your own culture like that?"

Metro shrugged. "It's just a little joke."

"There's a female version," Tump said. "It goes like this: My name is Lula. I work at the school-la. I make-ee five dollars a day. I go to see Rex. He give me some sex. And take my five dollars away."

Metro laughed so hard that he sprayed beer across the patio.

Lindsay gasped. "This is pitiful, to perpetuate these racial stereotypes in this day and age. If you were a minority, Tump, you wouldn't think it so funny."

"I'm more of a minority than anybody in the band," Tump assured her. "I'm Indian."

"Dot-head or feather-head?" Trusty Joe asked.

Tump frowned at him. "Cherokee."

"Full blood?" Lindsay asked.

Tump shrugged. "There were probably a couple of pale faces in the woodpile a generation or so back. I'm mostly Indian."

"Me, too, *tambien*," Metro claimed.

"You're Mexican," Trusty Joe argued. "You ain't Indian."

"Hey, do I look *puro* Spanish? I got *Indio* blood. Mayan. My ancestors used to sacrifice virgins, man."

"We got somethin' in common then," Tump said. "I've sacrificed a few virginities in my time, too."

"Lord, have mercy," Lindsay said. "No wonder none of you have girl-friends."

"I've got girlfriends!" Metro insisted. "A bunch of them, down in the Valley."

"Yeah, across the border in Boy's Town," Tump said.

Metro merely shrugged. "That's the best kind. They're cheaper."

"No doubt," Tump agreed.

"Good heavens!" Lindsay railed. "What about you, Creed?"

Taken by surprise, Creed was glad darkness had fallen. He doubted the band could see him blush from the living room light shining out through the windows. "Me? Shoppin' around."

"Uh-huh," Lindsay purred. "I've seen you operate, heartthrob. The groupies always dig the guitar player, right?"

"I wouldn't know. I've been in a slump lately."

Lindsay chuckled. "What qualifies as a slump to you? A couple of nights?"

"For starters." He tried warning Lindsay off with a glare but found her cool stare toying with him. "What about you, Trusty?" he said, deflecting the attention away from himself. "You got a girl?"

Trusty burst into tears. "My wife left me! I'm going through a divorce." He buried his face in his hands and sobbed.

"Oh, poor baby," Lindsay said, genuinely sympathetic. She got up to comfort him, putting an arm around his shoulders.

"That explains the cryin'," Luster said, finally joining the conversation. "What about the pukin'?"

"I have a spastic colon!" Trusty replied, mumbling into his palms.

Lindsay grimaced, took her arm off of his shoulder, and moved back to her former seat across the table.

CHAPTER

After a good cry, Trusty Joe rallied, and suggested they should help Luster clean up the table and the dishes.

"Good idea," Luster said. "Then we'll gather in the living room and convene this band meeting."

Half an hour later, with the band plus Sid and Kathy seated on the large, burgundy-colored, crushed-velour couch facing the fireplace, Luster stood before them, a fresh can of Old Milwaukee in his hand and a good oak fire crackling behind him.

"First of all," he began, "I want to apologize for my little hissy fit in the bus last night. It was our first real gig. I shouldn't have expected so much of you. We've only had a handful of rehearsals. I overreacted, and I'm sorry. Nobody's perfect, right?"

Creed, like the rest of the listeners, just stared up at him.

"Right?" Luster demanded.

"Right," Creed said, along with everyone else on the couch.

"So, you forgive me. Right?"

"Right."

"All right. Forgiveness is important. It's everything. Especially in a band. Especially in *this* band." He began to chuckle. "I mean, look at us, for Christ's sake! We're all imperfect. Lindsay, you're never on time. Metro, you're just a kid. You don't have a clue. Trusty's either blubberin' or pukin' half the time. And I'm sure Tump has a personality somewhere behind those shades. And Creed . . . Well, you've got to admit he's well-nigh perfect, like me. But hell, that's more aggravating than being all screwed up, like the rest of y'all. Nobody likes a near-perfect son-of-a-bitch!"

He paused to take a long gulp from his beer can. "I mean, we are *some-*

thin', ain't we? Look at us. We got a colored gal, a Meskin kid, a Wild Indian, and three white crackers."

"I prefer the term *honky*, if you're going to go the *colored* route," Lindsay warned.

Luster continued: "Metro thinks I'm old enough to be his great-grandfather, and the rest of you are scattered in between me and Metro. So, we got all ages, all these races, all three genders, and I'm afraid to even get into religion and politics."

"What do you mean *three* genders?" Trusty Joe asked.

"Just making sure you're paying attention. Here's my point: If it wasn't for this band, would we ever sit down to supper together? Would we even say howdy to one another on the street? That's the power of music. It brings people together, allows us to set our differences aside. It's important. So . . ." He took another drink of his beer and sat down on the fireplace hearth.

"Driving the bus home last night, I had an epiphany. I've been looking at this whole thing wrong. I've been thinking it's all about *my* comeback, *my* rebirth, *my* resurrection. *Me, me, me.* That's bullshit. What I did in the past is done. Everything has changed now. The business is completely different. The fans are younger. The sound is new. This isn't a rebirth, it's a whole new conception. This is an emergence. An emergency emergence! This is a rare and wonderful opportunity to create something original. And so, it's not about me anymore. It's about *us. Our* band. *Our* sound. *Our* music."

The couch crew stared as Luster guzzled the rest of his beer.

Trusty Joe broke the silence. "You mean, we're not going to play your songs anymore?"

"Well, let's not get nutty," Luster said. "Of course we're going to play my songs. They're classics. They're great. But we don't have to play 'em just like the old forty-fives and seventy-eights anymore. We can let 'em evolve—maybe put some of this new progressive-country flare to 'em. Change a tempo, add some harmonies. Who knows? We'll rearrange, re-produce. Let 'em breathe!"

"Let's play some reggae, man!" Metro said. "Like Bob Marley doin' Dylan!"

Tump elbowed him. "Easy, kid."

"Reggae?" Luster snorted. "Maybe. Who knows? Now listen, there's something else, too. Allow me to introduce our new manager, Kathy Music."

Kathy rose from the couch and stepped in front of the fireplace. "Hi," she said. "My name's Kathy Music. It really is. It's German. But I don't have any musical talent, like the rest of you. Okay . . . I don't even know where to start." She looked at Luster.

"Start with yesterday."

She nodded. "Okay. I'm an accountant. Or at least I was until yesterday, when I got my pink slip."

"Pink what?" Metro asked.

"I got laid off."

"Groovy!" Metro said, approvingly.

"Laid *off*," Tump explained, "not laid. She got fired, terminated."

"Made redundant, as they say in England," Trusty Joe added.

"Would y'all shut up and let the lady talk?" Luster ordered.

"Okay," Kathy said. "So, I was bummed. Really bummed. Then I heard about the concert last night, so I went to the show, and wow! So, I went to the bus to buy an album, but Luster said he didn't have any for sale. Oh, my God! I couldn't believe it! You should have product for sale. This band should be playing large venues, not smoky little dives. So, it occurred to me that I have a three-month severance package from my firm. So, I've got three months to make this band profitable. If I can make the band make money, and begin paying back the I.R.S. what Luster owes, Luster said I can stay on full-time as manager!" Her cute little shrug said, *Well, what do y'all think?*

"All that in three months?" Tump said, dubiously.

"I know. It sounds crazy. But deadlines are good. We need a sense of urgency to make this work. Even Mr. Larue has agreed to give us three months to turn things around."

"At peril of my own employ, I might add," Larue said, rather heroically.

"Turn things around?" Lindsay said. "You have to be heading in a direction to turn around. We haven't been going anywhere."

"Sure we have," Luster said. "We've been headin' straight down the crapper!" His right index finger described a downward spiral. "So Kathy is gonna turn us around, straight up out of the sewers of honky-tonk hell!" His hand shot toward the ceiling in meteoric fashion.

"I know," Kathy said, as if reading minds. "It sounds like a pie-in-the-sky pipe dream. But I believe I can do this. We can."

"All right," Creed said. "So we need product. Why not put together a best of Luster Burnett album?"

"Great idea!" Luster said. "Except, I don't own the rights to the masters. Those belong to three different record labels, and none of them will release the rights. So we can't use the original studio tracks."

"So let's get in the studio and cut the songs over," Lindsay suggested.

"Brilliant! Except that I don't own all the songwriting and publishing rights to all of my songs anymore. When I quit the business, years ago, I knew I couldn't leave the boys in my band stranded, without an income. So I gave every one them one of my hit songs. They drew the titles from a hat. They get the royalties, not me. So recording those songs won't earn me any money."

"How many songs do you still own?" Creed asked.

"Only six of my big hits."

"That's not much of an album," Tump grumbled.

"No, it's not. So . . . We need more songs. We need to write more new stuff. All of us. Me and Creed have already come up with 'Fair Thee Well.' We need more fresh material to compliment my old standards. And we've got good singers in this band, too. Not great, like me, but good. Lindsay, Creed, Trusty, you can sing lead on some songs. It'll be more of a band project, not just a solo album."

"You want me to sing lead?" Trusty said, in a panic.

"If you think you can get through a song without pukin'."

"I can sing, too," Metro said.

"I can't sing, and I can prove it," Tump added.

"If it sounds good, we'll do it. The point is, if we have some new songs, I won't have to bullshit the audience so much to fill a two-hour set, and we can flesh out a ten- to twelve-track LP. We get all that done in three months, and we're on our way."

"That sounds rosy, Luster honey, but I got bills to pay," Lindsay said. "I can't wait three months for a paycheck."

"Mr. Larue has released enough cash from the auction to put you all on salary for three months," Kathy said. "Not much, but it should be enough for your bills. Plus, there will be bonuses for live shows."

"And a cut of the royalties when we get the record released," Luster added.

Silence filled the living room, save for the crackle of the fireplace. Creed decided to break it: "Well, what the hell are we waitin' for then? Let's vote on it."

"Good idea," Luster said. "All in favor say 'Screw Nashville.'"

A resounding "*Screw Nashville*" rang through the living room, followed by laughter from the band.

"I love democracy. All right, there's one more thing. We've got to rename the band. It's not all about me anymore, so we can't just keep calling ourselves the Luster Burnett Band. So here's what we're going to do. We're going to brainstorm. There are no stupid ideas, all right? When you're brainstorming, you just throw anything out there. The concept is that we will arrive at an intelligence that is greater than the sum of our parts."

Tump snorted. "That would put us somewhere between moron and village idiot."

"So what do you got?" Luster urged. "Somebody throw an idea out there. Anybody."

The band members stared at the fire.

"Oh, come on, you chickenshits! Who's got the balls to get the brainstorm started? Somebody say something. We need an identity. Some name that says who we are and what we do. Something that describes our essence in one word, one syllable, maybe even one breath."

"Band." Tump said.

"Okay!" Luster flashed a thumbs-up sign. "Gotta start somewhere. Too generic, though."

"Spelled B, A, N, N, E, D," Tump explained.

"Nice try, Tonto. Who else has somethin'?"

"Luster and the Home Wreckers?" Trusty said, apologetically.

"All right!" Luster cheered.

"You like it?"

"No, I hate it. It's too negative. Throw something else out there, though. Don't be shy, y'all!"

"I always wanted to start a band called Raven and The Maniacs," Lindsay purred.

"You can do that after I'm dead Miss LockETTE."

"Raw," Tump suggested. "It's like War, backwards."

"I prefer Medium Rare," Lindsay said.

Trusty: "Well Done!"

"That's good," Luster said. "I mean the brainstorming is good. The band names are terrible, but that's all right. Keep it going. What else you got?"

"I've been listening to the Thirteenth Floor Elevators," Creed said.

"How about Luster Burnett and the Escalators? That's what we do. Or what we should do. Escalate through the show, right to the top!"

"That's good, but you're intellectualizing. Just blurt something out!"

"Flirt Alert!" Metro yelled. "It rhymes."

"I like it!" Lindsay said.

"Well, then why don't you two go start your own girl band," Trusty suggested.

"Yeah, kid," Tump said, "just let the grown-ups handle this."

"Don't criticize!" Luster said. "It's okay to throw stupid shit like Flirt Alert out there. We're brainstorming!"

"I still think it should be Luster Burnett *and* something," Creed insisted. "Luster's our ticket. He's the focus."

"You're still intellectualizing!" Luster scolded. "Just brainstorm!"

"Well, then, how about Luster Burnett and the Brainstormers?" Lindsay said.

"Close," Luster said. "Hell, somebody jot that one down. What else?"

Kathy: "The Bean Counters! Sorry, I got carried away. I won't jot that one down."

"You're supposed to get carried away. What else?"

"I always wanted to name a band The Ghost Town Council," Trusty said. "Like it's the town council in a ghost town. Like, they're all ghosts!"

"Okay for a cowboy band, but not us. What else? Come on! This is not even a breeze. We need a storm!"

Trusty: "The Barn Stormers!"

Tump: "The Storm Stalkers!"

Metro: "Luster y Los Locos!"

Creed: "The Luster-Tones."

"Jot it down. No, never mind."

"You guys are really creative," Kathy said.

Sid: "The Exemptions."

Luster laughed. "I wish."

Lindsay: "The Deductions."

"Get off the tax thing. It's about music."

"I still like Flirt Alert," Lindsay said.

"We don't play bubblegum pop," Tump said.

Trusty: "The Hayseeds."

"Too country."

Tump: "The Hempseeds."

"Too hip."

"The Bolters," Kathy said. "Like a lightning bolt."

"Huh?" Sid said.

"Sorry."

"Don't apologize! What else?"

"Maybe we should sleep on it," Tump mumbled.

"I've got it," Creed said, softly.

Trusty: "The Dream-Tones."

"No more -*Tones*. It's too old-fashioned."

"I've got it," Creed repeated.

"Metro y Los Mysteriosos."

"It ain't all about you, kid."

"The Mystics?" Lindsay said.

"I kinda like that. Write it down."

Lindsay beamed.

"The Mysti-Cats," Trusty added.

"No more -*Cats, -Tones*, or -*Notes!*"

"The Epiphanies," Tump said.

"I'm tellin' y'all, I've got it."

Trusty: "Luster, you like cards, right? How about Royal Straight?"

Tump: "How 'bout The Straight Flushes?"

"Ace in the Hole?" Lindsay said. "No, never mind, that would never catch on."

Trusty: "The Imperfections."

"Do y'all want to hear the band name, or not?" Creed said. He reached into the cooler for another beer.

"While you're in there," Luster replied. He took a beer from Creed. "Okay, so tell us the band name, Hoss."

"This epiphany of yours," Creed said. "Exactly what was it?"

"I told you. It ain't all about me."

"I think you're holdin' out on us, Boss. There's something more to it."

Luster opened the beer. "Yeah? Like what?"

"You don't want to do this forever, do you?"

Luster shrugged. "Nothin' very good, or nothin' very bad, ever lasts very long." He took a long drink.

"You want to make your comeback with style, with dignity. You want to pay your taxes. Then you want to go back to ranching and collecting royalties."

Luster sighed. "You're pretty sharp, aren't you, Hoss?"

Creed opened his beer, took a long swig, felt the cold liquid pour down his throat. "But you don't want to leave your band high and dry. You want us to be able to go on without you when you're done."

"I always take care of my band."

"So what we need is a name that will carry us through the Luster Burnett era, on into the next phase of the band. You ready to hear it?"

"You've got my attention."

Creed watched every ear in the room lean his way. "We'll start out Luster Burnett and The . . ." He held up his index finger. "I'll tell you in a second. As we phase Luster out, we use his initials: L.B. and the . . .'"

"You're killin' us, kid. And the *what*?"

"What's L.B. an abbreviation for?" Creed quizzed.

"A pound?" Kathy said.

"The Pounds?" Trusty whined.

Creed smirked. "Luster Burnett and the *Pounders*." He said it with authority. "L.B. and the Pounders. The Pounders."

"Los Pounders," Metro said, trying the name on for size.

"We pound out the tunes. We pound out the beat. We pound the pavement. We pound the bricks. We pound our fists, and sometimes we pound our heads against the wall, but we just keep on *poundin'*!"

"We *com*-pound the interest!" Sid said, cracking himself up.

"We pound that poon-tang," Tump said low, to Metro.

"*Seguro que*, hell, yeah!"

"Beats Flirt Alert," Trusty allowed.

"Any objections?" Luster said. He waited. The fire crackled. "All right, then. We are now Luster Burnett and The Pounders. From now on, we write by day and rehearse by night, starting tomorrow. Y'all are welcome to stay here tonight if you want to. I'm going to Jollyville to win us some road money. Creed, you coming?"

"You bet your boots," Creed said, feeling cocky.

"What's in Jollyville?" Tump asked.

"Liquor and poker."

"Well, I'd sure like to meet her."

Kathy Music gasped and laughed. "Y'all are so randy! We never talked like that at my office!"

"Welcome to the other side," Lindsay said.

Luster shrugged. "I 'magine we can get you in if you want to go, Tump."

"Can I watch TV?" Metro asked.

"Make yourself at home." Luster grabbed a denim jacket, faded and worn. "All of you, pick a room and move in for the next three months. This home now belongs to the Pounders."

"I'm going to sleep in the bus," Lindsay said. "I cannot abide a bunch of men snoring."

"Fine, you can have the bus," Luster agreed. He pulled the jacket on and grabbed his felt hat. "Creed. Tump. Load up!"

25
CHAPTER

When the phone finally rang, Franco was ready. He slipped on a pair of yellow rubber gloves and picked up the receiver.

"Speak," he ordered, as if talking to a dog.

As expected, he heard Lieutenant Jake Harbaugh's voice on the other end of the line: "Yeah, it's me."

"Where the hell are you?"

"A phone booth in Llano."

"You made good time. I'm impressed. You're about twenty minutes away."

Franco gave him the directions to the lake house, hung up the phone, and ran some hot water in the kitchen sink. He began slowly washing dishes that were already clean, rinsing each dish methodically, placing it in the rack beside the sink to drain and dry.

Harbaugh showed up in due time. Franco met him in the driveway, opened the garage door, and waved him in, still wearing the rubber gloves. Harbaugh parked his Toyota Land Cruiser in the garage next to Franco's Shelby GT. Franco closed the garage door.

"You hauled ass," Franco said, as Harbaugh opened the vehicle door. "I didn't expect you for an hour or two."

"Figured I'd better get here. Figured you might need this." Harbaugh stepped out of the Toyota with the briefcase, looking uneasily at the plastic gloves.

"Come on in, I was just washing the dishes." He turned his back on the cop and led the way into the house. "Grab a beer in the fridge." As he continued to wash the dishes he had left in the sink, he looked out at the dreary night through the kitchen window. A spring storm had blown in all rainy and cool. The neighbors were holed up in their lake houses. He heard the refrigerator door open and close behind him, and refocused his eyes on the windowpane, using it to watch Harbaugh's reflection as the big man moved through the kitchen behind him. "Long drive, huh?"

"Yeah, hell of a long drive. What do you want me to do with this?"

Franco looked over his shoulder and saw Harbaugh holding the briefcase in one hand, a beer in the other. "Oh, put it on the table. Take a load off."

Harbaugh sat at the table. "You always wear rubber gloves to wash the dishes?"

Franco chuckled. "Usually, I don't have to wash the damn dishes. I got people to do that. The soap irritates my skin. Hey, I'm a tough guy, but I got tender skin. What can I say?" He heard the sound of Harbaugh guzzling beer from the bottle.

"So, Franco, are we okay?"

Franco looked over his shoulder. "What? Give me a break. I was in a shitty mood on the phone yesterday. Stuck here in Texas? You'd be pissed, too. Don't worry about it."

"So, we're going fishing?"

"We gotta find the boat that took your ex-girlfriend out onto the lake. I don't want to look like some goombah from Vegas, out for a cruise, you know what I mean? People fish on this lake. But I don't know shit from fishing, so you're gonna show me."

"Crappy weather for it."

"It'll blow over. You know what's in the case?"

"No."

"You didn't look?"

"It wasn't none of my business."

"Go ahead and open it. The combination is twenty-two fifty." In a moment, Franco heard the latches open. His heart started beating harder. He took a couple deep breaths to calm himself.

"Whoa. Lotsa cash."

"Yeah. How about the piece?"

"It's in here."

"Good. I had to ditch my last one. Pick it up. Check it out for me." Franco watched the reflection in the window as Harbaugh lifted the twenty-two autoloader out of the briefcase, his big hand wrapping around the small grip, his trigger finger slipping into the guard. Franco could see that there was no ammo clip in it. "Put the mag in."

Harbaugh picked up the magazine and shoved it into the bottom of the grip.

"What do you think?"

Harbaugh shrugged. "It's a twenty-two."

Franco chuckled. "Yeah, you cops like your hand cannons, don't you?" He grabbed a towel to dry the gloves he was wearing. His heart pounded again.

"A pop gun like this wouldn't spook a perp much."

"When I use my piece, it's not to spook somebody. I rely on silence. And what I lack in fire power, I make up for with accuracy."

Harbaugh nodded. "Then this is a good piece for what you do. Baretta. Got a silencer on it."

Franco turned. "No shit? Baretta?" He reached for the handgun. Harbaugh handed it to him. Franco jacked a round into the chamber, pretended to flip the safety on. "I carry mine cocked and locked. You?"

"It's the only way."

"People say it's dangerous." Franco shrugged.

Harbaugh snorted. He was beginning to relax. "I wouldn't carry a piece that wasn't dangerous."

"Exactly." Franco was looking down the gun sight, aiming the pistol at nothing in particular across the kitchen. "By the way, the cash is for you. For keeping your mouth shut."

"No shit!" Harbaugh said. He reached for a stack of bills.

Franco swung the silencer up next to Harbaugh's temple and pulled the trigger. The big cop's head jerked away from the impact of the bullet, a compact stream of blood gushed from the entry wound, like water from a drinking fountain. Harbaugh's whole body went limp and he fell sideways out of the chair, bumping his chin against the kitchen table as he crumpled to the floor.

Franco stood over him, panting, resisting another shot. Very few suicides got off a second round. But the big man was still breathing. "Come on, die, damn it!" Franco growled. He noticed that Harbaugh's jacket had fallen away from his hip to reveal his service piece in the holster—a nine millimeter.

It took a minute for the big man to bleed out and stop breathing. Franco used that time to collect himself. He placed the Baretta on the floor, next to the corpse's hand. Harbaugh's prints were already on it, as planned. He pulled the blood-spattered rubber gloves off inside-out and placed them carefully in a plastic trash bag. He then pulled on a new pair of rubber gloves. He had spent all day wiping his fingerprints away all over the house, and wasn't about to leave any fresh ones now. He took the credit card he had used to rent the house from his pocket and slipped it into the outside pocket of Harbaugh's blazer.

Reaching carefully into the briefcase, he opened the inside pocket and removed the envelope Papa Martini had hidden there. He opened the envelope and looked at the typewritten suicide note, prepared by another cop on the family payroll, using the typewriter in Harbaugh's own office:

I, Jake Harbaugh, am responsible for the deaths of Rosa Martini and Celinda Valenzuela. I killed them both. I sank the boat I used to murder Rosa. It will never be found. I could not tolerate Rosa's rejection. Celinda knew too much. I thought I could live with what I have done, but I cannot. I don't expect to see Rosa in heaven. I am sure I am going to hell.

Smirking at the last touch, Franco placed the note at the far end of the kitchen table where he saw no blood. It wouldn't make sense to put it on top of the blood. Now he had to watch where he stepped as he vacated the kitchen. He didn't want to leave any bloody footprints for the cops to wonder about. He withdrew carefully, taking the trash bag with the bloody gloves, leaving the dishwater in the sink, turning off lights as he left.

He opened the garage door and backed his Shelby out, then got out to close the garage door again. The rain would wash away his tire tracks. Perfect. Textbook. He drove thirty minutes to the other side of the lake where he had rented a second lake house, using a different credit card, also untraceable. He had crumpled newspaper and kindling waiting in the fireplace under a few bigger logs. He started the fire and burned the clothing he had been wearing during the hit, including the bloody gloves.

Tomorrow, the cleaning company would find the dead body. The cops would probably close the case, even if they didn't buy the suicide. It was just too convenient. They didn't really want to tangle with the mob. The schmuck who owned the boat would be confused, but relieved. He would come out of hiding. The cops would quit looking for him. But Franco would not.

26
CHAPTER

Hooley walked through the back door of his house, flipped the light switch on, and hung his Resistol on the deer antlers beside the door. He went straight to the bar and poured a tumbler nearly full with straight bourbon. Good ol' Jim Beam. Decent whiskey, affordable price. He took a sip, then pulled his boots off with the bootjack on the floor.

Long day. He had spent much of it sifting through dead-end leads on the antique boat. Dozens of citizens—some well-meaning, some nuttier than fruitcakes, some just pathetically lonely—had called in tips on antique boat owners. None of the tips had proven useful. Hooley had also been searching Texas Parks and Wildlife boat registration records, antique boat clubs, title searches. He had turned up absolutely nothing. His assistant, Lucille, was looking, too, in her spare time at the department, but had also come up with zilch. His brain was numb and his eyes ached from poring through records, files, and newspaper articles on microfilm. He was beginning to doubt whether there was even a needle in the haystack he was searching.

He sat down in his La-Z-Boy recliner and levered the footrest to full extension. This would probably be another night of sleeping in the recliner, he thought. He was already exhausted, and the whiskey would only send him over the edge into fitful slumber.

Glancing at the clock, he saw the ten o'clock news had been on for five or six minutes already. He reached for his remote and clicked the television on. At least he could catch the weather. Sports didn't interest him much this time of year. Football season was over, and baseball hadn't begun. Basketball? Not his game.

As the picture faded in, he saw the gorgeous blond newscaster staring into the camera, her blue eyes and red lips glistening. Could you just imagine? He took a gulp of whiskey, felt the welcome warmth plunging into his empty stomach. He grabbed a Swisher Sweet cigar and lit it. Well, that was one good thing about his divorce. He could smoke a damn cigar in his house if he wanted.

What was she talking about? She was smiling, so it had to be a light story of some kind. He turned the volume up with the remote.

"*. . . our news office has been deluged with calls about our exclusive coverage of the comeback of legendary country music singer Luster Burnett, who came out of retirement to perform at an Austin-area location last night . . .*"

Hooley smirked. Be damned! Luster Burnett! He was still alive? He watched the film of the band playing at some honky-tonk. That was Luster Burnett? He scarcely recognized the man from the old days. Sounded as if he could still sing. He wasn't so sure about the crappy band playing in the background. He took another swallow. He always liked that song, though he couldn't remember the title of it right now. Come to think of it, he had heard three or four Luster Burnett oldies on the radio today. Now he understood why.

The commercial break came. He turned the volume back down. It was that idiotic commercial with the dancing cigarette pack singing "*. . . taste me, taste me, come on and taste me . . .*" He turned the volume back up when the Ford pickup truck ad came on. He sure would like to have a new one, but knew he couldn't afford it. The judge had given Hooley's wife half the house, so he had a mortgage again, though he had already paid the house off once. There wasn't enough left over for a new truck payment, that was for sure.

Blondie was back, her fun-story face gone now, her eyes all serious-looking. She was covering the fatal car wreck on twenty-two-twenty-two. Hooley had heard that chatter on the radio today. Another bad one on that stretch of road. "*Jim,*" she said, having wrapped up the gory details.

The camera went to Jim: "*The Lower Colorado River Authority will begin lowering the water level on Lake L.B.J. tomorrow to repair the hydroelectric generating station in Wirtz Dam. The lake level will remain down for two weeks. An L.C.R.A. spokesman said this would give residents around the lake an unexpected opportunity to repair and maintain docks, boathouses, and other structures normally underwater . . .*"

Hooley shot out of his La-Z-Boy, sloshing whiskey. Why the hell hadn't somebody called him? Didn't they know he was looking for a boat, possibly sunk in that lake? He charged over to the phone as he dug for his wallet in his hip pocket. He produced Mel Doolittle's card, his home phone number handwritten on the back.

Three rings. The answering machine kicked in. Hooley hung up. The number for that cotton-picking portable spy phone was also scrawled on the back of the card. What the hell. Worth a try. One ring, and Mel picked up.

"*Doolittle.*"

"You ready to go fishin' again?"

"*Hooley?*"

"In living color. Get on the first flight to Austin tomorrow. They're lowering the lake level."

"*For us?*"

"Yeah, I told 'em to," he said, the sarcasm thick in his voice. "No, they have to fix hydrogenerators in the dam. Can you get here early?"

"*Yeah, sure. I'm on stakeout, but I'll turn it over to my partner.*"

"Oh, yeah, your partner. Tell Samantha I said howdy."

"*Right. I will.*"

"Anything developing in Vegas?"

"*Maybe. A couple of key people have disappeared.*"

"Yeah? Who?"

"*I'll tell you whom tomorrow.*"

"I'll pick you up at the airport. First flight from Vegas. Hey, are you really on your spy phone right now?"

"*Yeah, it works great here in the civilized world.*"

"I'll be damned. See you at the airport. With any luck, we can bust this case wide open tomorrow."

CHAPTER

Creed pulled his Good Times van into the usual Jollyville location for the floating poker game—a house on the edge of town, secluded in a creek valley, hidden by thick cedars and oaks. The pasture used as a parking lot was not even half full, as they had arrived rather early—around midnight.

As he got out of the van, along with Luster and Tump, he grabbed the purple velvet Crown Royal bag that held his poker chips from last week. The three of them ambled up to the door, where a burly youth stood guard—not the same one who had gotten his scalp creased last week, but a tougher-looking rascal.

"Did you get the password for this week?" Creed asked.

"Yeah, I called Gordy the day after the shootout."

"Shootout?" Tump said, the concern obvious in his voice.

As they stepped up to the doorman, Luster said, "We don't need no stinking badges."

The young man frowned. "Gordy's been expecting you. Wait here." He stepped inside and locked the door.

"What the hell's going on?" Creed said. "They owe us money." He rattled the chips in the Crown Royal bag.

"I'm sure we'll sort it out with Gordy. Don't lose your temper till I tell you to."

In a moment, Gordy came to the door and stepped outside with the guard. All smiles, he shook Luster's hand. "Good to see you, my friend."

"Good to see you, too, Gordy. It would be even better to see you cashing in my chips from last week."

"Can't do that," Gordy said.

"Why the hell not?"

Gordy shrugged nonchalantly. "I listen to the radio. I watch the TV.

I seen you boys on the news. Run on to a little bad luck with the I.R.S., I understand."

"What's that got to do with poker?"

"You're over ten grand in the hole with me, friend."

"I've always paid my markers. You know that."

"Yeah, when you had something to pay with. You're broke. No more credit. You don't play till you pay."

"Come on, Gordy. I finally broke my streak of bad luck at the tables last week. I'm on a roll. Let me win the money back."

Gordy shook his head. "You're too big of a risk now."

"What about me?" Creed said. He rattled the Crown Royal bag. "You owe me from last week. I'm not in the hole with you."

Gordy took the chips. "You work for him, right?" He nodded toward Luster. "I'll apply this to what he owes."

"The hell you will! You owe *me* that money!"

The burly guard squared off in Creed's face. Creed was a split second away from taking him down with a head butt to the bridge of his nose, or knee to his groin.

"Easy, Creed," Luster warned.

Creed stood his ground, but resisted further aggression.

Gordy looked at Tump. "Who's this? Did you bring your goon with you?"

"Close," Luster said. "He's our bass player. Now, let's all just settle down and talk this over. Gordy, you can't put the kid's chips on my account. He won fair and square last week, before the shootin' started."

"Shootin'?" Tump groaned.

"All right, I'll pay him off," Gordy said. "But he can't play. Nobody wants his trigger-happy ass in the game."

"If it hadn't been for my happy trigger, we all would have been robbed, or worse."

"Yeah, you're a regular Buffalo Bill Earp," Gordy said. "You almost got us all arrested."

"Don't you mean Wyatt?" Tump asked.

"Buffalo Bill Wyatt. Whatever. How much did you win last week, Billy Holliday?"

"Are you going for Doc Holliday or Billy the Kid?" Tump asked.

"Eleven hundred," Creed said. "You can count the chips."

"I trust you. Easy, now, I'm reaching for my wad." Slowly, Gordy pulled a fold of bills from the breast pocket of his jacket and peeled off eleven one-hundred-dollar notes. "You boys need to find another game in another town. And Luster, you need to pay up, or I'll have to send a collector to visit you. Neither one of us wants that."

"I always pay my markers."

"I made a few calls. You've got markers to pay from Lake Charles to Reno. Just make sure you pay mine first. I know where you live."

"No need to threaten me," Luster said. "Everybody's going to get paid."

"Don't make me wait too long."

"Well, nice meeting you both," Tump drawled, "but we've got to be running along now."

Creed let Tump drag him away by the sleeve. He had his money. That would get the band down the road to the next gig, wherever that might be. He took a few deep breaths on the way to the van to let his temper simmer down. Steering the van up the gravel drive, Creed noticed that Tump was keeping an eye trained out the rear window. When they hit the pavement, he finally turned forward.

"So let me get this straight," he said. "Last week, you two went to a gun-fight, and a poker game broke out?"

"Something like that," Luster replied.

28
CHAPTER

Hooley spotted Special Agent Mel Doolittle waiting on the sidewalk in front of the terminal, holding his suitcase, his briefcase, and his spy phone. Hooley stopped his truck, pulling the bass boat on the trailer behind, just long enough to let Mel jump in. They shook hands.

"I brought my lucky fishing hat," Mel said, smiling.

Hooley had more pressing issues on his mind. "I need you to brief me on the missing persons you mentioned last night."

The smile slipped from Mel's face. "But enough small talk. Okay. About the time Rosa fled Vegas, a casino manager by the name of Bert Mathers disappeared. He hasn't been seen since."

"From one of Paulo Martini's casinos?"

"Exactly. He was the manager of The Castilian."

Hooley ground his teeth. "You reckon maybe Rosa could have told us what happened to him?"

Mel shrugged. "That's one possible scenario. Maybe she saw something she wasn't supposed to see."

"Who else is missing in action?"

"A while back, Rosa was dating a lieutenant in the Las Vegas Police Department. We've been keeping tabs on him since Rosa's death. Yesterday, he took an emergency leave of absence and dropped off the radar."

"I thought you were keeping tabs on him."

Chagrinned, Mel said, "He gave us the slip."

"His name wouldn't be Lieutenant Jake Harbaugh, would it?"

Mel looked truly shocked. "Yeah. How'd you . . . ?"

"He was found dead about half an hour ago in a lake house overlooking our favorite fishing hole. There's a suicide note. I told them not to touch a thing and we'd be right there."

Mel began clawing at the latches to the leather case holding his spy phone. "I've got to call my partner—get a warrant to search Harbaugh's place in Vegas." He yanked the receiver from the portable phone and listened to the headset. "Hey, I actually have a dial tone!" He began hurriedly punching in numbers. "Hooley, pull over, will you? I don't want to loose this connection."

Without signaling, Hooley changed two lanes in front of honking traffic and whipped into the parking lot of a Circle K store and gas station. He watched as Mel listened to his phone, then shook the box and cursed.

"Go back a couple of blocks," Mel suggested. "There was a signal back there."

Hooley just stared at him.

"Just two blocks," Mel pleaded.

"Hey, Slick. You recognize that antique right outside your door?"

Mel turned and looked at the phone booth Hooley had deliberately pulled up next to.

The young agent shoved his spy phone aside and opened the truck door, too embarrassed to make eye contact with Hooley. He jumped out and slammed the door unnecessarily hard. He reached into his pocket as he stepped into the phone booth. His hand still in his pocket, he hung his head. Slowly, he trudged back to the truck and opened the door.

"Sorry I slammed the door so hard. I forgot it's your private vehicle."

"Yeah." Hooley was shifting in the seat, reaching into his pocket. "Anything else you want to say?"

Mel nodded and rolled his eyes. "May I borrow a quarter?"

Hooley chuckled and handed him the coin. Mel clicked the door closed and turned toward the phone booth.

An hour later, having driven ninety miles per hour out to Sunset Shores, Hooley pulled his bass boat past half a dozen squad cars from various agencies and parked in front of the crime scene. He nodded at the deputy sheriff guarding the rental house and entered through the open garage, Mel on his heels with his briefcase.

"That's Harbaugh's Land Cruiser, all right," Mel said.

Stepping through the open door to the kitchen, Hooley stopped at first sight of the corpse lying on the floor, hair caked with dried blood that had pooled on the linoleum, then blackened around the head like a satanic halo. He looked back at the deputy. "Has anybody been in here?"

"Nobody's taken one step past where you're standing."

Hooley stepped aside to let Mel in. "Well, Special Agent Doolittle. This looks like a job for the F.B.I."

Mel entered the room carefully, eyeing the dead body like a man walking around a rattlesnake, keeping his distance. "That's Harbaugh." He put his briefcase on the kitchen counter, opened it, and removed an insta-matic camera with a flash.

"The D.P.S. photographer's on the way."

Mel nodded. "I just want a few shots of my own."

"Ah, memories," Hooley jested.

Mel slipped on a pair of surgical gloves and half-circumnavigated the body, taking flash shots and winding the camera with his thumb. He knelt as close to the body as he could without treading on dried droplets of blood. "Interesting."

"What do you see?"

"There's blood spatter all over the weapon in his hand, but only a drop or two on his hand."

"Imagine that."

Mel backtracked for a closer look at the suicide note. Carefully, he lifted the piece of paper by one corner. He put the camera back in his briefcase, and removed a magnifying glass.

"Whatcha got there, Sherlock?"

Mel was looking alternately at the back of the note, then the tabletop, then the note again. "There's a single droplet of blood on the *back* of this note. The paper picked it up from the tabletop."

"So he put a bullet in his own brain, *then* laid the note down. Tough guy. Look what he supposedly shot himself with."

Mel nodded. "A twenty-two Baretta auto with a silencer."

"Didn't want to disturb the neighbors. This is bullshit. He's wearing his sidearm. What is that? A forty-five?"

"Nine millimeter," Mel said.

"If you were gonna end it all, would you trust a plinky little twenty-two, or do the job right with your nine mil?"

"Harbaugh wasn't the type to do himself in, anyway."

"Frank's been here," Hooley announced.

"Franco?"

"That's what I said. I'll have the boys dust the place for prints and take enough pictures for a class yearbook. Doc Brewster will have an autopsy done by the end of the day. What else do you need to do?"

"I want to talk to the cleaning lady, and the company that rented the lake house."

"You do that. I'll launch the bass boat."

Hooley launched his boat, noticing that the lake level had already dropped nearly a foot from his last visit here. When Mel had wrapped up his interviews, he trotted to the dock from the nearby crime scene and jumped in the boat. Hooley motored out past the snag that had caused Rosa's boat wreck, a little over a week ago, now standing a foot above the dropping water level.

"I've been thinking about The Crew's Inn," Mel said, shouting over the whine of the outboard. "If I wanted to boat to the bar, instead of drive—especially at night—I wouldn't want to have to go very far."

Hooley nodded. "Makes sense to me."

"You remember where that old fart accused us of being shithead Republicans?"

"Yep."

"That's a likely neighborhood from which to go on a boat ride to the bar."

"The most likely, I'd say. That's where we're headed."

"Are we going to be able to get back to the boat ramp, with the lake dropping like this?"

"I know the channels. Leave the driving to ol' Hooley."

They motored as fast as they dared, considering the lowering of the lake giving rise to newly emerging obstacles. Pulling into Shithead Republican Cove, Hooley killed the outboard and dropped his electric trolling motor off the bow of the boat where he could sit in the swivel chair up front and cast his lures.

"So, you're really gonna fish?" Mel said.

"If you'd been fishin' as long as I have, kid, you could feel around underwater with your lure like it was your own hand." He made a cast as he rounded a bend in the channel flanked on both sides by lake houses. "Hey, look ahead. It's our ol' pal."

The old man was puttering around his dock, looking over newly exposed timbers and concrete. When he saw Hooley and Mel coming, he retreated to his house. The lawmen continued to troll, coming to the high-dollar neighborhood where the fancy boathouses faced the channel with doors like garage doors. Most of the doors were closed, but with the lowering of the lake, the fishermen could begin to see under them, into the private boat slips. Some were empty. Some housed vessels, hanging from boat lifts. None yet revealed the old wooden craft they sought.

Hooley entertained himself by expertly flipping his lure underhanded through the narrow horizontal gaps created between the garage doors and the dropping waterline. Mel tried to emulate the technique, but kept slamming his lure into the closed doors, missing the open gap below them.

"Nice try, Slick."

"I'll get it. I just need a few more practice throws."

"Do you always fire a warning shot, too?"

"I've never had to fire my weapon at anybody. You?"

Hooley made a perfect cast and shrugged. "A few times, over the years. The thing is, you've got to be ready to do it when the time comes. Ain't no second place in a gunfight."

Mel finally made a textbook cast, just under the bottom of a boathouse door, far into the empty stall behind it. "Hey, look at that cast!" he said.

"Beginner's luck."

"Uh-oh. I'm snagged on something."

Hooley killed the trolling motor with the foot switch. "I'll back up. Maybe you can pull it loose." He maneuvered back down the channel a few feet, the way he had come, but Mel's lure was still snagged on something underwater.

"It feels like I'm hooked on something that I can lift a foot or so, then it hangs up," Mel said.

"Let me get you closer. Reach your rod up into the boat slip and lift it straight up."

Mel followed the suggestion. "It feels like it came loose," he said, reeling, the rod still bent.

"Reel it in. See what you got."

Mel lifted a small, flared, bell-shaped object into view, covered with silt. It was precariously lodged on the point of his fishing lure's hook.

"What the hell is that?" Mel asked.

"A piece of an air horn," Hooley said, motioning for Mel to swing the object over to him at the end of the fishing pole. "You screw a can of compressed air onto the bottom of this thing."

Mel nodded. "A noisemaker. Like some people would use at a ball game."

He dislodged the hook from the horn. "Or in a boat at night, to warn off other boaters in the dark."

"What do you think it was doing down there?"

Hooley shrugged. "Either somebody accidentally dropped it overboard, or . . ."

"Or the rest of the boat's down there, too?"

"Let's troll on through this channel. We'll come back here for another look when the lake drops a little more."

They searched the rest of the neighborhood, feeling about underwater with fishing lures. Mel caught a three-pound bass up the channel, causing Hooley to forget, momentarily, the crime scene he had witnessed this morning, the deaths of two young women, the frustration of a case unsolved. When this was over, he thought, he needed to take a good long fishing trip somewhere far away.

Hours later, having searched the entire convoluted shoreline of the lakeside community, the battery of the trolling motor now waning, they returned to the enclosed boat slip that had yielded the air horn. Approaching the place, Hooley saw that the lake level had now dropped more than two feet below the bottom of the garage door.

"I wouldn't have thought a lake this size could drop this fast," Mel remarked as they moved slowly to the fatigued groan of the trolling motor.

"That's the good ol' L.C.R.A. When one of their moneymakers breaks down they'll waste no time droppin' the lake to get that generator ginnin' again."

"The hydroelectric turbine?"

"That's the moneymaker I'm talkin' about, kid." He reached into a compartment below the steering wheel of the boat and produced a flashlight, which he tossed to Mel. "Crane your neck up under that door, and take a gander."

"Don't mind if I do." Mel dropped to his belly on the rear fishing platform of the bass boat, and switched on the standard police-issue mag light. As Hooley eased the boat up to the gap between the door and lake surface, Mel twisted his shoulders off the edge of the vessel to get his entire head up under the door so the blinding light of day wouldn't interfere with his sight.

Hooley watched for several seconds as Mel angled the light around. The young federal agent said nothing, though several more seconds passed. Hooley knew by now that Mel was a pretty quick study. He could have assessed the place for evidence at a glance. Yet his head remained under the door in what had to be an uncomfortable position, even for a young man, for several more long seconds.

Hooley tried not to let his imagination carry him toward a disappointment, yet he could not help feeling he was about to round a corner in this case. He waited. "Well?" he finally shouted.

Mel drew his head out of the boat slip and rolled over on the deck, a blank expression on his face. "I'll be damned."

"You will be if you don't tell me what you saw in there."

Mel sat up and set his jaw as if to ready himself for a coming marathon, and began to list his findings. "Windshield. Shattered. Bullet hole."

"No shit?"

"One more thing."

"Well? What?"

"Long black hair stuck in the broken glass."

Hooley felt that sadness again: the almost crushing feeling of loss as he imagined Rosa's last violent moments alive. But now he sensed something new accompanying the sorrow. It was just a spark, but it felt like hope.

Creed felt the nudge on his shoulder and woke to the smells of burnt flesh and gunpowder as he reached for his sidearm and threw a fist at whomever had touched him.

"Easy, Hoss," said Luster's voice.

Panting, Creed found himself sitting up on Luster's living room couch, having crashed there after their return from the Jollyville poker game. It didn't help that Luster was holding a shotgun. Creed's heart was pounding, which made him think about the appropriate nature of the new band name: The Pounders. "What the hell's goin' on?"

"You know how to talk turkey?"

"What?" It seemed like the middle of the night. The only light came from the kitchen.

Luster produced a small wooden box and, cradling the shotgun in the crook of his elbow, made the chalked lid of the box chirp turkey calls from the rim.

Creed focused on a cheap electric timepiece on the mantel—the replacement for the auctioned grandfather clock that once stood against the wall. It was about an hour before dawn. He nodded at Luster. "I used to hunt with my grandpa."

"Good. You can call a gobbler up for me. Broke as we are, we've got to live off the land!" He chuckled. "Come on, there's coffee on in the kitchen."

After coffee, Creed climbed into the passenger seat of Luster's pickup truck and they drove down a dirt lane toward the back pasture of the ranch.

"What all did you and your grandpa hunt?" Luster asked, as he drove slowly, sipping a cup of black coffee.

Through the oaks, Creed watched the pastel dawn creeping into the sky. "Turkey, deer, ducks, cottontails, squirrels, wild hogs . . ." He smiled to think of those hunts with his grandfather.

"I guess y'all did your share of fishin' in the Piney Woods, too."

"Oh, hell, yeah. We ran trotlines for cats. Used cane poles for panfish. We ate everything from grindles to gaspergous. When I could finally afford a rod and reel, I started catching a lot of bass."

"Don't lose that. Don't let the music business take over your whole life. I've seen too many musicians get hooked on it like a drug to where that's all they do is travel and play. They got no other life. Then they start poppin' those pills to keep going. Drinking. Hell, that's what happened to Hank." He switched hands with his coffee cup, holding the wheel with his knee as he downshifted through a muddy stretch of road.

"It tends to take over your life." He was thinking of Dixie and how she wanted no part of anything but the next show.

"Don't let it consume you like that. It ain't worth it. The music is important, that's true. People need it. But you've got to stay well rounded. You've got to have other interests. I don't care if it's huntin' and fishin' or golf or stamp collecting."

"I do need to dust off the ol' Zebco."

"Especially if you're a writer. A man should travel, read, do things, see the world. Then you'll have something to write songs about."

"I hear you, Boss."

"This is the place," Luster said, coasting to a stop and shutting off the truck. "We'll walk the rest of the way." He handed the turkey call to Creed.

Creed got out and clicked the door closed, assuming the game might be within earshot of a slamming door. Luster did the same after pulling his over-and-under twelve-gauge off the gun rack in front of the rear windshield. Creed followed Luster down a cow trail to a clearing in the woods. They sat on the ground and leaned their backs against oak trees, with the thorny leaves of some low-lying agarita bushes obscuring all but their faces. Creed was wearing his army field jacket, which he reasoned would blend in well enough with the woods at his back. Luster wore a flannel coat in green plaid. The light from the east had sufficiently illuminated the small clearing in front of them.

"The roost is a couple hundred yards away, in the creek bottom," Luster whispered. "See what you can call up."

With his first hen call on the wooden box, a gobbler answered, his mating call echoing through the cypress branches. Over the next half hour,

Creed worked the tom in patiently, growing more excited as the gobbler's voice got closer. Finally, the large bird appeared at the far edge of the clearing. Luster had his shotgun ready, the forestock resting on his knee. A ray of sunshine knifed through the woods, spotlighting the gobbler as he fanned his tail and strutted. Creed was glad Luster had wakened him. The air in his nostrils felt cool and clean.

Scarcely moving his hand on the box, Creed chirped plaintive hen calls until the gobbler strutted within range. A blast from the shotgun flipped the turkey over backward where it lay quivering in the throes of death. It reminded Creed of the enemy soldier he had shot that night outside the hooch at Fire Base Bronco. Probably some rice farmer's son.

"Good work!" Luster said.

They retrieved the bird and ambled back toward the truck.

"Did you know Ben Franklin wanted the wild turkey to be the national bird?" Luster said.

"No, I never heard that."

"Yeah, he said the turkey was a little vain and silly but was a bird of courage who would run a Red Coat clean out of the farmyard. Good thing ol' Ben lost that campaign."

"How come?"

"Bald eagle don't eat near as good as wild turkey."

Creed chuckled. "Yeah, Bald Eagle Liquor doesn't have much of a ring to it, either."

They reached the truck, threw the bird in the back, and started home. As they drove back to the ranch house, Luster said, "There's something else I forgot to tell the band last night."

What now? Creed thought. "Yeah?"

"I had to make a deal with Sid. He gets to sing one song with the band as a guest singer."

Creed groaned. "Can he sing?"

"Probably not. But don't worry, I got it figured. You give up your mic and step off the stage while he sings. We'll keep Sid's voice in the monitor, so he can hear himself. But you'll have a mic backstage, and we'll patch your voice into the main speakers out front. The band will have to listen to Sid onstage, but the audience will hear you."

"You're serious?"

"We got no choice, Hoss. It was the only way I could get the three months grace period out of him."

Creed sighed. "This is turning into the weirdest band in the business."

At the ranch house, Luster cleaned and plucked the turkey while Creed cooked up some bacon and eggs. The entire band, plus Kathy Music, had stayed the night at Luster's place, vowing to get a fresh start on songwriting and rehearsing in the morning. Now the smells of coffee and bacon began to lure them from their rooms.

Kathy came out of her guest room wearing yesterday's clothes, no makeup on her face. She didn't wear much makeup anyway, Creed thought, and didn't need any. She had a cute, sleepy-eyed look about her. Creed admitted to himself that he had thought about waking up with her, but not exactly like this.

"You're quite the cook," she purred as she loaded up a plate at the stove.

Creed was still scrambling eggs and flipping bacon. "I can squash bugs and lift heavy things, too."

She smiled, and raised a sleepy eyebrow. "But do you do dishes?"

Creed began snapping his fingers. "*But do you do dishes,*" he sang, lending an impromptu blues melody to the lyric. "*But do you do dishes,*" he repeated. "Got a nice ring to it. We should write that together."

"You're a live wire in the morning."

"I've been up for hours. Luster woke me early and we went turkey hunting."

"Really? Anyway, you're avoiding the question. Do you do dishes, or not?"

"*Do you do dishes, or not?*" he sang.

"I'll do the dishes," Trusty Joe said, having wandered into the kitchen from a bed, or a sofa, or a floor somewhere in the house. "Then I'm gonna go out to the barn and visit with Baldy."

Kathy carried her plate to the kitchen table and sat down. "I need to have a meeting with you after breakfast," she said to Creed.

"Okay," he said. "About what?"

"I woke up this morning worrying that I've bitten off more than I can chew. I need a crash course in music business one-oh-one."

"I'll meet you on the patio after breakfast."

Later, as Trusty Joe washed dishes, Lindsay finally woke up, but said she never ate breakfast anyway. She had a cup of coffee and went to the studio with Tump and Metro to work on some song idea she had come up with in her sleep.

Kathy was waiting with a notepad and a pen when Creed showed up at the patio table.

"Shall we call this meeting to order?" she said, the coffee having kick-started her cheerleader demeanor.

He nodded and sat down, his hands cradling the warmth of yet another cup of black brew.

"Where do I start?" she asked.

"A band needs four things to function." He held up four fingers as a visual aid. "If we had a big record label deal, there would be a department for each of the four things. In our case, you're going to have to arrange it all yourself."

"I'm not afraid of work. What are the four things?" Her pen hovered above the legal pad.

He began the list, going slowly enough for her to scribble as he spoke. "Live gigs . . . radio airplay . . . retail distribution . . . marketing."

"Got it. Go on . . ."

"Live gigs: With Luster's name, you should be able to find an Austin talent agency to book the band, so you won't have to do that all yourself. Once you land a booking agency, let's say they book the band in . . ." he shrugged. "Des Moines, Iowa."

"Oh, Des Moines is so lovely this time of year."

"A couple of weeks before the gig there, the local country-western radio station needs to start playing the hell out of our record."

"Okay. How do I get them to do that? Pay them?"

"No, that's illegal. That's called payola. No, you've got to call the program director once a day. Charm the hell out of him."

"Charm . . . program . . . director," she muttered as she scribbled. "How do I know who the program director is?"

"There's a list somewhere—some radio station association, or something. You'll have to figure it out."

"Okay."

"Talk up the great Luster Burnett, and his comeback, blah, blah, blah . . ."

"Blah, blah, blah," she wrote.

"We'll press some singles and send them out to all the country radio stations, including the one in Des Moines. You have to time it to where you call the PD the day the single arrives so they don't just chuck it in the trash."

"What's the single going to be?"

Creed shrugged. "Whatever song turns out best on the LP. So, the PD puts the single on the playlist and the deejays start spinning the disc a couple of weeks before the live gig in Des Moines."

"Spin . . . the . . . disc," she repeated. The ballpoint seemed to speak the words on the paper. "I love the jargon in this business!"

"Now we've got the live gig and radio airplay lined up, so we need to make sure the record stores in Des Moines have the LP for sale."

"L.B.'s LP," she whispered, underlining the note.

"People hear the record on the radio, and they'll want to buy it. We need to find a record distributor to handle that. Shouldn't be too hard with Luster's name attached to the project."

"Got it."

"So, all that's left to do in Des Moines is handle advertising and publicity. Problem is, we have no advertising budget, so we're going to have to get creative with the publicity. Call the entertainment writer at the *Des Moines Register.*"

"You know the name of the paper there?"

"I just pulled that out of my . . . hat. Let the newspaper in on this scoop—the comeback of the legendary Luster Burnett. You'll need to write up a press release, too, full of colorful quotes from Luster, whether he said them or not."

"I don't know how to write a press release," she admitted.

"Go talk to some flunky editor at the Austin Mistakesman," he said, bastardizing the name of the *Statesman.*

"Mistakesman!" She laughed. "That's funny!"

"Yeah, well, don't share the joke with them. Get some sample press releases from them. You'll figure it out. It's just journalism. How hard could it be? Who, what, where, when, why, and how. It ain't rocket surgery."

"Rocket surgery! You're hilarious, Creed," she said, scribbling.

"Yeah, I'm a one-man riot."

"Okay, that's all four things in Des Moines."

"Multiply that by every other town where we're booked to play. And make sure the booking agent routes the gigs—logistically, geographically."

"Route . . . the . . . gigs."

"Even in towns where we're not playing live, we need to work the radio, retail, and publicity angles."

She looked up at him, biting her lower lip. "Anything else?"

"Those are the basics. That's good for now."

"So, first I should . . ."

"Find a talent agency to book the gigs. They work on commission. Look in the yellow pages. Meanwhile, Luster and I will work on getting the album recorded."

She clicked the little button at the end of her ballpoint pen, punctuating the end of the meeting. "I'm going to town. By the end of this day, we'll have a booking agency and a press release."

"We'll need photos with that press release."

Kathy screamed.

"Sorry. The photos can wait."

"What is that thing?" she squealed.

Creed followed her eyes and looked over his shoulder to see Luster carrying the wild turkey, gutted and plucked, head and feet still attached.

"Supper," he said.

Kathy scribbled a note on her pad. "Bring pizza," she said, marching away to conquer the music business.

Trusty Joe galloped down the creek bank on Ol' Baldy.

"I guess I'm gonna have to give that horse to Trusty," Luster said. "Which means I've got to give everybody in the band something of equal value. Y'all are like the kids I never had. I've got to treat you all equally."

"You don't have to give me anything," Creed said. "The salary's more than I expected."

"I knew you'd say that. Start me a fire in the smoker, will you? I want to put about two hours of smoke on ol' Tom, here, before we wrap him in foil."

Creed helped Luster gather kindling and some mesquite wood to get a slow-burning fire started in the smoker. The smoker was built on a trailer, a custom-made affair built by a welder out of a steel tank of some kind. Creed noticed that the tires were flat on the trailer.

"Good thing the smoker didn't sell in the auction," he said.

"I let the air out of the tires," Luster admitted. "Figured nobody would want it unless they could just back up to it and haul it off."

They placed the harvested game bird in the smoker and stepped back to watch with outdoorsmanly satisfaction as the smoke boiled out of the cracks around the lid.

"Did you get our manager educated?"

"Took all of five minutes for me to teach her everything I know about the music business."

"Good. That's no longer our worry. Our job is to make music. If we do it well, it'll find the cracks in the smoker and seep out into the world." He spread his arms and wiggled his fingers for effect.

"Maybe somebody will catch wind of it."

"Don't belabor the metaphor," Luster warned.

"Right. You got any idea where we might record an album on spec?"

"You know Nigel Buttery?"

"At Bee Creek Studios?"

"No, the other Nigel Buttery. Yes, at Bee Creek. He owes me a favor."

"Yeah? How big a favor?"

"I loaned him all my vintage microphones before the I.R.S. sent Sid to harass me. There are some things that are too valuable to be auctioned off for back taxes. He's also holding a few guitars and a couple of amps for me. All great studio stuff."

"Maybe we should drop by."

"Let's load up, Hoss."

"I'm with you, Boss."

A twenty-minute drive in the pickup delivered Creed and Luster to Bee Creek Recording Studio, located in a converted farmhouse near the village of Bee Creek, west of Austin.

Though by musician's time it was still early, Creed found the front door to the studio unlocked. He opened it. "Nigel?" he called out.

Nigel Buttery, a transplant from England, looked out of the control room door to see Creed and Luster enter. "Here's a brace of rogues!" he announced.

Creed always wondered if they really talked like that in England, or if Nigel simply laid it on thick for the Texans.

Nigel greeted them with a toothsome smile that complemented the wild, wavy shocks of golden hair streaming from his scalp—hair for which many women would commit larcenous acts to possess. Creed remembered that Nigel had a hip, European way of shaking hands. Luster refused to participate in any of that, and offered nothing beyond the old-fashioned pressing of palm flesh.

The three of them made small talk about Luster's comeback and the new band for a while. Of course, Nigel had seen the clip on the evening news.

"Bloody awful audio on that news footage."

"No, we actually sounded that bad in real life," Luster admitted. "But we're better now."

"Super! Ready to record, I gather."

"We ain't got no money, and we need a new album yesterday," Luster said.

"Yesterday would have been fine. But today and the rest of this week, I've got the Lost Gonzo Band coming in for some tracks. Next week, I'm cutting jingles with an ad agency. That's where the real money is, you know. In fact, the next six weeks are booked solid."

"Damn," Luster said, sadly. He looked at Creed. "I guess we'd better gather up those old mics and head over to Willie's studio."

"Listen, I've got a spendid idea!" Nigel sang. "My weekends are free and I've got a superb system for recording live shows. I'll bring it to one of your gigs, and you'll have an instant album, mixed and mastered, in a fraction of the time it would take to cut it in a studio. For a fraction of the cost, I might add."

Creed looked at Luster. "Live?" he said, suspiciously.

Luster cocked his head. "I don't know. Our band is pretty raw."

"I'll do it on speculation. You can cut me in on record sales until my time is paid off."

Creed shrugged. "Suits our budget."

"The raw sound is all the rage," Nigel insisted. "You've heard *Frampton Comes Alive*?"

"Can't say that I have," Luster admitted.

"It's all over pop radio," Creed explained. "This guy never hit it big with his studio stuff, but his live record is selling faster than they can stock it."

"Raw, huh?" Luster was pondering.

"Tump said it last night. It's like war, backwards."

"Luster Burnett and The Pounders. *Raw*."

"That's the name of the bloody album! Bloody *Raw*!"

"Without the *bloody*," Creed said, for reassurance.

"Of course. I only said *bloody* for emphasis. You've noticed I'm British?"

"It's a deal, Nigel. Now, all we need is a live gig somewhere. I'll call you as soon as we get one."

"So, I can hold on to the Neuman and the Sennheiser?"

"Consider it a semipermanent loan. Collateral on future royalties." Luster looked at his Timex and motioned for Creed to follow him out of the studio. "Come on, Hoss, we've got to go wrap some aluminum foil around that turkey in the smoker."

Nigel burst into laughter. "I do love your Texas colloquialisms!"

Creed smiled. "That's always been one of my favorites, too."

Luster had one foot through the door. "Adios, Nigel!"

"Right, then! Cheerio!"

"Fruit Loops back at'cha," Creed replied.

CHAPTER 30

Hooley looked up from his desk as Mel entered, the young F.B.I. agent looking over the ranger's office as if investigating the place.

"The press is out front," Mel warned. "They're waiting for you."

"Like vultures to dead meat," Hooley replied, shoving a file folder at Mel.

"What's this?"

"The official report from the lab. The only prints they got were Harbaugh's, and they were found only on the door coming in from the garage, and on the murder weapon."

"That's it?" Mel said, leafing through the report.

"The rest of the place was clean, slick as a whistle, upstairs and down."

"That's too clean."

"Yeah. Did you track down the owner of the lake house?" Hooley asked, referring to the fancy place in the cove where the wrecked wooden boat had been located.

"Finally." Mel pulled a notepad from the inside pocket of his black blazer. "One Charles Biggerstaff." He lifted his portable phone as if submitting evidence. "I caught him on the phone at his golf course clubhouse. He had an eight o'clock tee time."

"Country club member?"

"Yep. Conroe, Texas. North of Houston."

"I know where Conroe is."

"I've got a one thirty flight booked to Houston. I'll interview Biggerstaff this afternoon."

"What do we know about him?"

"He's an entrepreneur and an inventor. His company manufactures some kind of drilling equipment."

"Oil patch?"

"I don't know if he makes patches or what, but I'll find out."

"You do that, Slick. By the way, *oil patch* is slang for the oil field."

"Oh." Mel grabbed his pen and scribbled something down on his notepad. "What about the autopsy on our supposed suicide?"

Hooley stood. "Doc Brewster's waiting on us right now over at the county morgue."

The phone rang. Reluctantly, Hooley answered it: "Captain Johnson."

"Hooley, it's Dolph."

"Good mornin', Governor. I'm gonna put you on speakerphone. I've got Special Agent Doolittle here with me." He pushed a button and put the phone in the speaker cradle.

"Congratulations to both of you. I hear you solved the case."

"Who told you that hogwash? We found a body and a note, but it's all fishy."

"I'm going to ask you for a favor."

Hooley looked at Mel. "Aw, shit," he growled, under his breath.

"Make a statement to the press. Make it look like the case is closed."

"Dolph, you know we can't do that."

"I didn't say close the case. I said make it look like the case is closed. Put an end to this serial-killer hysteria. It's bad for Texas."

Hooley sighed. "I've got to go to an autopsy briefing, Governor. I'll do what I can for you."

"It's the right thing to do, Hooley. What if some copy-cat nut wanted in on the publicity?"

"That's far-fetched, but I guess it's possible. We'll see what Doc Brewster says about the autopsy. Maybe we can give the press just enough information to calm the public."

"Thanks, Captain."

"Have a splendid day, Governor." Hooley pushed the button and hung the phone back on the hook. He looked at Mel. "All those hysterical sorority girls have rich daddies and a lot of 'em contribute to political campaigns."

"How often does he call you?"

"Doesn't your boss ever call you?"

"Jimmy Carter?"

"Yeah."

"Not yet."

"How would you know? He might be trying to ring that spy phone of yours right now."

"It works here," Mel said defensively. "I just put a call into Samantha. By the way, she got the faxed image of the suicide note and said the print appears to match the type on Harbaugh's typewriter, but the lab needs the actual note to be sure."

Hooley raised his eyebrows. "No shit? The spy phone actually works here in the building?"

"Yeah, it works fine."

"Humph. Really?"

Mel nodded with some authority. "It's got a great signal here."

Hooley reached for his hat on the rack. "You ready to go over to the morgue and talk to Doc Brewster?"

"Sure."

"All right, but first we're gonna put that phone of yours to use."

"What do you mean?"

"Just follow me." Hooley left his office and turned toward the front desk of D.P.S. headquarters. Ahead, in the hallway, he saw a fellow Texas Ranger step out of a doorway, and braced himself for trouble. He was pretty sure Ranger J. D. Barlow was a clansman in his spare time.

"Hey, Hooley, where'd you buy the colored boy?" Barlow drawled.

Hooley saw Mel immediately hump up like a bronc about to buck. At the same time, a black state trooper stuck his head out of a nearby office door and looked at Mel, all but asking what he planned to do about the racist statement.

"First of all," Hooley said, stepping between Mel and Barlow to cut the fuse to the powder keg, "he's a grown man. Second, what do you mean by calling him colored? He's black."

"That's exactly what I mean by colored. And that's puttin' it nice."

"This is Special Agent Mel Doolittle of the F.B.I. He was born black and he'll die black. You, on the other hand . . . You call yourself a white man, right, J.D.?"

"Mighty white of you to notice."

"I've seen you turn red when you're mad and blue when you're cold. You turned yella that time you had the jaundice. You turned green with envy when I made captain ahead of you. And you call *him* colored?" He jutted his thumb at Mel.

The black trooper in the doorway started laughing, letting Mel off the hook. Barlow was befuddled, and effectively silenced. He waved his hand at Hooley as he turned back into his office and muttered something—probably a slur.

Hooley and Mel resumed their walk down the hallway.

"Green with envy," Mel said, his voice still tense. "That was a nice touch."

"He really did get the jaundice one time, too. Turned yella as a squash."

"We were talking about the portable phone."

"Oh, yeah . . ." Hooley led the way to Lucille's desk. Looking through the glass doors in the front of the building, he could see the news vans camped outside, a cluster of reporters waiting to pounce on him as he emerged from the building. "Lucille, darlin', this is Special Agent Mel Doolittle of the F.B.I."

"Do tell?" Lucille said, daintily offering her hand to Mel, her eyelashes blinking seductively.

"Can you keep a phone line clear for him to use? He's gonna have to make a call here, directly."

"Line four is all yours, honey."

"All right, Mel, I'm gonna go out there and talk to them newshounds. Sooner or later, they're gonna ask me something I don't want to answer. When that happens, I'm gonna take my hat off, and run my hand back over my head, like this . . ." He demonstrated, theatrically. "When I do that, you call me on the spy phone immediately."

"Okay. What do you want me to say to you?"

"You don't have to say a damn thing. Just make the phone ring."

Mel nodded. "Got it."

Hooley turned to Lucille. "How do I look?"

She glanced up and down his frame. "Button your jacket and stand up straight. There, that's better. Now you look like the voice of authority."

Hooley turned to Mel. "What do you think, sumo-come-lately?"

Mel nodded. "You look like a know-it-all to me, too."

Hooley smirked, impressed with himself. "Good. Remember what I told you. Look for the signal." Hooley grabbed the experimental F.B.I. phone and marched for the entrance, pushing his way through the glass doors to greet the reporters.

"Mornin', ladies," he said to the mostly male gathering. "And gentle-men." He coughed. "And members of the press." He placed the spy phone at his feet on the sidewalk. "I have a brief statement to make, then I'll take a few questions." He paused, remembered to stand up straight.

"In case you don't know, I'm Texas Ranger Captain Hooley Johnson. Yesterday, the body of a deceased white male was found in a house near Lake L.B.J. An apparent suicide. There was a suicide note. The body was found by an employee of a cleaning company who went there to clean the house. It was a rental house on the lake. The cleaning company notified the Burnet Country Sheriff's Department, who notified the Texas D.P.S."

Hooley took his tally book out of his pocket and flipped it open to make it look as if he would refer to some notes or something.

"The identity of the deceased is being withheld until family members can be contacted, but I can tell you that the victim was a white male from Nevada. As I mentioned, there was a suicide note. It was typed on a typewriter. A connection between the note and a typewriter owned by the deceased has already been established, but not confirmed. Now, in this suicide note, the victim appears to confess to killing two young women who died tragically last week in our area. Both women were formerly members of the same college sorority. I'm sure you're familiar with those cases."

He put his tally book away and picked up the spy phone case. "Now, as you know, the D.P.S. and the Texas Rangers are cooperating with the F.B.I. in this investigation, so we have access to the latest technology, and we're gonna get to the bottom of this thing. Any questions?"

A local newspaper reporter was quick to raise his hand. "So, is the official ruling suicide, or something else?"

"No official ruling on that, yet, Joe. We're waiting on the autopsy report."

"Who's doing the autopsy?" some out-of-town reporter asked.

"That would be the Travis County Medical Examiner, Dr. Brewster."

"What's Dr. Brewster's first name?"

"His first name is, uh . . . Doc." Hooley smiled to the chuckles among the reporters.

A young television reporter from Houston raised a hand. "What condition was the corpse in?"

"Last I checked, he was still dead."

The reporters laughed.

The blushing TV reporter rephrased: "What was the cause of death?"

"It appeared to be a single gunshot wound to the head, but the official autopsy report hasn't been released."

A crime reporter from the *Dallas Morning News* waved a ballpoint. "What's the connection between the deceased and the two sorority girls?"

"Good question, Bud. The deceased apparently had a personal relationship with one of the young women."

"Which one?"

"He was a white male from *Nevada*. That's all I can tell you right now."

"Hooley, is there some kind of organized crime connection with this death?"

Hooley shook his head. "Not at this time. The investigation is still going on." He was fingering the latches to the spy phone case.

A young reporter from the local TV news tossed her blonde hair at Hooley. "Captain Johnson, does this mean that the cases of Rosabella Martini and Celinda Valenzuela have been closed?"

Hooley put the phone down, removed his hat, ran his fingers back through his short-cropped hair, returned the hat, and picked the phone back up. "Those investigations are ongoing, Susanne."

The attractive blonde persisted, flashing a wry smile. "What's your gut feeling, Captain? Do you believe this deceased man from Nevada is, indeed, responsible for the deaths of those two young women?"

"Susanne, there are a lot of unanswered questions in this complicated case. Right now, the only gut feeling I have is that I should have skipped the jalapeños with my huevos rancheros this mornin'." He thumped a fist against his chest and feigned a silent belch to the amusement of the reporters. Had Mel missed the signal? Why wasn't the spy phone ringing? The damn thing probably didn't even work.

Susanne the bombshell anchorwoman refused to relent. "Captain, with all the hysteria over a possible sorority serial killer on the loose, or a rogue mob hit man gone berserk, can you give us any information that will help calm the public?"

Hooley sighed. The reporters waited in silence, their pens poised, microphones aimed at his face. Finally, the phone rang. Hooley opened the case and yanked the phone receiver out.

"Captain Johnson."

He heard Mel's voice: "*Smile, you're on* Candid Camera."

Hooley didn't have to fake his surprise. He frowned. "No shit?" he said into the phone. "I'll be right there." He jammed the phone set back into the case and turned away from the clambering reporters, each of whom begged for another tidbit. "Gotta go," he said, over his shoulder, as he pushed through the glass doors, shutting the reporters out.

"Good work, Mel. Come on, let's slip out the back door. I hid my truck behind the Dumpsters."

"Good-bye, Agent Doolittle . . ." Lucille purred.

Arriving at the county morgue, they walked briskly through the building to the autopsy facilities. Brewster greeted them with handshakes—cold, like a dead man's hand.

"Agent Doolittle's got a flight to catch, Doc," said Hooley. "What do you got for us?"

"I want to show you a couple of things." He led them back into the operating room to look over the dissected human body on the aluminum table. He made a pistol of his right hand, the index finger being the gun barrel. "Make like you're gonna shoot yourself in the head," he suggested.

Hooley held his own finger to his head, and slapped Mel on the shoulder. Mel played along.

"Check the angle of the bullet path. Pretty much horizontal, right? Maybe even angling upward a little?"

"Right," Hooley said.

"With the victim, the bullet angled downward. It's difficult to even hold a gun to your own head in that position. The wound was to the right temple. Now, look at his right hand. Virtually no blood spatter. Blood spatter all over the weapon, but only a droplet or two on the victim's hand, which was, supposedly, holding the gun."

Hooley lowered his fake gun from his head. "You're lookin' at the choir, preacher."

"My opinion is that the victim was seated at the kitchen table. Someone standing above him put the gun to his temple and shot him. The bullet angled down through the cerebral hemisphere. The victim probably never knew what hit him."

"Of course, none of this is official until you finish your written report, right, Doc?"

Brewster narrowed his eyes at the ranger, removed his glasses, and polished them on his lab coat. "I suppose."

"A report like that is not something you want to rush, right?"

Brewster shrugged. "I'm in no particular hurry."

Hooley turned to Mel. "I mean, it might take a couple days to get the wording just right, I would think."

Mel nodded. "All that medical terminology. Yeah, two days, at least."

Brewster smiled with one side of his mouth as he replaced his spectacles. "I was just about to say I'll have the report ready in forty-eight hours."

"Thanks, Doc. Come on, Mel, I'll get you to the airport. Then, I've got to hightail it out to Lake L.B.J. The county is pulling that old wooden boat out of the water this afternoon."

31

CHAPTER

Franco stepped out of his rented lake house and felt an unexpected chill. Freakin' Texas weather. Earlier, just before dawn, he had stepped out to steal the newspaper from the neighbor's driveway. The temperature had to have been almost seventy. Now the skies had cleared, bringing out the sun. It looked warmer, but it was actually colder. He went back inside for the hooded warm-up jacket he had bought at Sports Nation in Austin.

Zipping the jacket up, he began jogging down the quiet lake community street. It was a weird place. Like a ghost town. He had learned that most of these houses belonged to absentee owners who lived in Houston, Austin, or San Antonio. The few residents who actually lived here full-time were old, retired farts who spent most of their time locked up in their houses, staring at the boob tube. This had to be the dullest place on earth. He missed Vegas, and couldn't wait to get this business over with so he could go home.

It was all but done, he thought. He had given the ranger and the fed a murderer, complete with a confession on a suicide note typed on the murderer's own typewriter in his office at the Las Vegas Police Department. The cops would go to the press, claiming they had solved the mystery. Case closed. The boat driver who knew too much would come out of hiding—probably for a beer at The Crew's Inn. Franco had someone in place there watching for the guy to reappear—a nephew from Vegas who had won a bartending job at The Crew's Inn. The nephew knew what kind of guy to look for. Tall, with long hair—or maybe a fresh haircut. A guy that played too much country music on the jukebox. As far as Franco was concerned, half a verse was too much country music. Anyway, the nephew was on the job, and once Franco could finger the stupid puke who had wrecked his vintage boat trying to help Rosa escape, he'd plan the hit and whack him.

Then it was back to Vegas, and the life he loved. He could hardly wait. He hadn't had a decent meal in almost two weeks. He had a jones for a good bottle of Italian red. As he jogged down the street, he thought about the choices in his personal wine cellar. When he got home, he was going to light a Cuban in the hot tub and open a bottle of Montepulciano d'Abruzzo he had been saving for years. Then he was going to call a couple of party girls from the strip club and open his stash of smack. He only used the stuff for recreational purposes. He liked to remain clearheaded while he was working.

Continuing his morning run, he pulled some dark sunglasses from his pocket and slipped them on. The cold wind was chilling his ears, so he yanked the knit cap down lower over his shaved head. He turned a corner and headed for a part of the neighborhood that ran along the channel leading from the lake. You never knew what you might see. Maybe an open garage door with a damaged wooden boat on a trailer or something. Didn't hurt to look around while he was keeping in shape.

Rounding a curve in the street, he noticed three squad cars in front of a house up ahead, red and blue lights blinking. A crane had been hauled in on a large flatbed trailer. It was now off the trailer and positioned beside the house, braced with four tubular legs spread wide on steel-pad feet. Its boom reached behind the house, lifting something, the cable taut with weight. A few neighbors had emerged from houses to stand in the yards, rooted like shrubs, staring as they stood motionless in the slouched pose of the elderly, bellies forward, mouths hanging open.

Franco's trot slowed as he took in the scene. The squad cars belonged to the County Sheriff's Department. As he neared the house, an object came into view above the roof at the end of the cable, the crane's diesel motor revving to lift it over the house. Though covered with muck and algae that dripped onto the roof of the house as the crane lifted it over, Franco could tell that it was a boat. And not just any boat, either, but a battered old woody! His heart raced, and it wasn't from the run.

Jogging by the squad cars, he made out the brand name of the vessel in slime-covered chrome on the side: *Correct Craft.* The hull was bashed in pretty badly. The windshield was shattered. He even made out his own bullet hole. As he trotted on by, he glanced at the name on the mailbox: Biggerstaff. The address was 335 Channel View.

A smaller flatbed awaited the boat, attached to a pickup truck with a D.P.S. paint job. Tarps waited to cover the evidence. A trooper with a camera took numerous photos as the boat swung toward the waiting flatbed.

A Ford Ranger came around the corner ahead of Franco. He knew the truck. It belonged to the Texas Ranger, Johnson. It accelerated alarmingly toward the scene, and then skidded to a halt. The ranger leapt out, leaving his door open and his engine running.

"Goddamnit!" the lawman bellowed. "I said keep it low profile! Get these county vehicles out of here! Turn those strobe lights off!"

The photographer got a couple of good shots of the ranger cussing the deputies up and down, ranting in the front yard of the house in question.

Franco saw the ranger look at him as he jogged by. They both wore sunglasses, like two poker players avoiding eye contact across a table. Franco forced himself to maintain his trot—just a citizen out for a casual jog. But he couldn't resist flipping the hood of the jogging suit up as a shield against the lawman's eyes that he felt drilling into the back of his head. He heard the shutter of the camera clicking more photos as the ranger started cursing again.

Franco turned on the first cross street he came to. Once out of sight, he switched his pace to an all-out sprint and arrived at his rental house winded. He ran right up to the front door and entered. Once inside, he whipped the hood off his head, then the knit cap and sunglasses, his burning lungs appreciating the warm air inside the house. Still panting, he stepped up to the window that faced the street and pulled a crack in the Venetian blinds so he could look outside.

He saw the Ford pickup trolling down the street. He narrowed the crack he had pulled in the Venetian blinds. Had the ranger seen him run this way? His heart pounded. What would he do if good ol' Ranger Johnson came to the front door? The Ford continued to prowl on down the street, and he saw the lawman's eyes searching. Old-school lawman. Hunch follower. He made Franco nervous, and that was rare. But for now, the pickup and the Texas Ranger were gone. No damage done.

Franco headed for the shower. There was work to do. He had to find the owner of 335 Channel View. Biggerstaff. The cops were already ahead of him on that. They had obviously secured a warrant to lift the Correct Craft out of the drink. They were probably interviewing the owner of the house right now. He didn't want to have to call Papa Martini on this. He stripped and stepped into the warm water spraying from the nozzle. By the time he came out of the shower stall, he had a plan.

Wrapped in a towel, Franco picked up the phone and called the information operator for the number to the county courthouse. Dialing the courthouse next, he got a receptionist on the other end, and in his best Texas drawl, said he needed to find the owner of a piece of property. The receptionist connected him with the county tax assessor-collector.

"Yeah, ma'am," he said. "I'm trying to find my neighbor across the way, Mr. Biggerstaff. I'm keeping an eye on his lake house for him. He doesn't live here full-time. We all watch out for each other over here in Blue Cove. Anyway, I need to find a number on him. It's three thirty-five Channel View. Name's Biggerstaff."

"Sir, you'll have to come down to the courthouse and pull those records," the woman said.

"Oh. Well, here's the deal. I'm a disabled World War II vet. I'm in a wheelchair, and it's an ordeal gettin' around. I'd have to call my son up from Austin, and by then, you know, it could be too late to help my neighbor."

After a pause, the woman said, "Now, why is it you want this information?"

"Oh, I saw some strangers hangin' around his place. I'm the only one who lives full-time on this street. It's all lake houses, you know. Weekenders. So I'm the friendly neighborhood watchman. They count on me. I just want to call Mr. Biggerstaff and ask if these strangers are supposed to be in his weekend house, but I can't find his number anywhere. His name is Biggerstaff. Can't recall his first name."

The woman sighed. "Okay, let me put you on hold."

Franco grimaced. That could mean a lot of things. Was she going to get the records, or her supervisor? The sheriff's office might be right next door to the county tax assessor-collector, for all he knew. Maybe she had heard the dispatches on the police scanner all morning long singing out "Channel View Lane." Maybe he should have made this call from a pay phone. He gritted his teeth, and busied himself by drying off, then found a pen and a scrap of paper, in case the woman actually came through.

"Still there?" the woman finally said.

"Yes, ma'am."

"Three thirty-five Channel View, right?"

"Yes, ma'am."

"That belongs to a Charles Biggerstaff. He lives in Conroe."

"Oh, yeah, they call him Chuck. Oh, thank you so much, darlin'. Do you have a number for ol' Chuck?"

"Sure. Seven, one, three . . ."

Franco scribbled as she quoted the exchange. "Thanks again. It's probably nothin', but it doesn't hurt to call, you know what I mean?"

"Yes, sir. You have a good day, now, you hear?"

"Thank you, and you do the same." He slammed the phone down, held it there for a second, and picked it back up. He dialed the number for Charles Biggerstaff. He doubted that the feds had had time to get a subpoena to bug the phone line, and he knew he might be running out of chances to get to Biggerstaff first, so he was willing to call from the rental house rather than a pay phone somewhere. Anyway, he could bug out of this rental place within minutes if he had to.

The phone rang twice. "*Biggerstaff,*" said a voice on the other end.

"Charles Biggerstaff?"

"*Yeah, who's this?*"

"Mr. Biggerstaff, my name is John Rogers, I'm a lawyer assigned to your case by your insurance company."

"*What case?*"

"The boat."

"*I haven't even put in a claim. I didn't even know the boat was wrecked until yesterday.*"

"Well, apparently, you're the last one to find out. You're being sued by the family of the deceased. They put in the claim. Have you talked to the police yet?"

"*No. An F.B.I. agent is supposed to be here in about an hour.*"

"Special Agent Doolittle?"

"*Yeah.*" He sounded surprised.

"I talked to him already. When he gets there, don't let him in. Don't tell him a thing."

"*But he's on his way from Austin.*"

"Don't talk to him, Mr. Biggerstaff. He doesn't have your best interest at heart. I do. Sir, you could be in real trouble. The girl that was killed on board your boat was from a mob family in Las Vegas. They play hardball. Do you understand what I'm saying?"

The line went silent for several seconds. "*Mob?*"

"The Mafia."

"*I know what the mob means,*" he said, clearly exasperated.

"So who was driving the boat that night, Mr. Biggerstaff?"

"*I wouldn't know. I haven't been to that lake house in months. I was at a chamber of commerce banquet that night. I have hundreds of witnesses.*"

"All right, then, listen carefully. Tell the F.B.I. that your lawyer advised you not to say anything. Tell them we'll set up a meeting with them soon."

"*That's gonna look funny.*"

"I can't help you if you don't cooperate, Mr. Biggerstaff."

He mumbled a curse at the other end of the line. "*Okay, I won't talk to the agent.*"

"You've got good reason. Tell them you're concerned about the Mafia angle. Tell them you need time to confer with your lawyers."

"*How did the girl's family know to file a claim? How did they find out about the boat before I did?*"

"It's the Mafia. They have ways of making people talk."

"*Shit.*"

"Now, Mr. Biggerstaff, I need to know who was driving that boat that night."

"*I have no way of knowing that. I wasn't there.*"

"Remember, everything you tell me is strictly confidential. I'm your lawyer, assigned by your insurance company. The sooner you tell me everything you know about this case, the sooner we can settle this thing, and you can get on with your life. Is there anyone else with access to the house?"

"*Well . . .*"

"Yes?"

"*My son. I haven't spoken to him in years. We had what you might call a falling out. He has a key to the house. But that doesn't mean it was him.*"

"Of course not. It probably wasn't. It was probably some kids out for a joy ride in a stolen boat. There's been a rash of that sort of thing on that lake, I'm told. What's your son's name?" Franco waited. He could feel the answer coming.

"*Charles The Third.*"

He clinched his fist. "And where does Charles live?"

"*I have no idea. I told you I haven't spoken to him in years. That boy has always been trouble. Always.*"

"Where did he live the last time you spoke to him?"

"*Somewhere near Austin. He fancies himself a musician. Lives off his trust fund. Never has worked a solid day in his life. He doesn't go by his real name, either. He uses some stupid stage name. I can't even remember what it is."*

"I'm going to need to know that. Here's what I want you to do, Mr. Biggerstaff. Take down this toll free number: One, eight-hundred . . . Are you writing this down?"

"Yeah, yeah . . . Eight hundred . . ."

Franco quoted the rest of the Martini family's toll free number, which came in handy for all sorts of things. "You'll get a generic answering machine. I want you to say, 'Hey, I remembered that guy's nickname I couldn't think of. They call him, blah, blah, blah . . .' Then hang up. Do you understand? Your phones will probably be bugged by the feds when you turn them down for an interview, so don't let on that it has anything to do with this case. Act like you're just calling an old friend. I need to know your son's stage name as soon as possible so we can find him and establish his alibi."

"Wouldn't it be better to let the F.B.I. do that?"

"No. Absolutely not. Don't be naive, Mr. Biggerstaff. The cops don't always care if they get the right guy, as long as they get a conviction. If I get to your son first, he *will* have an alibi. Anyway, if the feds finger your son, the mob will find out about it, and your son will be in real danger then. So let our firm handle this. This is what we do."

"This is a nightmare."

"Yes, it is. This is the reason you need me. I will fix this for you, and your insurance company will foot the bill. This is the reason you've paid those premiums all these years."

Biggerstaff moaned at the other end of the line. *"Okay. So I'll track down Charlie's stage name. Maybe my wife remembers. Then what do you want me to do?"*

"Call the information into the toll free number I gave you."

"I got that! What then?"

"Go out and play a round of golf, or go fishing, or see a movie with your wife."

"Are you serious?"

"You've done nothing wrong. You're not guilty and you're not worried, so go about your business as usual. Whatever you enjoy in your spare time."

"That would be golf."

"Keep it in the fairway."

"All right. Thanks."

"Don't mention it. I'll be calling you within forty-eight hours to set up a meeting with you. In the meantime, don't talk to anybody other than me."

"Okay. Thanks, Mr . . ."

"Rogers. John Rogers. Call that eight hundred number. Otherwise, don't call me, I'll call you."

"Okay. I'll do it."

Franco hung up the phone. The gullibility of people sometimes amazed him. He had honed it to a science. Create fear, then offer a way out of it.

His next call: the information operator. How many Charles Biggerstaffs could there be in Austin, Texas? He could taste the end of this ordeal on the tip of his tongue, and it tasted like blood.

CHAPTER

The groove felt surprisingly good. Creed had thrown his partially finished song, "My Luck Is Gonna Change," out to the band to finish. Tump and Trusty Joe had jumped all over it, bandying lyrics back and forth like Ping-Pong balls. Then Trusty had suggested changing "the point of view of the listener."

"What do you mean by that?" Tump had asked.

"Instead of saying 'Then I saw you standing by the roadside . . . ,' say 'Then I saw *her* standing by the roadside. . . .' Makes it less of a love song, and more of a story song."

Tump had nodded. "So we're not singing *to* her anymore, we're singing *about* her."

"Exactly."

"So we can say whatever we want, without pissin' her off. I like it."

Creed had shrugged his agreement, and they had gone back to parrying rhymes, the song morphing into a story about getting lucky more so than meeting the woman of one's dreams. It was a blues grinder, after all, so the story fit the feel. They created two more verses within thirty minutes.

As a simple three-chord blues shuffle, it was easy for the band to learn. They had played it through all of half a dozen times now, and it already sounded album-ready. Though it felt good, Creed had no delusions about it. It would probably never see airplay on the radio, but it was a respectable album filler, and a solid song. It would help to shape this band into something other than just a classic country comeback combo for Luster Burnett. It tapped into the unwritten Austin, Texas, Freedom-to-Play-Whatever Act. It was a bluesy biker song with an outlaw feel.

Moreover, Luster liked it. He had blues influences in his background and played a solid rhythm guitar to the tune, and even sang harmonies. Creed couldn't believe it. Here he was, on salary, in rehearsal, with the great Luster Burnett singing backup vocals behind him! He felt he was finally back in the business.

As the song ground to a tight, pounding finale, Kathy Music burst into the studio, all smiles, clearly excited about something. Her mere presence took Creed's breath away. He knew he should get over that.

"Wow!" she said. "Cool song!"

"It's our new theme song," Luster announced. "Our luck *is* gonna change."

"It sure is!" Kathy sang. "I have news! Band meeting in the dining room!" She clapped her hands and did a couple of cheerleader bounces.

The band members sat and stared at her.

"I brought pizza!"

Metro threw his sticks over his shoulder and led the retreat from the studio, through the living room. Creed brought up the rear, after Luster, who had paused to get both of them a beer from the cooler. By the time Creed stepped into the dining room, he saw that the hungry musicians had already ransacked the pizza boxes. That was fine with him. He waited as Luster carved slices from the smoked wild turkey breast, and set out serving dishes of mashed potatoes and green beans. He and Luster enjoyed their own home cooking while the rest of the band bolted the junk food.

"Turned out good, Boss," he said to Luster.

Luster shrugged. "I've made better, but it'll eat." He leaned in closer to Creed, and spoke low. "It'll make a better turd than that gut bomb they're devouring."

"Like possums eatin' shit out of a hair oil can," he replied, quoting his grandfather, though he had never seen a hair oil can and never understood how shit might end up in one for a possum to eat.

Luster snickered along with him as they both chewed on the turkey— smoky and flavorful, but rather dry.

"What are you two conspiring about down there?" Kathy said from the other end of the table.

Creed swallowed hard. "Just wondering about your news. Thought you had an announcement."

"And so I do!" She attempted to compose herself. "Luster Burnett and The Pounders now have a booking agent! Tomahawk Talent Agency, in

Austin, Texas! She began clapping her hands to lead the band, grudgingly, into an infectious round of applause.

Creed nodded. It was a respectable agency, booking some good acts, a couple of which toured nationwide.

"But that's not all!" Kathy continued, barely able to contain herself. "We also have a gig! A really good booking! You're gonna love this!" she sang, pausing for affect.

"So . . ." Lindsay said, her languid delivery the antithesis of Kathy's enthusiasm.

"This Saturday . . ." Kathy began.

"So soon?" Trusty blurted, sounding nervous.

"Houston, Texas . . ."

"Spit it out, girl," Lindsay ordered.

"Jefferson Stadium . . ."

"Big venue," Tump offered.

"Four bands. We're the opener. The headliner is Dixie Houston!" Kathy raised her fist triumphantly.

Creed felt as if someone had kicked him in the stomach.

"Creed's ex?" Metro said. "She's fine!"

"She's not my ex," Creed growled. "We were never married."

"You two are still friends, right?" Kathy said.

"Doesn't matter. A gig is a gig."

"How did you manage that on such short notice?" Luster asked.

"That part was pure luck. There was a cancellation. They were scrambling to fill it when I walked into their office without an appointment."

"Who canceled?" Tump asked.

"George Jones."

"Of course."

"So now it's us, Mickey Gilley, Charlie Daniels, and Dixie Houston. They've sold over twenty thousand tickets!"

"Oh, God," Trusty Joe groaned, holding his stomach.

"Good money, then?" Luster asked.

Kathy's enthusiasm plunged into uncertainty. "They offered ten grand. I countered with fifteen, and they took it," she said, more as a question than a statement.

"Holy shit!" Metro cried.

Luster shrugged and nodded. "That'll get us to the next gig. It's a good step. Great job, Music!"

The band burst into excited conversation, but Creed was still grappling with the idea of opening the show for the warm-up act for the lead-in artist for Dixie. Was she ever going rub his nose in that. He had often thought of running into Dixie out on the road again, somewhere, after he got his career back on track. But now it was actually going to happen. The saving grace here was that he was the band leader for a legend. And he truly believed that this band was going to kick some serious ass in that stadium. Provided Lindsay could get her makeup on in time, and Trusty Joe didn't puke on the soundman.

He looked up at Kathy, who was waiting for his reaction. He gave her a grin and a thumbs-up. That seemed to make her day. This Kathy Music was well-nigh the opposite of Dixie Houston. She might be good for him. Creed flinched, and shook the thought off. She was off limits. No relationships within the band. Period.

Later, while Creed was talking about bands and music with Lindsay, Kathy approached the two of them and asked Creed to step outside to the patio.

"Feel free to interrupt," Lindsay said, her voice dripping with sarcasm. She turned and strutted away.

The cutest confused smirk Creed had ever seen shaped Kathy's face.

"Is she mad at me?" Kathy asked.

"Don't worry about her. She woke up on the wrong side of the bus." Creed feared, however, that Lindsay was a bit jealous. He and Lindsay had shared that one night in his bed, after all—the night he couldn't remember.

Kathy led the way outside and sat on the picnic table. "Tomahawk wants a stage plot for the Houston show."

"Okay. What format?" Creed replied.

"I don't even know what a stage plot is," she admitted.

He chuckled. "I'll help you draw one up. It's just an overhead view of where each player stands onstage, so the sound crew onstage will know where to set amps and microphones and monitors."

"Monitors?"

"The little floor speakers that point back at the band, so we can hear ourselves."

Kathy sighed. "I have so much to learn."

"We all do, darlin'."

She shifted on the table. "You're not upset about playing with Dixie again, are you?"

"I'm not playing with Dixie. I'm playing with L.B. and The Pounders."

"You know what I mean. Do you miss her?"

"Hell, no. Well, maybe the old days, before she changed." He felt comfortable talking about this with Kathy for some reason. It was the first time he had talked about Dixie with anybody since Uncle Sam forced their breakup.

"How did she change?"

"The stardom went to her head. She liked the attention too much. And she went overboard on the lifestyle. It started with whiskey before the gig, but it got out of hand real quick. She'd wake up about noon and fire up a joint. She drank all day. Even kept a bottle of vodka under her pillow at night. Hard drugs didn't scare her, either. She was just getting in to all that when I got drafted. Mescaline, mushrooms, acid . . . I don't know that she ever stuck a needle in her arm, but I wouldn't put it past her."

"I'm sorry, Creed."

He looked at her, befuddled. "About what?"

"I'm sorry I booked the gig without checking with you. And I'm just sorry you're hurting."

He scoffed, forced a grin with one side of his mouth. "I got over Dixie Houston a long time ago." He knew that was not completely true. "Anyway, this is a great booking for the band, and you'd have been crazy not to jump on it immediately, like you did."

Kathy sighed, clearly relieved. She looked at her watch. "Oh! I have to go!"

Though disappointed, Creed figured it best that she should leave. He escorted her back into the living room. "Where do you have to go this time of night?"

"A record distributor I talked to on the phone today is going to be at an album release at Threadgill's for one of the artists they handle. They want me to meet them there. They're really excited about Luster's comeback."

"You mean Luster Burnett and The Pounders."

"They don't know they're excited about The Pounders yet, but they will be after tonight."

"Which distributor is it?"

"Clear Water."

"Wow. They're big."

"I think they want to distribute Luster's new project."

"You mean the one we haven't recorded yet?"

A cute little grimace wrinkled her features. "What should I tell them about that?"

"Tell them it'll be a live album of the Houston gig. We arranged that today with Bee Cave Studios."

"Oh! Far out!"

"Tell them we'll get them two backstage passes."

"Can we do that?"

"Tomahawk can."

"Okay. Can you help me with the stage plot in the morning?"

"I'll be right here. We rehearse at ten."

"I'll meet you at nine." She smiled. "Bye, Creed."

As Kathy turned away, Lindsay sauntered out of the kitchen. "Bye, Creed," she purred, breathily.

"What?"

"Are you trying to make me jealous?" Lindsay prodded.

"Make you . . . No! That was all about business."

"You two aren't fooling anyone. I'm just glad I got to sleep with you first."

Creed cringed inwardly. "You're not going to tell anybody about that are you?"

"You mean, am I going to tell Miss Music?"

"No, I mean *anybody*. It wouldn't look right."

"Maybe I should tell her, so I can have you all to myself."

Creed was really getting nervous now. "Come on, Lindsay . . . This band is just coming together. Let's not mess it up."

Lindsay chuckled, a strangely deep chortle for such a dainty woman. "Relax, Creed. I have to confess something to you. Nothing happened that night. You went to bed, leaving the rest of us on the deck. I was going to crash outside, but I got cold, and those guys started snoring. So, I slipped inside and crawled under the covers with you. I didn't even take all my clothes off. And I didn't see you in all your glory."

He grinned. "You've been yankin' my chain."

"That's all I yanked. I promise. I thought I'd better tell you, since you're sweet on the bean counter."

Creed scoffed. "I ain't sweet on her. Please . . ."

"You are sweet as buttermilk pie on that white girl. Don't lie to Lindsay."

"What makes you think . . . Come on . . ."

"Hey, listen . . ." Lindsay warned, cupping her hand behind her ear.

Creed strained to hear. At the front door, he could hear the voices of both Tump and Kathy, yet could not make out what they were saying.

"Come on," Lindsay whispered, urging Creed to get closer so they could eavesdrop.

Creed's curiosity forbade resistance. He and Lindsay stepped closer to the front hallway so they could listen around the corner. He heard Tump's booming voice, booze-amplified:

"So, how are you liking your new job as a band manager?" he slurred.

"I like it fine," Kathy said. "I'm having fun."

"What else do you like? What else is fun to you?"

"What are you getting at?"

"Do you like screwin'?"

There was a pause, and Creed held his breath, waiting to see how Kathy would handle this, wondering if at any moment he'd have to beat the crap out of his bass player should Tump push the subject too far. He could already feel his fists clenching.

"As a matter of fact," Kathy replied, coolly, "I do. And I'm real good at it. Oh, but wait . . . You didn't mean with you, did you?"

"Very funny. Anyway, why not with me?"

"For starters, you're boorish and slovenly."

"The hell I am. I'm Irish and Czech. You can ask my parents."

"I thought you said you were Indian."

"I am . . . Some . . . So, you got a boyfriend?"

"No, just someone I'm interested in, and you're not him. Sober up, Tump. Get a grip on reality."

Creed could hear her car keys jingling as she stormed away. He heard Tump sigh. The door to the Carmen Ghia slammed and the car started.

Lindsay looked at Creed and smiled. "Looks like she's just as smitten with you as you are with her."

Creed could not help smiling back. "You ain't shittin' she's smitten."

33
CHAPTER

Franco had no further reason to occupy the lake house, so he packed up, wiped the place free of his fingerprints, and drove to Austin where he checked himself into a nice hotel downtown, an old place called The Driskill. He ordered a steak and a pretty decent bottle of cabernet from room service. He watched television as he ate and slurped his wine. One thing about these Texans, they knew how to cook a steak.

After supper, he went down to the hotel lobby to use one of the pay phones. He put in a call to Papa Martini. By habit, they made a little small talk first, to bore the cops in case the phone was bugged.

"Hey, bambino, that friend of yours remembered his buddy's nickname," Papa threw into the conversation.

"Yeah?" Franco reached for a notepad. He scribbled the name down as Papa threw it casually his way. As Biggerstaff had bemoaned to him, it was a rather stupid stage name. "Hey, Pop, do we have an associate in Austin, Texas?"

"Yeah, we got a guy looking into opening a franchise there. Why?"

"Just wondering. Maybe he can help my buddy find this guy with the nickname. He's a musician."

"Why's your pal looking for him?"

"Hell, I don't know. I guess he misses him."

"Yeah, I miss you, too, kid. You coming home soon?"

"I hope so, Pop. I just need to find this guy for my buddy." On the other end, he heard his father's rasping cough, and another telephone ringing.

"Gotta go. My other line is ringing."

"Ciao, Pop."

Franco hung up the phone and trudged back upstairs to his room. *The Tonight Show* was on TV. Johnny's guest was Charo, and she was shaking her ass. What a bimbo. He turned the television off. So, Austin was sup-posed to be some kind of live music hot spot, he had heard. He decided to change clothes and take a walk down Sixth Street, where a few bars fea-tured live bands. He could pretend to be a music fan if he had to. Maybe he could ask around about Charles Biggerstaff Jr. of the stupid stage name. It was a long shot, but his luck had changed, and besides, a few beers sounded like a good idea.

CHAPTER

Hooley stood hunched over the evidence in his office, leaning on palms placed flat on the table across which his notes, maps, autopsy reports, and photographs were scattered. He felt the frustration like knotted ropes between his shoulder blades. The case had stalled again, and his patience was wearing thin.

Finding the boat had seemed like the big break. Then Mel had come dragging back from Conroe in defeat. Charles Biggerstaff had shut down like a rusted bear trap, refusing to even let Mel in the door, claiming his lawyer had advised him against the meeting, promising to contact the F.B.I. soon for an interview—with his lawyer present.

"They got to him," Mel had said.

"Who?"

"The family."

"The Martinis? How the hell did they know?"

"I don't know. But Biggerstaff flat out said he was afraid for his wife and family, so they obviously got to him."

Now Hooley was wondering what he had missed, wondering how Franco had found Biggerstaff so soon, wondering who would die next if he didn't solve this case pronto. No pressure there. Just another corpse for Doc Brewster to shake his head over. Just another phone call from the governor. Just another failure to protect and serve.

Hooley stood straight, and pushed at the small of his back. He turned to the window, remembering that there was a world outside of his table strewn with evidence, albeit a view of the impoundment lot.

"Okay," he said to himself, "what do you got to work with?" The latest attempt to carry the case forward was a subpoena to obtain Charles Biggerstaff's phone records. That had been executed, and the phone records obtained. Hooley had turned them over to his unofficial assistant, Lucille, to analyze. He thought about walking up to reception to see how she was coming with that when—as if she had read his mind—he heard a pair of heels clicking rapidly toward his office door, getting louder.

"Hooley," she said, stepping through the door with the records in her hand. "I traced all the calls."

"And?"

She shrugged. "They all seem like normal business calls or personal calls. Except . . ."

"Yeah?"

"After the boat was found, there are a couple of odd ones." She put the records on his desk and pointed out two calls she had circled. "While you were lifting that boat out of the lake, Biggerstaff got an incoming call from the same neighborhood."

"The same neighborhood as Biggerstaff's lake house?"

"Yes, the Blue Cove neighborhood. I traced that number, too. It's a rental. The owners rent it to tourists, by the weekend or the week, usually. Here's the address." She pointed to her notes. "I wrote down the lake house rental company's number for you here. They said they'd open the house for you to look around. By the way, it's the same company that handled the rental house where Harbaugh's body was found. They said they never saw who rented the house, that it was handled over the phone."

"You don't say. What's this other call you circled?" He tapped the list of phone calls with his long trigger finger.

"That's an outgoing call, made from Charles Biggerstaff's house in Conroe, the night after you pulled the boat out of the lake. It was made to a toll-free number. I traced it to Las Vegas, Nevada, but I don't know yet who owns the number."

"I'll put your boyfriend, Mel, on it."

"I wish," Lucille said, her eyes flashing. "Has he gone back to Vegas?"

"Yeah, maybe you should go out there and try your luck."

"I don't usually gamble. But . . ."

Hooley forced a chuckle, though he felt no smile on his face. "Thanks, sugar. That's real good work."

"Call me if you need anything else." She left his office and clicked on down the hall.

What next? What about this rental house in Blue Cove? He had a hunch it had been vacated by now, but he knew he had to follow up on it. He sat down at his desk and grabbed the phone. He called the county sheriff's office and told them to watch the place until he got there. Then he called the rental company and told them to meet him there with the key in an hour.

He took his tally book from his pocket and flipped through it until he found Mel's spy phone number.

"*Doolittle.*" Mel said, answering Hooley's call.

"This is Hooley. Got a toll-free phone number for you to track down. It's a Vegas number."

"*Okay. Why?*"

"Biggerstaff called this number from his house after he sent you packin'."

"*Go ahead. I'm ready.*"

Hooley quoted the number to him. "How's the weather out there?"

"*Sunny. There?*"

"Chamber-of-commerce perfect. It's Texas in the spring, though. Could change to hail and twisters any minute."

"*Any new leads?*"

"I'm going to check one out, I'll call you back this afternoon."

"*Be careful, Hooley.*"

"That's my policy, stud. Give my love to Samantha." He hung up the phone, got up from his chair, and grabbed his hat. He looked back at the evidence spread across the table. What had he missed? What was he leaving undone now?

His eyes fell on the stack of photos from the confiscation of the wrecked Correct Craft. He hadn't even picked them up to thumb through them yet. What was the point? He had been there in person. What could a photo possibly reveal that his own eyes hadn't seen?

"A picture's worth a thousand words," he muttered to himself. What would it hurt to look at them? "Leave no stone unturned." He was thinking in clichés. Brain must be tired. He took his hat back off and picked up the stack of photos.

There were shots of the drained lake channel, the dock, the wrecked boat resting on the muddy lake bed, the crane lowering its hook into position, the boat being dragged out of the boat house and lifted from the muddy bed of the lake. The boat going over the roof of the Biggerstaff lakehouse.

"Oh, my Lord . . ." Hooley said. Here was a shot that the photographer had taken of Hooley himself, jumping out of his truck to cuss the county deputies up and down for creating a spectacle of what should have been a low-profile impoundment. The likeness scared even himself. He never knew he had so much anger in his face. It was ugly. He felt ashamed of that outburst now. He regretted that the camera had caught it. It was not pleasant to look upon.

He flipped to the next photo, found a profile shot of his scowling face.

"Hey, what the . . ." Hooley looked closer. In the background. There was that guy. He had all but forgotten about the jogger. In this shot, the runner was looking back at Hooley over his shoulder, wearing shades and a knit cap.

He shuffled the shot aside and found the next photo in the series. Now the jogger had his back turned, and had flipped his hood up over his head. Why would he do that? It had been rather cold that morning, but why just then would the runner go with the hood? Hooley squinted. There was something white on the back of the dark material of the hood. A sticker of some kind? He stepped over to his desk and found a magnifying glass. He got it focused on the back of the hood. Yes, it appeared to be a price tag or some such thing glued to the hood. A new running suit?

He looked at his watch. He needed to get out to Blue Cove to look at that lake rental. He grabbed his hat, and the two photos of the jogger, and turned up the hall toward reception. He found Lucille at her desk.

"One more favor, darlin'. Get the photographers to blow up this picture. Especially that tag on the back of this guy's hood."

She frowned, obviously doubtful of the significance of such a request. "If you say so."

"And fax this one where the jogger's looking back at the camera to Mel's office. Ask him if that looks like Franco."

"Holy Lord in Heaven!" Lucille said.

"What?"

"You don't photograph well when you're angry."

Hooley frowned. "Have 'em crop me out before you fax it."

CHAPTER

The booking had come in from a beer joint outside of La Grange called The Red Rooster. It didn't pay well, but Luster and Creed had decided the band could use the practice for the Houston gig. Besides, La Grange was on the way to Houston. They could make the trip in the bus and feel like a real touring band. Almost.

Arriving, they found a dirty little dive and a crappy little sound system that Creed somehow made to function beyond its capability. Creed met the owner, a bulky tough named Karl who had scars on his neck and face that Creed could only explain as the creations of a prison shiv or hand-to-hand combat in 'Nam.

The bar soon filled up with Luster Burnett fans and the air turned so smoky that it clouded the view across the small room. As he played, Creed was thinking about the thousand dollars they had been promised for this gig. The cover charge was five bucks. He counted heads. There were maybe a hundred and twenty drunken honkies in the place. Didn't add up. The owner was going to have to dip into his bar sales, and owners were sometimes reluctant to do so. Still, Kathy had received a signed contract from the Tomahawk Talent Agency that guaranteed the band one grand. That, minus the twenty percent agent fee, would provide gas, motel, and meal money to Houston.

In spite of the cruddy surrounds, the band played well and the crowd remained enthusiastic and surprisingly well behaved, except for two unrelated fistfights and one random hair pulling. There were a couple comments made about a black girl, a Mexican kid, and a long-haired cowboy being allowed in the bar, but talent won over even the gossamer mind-sets of the rednecks, and last call came and passed without any bloodshed.

To Creed's relief, the county sheriff showed up with two deputies for the last set. Creed thought him rather young to have been elected sheriff, but noticed a U.S. Marine Corp tattoo on his oversized forearm and knew the lawman was a Vietnam vet. He figured him for an ex-commissioned officer, as he carried a Model 1911 Colt .45, a favorite sidearm of Marine officers in 'Nam, and the same handgun Creed had brought home from his tour in the war.

"I've waited my whole life to meet you," the sheriff said to Luster after the gig. "It's a pleasure to shake your hand."

"The pleasure's all mine." Luster didn't have to voice his appreciation for the protection the law provided at the end of the show in a place like this.

"Y'all gonna spend the night here?"

"No, we're gonna hook up the ass wagon and head on to Houston. Got a big show there tomorrow night."

"I'd say that's a good idea. Who's drivin'?"

"I am," Creed said.

The sheriff looked him over. "You been drinkin'?"

"Did I play like I've been drinkin'?" He smiled.

The lawman narrowed his eyes at Creed, but returned the smile. "You handle that bus like your guitar, and you'll be fine."

"*Semper Fi,* sir."

"Corps?"

"Army."

"Close enough. Carry on."

Later, with Lindsay and Metro hidden safely aboard the bus, Creed waved to the county law as they left, and went back into the Red Rooster to make sure about the pay. As band manager, it was Kathy's job to collect, of course, but Creed predicted she might appreciate some backup in this rough joint.

Tump and Trusty were drinking at the bar when Creed came back in.

"Great gig, huh?" Trusty said, seeking Creed's approval.

"Yeah, not bad." He patted the nerve-racked fiddler on the shoulder. "It helps when Tump and Metro lock in like that, huh?"

Tump grunted and shot another jigger of whiskey, tapping the shot glass on the bar to get the bartender's attention.

"Where's Luster and Kathy?" he asked.

"They went to get paid," Trusty said.

Creed had already familiarized himself with the layout of the joint. He knew where the office was. He glanced at the bartender, who was washing shot glasses in dirty water and throwing beer bottles noisily into a large metal trash can. Creed saw his cash register drawer open and empty. The place smelled like stale beer, smoke, urine, and puke. He couldn't wait to get out of this dump.

Passing by the bar, he stepped into a dark hallway that led to the owner's office. He checked the pull of his automatic tucked in the back of his jeans. A light came from the open doorway of the owner's office. He heard voices—Kathy, Luster, and the owner.

He tiptoed down the hall and listened.

"Well, you can't get blood out of a goddamn turnip," Karl's voice was saying.

Kathy: "And we didn't just fall off the turnip truck, either."

Her spunk impressed Creed, but he didn't like the tone of the confrontation.

"Let's go over this again," Luster said, remaining the calm voice of reason. "You've got the contract right there in front of you. You signed it. It guarantees us a thousand dollars for this show."

"That was an obvious mistake," Karl complained. "It should have guaranteed you the door *up to* a thousand dollars. The door only took in six hundred."

"You signed the contract," Kathy scolded. "You should have read it more carefully. You owe us four hundred more dollars and we're not leaving without it!"

"What am I supposed to do?" Karl said. "Pull it out of my ass?"

As Creed walked back toward the bar, he heard Luster continuing to play good cop: "I'd say you sold several thousand dollars worth of beer tonight . . ."

Creed stepped out of the hallway and back into the barroom. "Hey!" he said to the bartender. "I need to talk to you."

"What do you want? I'm a little busy here."

Creed drew his autoloader and cocked it. The bartender heard it, and looked. Tump and Trusty also turned—Trusty shocked, Tump bemused.

"Are you armed?" Creed said.

The bartender shook his head.

"Come here. Get your hands up."

"Are you robbin' me?" The barkeep lumbered out from behind his bar.

"Just gettin' paid. Assume the position." Creed noted that the barkeep knew what that meant. He leaned on his own bar and Creed quickly patted him down in the obvious places. "Where does your boss keep the cash?"

The bartender looked at the muzzle of the forty-five. "Bottom left-hand desk drawer. The drawer that locks. Can you get my last week's pay, too? I've been livin' on tips."

"You're on your own there, Slick. Now get in the men's room and stay there. Tump, Trusty . . . Don't let him out of the crapper."

Tump got up from his bar stool and grabbed a pool cue off the rack. Trusty just stared, his mouth hanging open.

"Easy, boys," said the barkeep as he headed for the men's room. "You won't have any trouble from me."

Tump tossed a second pool cue at Trusty. "Go outside and watch the men's room window. Don't let him out of there."

Trusty caught the cue stick and ran for the front door.

Creed slipped back down the hallway, pausing to listen long enough to determine that the stalemate still held fast, the owner refusing to pay, in spite of the contract he had signed.

Karl: ". . . your slick, big-city booking agents and their tricky, goddamn contracts."

Luster: "Son, I am ten times the country boy you are, and where I come from a deal is a deal."

Creed eased the hammer down on his sidearm so that he could recock it in Karl's fat, red face when the moment came. The sound of that hammer latching back always had a stirring effect. He peeked into the doorway to check out the best approach.

"I'll tell you what," Karl was saying. "Let me see what I can find in here." With that, the seedy barman opened a drawer, pulled out an ancient little revolver, and lay it on the desktop for all to see. "Oh, well, lookie there!"

Perfect. Creed charged in, his automatic leading the way. Luster quickly gathered his intent, and reached for the revolver on Karl's desk. Kathy gasped. Karl rolled back in his chair, his hands reaching for the ceiling. The moment came. Creed cocked the weapon in Karl's face.

"Whoa, now!" the bar owner said.

"Roll your fat ass over in the corner and shut up!" Creed ordered.

Karl scooted his wheeled office chair up against a stack of beer cases.

"Cover him, Boss."

"I got him, Hoss."

"Kathy, stand over here, please," Creed said.

With half of the room cleared the way he wanted it, Creed angled his muzzle down toward the lock on the desk drawer and blasted a bullet hole in its place.

Kathy screamed. "Sorry, I wasn't ready for that."

Creed forced the wrecked drawer open, grinning at the gunpowder smoke that stung his nostrils.

"Kathy, you want to count out what he owes us?"

Coolly, she grabbed a stack of twenties. "Uh-oh. This stack has a bullet hole in it from somewhere." She left the damaged twenties on the desk, reached in for another stack, and began counting with bank-teller precision.

Creed heard footsteps coming rapidly down the hallway. Trusty Joe's face appeared, eyes wide. "Everything okay?" He had a pool stick in his hand, holding it at the ready like a club.

"We're fine. Go back to your post."

Trusty scurried away as Kathy finished counting the four hundred. "I've got it, Creed." She shook her finger at the bar owner. "You messed with the wrong band, mister!"

Karl frowned, and rolled his eyes. He was getting tired of holding his hands up.

Creed grabbed the cord leading to the telephone on the desk, took a couple wraps around his fist, and ripped it from the wall.

"Now, why'd you have to do that?" Karl groaned. "What am I gonna do, call the sheriff? That son-of-a-bitch hates me."

"Well, he loves us!" Luster sang. "But you won't be callin' any of your gun-totin' redneck pals or inbred cousins now, either, will you?"

"No need to get personal!"

"Stepping out of this bar before we're gone down the road a good piece would not be healthy," Creed warned.

Kathy shook the money at the owner. "Nice doing business with you, Karl," she said with royal sarcasm.

They all backed out of the office, into the hallway.

"You'll never play the Red Rooster again, you cocksuckers!" Karl shouted after them.

Passing through the barroom, they collected Tump. Kathy was tugging at the cord of the phone behind the bar, so Tump angled her way, grabbed it, and helped her pull it loose. He also grabbed a bottle of scotch for the road. As they passed through the front door, Tump whistled for Trusty, who came running from the men's room window.

Luster was the last to exit the building, guarding the retreat with his captured revolver. "See if the bus will start, Hoss!" he ordered.

Creed jumped aboard and cranked the ignition. The starter growled, but the Detroit diesel refused to fire. He heard Kathy praying behind him. He tried the ignition again and the engine turned over. Luster chunked the revolver onto the roof of the saloon and jumped aboard the Silver Eagle. Creed drove off with the muzzle of his pistol stuck out of the driver's window, but saw no one emerge from the dark saloon. Trusty Joe Crooke started howling like some kind of desperado who had just robbed a train. He still had the pool cue in his hand as a souvenir.

An hour later, Creed was watching the white lines roll past the bus, safely out of the county and onto Interstate 10. Metro, Trusty, and Lindsay had found bunks and turned in. Tump was sitting right behind Creed at the bus's Formica-covered dinette table. Having drunk half his bottle of scotch, he started blubbering about some vague, horrible thing he had done.

Kathy sat beside him. Creed could keep an eye on her in the rearview, the headlights of oncoming cars painting weird patterns on her pretty face.

"What are you talking about, Tump?" Kathy asked him.

"I didn't mean to, Mama. I swear, I didn't mean to . . ." he slurred, then passed out with his face on the dinette table of the rocking bus.

"Is he going to be all right?" Kathy asked.

"As long as he doesn't start drinkin' like that before the gig, he'll be all right," Luster said, cracking open a beer. He sat in the front, right-hand bench seat where Creed could glance at him over his shoulder.

"I didn't mean as a band member," Kathy said. "I meant as a human being."

Luster shrugged. "He's a bass player, not a human being." He laughed along with Creed. "Anyway, he's a grown man. I've seen worse."

Kathy sighed. "Okay . . . That was crazy tonight. Does that happen often?"

Creed spoke over his shoulder as he drove. "Tomahawk should have known better than to book that gig. You need to chew some ass over there, Kathy. Tell them no more honky dives."

"I will!" She took the beer Luster gave her. "Have you ever seen anything like that before, Luster?"

"Here and there," he admitted. "More so in the old days."

"What about that shootout outside of Fort Worth?" Creed asked. "Any truth to that?"

Luster pretended to search his memory. "Oh, on the Jacksboro Highway? Aw, that was no big deal."

"Shootout?" Kathy said, intrigued.

Luster chuckled a little and leaned back in his seat. "There was a rough strip of nightclubs out there in those days. I had some money coming in, so I bought one of those clubs. I had figured out that if you own the bar, you don't have to audition. So when I was off tour, I always had a place to play if I wanted to."

"What did your wife think about owning a bar?" Kathy said, her upper lip a cute snarl in Creed's mirror.

"She didn't like it. I asked her if she wanted to run the bar with me, and she said, 'No way! You'd be PR, and I'd be peon!' She refused to have anything to do with it. I should have listened to her in the first place. That place almost got me killed."

"What happened?" Kathy scooted to the edge of her perch.

"Well, the mob was trying to move in on the Jacksboro Highway and take over the whole strip. One day, this little piss-ant Mafia wannabe punk who called himself Josh Gold, or Goldie, came into my bar—I called it Luster's Last Stand—real clever, huh? Anyway, this Goldie character came in there and tried to extort some protection money from me. I threw him out by the scruff of his neck.

"Next thing you know, he comes back with two thugs. I got the drop on 'em with a scattergun. I marched 'em out into the parking lot and told 'em I'd give 'em ten seconds head start, and that bird shot would hurt a lot less the farther away they got. I peppered their asses pretty good with some number nine pellets. Didn't hurt 'em much, but I had made my statement."

"That was the gunfight?" Kathy said.

"No, that was just the prelude. Goldie came back and tried to ambush me in the parking lot a few nights later. He was trying to make a name for himself as a mobster, and I had embarrassed him pretty bad. He was out for blood. The two of us shot up the parking lot pretty good until I got off a lucky shot on a ricochet and caught him in the butt cheek. He was hurtin' so bad he couldn't run. My car had a flat tire from a bullet hole, so we took his car, and I drove him to the hospital."

Creed cracked up, the bus careening around a curve, the wheel wallowing around the steering column in his hand. "You shot the guy, then drove him to the hospital in his own car?"

"Seemed like the right thing to do. I gave Goldie enough time to get out of Texas, and then put in a police report, so he couldn't rightly come back and mess with me again without flirting with some jail time. Last I heard, he was out in Vegas, working as a collector for some casino boss."

"Well, that was exciting tonight," Kathy said, "but I'd prefer not having to do that again."

"You stood right in there with us," Creed said. "You did good."

"Creed's right. You showed some spunk with that big peckerwood, Karl."

"I can stand my ground if I'm sure I'm right. We had a contract. Still, we need to be playing a higher class of venue."

"To say the least. I felt like I was back in a garage band back there."

"Aw, just think how nice Houston will feel by contrast," Luster said, always looking for a bright side.

Kathy yawned. "No doubt. I'm going to crawl up into the top bunk and get some rest for tomorrow, gentlemen. I'll see you two in the morning."

Creed glanced over his shoulder long enough to wink and smile at the band manager, then trained his eyes back on the highway.

After she walked aft, bouncing side-to-side in the swaying bus, Luster handed Creed a beer—his first of the night.

"You reckon you ought to be winking at our band manager that way?"

"I had something in my eye."

"Right."

36
CHAPTER

Franco had been told by his admiring colleagues in organized crime that he had eyes in the back of his head. There was no truth to that, in a literal sense, of course. But in many ways, Franco could sense what was going on behind him, without the benefit of another set of eyes trained aft. It was just common sense born of a desire for self-preservation. Franco considered his life just too good to leave behind. He was not going to be blind-sided.

So, how did he do it? Well, first of all, you didn't sit with your back to the room. The famous old-west gunfighter Wild Bill Hickock knew that rule, had violated it once, and lost his life because of it. You sat with your back to the wall—better yet, a corner. And you didn't sit with your back to a window where somebody could whack you from outside.

That much was simple. That was putting yourself in a place where you didn't really need eyes in the back of your head. But when you got up from that table and walked out onto the street, you had better know how to see, smell, hear, and feel what was going on behind you.

Take tonight for example. Standing at the bar in a place called Maggae Mae's on Sixth Street, using the mirror behind the bar to watch his back, Franco had spotted the guy in the arm sling staring at him. Franco had been asking around for a couple days about Charles Biggerstaff Jr. of the stupid stage name. So far, no one knew, or even knew of, a musician by that name. Maybe Junior had changed his stupid stage name by now. Maybe word had gotten around that someone was asking. Maybe that was Junior in the arm sling.

In the mirror, he watched the guy in the sling using his lips to pull a smoke from a green-colored pack of cigarettes in his good hand. Franco paid his bar tab and stuffed a dollar bill into the tip jar. Average tip. He was just an average guy, having a beer. Or at least that's what he wanted these hicks to think. He turned and started walking toward the door. A songwriter named Willis Allen something-or-other was singing his last song. Something about muskrats. This town was weird. They called this music? If it didn't have a horn section, Franco didn't see the sense in listening to it.

As he approached the exit, he glanced up at the big plate-glass windows facing the street. Instead of looking through them, Franco looked into them. He caught glimpses of the reflection of that white arm sling moving in behind him.

Leaving the bar, he turned left onto the sidewalk. He walked for a few seconds to give Sling a chance to step out of the bar, if indeed the guy intended to tail him. Franco weaved a little to give the impression he was drunk, which he wasn't, of course. That would give Sling a false sense of advantage if he intended anything rough. He took his hotel room key from his pocket.

He walked under a streetlight, tripped intentionally over a seam in the sidewalk, and dropped his room key. He bent over to pick it up. There, looking behind him upside-down, he saw Sling prowling along in tow. He knew, under the streetlight, that the amateur wouldn't see his shadowed eyes, and it only took a glance to know he was being tailed.

A car was coming down the street, so Franco decided to cross in front of it, stumbling blindly, like a drunk, into the path of the automobile. The driver slammed on the brakes, honked, swerved, cursed. The car wasn't really that close, and he knew he could have leapt clear even if the driver had failed to notice him. He turned and shot the bird at the driver, but was really using the opportunity to get a look at the guy tailing him. How big was he? How sober? Why was his arm in a sling? How could he take this guy down?

The other reason for crossing in front of the car was to determine whether Sling would cross the street, too. If so, there was no doubt the bum was up to something. And indeed Franco glanced back to see Sling crossing the street to stay behind him. He was getting closer, too, coming up from behind, smoking his cigarette.

Now Franco used the reflections in chrome bumpers, side mirrors of cars, and angled storefront windows to keep tabs behind him. Even the glass windows across the street told him that Sling was gradually closing in on him. That white sling stood out nicely. He slowed down to give the impression that he was oblivious to the tail. A breeze whipped down the street from behind, and he could smell Sling's cigarette smoke. Menthols. What a puke.

They were far enough away from the noise of the late-night bars that Franco could now distinguish his pursuer's footsteps. That's how close the guy was. Sounded like boots. The heels clicked, the soles slid like sandpaper. Still, he pretended to be unaware. The Driskill Hotel was just over the next cross street: Brazos.

Reaching Brazos Street, Franco ducked right around the corner. He stopped, glanced both ways up and down Brazos for witnesses—especially cops. The street was empty. The last streetlight he had passed was now casting Sling's shadow on the Sixth Street sidewalk. He saw the menthol cigarette butt flip smoking into the gutter. He knew exactly when Sling would round the corner. And here he came . . .

Franco cocked his automatic in the gimp's shocked face, grabbed his shirt, and slung him around the corner, taking his feet out from under him by tripping him over his own leg planted solidly on the sidewalk. Sling's butt hit the concrete, the back of his head slamming against a brick wall, his breath *oofing* out of him.

"Why the hell are you following me?"

"I wasn't," the startled amateur wheezed. "I was . . . Just going to my car."

"Why are you wearing that sling?"

"Got a busted collarbone."

Franco used his pistol barrel to whack the guy's collarbone.

"Ow!" he howled.

"Don't mess with me. You were following me. Why?"

"I just wanted to talk to you."

"What would I possibly want to talk to you about?"

"I heard you say you were looking for some guy. A musician."

"So what?"

"Maybe I can help you."

Franco heard a vehicle turn the corner to his left, looked up Brazos and saw the patrol car coming down the street. "Shit," he said, quickly locking the safety on his piece and slipping it into pants. "Act drunk," he ordered, hoisting Sling from the sidewalk to his feet.

The patrol car slowed. "What's going on here?" the cop demanded through the open window.

"My buddy fell down," Franco claimed.

"Y'all been drinkin'?"

"He's getting married tomorrow. I'm taking him up to his hotel room now." Franco pointed to the Driskill.

The cop frowned. "If I see you two on the street again, he'll be getting married in jail."

"Don't worry, sir. He's marrying my sister. She'd kill me if I let that happen." He watched the car turn onto Sixth Street and head toward easier collars near the bars. "Ya hick," Franco added.

"So," Sling said, rubbing the back of his head.

"Come up to the room and tell me more. And take that sling off. You stick out like a sore arm."

"It hurts if I take it off," he complained.

Franco thumped him on the collarbone again.

"Ow!"

"Take it off!"

Sling obeyed, and they walked into the century-old Victorian hotel, across the marble floors, past the reception desk, and up the stairs to the second floor. Entering his room, Franco motioned for Sling to sit down in a padded leather chair. At the mini bar, he poured himself a tumbler of bourbon and dropped an ice cube into it, but did not offer one to his guest. He sat on the sofa facing Sling's chair, his briefcase at his elbow on the end table.

"What's your name?"

"They call me Jimmy the Hand."

Franco laughed, disparagingly. "I don't care what *they* call you. Your name is now Sling. So, what can you tell me, Sling?"

"What's it worth?"

Franco smirked and pulled his briefcase onto his lap. He opened it, the contents shielded from Sling's view by the open lid. "What's it worth? Well, let's see. One hundred . . . Two hundred . . ." he pretended to count cash as he screwed a silencer onto the muzzle of a twenty-two. "Is it worth you leaving here alive?" He shut the briefcase lid and pointed the piece at Sling's face.

Cross-eyed, the rank amateur swallowed hard. "I know where you can find the guy you're looking for. The musician."

"Yeah?"

"He's playing in a band with some old country singer trying to make a comeback—a guy named Luster Burnett."

"Yeah?"

"I seen the band play. I heard the guy's name in the introductions."

"The stupid stage name?"

"Yes, sir. But I didn't catch which guy in the band was the guy. I just heard the name."

In spite of his suspicious nature, Franco tended to believe this guy. He was too stupid to lie convincingly. He fought back the urge to smile. This was the breakthrough he'd hunted for day upon day now. He put the weapon down on top of the briefcase lid. Now, what to do about Sling?

"Why would you want to help me, Sling?"

Sling shrugged. "I got a grudge against one of the guys in the same band. I thought if you were after this other guy, maybe we could work together."

"I never said I was *after* him. I just said I wanted to find an old buddy, and that was his stupid stage name."

"I had a hunch you were after the guy, like he owed you money, or something worse even."

Franco raised his eyebrows. That was the first intelligent thing this idiot had said all night. "So why do you have a grudge against this other guy in the band?"

Sling pointed at his collarbone. "He did this."

Franco chuckled. "You let a musician kick your ass?"

"He didn't kick my ass. He shot me. It was a robbery at a poker game. I don't know how the guy got the drop on me so fast, but I'm lucky I was wearing a vest."

"Wait a minute . . . Who was robbing who at this poker game?"

"I was robbing the poker game. Or trying to. This guy shot me, and my wingmen dragged me away. Lucky we weren't killed because there was bullets flyin' everywhere."

"Hang on, hang on . . . Where was this poker game?"

"South of town. But it's a floating game, so it moves every week."

"So you tried to rob the game and got shot instead? Dipshit."

"I don't know how the guy pulled on me so fast."

"You fancy yourself a gunslinger, Sling?"

Sling shrugged. "I've knocked over some liquor stores and gas stations."

"You ever do time?"

He nodded. "Five years for attempted robbery."

Franco narrowed his eyes. Something didn't make sense here. Sure, he had been asking around about Junior Biggerstaff. But for this small-timer to just approach him out of the blue seemed too good to be true.

"You know, you're an idiot. What if I was a cop?"

"I know you're not a cop," Sling said, looking suddenly worried, as if he'd just said too much.

"How do you know that?"

"I know who you are. You might say I'm a fan."

"A fan? What am I, a rock star?"

"I've studied up on you guys in Vegas. You're Franco Martini. It's my dream to work for you some day."

"And that's why you followed me?"

"Yes, sir. And . . ."

"Spit it out."

"I know why you're in town. I seen it on the news. Your cousin was the girl who bought it on the lake."

Franco nodded. "Poor, sweet Rosabella. I miss her so much." His voice was monotone.

"You're looking for the guy who did her in."

"And you're looking for the guy who shot you at the robbery."

"Might even be the same guy. At least, they're in the same band."

Franco bolted the rest of his bourbon. "Sling . . ." He hoped he would not live to regret what he was about to say. "You're hired." He tossed a couple hundred dollars to his new employee.

"What's this for?"

"Operating capital. Now listen, you puke. You do what I say, and only what I say. If you screw up, I'll kill you. Got it?"

Sling grinned and nodded as he picked up the cash. "This is a dream come true!"

CHAPTER

Hooley arrived at D.P.S. headquarters, switched his truck motor off in the parking lot, and just sat there, bits of evidence swirling like whirlwinds in his mind. The leads had all unraveled again, like a busted lariat, its ends dwindling to twisted cords, then to threads that tapered away to nothing.

The anticlimactic raid on the lake rental house yesterday had revealed nothing other than a great dearth of fingerprints. That was enough to suggest to Hooley that Franco had been there, but not nearly enough to prove it. If Biggerstaff didn't have a change of heart soon, and start cooperating, Hooley didn't know what he was going to do to carry this case forward. The only lead he still had out there was the blurry photo of the back of some runner's hood. He had a hunch that runner was Franco, but hunches alone seldom won arrest warrants or subpoenas.

He stepped out and slammed the door of his truck, wincing at the unnecessarily loud metallic thump. His grandfather would have scolded him something fierce for slamming a vehicle door that hard. It was just the distraction of this case. He wasn't himself. He had hardly slept at all last night, running the facts through his mind over and over, wondering what he had missed. He couldn't get the nagging thought out of his mind that Franco Martini still had one more person on his hit list—the driver of the wrecked Correct Craft. What if Franco had already found him?

Entering the building, he marched to Lucille's reception desk and whipped his shades off. "Mornin', Sunshine," he growled.

Lucille looked up from her typing. "Oh, heavens. You look exhausted."

"Occupational hazard. Any messages?"

She reached for a leaf of paper. "Yes, Mel said the photo looks like it *could* be Franco, but positive ID was inconclusive. And the toll-free number

Biggerstaff called from his house is registered to a construction contrac-
tor in Las Vegas. Mel suspects it's a mob cover, but he can't prove it."

Hooley slumped. "So we got nothin' new?"

"We've got this," she said, handing a photo to the ranger. "It's the shot
of the back of the jogger's hood, blown up as large as the photographer
could make it."

Hooley blinked at it. "What is that?"

"It's a fifty-percent-off sale sticker from Sports Nation."

Hooley turned the photo sideways, walled his eyes at it. "How can
you tell?"

"I buy my niece's softball team uniforms there. I recognized the logo,
even though it's blurry blown up like that."

"Sports Nation. I've seen their commercials on TV. Where's the nearest
franchise?"

"We only have one in town. Near Lamar and Riverside."

Hooley searched the map of Austin he kept in his head. "That ain't far
from Celinda's apartment."

Lucille smiled. "Only a few blocks. I took the liberty of calling the store
manager. They recently installed some new video surveillance cameras to
catch shoplifters and watch the cash register in case of a robbery."

"Video? They got tapes?"

Lucille nodded. "Their tapes go back three weeks. The manager said
he'd be happy to cooperate."

Hooley felt his smile muscles tugging at his face for the first time in
days. "So, how's the team doing?"

"What team?"

"Your niece's softball team?"

"Not bad. We're three and oh."

"Do you coach?"

"I do. I was a pitcher in high school."

"You are full of surprises, Sunshine. I'm on my way to Sports Nation."

"The manager's name is Barry Kincaid," she sang out after him. "He'll
be waiting for you."

Barry Kincaid proved enthusiastically helpful. A former college linebacker
turned retailer, he still carried himself with athletic vigor, and looked as if
he still worked out with weights and on the track. Greeting Hooley at the

storefront, he first pointed out where the surveillance camera was hidden above the checkout lane, its lens barely visible, peeking out through a hole in the ceiling tile.

"I saw you on TV the other day. Is this about what I think it's about?" Kincaid showed Hooley to the offices located adjacent to the store's large warehouse of sporting goods.

"Just trying to wrap up a case," Hooley claimed, avoiding the question.

"Well, I hope we can help," Kincaid said, stopping in front of a television monitor on a rack, connected by cables to a metal box on the shelf below it. "The surveillance videos are stored on these tapes. Your secretary said you'd probably be looking at these four." He handed four cassettes to Hooley. "A couple of Saturdays back?"

"My secretary is always right." Hooley turned the plastic cassettes and held them uncertainly, not sure what to do with them next. He had seen these things in use, but had no experience with them. For a man who started his ranger career reading hoofprints in the sand, this technological stuff came painfully slow to him.

"That's the day that girl was killed down the street, isn't it?" Kincaid prodded. "And the day her friend was found dead on the lake?"

"Crime investigation is ninety percent eliminating false leads," Hooley claimed. "Just do me a favor and keep this quiet. I can do without the public hysteria, you know what I mean?"

"Oh, sure," Kincaid agreed. "I won't speak a word of it."

"Now, how the hell do you look at the pictures on this contraption?"

Kincaid smiled and took the cassette tapes back from the ranger. He turned on the monitor and the tape player, slipped the tape into a slot. "You're lucky your secretary called today. A couple more days, and these tapes would have been recycled. We record over them after a couple of weeks. Here it goes. It starts at nine o'clock, when the store opens. The time and date are shown here." He pointed to some digits at the bottom right-hand corner of the monitor screen. "Each tape covers two hours. That's a total of eight hours until closing time."

"I guess I better get comfortable, then." Hooley took off his hat and pulled up a chair under the fluorescent lights in the windowless office.

"You can view it in fast forward," Kincaid said, showing Hooley the appropriate button. "That'll save you some time. Then, if you see something, you can push play. Rewind . . . Watch it again . . . Whatever. Just don't push record, or you'll tape over it."

"I think I got it." Hooley was impressed by the clarity of the video. It wasn't quite movie-quality, but close.

"Give me a shout if you need something," Kincaid said. "I've got to get back out front. Oh! One more thing. You can tell about how tall each customer is. That shelf behind the customer is six feet high. See what I mean?"

"Yeah, thanks. I appreciate it." Hooley settled in and began viewing the day in question in fast-forward, slowing the tape to real time whenever he saw something the least bit suspicious. He was near the end of the first two-hour tape when the rapid-motion image of a burly bald man leapt out at him. He hit play to slow the tape down as the man turned and left the cash register with his purchase.

Leery of that record button, Hooley carefully pushed rewind and watched the figure reappear in reverse high speed. He let the machine run backward until the customer backed away, waited a few seconds more, then hit the play button again. He noted the time: 10:20 a.m.

The customer stepped up to the counter with a number of items, including a hooded warm-up outfit. Franco! It had to be him. He was five-foot-nine or so. Bald. Muscular. Damn it, though, he was wearing sunglasses. Wait . . . Franco took the shades off to look at his wallet and pull out the cash. Damn it. Cash. No credit card numbers to trace.

"Come on, look up, Franco," Hooley mumbled, his stomach gathering butterflies, his heartbeat racing.

As if on cue, Franco looked up and smiled at the girl at the cash register. The son-of-a-bitch smiled! He had, in all likelihood, just killed a girl about that age, or was getting ready to. He looked right at the camera lens, though he couldn't know it was there. It chilled Hooley. The guy's eyes were vacant—a ghostly light gray on this black-and-white video. He made his purchase, replaced his shades, and left with his bagged items.

Hooley watched it three more times, then ejected the tape. He took the cassette back to the front of the store. "Hey, Sport," he said to Barry Kincaid. "I'll need to take this tape with me as evidence."

"Sure," Kincaid said. He stepped close to Hooley and whispered. "Is the murderer on there? Was he here, in my store?"

"Too soon to tell. Like I said . . ."

"Yeah, yeah . . . ninety percent eliminating false leads." Kincaid gave Hooley a knowing smile and handed him a business card. "Call me if I can help you with anything else."

Back at D.P.S. headquarters, Hooley handed the cassette to Lucille. "Ten-twenty a.m. We got about forty-five seconds of a guy that fits the description of Franco Martini."

"Really!" Lucille said, wide-eyed, and smiling all at once.

"I wouldn't kid you about this, darlin'. I need a still photo of the best shot of him with his sunglasses off, looking up. Fax it to Mel. See if we can get a positive ID."

"Yes, sir!" Lucille said, excited about the developments. "What are you going to do next?"

"It's time to tighten the cinch on this pony. I'm gonna drive to Conroe and catch Charles Biggerstaff someplace where I can look him in the eye."

"Hooley! You're exhausted! You should go home and go to sleep!"

"Can't. I can feel this thing trying to wrap itself up. I should have gone to Conroe in the first place, instead of Mel. He's a good young cop, but he don't know how to talk Texan to an oilman. I'm goin' down there."

"Promise me you'll pull over and take a nap if you get too tired to drive."

"Yeah, sure . . ."

"Hooley! Look at me!" she scolded.

"Okay, I promise! Good God, we might as well get married if you're gonna use that tone of voice."

Lucille beamed her widest smile. "Hooley! Are you proposing?"

He laughed from his gut. "Now, wouldn't that harelip the governor?"

"In this day and age?"

"Maybe you're right," he flirted. "Hell, it probably won't be long until we have a colored . . . excuse me, *African-American* governor."

"You'd vote for Barbara Jordan?"

"I'm talkin' about *you*. You'd get my vote any day, sugar."

"Hooley, you had better get on out of here right now, before I start to listen to your nonsense."

He grinned and winked at her. "Right, as usual, good-lookin'. If you hear from Mel, leave a message on my home machine, will you?"

"Mel who?" she said, her false eyelashes all aflutter. "Just kidding. Of course I will."

Two hours later, near College Station, Hooley remembered his promise to pull over for a siesta if he got too tired. He parked under the shade of an

oak tree. He dozed off, chuckling about the crazy idea of flirting with Lucille in broad daylight at the office.

Franco answered the phone on the first ring. "Hello?" He sucked his teeth,
having just finished his lunch. Chicken cordon bleu. Room service. Not
bad.

"It's Sling."

"What do you want?"

"Got some information for you."

"Cough it up. I got better things to do than shoot the shit with you."

"The band—the old guy, Luster Burnett . . ."

"Yeah?"

"They're part of a big country music concert in Houston tonight. At Jefferson Stadium."

"You're sure?"

"Positive. I found their booking agency. They're opening the concert.
About seven."

"Seven o'clock?" Franco looked at his watch. He knew Houston had to
be an hour or two away. Still, he could possibly make it.

"Yeah. You want me to go with you?"

"Hell, no. Stay by your phone. I'll call you when I need more details. So
tell me, you asked the booking agent which guy in the band is our guy?"

"I did, but they didn't know."

"How the hell could they not know? Did they book the act, or not?"

"They said they just signed the act up a couple days ago, and they don't
have the bios yet."

"Damn. All right, wait by the phone. If I call, you better be there." He
hung up the phone and jumped out of his chair, grabbing the keys to his
rental car.

CHAPTER

The old Silver Eagle had arrived belching black smoke. Creed had intentionally parked it a safe distance from Dixie's band's three shining Prevost tour buses to avoid the obvious comparison with The Pounders' clunker.

He had met with the soundman for the concert, Hutch, whom he knew and liked from his days with Dixie Creed. Hutch agreed to let Nigel Buttery of Bee Cave Studios patch into the mixing console to record Luster's set. A detail-oriented technological genius, Hutch had taught Creed volumes on how to wring every last morsel of sweet music from a sound system. Even so, Creed was well aware that he had learned only a fraction of what Hutch knew about sound, speakers, mics, amps, effects, phase, feedback, mixes, reverbs, slapback, echo, EQ . . .

Nigel and Hutch had spent half an hour hooking up cables to patch in the twenty-four-track tape machine Nigel had hauled from Bee Cave. It was about the size of a typical kitchen stove. They worked as if reading each other's minds, as both were well-trained soundmen. Otherwise, they didn't have much to talk about, Nigel being an urban British cat, and Hutch a country boy from Arkansas. Luckily Creed was there to translate when they hit a language barrier.

"Let's just not let Dixie know we're doin' this," Hutch had suggested, as he and Nigel finished the process.

"Forgiveness is easier to get than permission," Nigel agreed in his singsong British accent. "Still, let's hope no one gets made redundant over this taping."

Hutch looked at Creed.

"Wouldn't want to get anybody fired over this," Creed explained.

"That's what I just said," Nigel snapped, irritably.

"Seriously, Hutch, I hope it won't cause you any trouble."

"Trouble? Creed, this whole tour has been nothing but trouble. Dixie has turned into the prima donna from hell. You got out of this band just in time."

"Yeah, looks like y'all are sufferin' through it with your three buses and four semis full of stage gear."

"Hey, I'd gladly ditch it all to go on tour with you and Luster Burnett right now. I mean, Luster Burnett, man! I envy you, dude."

"Right!" Nigel blurted. "So . . . let's wrap some foil on this turkey!"

Hutch angled his puzzled eyes toward Creed.

"Time for sound check," Creed translated.

"I didn't know you spoke British," Hutch muttered.

"I'll get the band."

The sound check had gone flawlessly, with Hutch on the side of Luster and The Pounders. The band had retired to the bus to relax and get mentally ready for the gig. Knowing they were recording the set for the live album, the band members remained on good behavior, sipping coffee, tea, soft drinks, or water. Creed sat sideways in the driver's seat, answering Kathy Music's endless questions about distribution, radio, booking, routing . . . Tump and Metro stood outside the open door to the bus, smoking cigarettes and trading dirty jokes. Lindsay sat at the dinette, staring into a lighted makeup mirror she had brought with her, expertly painting on her eyeliner. Luster was napping in his private bunk in the rear of the bus.

To Creed, they all seemed confident and prepared, with the expected exception of Trusty Joe, who was a nervous wreck, wringing his hands and biting his lip on the edge of his bunk, swirling ever deeper into his private hell of insecurity. His face looked almost green.

Finally, Luster came out of his tiny suite at the back of the bus, a beer in his hand, and a Navaho blanket thrown conspicuously over his shoulder. "Everybody dressed and ready? Good," he said, not waiting for the answer. "All aboard. Quick meeting."

Creed called Tump and Metro onto the bus.

"I brought this blanket with me to show y'all," he began. "It was given to me by a tribal elder on the Navaho rez in New Mexico, years ago. I played a fund-raiser for them so they could build a new school, and the elder took a liking to me. He told me something about the Navahos, and their blankets." Luster held the blanket up by one end—zigzags of reds, yellows, and blues painting striking patterns.

"Look at this thing. The colors, the patterns. Look at the weave, the craftsmanship."

Lindsay looked up from her mirror. "That *is* a thing of beauty, LusSTAIR."

"But, look here, Miss LockETTE . . ." Luster pointed out a twist of wool protruding from one edge of the blanket. "The old Navaho told me that this imperfection in the design and making of his blanket is intentional. Perfection, he said, is unnaturally extreme. It's like a cold, closed box. He told me a thing that's perfect is unable to breathe. It can't live. After all, there is no perfection in nature. Not even a drop of rain is perfectly round. It moves. It lives. It breathes. In perfection there is no reality, and definitely no room for creativity. So the Navahos, when they make their blankets, always build in some little flaw."

Metro patted a shuffle on the chrome handrail leading up from the bus door.

"Interesting," Kathy said. "So . . ."

"So, we're recording a Navaho blanket this evenin', not some unnaturally perfect geometric shape. Let it breathe. Let it live. Embrace the imperfection. To err is human. It's organic. Feel it. Live it. Love it." Luster draped the blanket respectfully across the back of a padded seat. "Anyway, if you screw up too bad, we can overdub it in the studio. No pressure. Let's go have fun."

Creed waited for the band to file off of the bus, but noticed Trusty Joe still sitting on his bunk. "Trusty?"

Trusty stood and touched the vagrant thread protruding from the Navaho blanket. "This is me. I'm gonna be the imperfection."

Creed watched in dismay as Trusty started crying. He grabbed him by the arm. "Get off the bus, Trusty. Get some fresh air."

"It's Houston air!" he sobbed. "I hate Houston."

"Come on. You'll do fine . . ."

Once off the bus, Creed could hear the hum of the crowd that had gathered in the open-air football stadium often used as a concert venue. He saw the dread that the crowd noise painted on Trusty Joe's face. He felt like slapping Trusty around a little, but doubted that would help. Maybe he just needed to take Trusty's mind off the whole situation. He had to do something. He was band manager, and personnel issues fell under his list of responsibilities.

"Trusty, what would you rather be doing right now?" he asked.

"I like what I'm doing. I just don't like who I am."

Creed felt he could relate to that. "What if you were riding Ol' Baldy right now?"

Trusty immediately stopped blubbering. "I wish."

"Here's what I want you to do." He stopped at the bottom of the steel staircase leading up the backstage area. "When you step onto that stage, I want you to imagine stepping into the stirrup, and swinging your leg over the saddle."

"Yeah?" He dragged his sleeve across his nose.

"In your mind, I want you to put yourself astride that big beautiful horse, and show these people what you can do. I've seen you ride, and I've heard you play, man. You're a natural-born horseman, sure as you're a natural-born musician. You don't have to do this alone. Ol' Baldy will help you."

Trusty Joe drew himself up with something akin to hope. He swallowed hard and put on his game face. "Giddy up," he growled.

As Creed reached the top of the steps, he found Luster waiting for him. "Is he gonna be able to play?"

"I think so, Boss. I just gave him a pep talk."

"Good. Now here's the bad news. Sid is here."

"Oh, no. He doesn't want to sing, does he?"

"That's the deal we made. Clue the soundman in, okay? It'll be your voice going to tape, and your voice the audience hears during the show."

"Yeah, and what's going to happen when Sid hears my voice on the record, and not his?"

"He'll probably audit you or something, but you pay your taxes, right?"

"Very funny, Boss."

"We'll think of something by then. Right now, we have to let him sing, or he'll pull the plug on the whole project and send down the really mean tax dogs."

"All right, I'll go talk to Hutch."

"Better hurry. We go on in five minutes."

With no time to go around the long way, Creed jumped off the front of the six-foot-high stage, into the audience. He muscled his way through the crowd and ran up to Hutch's mixing console to tell him the bad news about Sid's fake vocal.

"You've got to be kiddin'?" Hutch said.

Once Creed convinced him that he was serious, Hutch sent an assistant to hook up another microphone in the wings off-stage. Creed raced back to the stage and began to climb up on it, when he was stopped by a burly security guard.

"I'm the guitar player," he said.

"Sure you are, bud. And I'll be backing you up on the banjo."

"No, really."

"Back off!" the muscle man warned, putting his palm in Creed's chest.

Creed thought briefly about taking him down, but decided that would not make for a good opening act. About then, Luster stepped onto the darkened stage, ready to be introduced. Creed shouted at him, but couldn't get his attention over the crowd noise. So he took off his left boot, and when the muscular security guard wasn't looking, he threw it at Luster, hitting him in the shin.

Bemused, Luster looked for the source of the boot as fingers pointed at Creed and the security man descended on him.

"They won't let me onstage!" Creed said.

Luster scurried to the edge of the stage. "Hey, that's my guitar player," he shouted at the guard. "Help him up here."

The guard smirked and gave Creed a boost. "Sorry, man."

"Keep up the good work, dude."

Some local deejay began introducing the legendary Luster Burnett to an audience of more than ten thousand that had gathered early for the Dixie Houston show. Luckily, it was a lengthy intro, so Creed had time to scramble for his guitar. He strapped it on, turned it up, and tightened the B string to bring it into tune. The deejay was finishing his intro with . . .

". . . so ladies and gentlemen, without further adieu, the great Luster Burnett and The Pounders!"

Creed looked at his boot lying on the stage. No time for that right now. Metro clicked out the tempo for the opener with his sticks. Creed turned his volume halfway up and got in on the downbeat with a big Strat power chord. Suddenly, thoughts of Sid, Trusty Joe, the live recording, his errant boot, and just about everything else on his mind melted away. Nerves unwound. Tension twisted into positive energy. Damn, Hutch was a great soundman! Every cubic inch of atmosphere onstage filled with a perfect blend and balance. He was so thankful he had never said a harsh word to Hutch. Every member of the band plunged into the groove of the classic country hit. And then, Luster started to sing.

Creed looked up, almost surprised to see ten thousand faces staring back at the stage. This song was older than most of the fans, yet their looks of pleased astonishment told him his confidence in his band was well placed. Their expectations for the opening act were probably modest, but Creed could tell now that they were glad to have arrived early to stake their claim to turf in front of the footlights. He smiled at some kids on the front row. They smiled back. This was starting to feel like fun again.

Luster didn't speak a word to the audience until after the third song, and then Creed finally had a chance to pull his left boot on. He caught Lindsay's twinkling eyes as she laughed at him.

"So much for the old gold-and-platinum country," Luster was saying. "Do y'all want to hear some new outlaw music?"

Metro was already clicking out the beat for "I Believe My Luck Is Gonna Change." After three new tunes that seemed to get just as big of a rise out of the crowd as the old stuff, Luster began introducing a special guest from St. Louis, Sid "The Kid" Larue. Creed racked his Strat and slipped off the back of the stage as Sid nervously shuffled up to the microphone Creed had vacated. Backstage, Hutch's assistant waved him over to a corner and handed him a Shure 58 microphone.

"You know what we're doing, right?"

"I think so," the assistant said.

"Make sure the monitor man knows that that guy onstage needs to hear himself in the monitor."

"But your voice is in the mains, right?" the young trainee said.

"God, I hope so."

The intro done, it was time to sing, so Creed remembered that he was going to tape, dreamed up an imaginary audience to sing to, and let the lyrics rip. It was weird. He was backstage, singing to no one but a few confused stagehands, yet he could hear Sid's voice coming from the monitors onstage. Sid had been lectured repeatedly to sing the song exactly like the record and Creed did the same so that his vocal came out exactly on time with Sid's. To make things stranger, he could just barely hear the echo of his own voice out in the main speakers blasting sound out to the audience. He couldn't believe they were actually getting away with this.

The song done, Sid took a bow and turned to walk offstage. Creed passed him as he raced back to his guitar. "Good job, man."

"That was a kick!" Sid said. "The crowd loved it!"

"Thank you," Creed muttered to himself as he stuck his head through his guitar strap. He nodded at Metro, who clicked the tempo for the next tune, and cranked up his volume for one of Luster's golden oldies. With the worry over the Sid Larue fiasco behind him now, his instincts took over and he just played. Suddenly, he felt as if his hands were playing every instrument onstage. He felt something he had been missing since before the war. He was part of a band. A band! A real ensemble of six parts working together in one machine. Six parts, all intentionally flawed by their maker like a bunch of Navaho blankets, yet somehow seamlessly merging their talents together into an invisible spell cast over the masses. Music! Look at the power! It made people move, smile, dance, groove. Girls were swaying, waving their arms above their heads, undulating hips and shoulders like wisps of smoke rising from a snuffed candle. Guys were bobbing their heads, biting their lips, playing guitars made of air—part of the groove, part of the band in their own fantasy worlds.

God, it felt good! The vibes from the amps, the monitors, and the drums massaged him from every angle, lifted his weight from his feet until he felt as though he were floating. Metro was pounding the pedal under his right foot so hard that blasts of air were shooting out of the front of the kick drum and hitting Creed in the back of his calves, the force of the air plastering denim to flesh.

The next thing Creed knew, it was his spot for a lead break on guitar, and he found himself hanging his toes off the front of the stage—literally teetering on the brink, looking at the smiling face of a pretty girl right between the toes of his boots. He did a Chuck Berry shuffle over to Trusty Joe, who was poised to pick up the solo.

"Saddle up, Trusty!"

"Yee-ha!" the fiddler railed.

He thought about that talk Tump had had with Metro, back at Bud's Place—the discussion about the beat as a pocket. Metro had taken it to heart, because the groove was in his hip pocket now, somehow powerfully lazy. Luster was windmilling his guitar with his right arm, Lindsay was showing off her pearly whites along with her flawless swoops and stretches on the pedal steel. Trusty's hair was blowing back under his hat brim for some unexplainable reason.

And then, too soon, it was all but over. The last song had commenced. Creed caught some movement stage right and glanced that way to find his band manager, Kathy, standing there, looking perfectly, wholesomely gorgeous in a tie-dyed tee knotted around her waist to reveal her midriff above skin-tight, hip-hugging bell-bottoms, her hair falling over her shoulders. He smiled at her, and she took his breath away with the look she gave him.

Just as quickly, though, her expression changed to one of confused surprise as she looked beyond Creed to the left wing of the stage. Curious, Creed turned left and found the source of Kathy's shock. Dixie had come out of her bus in her nightgown—a skimpy one—to see who was rocking the stadium. When she recognized Creed, her mouth dropped open, and it occurred to Creed that Dixie probably had had no idea that he was working with Luster Burnett.

Dixie worked it wickedly. Having picked up on the flirtation between Creed and the gal in the tie-dye and bell-bottoms at stage right, she gave Creed one of those old come-hither looks and actually flashed her left breast at him as she adjusted her nighty. Creed grinned at her gall and shook his head. He knew as well as anyone in the world that she was trouble, and that he should tear his eyes away from her, but damned if she still didn't possess something of a spell over him. He knew it was foolishness, but he caught himself thinking . . . What if they patched things up? What if Luster and The Pounders toured with Dixie? What if he felt his naked skin pressed against hers again, after several years of separation?

He shook his head as if a bee had stung him and looked away from the shameless Dixie. He looked stage right for Kathy, but it was too late. She didn't play that game. That breathtaking look she had given him before Dixie arrived was gone like a bullet from a hair-triggered gun. Kathy wasn't even looking his way. She was gazing out over the audience, disappointment clear on her pretty face.

What had just happened? Creed had been simply doing his job, living and loving the dream onstage with a kick-ass band. It reminded him of a well-known fact. No matter how tight the music onstage, there would always be trouble waiting in the wings, and it was often disguised as a woman.

CHAPTER

Back on the old Silver Eagle, the band gathered and passed around cold beers, every member beaming. Metro was going on and on, in Spanish and English, about the size of the crowd and feel of the big stage. Lindsay and Tump were sitting together at the dinette, sharing a cigarette, both unable to erase their grins. Sid looked proud just to be a coattail clinger to the whole experience. Luster couldn't sit down. He slammed beer after celebratory beer, chiming in about the set like one of the kids in his band. Only he and Creed had ever played a stage that large. Trusty just looked relieved.

Kathy was smiling, but still refused to make eye contact with Creed. He tried not to let that bother him. He had done nothing wrong, other than maybe stare a little too long at a scantily clad old flame. What did he care if Kathy got jealous over it? She was off-limits, anyway. It wasn't as if they were going to have a relationship or something.

Someone was pounding on the bus door, so Creed looked out of the window to see Nigel Buttery. He opened the door and let the friendly Brit aboard.

"Nigel!" Luster said. "Well?"

The eyes of all the pickers turned toward their recording engineer.

"Right. Well, indeed." He looked at his wristwatch. "I've just returned from dinner, so let me know when you take the stage, and I'll go push the record button."

A sickening silence sucked all the joy out of the bus.

"No . . ." Tump warned, in a homicidal tone of voice.

"Kidding!" Nigel sang. "I've got it all on tape! Every marvelous note!"

Elation imploded tenfold into the Silver Eagle as Luster playfully shook his fist at the foreigner. Trusty tossed Nigel a brew.

"Oh, lovely. American beer. How quaint. In an al-you-MEN-ium can, no less."

"In America, that's aLUminum," Tump instructed.

"Isn't that what I said? Al-you-MEN-ium?"

"Hey, you're in Texas now," Metro chided. "Speak Spanish! *Cerveza in aluminio.* Just drink it, man!"

Nigel opened the can. "All right. Hip-hip and all that rot! To the best live album I've ever recorded!"

As the happy conversation filled the bus once more, Kathy stepped closer to Creed.

"You did a great job getting the band ready," she said. "And you played some amazing licks up there." She forced a smile.

"Thanks. But you booked the gig."

She nodded. "We've got a good team going here. I hope nobody messes it up."

"Me, too."

"I mean, certainly not you or me, but . . ."

"No, not us, of course. What would we do to mess it up? It's these other yahoos who worry me."

She nodded, glancing over the happy busload. "I hope the Sid situation doesn't become a problem. And I don't know how you pulled Trusty through. I thought he was going to have a heart attack before you gave him a pep talk."

"I didn't realize you knew I had talked to him."

"I don't miss much, Creed."

He grinned. "I'm learning that."

"So . . . the flasher backstage in the lingerie . . ."

He nodded. "Dixie."

"I thought that was her, but I wasn't sure without all the hairspray and makeup. Not to mention the lack of her usual push-up bra."

"Yeah" was all he could think of as a reply.

"She's jealous of you, you know. Professionally, I mean."

He chuckled. "I don't think so." He opened his arms as if to present the beat-up bus that The Pounders somehow kept rolling down the road. "What would she be jealous of?"

"Luster. You're the architect of his comeback. That has all kinds of country music credibility attached to it. You've got Luster, and now she wants him."

"Well, she can't have him."

"Let me make a prediction. She's going to offer Luster a touring deal. You'll be part of it at first, then she'll dump you like she did before, along with The Pounders, and claim the credit for Luster's comeback herself."

"How long have you been in the music business?" he asked, as if he didn't know.

"I've been in the money business long enough to see greed in someone's eyes. I saw the way she flirted with you, and I saw the way she looked at Luster. No offense, Creed, but she wants Luster more than she wants you."

"Luster won't go for that. He loves this band."

Kathy laughed. "He won't know what hit him! He's a man. She'll wrap him around her pinkie quicker than he can tune a G string. And, by *pinkie*, I don't necessarily mean her little finger."

Creed thought he might actually be blushing. "I'll warn him, but I don't think she'll make a move to take over the whole comeback."

At that moment, a stranger stepped into the open door of the bus. Creed recognized him as the bodyguard he had seen outside Dixie's bus.

"Excuse me," he said. "Mr. Burnett?"

"What can we do for you, son?" Luster said, opening another beer can.

"Dixie Houston would like to invite you to sing a duet with her during her show."

Creed grunted as Kathy elbowed him hard in the ribs.

"Really? Well, that's a nice offer, but what would we do?"

"One of your old standards. She knows several of them. And which one of you is Creed?"

"That would be me."

The bodyguard glanced at him. "Dixie wants you to do that one hit the two of you recorded together. I forget the name of it."

" 'Written in the Dust.' "

"Right. Can I tell her yes? She doesn't like to take no for an answer."

"I don't know," Creed said.

Kathy stuck her hand out, demanding a handshake from the bodyguard. "I'm the band manager. Tell Dixie they'd be glad to perform with her."

"Good. Thanks." The bodyguard nodded and left.

"Free publicity," Kathy explained to Luster.

"Wow," Metro said, nudging Luster on the shoulder. "A duo with Dixie. She's fine, man! *Masota!*"

"You sure this is a good idea?" Creed said to Kathy as the chatter returned to the bus.

"Just pay attention. I want you to see what she has up her satin sleeve. Don't fall for it, Creed. You and I have to hold this band together. I really don't want to go back to doing other people's taxes."

The bodyguard came back and explained the plan to Creed and Luster. Dixie was going to kick off with five of her hottest songs. On the sixth song, Creed was to join her onstage for "Written in the Dust." The seventh song would be the duet with Luster.

Darkness had fallen by the time Dixie took the stage. Strobe lights, black lights, and moving spotlights, some in vibrant colors, cast unnatural hues on the faces of the fans. Creed and Luster arrived backstage. Luster peeked out at the crowd.

"This ain't like any country show I ever played," he said.

"It's basically a rock concert with a little twang," Creed replied.

As the time approached, Creed was waiting in the wings, stage right, like he had been told. Dixie was shaking her ass at the crowd, making the redneck boys howl like wolves. She wore red hot pants and high-heeled cowboy boots, a sequined pink spaghetti strap top and a lavender cowgirl hat. Borrowing a bit from Tina Turner, she started gyrating through some choreography, flanked by two dancers of exactly the same size and build as Dixie herself, dressed all in pink so Dixie's scarlet hue would stand out.

Toward the end of the fifth song, she threw her lavender hat out into the audience, creating a fistfight between two frat boys, each of whom wanted the hat for his girl. Meanwhile, Dixie's hair, which had been stuffed up under the hat, now fell to her shoulders, and she shook it out in a move she had stolen from Janis Joplin.

When the fifth song ended, Dixie took a break to swill a vodka and tonic. Dabbing sweat away from her brow, she stepped up the mic. "Anybody ever heard of a song called 'Written in the Dust'?" she asked.

The rhythm player started the intro. Dixie turned to Creed and beckoned with a seductive curl of her finger. "Come here, hotshot!" she purred.

"Oh, God . . ." Creed muttered, already embarrassed by the shenanigans. As he walked into a spotlight, the stage manager handed him a microphone. He happened to look beyond Dixie and saw Kathy standing beside Luster, shaking her head in disgust. He joined Dixie and began singing.

It was like the old show from the old days, when Dixie would rub herself all over him while they sang. Except now, Creed had no guitar to hold, and didn't know what the hell to do with his hands. Out of his element in this dog-and-pony show, he felt awkward and foolish, especially knowing that Kathy was watching.

Still, it was showbiz, so Creed made the best of it, and sang his parts as well as ever. The harmonies sounded pretty good, though Dixie was so winded from all her shaking and grinding that she couldn't hold the notes out very long.

Thankfully, the former hit came to a merciful end. Dixie moved away from him and said, "Boys and girls, I wrote that song and recorded it with this man."

He took a little bow as she gestured toward him. Wait a minute! Did she just say *she* wrote the song?

"You know him now as the guitar player for the great, the legendary . . ."

As she turned left, Creed's spotlight shut down. In the dark, someone took his microphone away from him and pulled him offstage.

". . . the one and only Luster Burnett!"

The spot hit full on the icon and the crowd went wild with adulation. As Luster and Dixie began their duet, Creed felt his mouth still hanging open.

Kathy, having walked around backstage, stepped up beside Creed.

"Did she get anything on you?"

"About a pint of perfume," he admitted.

"Yeah, and a gallon of chagrin. I thought you wrote 'Written in the Dust.'"

"I did." His embarrassment was transmogrifying into anger.

"She never even mentioned your name onstage."

"Too winded from shakin' her ass, I guess."

"She's hell-bent on putting the cunt in country music, that's for sure."

They stood and listened as Luster and Dixie traded verses on one of the old hits Luster had given away the rights to years ago. Now she was hanging on the legend. Not rubbing up on him as she had done with Creed, but draping herself on him rather luxuriously. Luster seemed to be enjoying the hell out of it.

At the end of the song, Luster took a glorious bow to outrageous applause.

"Ladies and gentlemen," Dixie announced, "let the world know that Dixie Houston is bringing Luster Burnett back to country music fans, beginning right here, in Houston, Texas!"

Creed glanced at Kathy's I-told-you-so expression. "Okay, so you were right," he allowed.

"Maybe I shouldn't have booked this gig after all," Kathy moaned.

"Luster won't quit us for her. He's got too much integrity. Think about the live album we cut. You were right to book this show."

Dixie threw Luster a kiss as he walked offstage. "You'll be seeing more of Luster Burnett soon, on tour with Dixie, baby!"

"Does she always talk about herself in the third person?" Kathy said.

"Past, present, and future tense." He felt Kathy's hand slip around his arm. When he looked at her, he saw regret in her honest eyes.

"I'm sorry I made you do the song with her, Creed. You deserve better than that."

He shrugged, feeling his temper cool a little. "I guess I needed the reminder."

She smiled, and tossed her head toward the other side of the stage. "Come on, we better get over there and reclaim our legend."

40
CHAPTER

Franco was already fuming with frustration when he found the stadium and saw the lights from the concert. He had had no idea Houston was so far away from Austin. He thought Nevada was spread out. How big was this freakin' state? On top of all that, he had gotten stuck in no fewer than three traffic jams. He knew the concert would be almost over by now, and that Luster Burnett's band had already performed hours ago. Not that he cared to see any of these hicks play their music, but he had hoped to hear the band leader introduce the band members, so he could get a look at Charles Biggerstaff, Jr.—the guy with stupid stage name.

Still, he wasn't giving up. He would get backstage somehow, snoop around, ask some questions. The parking spaces near the stadium were all taken. He had to park a mile away and trot to the venue. The headline band was still playing. He had heard on the car radio that the headliner at the concert was Dixie what's-her-name. Franco wasn't a country music fan, but even he knew who Dixie was. She had a knack for attracting media attention.

Once he got to the stadium, he gravitated toward the backstage area, looking through a high chain-link fence at the band buses and tractor-trailer rigs that hauled the sound equipment around. He continued to prowl this perimeter until he found a guarded gate where roadies and venue personnel were coming and going. Each wore a laminated pass on a lanyard around his neck.

Gotta get a pass, Franco reasoned. He saw a guy with a press pass and a Nikon camera around his neck leaving the secure area through the guarded gate. Scrawny guy. Easy take-down. The guy was engrossed in a notepad as he walked into the parking lot. Probably a newspaper photographer with a deadline. Franco smirked. This guy was going to miss his deadline. This was going to feel pretty good. He could take his anger out on this shutterbug.

The poor bastard's Volkswagen Bug was parked in a dark spot in the lot. As the clueless photographer slipped his key into the door lock, Franco skulked up right behind him, checking over both shoulders for witnesses, finding none. "Excuse me," he said.

As the journalist turned, Franco broke his nose with a quick left jab and jacked his jaw with a right cross. The victim was out before he hit the asphalt beside the Volkswagen. Back in the stadium, the band ended a song and the crowd roared. Feeling clever, Franco took a bow.

Working the lanyard off around the blood from the photographer's nose, Franco tossed it on top of the car. He opened the unlocked door and muscled the little unconscious guy into the Volkswagen, slamming the door on him. He took the camera the victim had dropped. The notepad, too. He was a photographer with a press pass now.

The guard at the backstage gate looked at the press pass and nodded at Franco. He entered the compound and began to stroll around. The fancy buses caught his attention. He walked up to one with an open door.

"Yeah?" said a bodyguard.

"Looking for Luster Burnett's band."

"Not this bus, buddy." He pointed. "That old piece of shit parked down yonder."

"Thanks." Franco turned away. Had he actually said *yonder*? Hicks. He approached the antique bus, finding its door open, too. No security. He looked inside, finding the band members laughing, throwing back beers.

"Can we help you?" an attractive young woman asked.

"I'd like to get a photo of the band for the entertainment section." He held up the Nikon and the press pass.

"Sure!" the woman said.

A band member groaned a complaint, but they all filed off the bus and lined up for the camera.

"Which newspaper?" the woman asked.

"Houston."

"Okay. Which one?"

"Highest bidder. I'm freelance."

"Oh. How will we know when the photo comes out? We're putting together a press package."

"You got a card?" Franco asked. "I'll send you a clip."

"I'm all out of cards, but I'll write down my information," the woman said, climbing back into the bus.

"All right, everybody look at the camera," Franco said. He flashed a shot at them. "That ought to do it. Wait, don't move! I need everybody's name so I can identify all of you correctly." He pulled the notepad from his shirt pocket, along with a pen, and began writing down the names:

Metro Morales, Lindsay Lockett, Tump Taylor, Luster Burnett, Creed Mason, Trusty Joe Crooke.

"Thanks," he said, turning away with a grin.

"Wait!" The woman came out of the bus with her name and contact information handwritten on a scrap of paper.

"You won't forget now, will you, Mr . . ."

He tucked her note into his pocket. "Gotta get to the dark room. Deadlines."

"Hey, do you have a card?"

He shrugged his apology, noticed that the one called Creed was watching protectively over the young woman from the bottom step of the bus. "I'm all out, too. I'll contact you."

"What did you say your name was?"

"Franklin. Tom Franklin. I'll be in touch." He turned and walked away. *Jesus, what a pushy broad.*

As Franco headed for the gate, he saw some commotion there. Ambulance lights approached. A crowd had gathered around the scrawny photographer he had coldcocked. The band hit the last lick on a big finale, and Franco heard the shrill voice of that superstar, Dixie, saying, "Good night, Houston! Dixie loves you!"

"Oh, hell," he groaned. He couldn't exit through the backstage gate— not with the victim's camera and press pass around his neck. The little guy had come to quicker than he had thought. Still, he had the camera and press pass for now, so he decided to use them to get onstage, as if he intended to take some photos of the finale from the wings. He climbed the back stairs to the stage level. The starlet, Dixie, was still blowing kisses to a rowdy, adoring crowd. She was real slinky-looking—just the kind of woman Franco liked. As Dixie held everyone's attention, Franco decided to ditch the camera, dropping it into a box of microphone or speaker cables. Some roadie was going to get a new camera out of this deal. It would probably wind up in a pawnshop at the next town on the tour.

Dixie finally grew weary of taking her bows and strutted offstage, right toward Franco. As her entourage and the stagehands showered the starlet with compliments, Franco dug deep into his wallet for his actual Las Vegas business card. She approached him, and looked blankly toward him, expecting more approbation. Franco had other things to say:

"How would you like to play Vegas?"

Her eyes actually focused on him.

"I own the biggest casino in town." He tilted his card toward her. "I'll get you all the crank you can snort." He had her figured for a cokehead. Just look at those eyes.

Dixie smiled. "I'll have my agent call you." She reached for the card.

Franco snatched it back. "No agents. You want to play Vegas, you call me. *You* call *me*." He gave her the card, noticing that her smile lingered and her eyes clung to him. As her entourage dragged her away, he saw her mouth the word *Okay*.

He shrugged. That was a long shot. She had probably already dropped his card. The cleanup crew would sweep it up with the litter. On the other hand, a guy never knew. She might actually take the bait. Who wouldn't want to play the biggest casino in Vegas? *Vegas*, baby! She might prove useful to him in getting to the old-timer's band. Franco had done his homework, and knew there was a link between Dixie and that guitar player from the other band—the guy called Creed. If he could get the old-timer's band to Vegas—home turf—the stupid stage name would be a lot easier to deal with. He might even end up under a root ball of a pine tree on the ranch in the mountains.

Franco's moment of euphoria quickly wore off as he realized he now had no choice but to file out of the stadium with twenty thousand idiot country fans. *Great*. Still, he was in a much better mood than when he had arrived. He had obtained what he came for. This thing was a hair trigger's pull from being over. He knew who Charles Biggerstaff Jr. was now. He couldn't wait to call Papa and tell him the good news.

41
CHAPTER

Hooley sat in his truck, thinking, brooding, reminiscing, regretting . . . Hours had passed as he waited for one Charles Biggerstaff Sr. to return to his home. A stakeout gave a man a lot of time to think. He missed his ex-wife sometimes. Years ago, she used to greet him at the door, no matter how late. She'd get out of bed and make him dinner, or breakfast—whatever the hour called for. That was long ago.

He had busted some real bad ones over the years. Survived a few gunfights. His career was a distinguished one. But now he was staring an imminent retirement in the face. How was he going to get by on his pension? The divorce had decimated his savings. Gasoline prices were going up every day, and that drove the price of everything else up. He'd have to hire out as a private detective, he guessed.

He was listening to the radio, fighting off sleep. KIKK, "kick" radio. Pretty good country station. They played some of the good old stuff. Earlier tonight, sitting here in his truck down the street from Biggerstaff's mansion, he had heard a tribute to Luster Burnett. The deejay had said Luster was performing again, and was opening tonight at some stadium for Dixie what's-her-name, the country bombshell. Hooley briefly considered abandoning his stakeout and going to the concert. Now he regretted not doing it, for it was almost midnight and Biggerstaff had not returned home.

Hooley had arrived in the afternoon, walked up the door of the Biggerstaff home, and rung the doorbell. Mrs. Biggerstaff wouldn't let him in. Her husband had given her strict instructions not to talk to anyone. Where was Mr. Biggerstaff? Golfing. Which golf course? She had slammed the door in his face.

So now he was waiting, wondering if he had been spotted staking the place out, feeling all the boredom and loneliness and uselessness of his chosen career eat away at him inside. *To hell with it.* He reached for the key in the ignition. Somewhere in the neighborhood, he heard the acceleration of a big block engine. Hooley took his hand off the key. Headlights swooped around a corner, and a bronze Cadillac Coupe de Ville followed them into Biggerstaff's driveway, like a boat sailing into harbor.

Hooley was already out of his truck and trotting toward the Cadillac. Biggerstaff had popped the trunk open from inside. He stepped out, walked aft, and muscled his golf clubs out of the open boot. Sensing Hooley's approach, he looked over his shoulder, a sudden fear registering on his face.

Hooley had his badge out. "I'm a Texas Ranger. Hooley Johnson."

"Jesus! You scared the hell out of me!"

"Little nervous, Mr. Biggerstaff?"

"People don't lurk in the dark in this neighborhood." He slammed his trunk lid. "Now, you'll have to excuse me, it's late."

"Hold on. I came a long way to talk to you."

"My lawyer has instructed me not to talk to anybody," he said over his shoulder.

"This is off the record."

"Doesn't matter." He was lifting the garage door.

"You don't have one of those automatic openers? Fancy house like this?"

"The battery in my clicker went dead," he said, defensively.

"Dang, that's rough. About this lawyer of yours. Where can I have a word with him?"

"I'm not at liberty to say." Biggerstaff pushed the garage door up over his head.

"You can't even say who your own lawyer is?"

"He's not my lawyer. He's my insurance company's lawyer." Biggerstaff slammed the heavy golf bag into the corner of the garage and started pulling the garage door down, with himself inside, and Hooley outside.

Hooley caught the door and held it open. "Wait. Listen to me. They told you not to talk, but did they tell you that you weren't allowed to listen?"

Biggerstaff looked Hooley in the eye. He looked scared. "No. I guess they didn't tell me I couldn't listen."

"I'm going to reach into my shirt pocket for my card." He did so, Biggerstaff's eyes following his every move. He handed the card to Biggerstaff. "Don't lose that. You're gonna need it. Sooner or later, this thing is gonna blow up in your face, and you're gonna find yourself in a whole lot of trouble—with the law, or something worse. You know what I mean by something worse, don't you?"

Biggerstaff nodded, reluctantly.

"When that kind of trouble comes, who do you want on your side? The Texas Rangers, right? *Right?*"

"All right!"

"You sleep on it, Mr. Biggerstaff. If you can. Keep your doors and windows locked. Have your lawyer call me. Better yet, call me yourself, and I'll tell you what you're up against. Oh, and Mr. Biggerstaff . . ."

"Yeah?"

"Try to call me before you or somebody in your family ends up *dead*." He took his hand away from the garage door and took a step back.

Biggerstaff rolled the door downward, slamming it with a metallic crash that made the neighbor's poodle bark.

CHAPTER

Franco finally got free of the concert crowd and the resulting traffic jam and found a pay phone outside a supermarket. He happened to look up at the name of the store as he stepped into the phone booth.

"Piggly Wiggly? Are you kidding me?" he muttered.

He called Papa Martini.

"Who's this?" his father said, gruffly.

"Hey, Pop, it's me. What are you doing?"

"Pouring my third nightcap. Where the hell have you been?"

"I went to a country music concert in Houston."

"What, three weeks in Texas and you've turned into a friggin' redneck?"

Franco chuckled. "You've heard this young country singer, Dixie Houston, right?"

"I don't listen to that crap. You know that."

"But you've seen her on TV. Tits and ass and country twang. I know you've seen her."

"Yeah, maybe. So what?"

"She was good, that's all. The crowd loved her. And there was an old-timer who opened the show. I met the band."

The line was silent for a moment. *"Franco, the bug man came today. We're clean."*

Franco knew that the "bug man" was the family expert who regularly swept the Martini mansion and phone lines for surveillance devices. "You're sure."

"Dead sure. Where are you calling from?"

"A phone booth in Houston."

"That's my boy. Now, what the hell's going on?"

"I've been chasing down this lead the last couple of days. I didn't want to bother you about it until I knew it was the real deal. The guy driving the boat that night—the night Rosa bought it—I'm ninety-nine percent sure that he's a musician named Charles Biggerstaff Jr. He plays in a band with this old-timer trying to make a comeback in country music. That's the band I met tonight. I got a look at the guy."

"You looked at the guy who drove the boat?"

"Ninety-nine percent sure."

"Not good enough."

"Pop, I'll beat it out of him until I'm a hundred percent sure before I whack him."

"Okay, that's better. How are you gonna kidnap him?"

"I don't know yet. He's with this band all the time. I'll have to catch him alone somewhere."

"Who's the old timer making the comeback? The band leader?"

"Luster Burnett."

Papa was quiet for several seconds.

"Pop?"

Franco heard his father break into a wheezing fit of laughter that culminated in a coughing fit.

"Jesus, Pop. The smokes. You gotta cut back."

"Luster freakin' Burnett! Why didn't you say so?"

"Pop? What?"

"Come on home, Franco. We'll handle this from here now."

"But Pop, I found the guy. Ninety-nine percent sure."

"I said come home. I'll explain when you get here. We're gonna lure the rat right into the rat trap!"

Creed felt the bus shift and looked toward the open door to find Dixie's bodyguard stepping aboard. The guard looked past him, to Luster.

"Miss Houston extends an invitation for you to join the party on her bus."

"The whole band, or just Luster?" Kathy said, suspiciously.

"There's not enough room for the whole band." He looked at Creed. "She said you could come, too."

Luster got up. "Come on, Creed. Let's be neighborly."

"Don't go," Kathy whispered as the bodyguard shuffled off the bus and Luster walked forward.

Creed got up to follow Luster off the bus. "This is business. She's trying to steal my song, and she needs to know that I'm on to her."

Kathy got up, followed him off the bus, held him back as Luster walked toward Dixie's Prevost with the bodyguard.

"Let her have the damn song. You've got new stuff coming out now. A whole new live album."

"I can't let her have it. It's my property. If I don't fight it, she'll claim everything I ever wrote back during the Dixie Creed days. I'll end up like Luster, unable to record my own songs."

Kathy pouted and crossed her arms, guarding her heart. "You're sure that's all it is?"

"Are you kidding? After the way she treated me onstage? Besides, I better keep an eye on our legend."

"I don't like it, Creed. I wish I had never booked this gig."

He touched her, gently but firmly, cupping his palm around her arm. "When the album comes out, we'll forget Dixie was ever even here at this gig. Don't worry."

She sighed. "Be careful. She's a conniving, manipulative . . ." Kathy made a *b* with her lips, but stopped short of saying the word.

"I gotta catch up before they shut the door on our future." Creed winked at her and trotted away toward Dixie's bus slipping in just before the hydraulic door closed.

Inside, he smelled weed. Climbing up the steps, he saw one of Dixie's band members offering Luster a joint. Luster raised his hands, as if in a holdup. Dixie's guitar player—some Nashville cat Creed didn't know— slapped him on the back.

"You son-of-bitch!" the picker said, a smile on his face. "I hate your guts."

"Backatcha," Creed replied. "Hey, man, thanks for letting me plug into your rig. Those Twins were smokin'."

"Any time. You want a drink or something?" He stepped aside to reveal the bar that Dixie had obviously had custom-built into her bus.

Creed shrugged, poured himself a shot of Jack Daniel's. He looked aft to see that Dixie had showered and changed out of her show clothes into jeans and a white cotton button-down shirt, her hair wrapped up in a towel. She looked like the small-town girl Creed had once fallen in love with. She was holding Luster's hand, looking into his eyes and telling him God-knows-what-all. Creed ground his teeth. What if Kathy was right? What if Dixie was offering Luster a slot on her tour right now?

As if she sensed his bad vibes, Dixie looked Creed's way, caught his eye, smiled, and waved him over. He resented being summoned, but condescended to join the conversation with Luster and Dixie.

"Welcome to my custom Prevost bus, hotshot!" she began. "A hundred and five inches wide!"

Creed knew Dixie was competitive, but he never thought she'd throw a bus width in his face. This was the kind of thing touring acts talked about when trying to one-up one another. "Yeah, it's state of the art, Dixie."

"Better than that old ninety-six-incher you're making Luster ride in."

"Well, it ain't too wide," Luster said, "but at least it's short."

Dixie snorted a laugh. "Anyway, Creed, honey, I want to thank you for bringing this wonderful man into my life. Luster has been telling me that *you* are the genius behind his comeback. He says you've made it all happen for him."

"I don't know about that. It's a comeback for me, too, and I couldn't do it without Luster."

Dixie smiled, her eyes twinkling. "Well now, aren't you two just the cutest thing in the world with your little mutual-admiration society?"

"Never thought of us as cute," Luster admitted.

"Well, I want to help, too. I have some ideas for the three of us, and we need to get together tomorrow, when we're all sober, and work this thing out. It could be the biggest thing ever to hit country music. Shit, not just country. Outlaw-slash-crossover-slash-rockabilly-slash-progressive-country-slash-rock-and-frickin'-roll!"

"Slash science-fiction-bluegrass!" Luster said, mocking her.

"What, no coon-ass gospel?" Creed monotoned.

"You two are so funny. You're going to be a hoot to tour with."

One of the band members broke in to shake Luster's hand just then, and to ask for an autograph. With Luster thus distracted, Creed turned to Dixie.

"You made me look like fool onstage tonight."

"I beg your pardon?" she said, in a defensive tone.

"You know what I'm talkin' about. And what's this about you writing 'Written in the Dust'?"

She scoffed. "I never said that!"

"Yes, you did. Onstage."

"Well, if I did, it was a slip of the tongue. It's not like I don't have anything else to think about up there."

"I was the sole writer on all our Dixie-Creed stuff. You do remember that, right?"

"Shut up, Creed!" She pushed him playfully against the chest, but he was too solid to budge much. "Anyway, I let you on my stage, you ungrateful piece of shit! Who could ask for more than that?"

Someone in the band shouted from the front of the bus: "Hey, Dixie! We're waiting on you, baby!"

She turned to scream toward the band: "Dixie-baby's comin', boys!" She turned back to her guests, Luster having finished signing his autograph. "I'll see you two gentlemen tomorrow."

She skipped forward toward the waiting band members, one of whom handed her a rolled up hundred-dollar bill. With obvious familiarity, the drummer was chopping lines of white powder on a mirror taken from the wall and placed flat on the top of the bar.

"Is that what I think it is?" Luster said.

"What do you think it is?"

"Well, they ain't chalkin' up a turkey call. Let's get off this bus, Hoss."

"I'm with you, Boss."

Outside, in air as fresh as Houston could offer, Creed strolled with Luster back toward their own humble little tour bus.

"She don't waste time cuttin' deals, does she?"

Luster chuckled, put his hand on Creed's shoulder. "Hoss, that back yonder is everything I hate about the music business. I ain't even talkin' about the cocaine. I'm talkin' about the bullshit. Do you know how many times I've heard that speech about the biggest thing to hit country music since Jesus Christ learned to tune a fiddle? Makes me want to puke. We're gonna do this thing our own way, and we don't need no Dixie Houston to do it."

Creed felt a smile spread across his face. "I'm proud to hear you say that, Boss."

"All right. Now," he said, shifting gears, "has Kathy collected our pay?"

"Yeah, it's on the bus. Cash."

"Good, because I got us into a poker game tonight over in Sugar Land."

"How'd you do that?"

"I called Gordy. He gave me a number to call."

"Apparently he doesn't mind us shootin' up somebody else's game."

"I guess not. With any luck, we can parley the chump change from this piss-ant gig into some real road money. You in?"

"Like Flinn."

CHAPTER

Once Dixie's fleet of buses and semis faded from the rearview mirror, Creed began to enjoy the drive back from the Houston gig. In fact, it felt quite glorious, and he seemed to share the euphoria with the rest of the group. Each band member had a few thousand dollars in his or her pocket. The live album was in the can. The Dixie Houston nonsense had been forgotten. On top of all that, Creed had almost doubled his gig earnings at the Sugar Land poker game, and Luster had done even better. Even the bus was purring like a mountain lion today.

Creed figured he'd better enjoy the high morale while it lasted, considering the band didn't have another gig lined up. They had gotten a late start Sunday afternoon, as Creed and Luster hadn't returned to the bus until almost dawn. After a few hours of sleep, Creed was ready to drive, and they motored west on Interstate 10, past green pastures and highway medians choked with colorful wildflowers of blue, red, and yellow.

Kathy had bought a good Canon camera with her cut of the pay. Sid had given her a ride to The Galleria Mall to purchase it. Since there was no hurry getting back to Luster's ranch, Kathy had Creed pull the bus over at every likely photo op for album cover and publicity shots, including a junkyard, a field of wild flowers, a funky barbecue joint, a graveyard, an old bridge over the Brazos River, a biker bar parking lot full of Harleys. Lindsay insisted on changing clothes for every shoot.

When Trusty complained about waiting on her, she said, "What if we use one shot for the album, and another for the poster? I don't want folks thinking I just have one outfit! Kathy, hon, can I borrow your top?"

Late in the day, the mountain lion of a bus quit purring and started gasping near Bastrop. Creed managed to limp on in to a place called the Lost Pines Motel, where the band members rented individual rooms for a bit of overdue privacy. No one seemed too upset about the transportation breakdown. Creed diagnosed the problem as a fuel filter issue. He called Junior, at the bus yard.

"You didn't put a new filter on it?" Junior asked.

"I know," Creed lamented. "I don't know how the hell that slipped my mind."

"Good Lord, that filter's probably got crap in it from 'sixty-one. No wonder it clogged up on you."

"Do you have one in stock?"

"Yeah, hell, I'll drive one out there to you after work tonight."

Sid, who had been following along in his government-issue I.R.S. car, had to get back to Austin so he could get to work hassling delinquent taxpayers Monday morning, but made a beer run with Luster and Creed before he left the band stranded.

As Creed slid into the backseat of the sedan, Sid turned to look at him from behind the wheel. "This trip is off-the-record, understood?" He shot the same warning glare at Luster, who sat in the front passenger seat.

"What?" Luster replied. "Uncle Sugar doesn't allow the company car to haul beer for the taxpayer?"

"Who's Uncle Sugar?"

"He means Uncle Sam," Creed explained. "Don't worry. Your bootleggin' career will be our little secret."

Sid put the car in gear and pulled out onto the highway, heading for the edge of town where they were sure to find a store that carried cheap beer.

"You don't think we'd inform the feds on one of our own band members, do you?" Luster asked.

"Band member? Me?" Sid glanced nervously in his rearview mirrors, as if his I.R.S. supervisor might be tailing him or something.

"Yes, you. You sounded great on that song you sang last night. Like a real pro."

"Don't blow smoke up the taxman's ass, Luster. I'm no idiot. I know you guys didn't have my voice piped out to the audience."

"Huh?" Luster said, innocently.

"What gave you that impression?" Creed asked.

"The crowd liked it way too much. I've watched people watch me sing before. Nobody's ever liked me that much."

"Well, who do you think they were listening to?" Luster said.

"The guy in the backseat," Sid said, jutting his thumb aft. "You didn't think I'd notice that the lead guitar player left the stage during my one song?"

Creed and Luster remained silent, wondering where Sid was taking this issue.

Sid started laughing. "Relax, guys. I loved it. I wouldn't trade that moment on the big stage for anything. They thought it was me. The crowd thought that was my voice! Man, that was a rush!"

"You sold it," Luster said. "Where'd you come by that stage presence?"

"Cut the bullshit," Sid groaned. "Don't worry, I'm not going to make you guys fake it again. Somebody might catch on. As it is, I can claim, for the rest of my life, that I sang onstage with Luster Burnett!"

Luster pretended to scratch the back of his head so that he could flash an emphatic "okay" sign to Creed in the backseat. "You got a point, Sid. Hey, look, there's a neon Budweiser sign in that store window!"

After unloading the cases of beer at the Lost Pines Motel, Creed waved good-bye to Sid Larue as he motored off toward Austin. He was relieved to see Sid leave. Creed had suspected that Kathy might hitch a ride back to Austin with Sid. He was inwardly elated when she didn't. Even though she was off limits, he wanted her around tonight. Was that wrong? Today, he didn't know or care if it was right or wrong. He just felt something special when she was near, and didn't want that feeling to drive off with Sid.

Junior arrived after dark with the fuel filter and some tools Creed would need. He also made a heroic pizza run for the euphorically drunk band. Because Trusty Joe's room was closest to the parking lot, they had carried the beer there and iced it down in the bathtub, all but emptying the motel ice machine. There were cases and cases of beer—Schlitz, Old Milwaukee, Falstaff, Lone Star, Texas Pride, Shiner, Pearl, and Miller High Life. Every fifteen minutes or so, Trusty Joe, like a good host, would take the tiny ice bucket down to the motel ice machine and bring back another scoop to keep the brew properly cooled.

In Trusty's room, Creed kicked his boots off and sat on the bed, his legs outstretched, his back against the wall. There, he amused himself by watching and listening to the band members as they bolted pizza, guzzled beer, and talked about the Houston gig.

After a couple of brews, Junior got up to drive back to Austin. Again, Creed was almost giddy when Kathy didn't ask for a ride back to the city, though he knew she was anxious to get back to work on band business tomorrow.

After Junior left, Trusty Joe came weaving in with another bucket of ice and, as he dumped it in the bathtub, he began to sob. The other band members looked at one another, smirking. Trusty's frequent breakdowns had long since ceased to concern or even bother them. The trait had, in fact, become almost endearing.

Lindsay smashed a half-smoked Virginia Slim cigarette in the ashtray. "Trusty Joe, honey, what is it now?"

"It's melting!" the fiddler blurted.

"This ain't Alaska," Tump growled.

"Hey, I'll get the ice from now on, man." Metro sprang to his feet to take the bucket from his bandmate's hand. "You need to relax. You got too much stretch."

"Stress," Tump corrected.

Metro shrugged.

"No, you don't understand," Trusty Joe blubbered. "It's a metaphor. I don't want this to ever end!" Huge sobs came from his shuttering chest.

"Oh, that is so sweet." Lindsay rose to give Trusty a hug, her arms outstretched as she approached him.

But Trusty's sobbing suddenly turned to gagging and he slammed the bathroom door, which failed to fully hide the hideous sounds of his pizza-and-beer retching from within.

"Why is it every time I go to likin' him, he goes to pukin'?" Lindsay asked, her arms still open for the undelivered hug.

Luster got up and hollered through the bathroom door. "Be careful of the beer!"

Creed rose from the bed, sensing an end to the party. "I've got to get up early and fix the bus," he muttered. To his astonishment, Kathy sprang to her feet with him.

"I was hoping we'd shove off early," she said. "I've got so much work to do. Good night, everybody!"

"*Turn out the lights, the party's over,*" Tump sang in a baritone growl.

Luster shot an accusing glare at him. "I thought you said you couldn't sing and you could prove it!"

"I just did."

"The hell you say, that sounded pretty good. Didn't you think so, Lindsay?"

Lindsay put her finger to her chin thoughtfully. "It sounded like Johnny Cash making fun of Kris Kristofferson."

"We're gonna give you a microphone from now on," Luster promised. "Everybody likes Kristofferson and Cash."

"Cash never hurt my feelings," Tump agreed.

Creed shook his head as he stepped out of the room, followed closely by Kathy. They turned down the outdoor walkway toward their respective rooms, which were only a few doors apart. In any other situation, Creed would have reached for her hand by now, or wrapped his arm around her shoulders. Awkward. He saw her trying to warm her bare arms with her own palms.

"I wish I had a jacket to offer you," he said.

She shrugged. "We're almost to my room." She took her key from her pocket.

They were strolling very slowly. Creed took in a deep breath. "The smell of pines here reminds me of home."

"Aromas are powerful memory makers," she purred. "Did you know I grew up in the country?"

"No, I didn't. Where 'bouts?"

"Far from the pines," she said. "Outside of Seguin. Flatland farm country. When I moved to the city, I never realized how much I missed that upbringing, until one day, driving out near Cedar Park, I smelled a skunk that someone had hit with a car. A skunk! Of all the aromas to take me back, I never would have dreamed a skunk would do it, but the memories of the country came flooding back to me with that odor. I missed my childhood home so much at that moment that I had to pull over and weep like Trusty Joe Crooke."

Creed threw his head back and chuckled from his belly. "You didn't throw up, too, did you?"

She flashed him a smile. "Just a short cry."

They stopped in front of her door. Neither spoke for a moment. Creed looked at her face in the pale, fluorescent glow from a parking lot security light. Her eyelashes rose like stage curtains and her gaze met his. She was astonishingly desirable.

"I'm kind of like Trusty right now, myself. I don't want this to ever end. But, in a way . . ."

"You do want it to end?"

"No. Not at all, but . . ."

"What?"

"At moments like this—just you and me—it's frustrating."

Bashfully, she lowered her gaze to the concrete walk. "I know. I don't want you to think I'm that kind of girl, but I would have invited you in already. I mean, if things were different. If we didn't work together."

"Hell of a sacrifice to make for a damned ol' band, huh?"

She smiled. "I don't want to be the one to mess this up, and I know you don't, either. Let's just do our jobs, and see what happens."

He held his hand out to her, more as if to propose to her than to shake. She switched her room key from right to left and took his hand.

"Good night, Miss Music."

"Good night, Creed," she sighed.

He couldn't help bowing to kiss the back of her hand, then he turned quickly away and walked to his own room where he would lie awake for some time, wondering if he should go back and knock on her door, or call her room, or . . . No, he had left it—whatever it was—in its proper place.

44
CHAPTER

The next morning, up under the back of the bus, tightening down the fuel filter housing with a ratchet wrench, Creed heard footsteps and voices approaching the bus. He soon made out the familiar voices of Tump and Lindsay.

"So," Tump was saying. "What are you doing tonight?"

"I have plans."

Creed heard them loading their bags into the open luggage compartment near the back of the bus.

"I was hoping we could have a repeat performance of last night."

"That will never happen again, Tump. You caught me at a weak moment."

"There's a saying where I come from: *Once you go black, you'll never go back.*"

She laughed. "There's a saying where I come from, too: *If you ever go white, it's just overnight.*"

Suddenly, Creed's frustration overwhelmed him, and he came scrambling out from under the bus, oil and gravel all over him, the ratchet wrench still in his fist. He found Lindsay and Tump quite shocked to see him.

"Now listen here!" he lectured, as he rose to his feet. "I'm making sacrifices for this band. Big sacrifices. You two are not allowed to mess this up if I'm not!"

"Easy now, Creed, honey, we were just two ships passing in the night."

"Yeah," Tump added. "You wouldn't even know about it if you hadn't been eavesdropping."

Creed shook the tool at Tump. "I was fixing the bus!" He threw the wrench down and stalked away to his room to shower and pack.

That afternoon, pulling up to the ranch house, the band members went their separate ways with their pay, with orders to meet back at Luster's ranch on Wednesday for rehearsals and more writing sessions. Trusty Joe went to the barn to visit Baldy. Kathy gave Creed a wave and left to get photos developed. After the long drive, Creed was ready for a beer, and accepted Luster's invitation to drink a few brews on the patio.

First, Luster had to check in with Virginia, taking two beers with him to her grave. Holding his hat in his hand over her headstone, apparently telling her all about the Houston show, he finished his beers, and carried the empties back to the house.

"I'll be right with you, Hoss, I'm gonna check the phone machine."

"All right, Boss." After the long and loud weekend, Creed reveled in the silence of the patio overlooking Onion Creek. He sat there, enjoying the feel of the cold beer pouring down his throat and into his stomach. He thought about his longing for Kathy, the power of the band on the big Houston stage, the gall of Dixie. The rush of Onion Creek seemed to shush all his worries. He felt pretty good, all things considered.

"Hoss," Luster said, sticking his head out of the house. "You better come listen to these messages. Bring me a beer from the icebox."

Creed entered Luster's den, saw him push the button on the Code-A-Phone device. He tossed the legend a beer. The static gave way to a beep, followed by the messages:

"Luster. Nigel. I've got the tapes at the studio. Smashing stuff, old man! I shall have this mixed and mastered by the end of the week. Cheerio!"

"Cool," Creed said.

"That's the good news. The next one's from Gordy. I recognize his voice."

The machine beeped again.

"I heard you won big in Sugar Land, you ol' rascal! Hey, there's somethin' fishy goin' on. Somebody bought your markers from me. So I called around. The same somebody's bought all your gambling debts from New Mexico to Louisiana. That somebody's name is Josh Gold. Sound familiar? I thought you should know, but you didn't hear it from me."

"What the hell?"

"It gets stranger," Luster warned.

Beep!

"You remember me, you son-of-a-bitch?" The accent was from one of

those New York boroughs, maybe Queens or Brooklyn. *"You shot me in the ass with a forty-five in 'fifty-seven!"* Rasping laughter. *"I heard you were making a comeback. I own a piece of The Castilian, the biggest casino in Las Vegas. I bought all your markers so I own you now. But I'll make you a deal, big shot. You and your band play two nights at The Castilian, and we'll call it even. Rooms and meals on me. National publicity. You can promote your new live album. You really don't have a choice. Be here Friday."*

A seed of sickness in the pit of Creed's stomach began to replace the good buzz from the weekend. "How'd he know about the live album?"

"Keep listening."

Beep!

"Luster, my hero. This is Dixie-Baby. You naughty boy! You are a sneaky one, you ol' fox!" She giggled drunkenly. *"You recorded an album through my mixer at the Houston concert. According to my silly ol' record company lawyers, that means I own the masters to the album. So . . ."*

There was an excruciatingly long pause, then Creed heard the sound of ice cubes tinkling in a glass of something. Dixie gulped and gasped.

". . . Oh, I'm sure we can work something out. But you have to bring your band to Vegas this weekend. I have a gig for you. Two nights at The Castilian. You'll be opening for me. My manager already called your agent. Pack your bags for Vegas, baby!"

As the message ended, Creed put his elbows on Luster's desktop and let his face fall into his palms. He thought he might puke like Trusty. "Dixie," he growled.

"Don't worry about her, Hoss. She's a lightweight compared to me. I can handle her."

"She's gonna try to steal you from your own band."

"You have my word of honor as a southern gentleman that I won't let that happen. Hey, this ain't a bad deal, Creed. I'm gonna clear my gambling debts. We're gonna announce the new album. The band is still on salary, so why would they care? We're gonna play Vegas, Hoss! So Dixie owns a chunk of the album. So what?"

"So she can name her own price."

"I'm a horse trader and a gambler from way back, stud. I'll tell her we can always just cut the album over again, at some other gig."

"Yeah, but there was some kind of powerful vibe in the air at that show. We were *on*, in a real raw kind of way."

"The power is with the band, Hoss, not the venue. We did it once. We can do it again. Anyway, I'm confident I can cut a deal with that little lush, Dixie."

"Don't underestimate her. She's a world-class manipulator."

"And I'm a world-class badass! You worry too much. Now, what we need is about five hundred sample copies of the new album for the press. I'll make a few calls, and the casino will be crawling with all kinds of hacks and critics. Newspaper, radio, TV."

"Whoa, Boss, how are we gonna get five hundred discs by Friday?"

"Hell, today's only Monday. We start by lighting a fire under Nigel's ass. Then we slap a picture of the band on the album cover and go to press."

Creed loved the way Luster could simplify almost any issue. "Where are you gonna press that many discs in four days?"

"I know a guy in Nashville who can press five hundred overnight, and another guy who will fly them to Vegas for us. I'll put Kathy on it. The little gal is a miracle worker."

Creed was rubbing his brow, mulling this thing over, when the phone rang. Luster picked it up.

"Hello," he said. He listened for a moment, then looked up at Creed. "It's Kathy. She's at Tomahawk." Luster pointed the receiver toward Creed. Across the room he could hear her shrill cheerleader voice, clearly enraptured:

"We're going to Vegas! We're going to Vegas!"

45
CHAPTER

The guard recognized Franco's Cobra and scurried to swing open the driveway gate to Papa Martini's high-walled Las Vegas estate. He ignored the guard's nervous welcoming gesture and parked in the shade of a palm tree. Stepping out, he breathed in the dry desert air, a welcome contrast to the humidity of Texas.

He had driven home Sunday through Tuesday, slept in till almost noon this morning. It was Wednesday afternoon now, and he had been summoned to Papa's house for a meeting. Damn, it was good to be home! He felt great walking through the familiar entryway, down the hall to Papa's office.

Stepping in, he saw Papa with a drink in his hand, and a cigarette hanging from his lips, listening to some bullshit story by that blowhard, Josh Gold—everybody called him "Goldie."

"Pop!" he said, interrupting the story. "The smokes! Jesus! What did your doctor tell you?"

"Franco!" Papa set the drink down to bear hug his son. "You look like shit!"

"I've been in Texas—chicken-fried hell."

Goldie laughed like the buffoon that he was. "Texas, *sheesh*! That place was almost the death of me, boy, I tell you!"

Franco looked disdainfully at his father's old flunky. He never understood why his father liked the two-bit collector so much. Franco made it his business to know everyone's background in the inner circle. Back in his youth, Joshua Goldstein had been one of those Jewish brawlers from the Lower East Side—a tough thug with more ambition than brains. Not much on religion, Joshua Goldstein became Josh Gold and parted ways with the Jewish mob, throwing his allegiance over to La Cosa Nostra, where he soon became known as "Goldie."

One of his first assignments was to organize a protection racket in Dallas that came to a humiliating end when some redneck Texas club owner shot him up in a parking lot gunfight. Goldie had been reassigned to Vegas, where he had proven useful over the years as a closely supervised collector. Papa seemed to find Goldie's loud mouth highly entertaining, but it always grated on Franco, as did the fact that Goldie seemed to have no fear of him.

"Son, you want a whiskey?"

"Sure, Pop."

Papa snapped his fingers at Goldie, who hopped over to the bar and poured one on the rocks, delivering it dutifully to Franco. They all sat down in plush leather chairs facing one another.

"Franco, you're looking at the new front man for The Castilian," Papa said, gesturing toward the proud Josh Gold.

"You're shittin' me."

Goldie laughed.

"You've heard the story of Goldie in Dallas. How some club owner shot the hell out of him for trying to sell protection."

"Yeah," Franco said, sipping the bourbon. "That looks real good on the ol' résumé, huh Goldie?"

"Well," Papa continued, "the guy who shot him was none other than Luster Burnett."

Franco swallowed a gulp of fine bourbon. He took in the information, and began to nod. Now he understood why Papa had elevated Josh to the status of front man for The Castilian. "Now I get it. I knew there had to be a reason."

"Here's the deal," Papa said, his voice switching to his no-bullshit business mode. "I gave Goldie enough dough to buy up Burnett's gambling markers. Now Goldie has leverage. Better still, that country singer, Dixie Tits-and-Ass called the number you gave her. You were right about her. She's got pull on Burnett."

"Dixie called?"

Papa smirked at Franco. "Yeah, while you were driving home. What, you got a hard-on for the hick chick?"

Franco shrugged. "Some of that might be fun for the weekend, you know? So, the plan is to get Dixie to get Burnett to The Castilian, so we can deal with our problem?"

"It's already done. We just got the signed contracts from the agents on the fax machine. Both bands will be here day after tomorrow. Burnett's playing Friday and Saturday, opening for Dixie T-and-A. Friday, everything looks normal, so the band relaxes, everybody has a good time."

"I'm gonna bury the hatchet with Luster," Goldie said. "We're gonna become best pals."

"What happens Saturday?" Franco asked, ignoring Goldie.

"After the show on Saturday, Goldie takes the guy with the stupid stage name for a ride to the ranch for a horticulture lesson."

"Whore to what?" Goldie said.

"Tree planting, you imbecile. If anything goes wrong, Goldie has agreed to take the fall. But, hey, what could go wrong? These pukes are musicians. They don't have a clue."

"I'll handle the plans," Franco said, "and I want it planned out to the split second. You answer to me, Goldie, and if you don't, *you'll* be root fertilizer, *capice*?"

"Sure," Goldie said. "Ain't I always a good soldier?"

"This gives us a day to prepare," Franco said, getting to his feet, excited about the prospect of putting the entire Rosa problem to rest for good. "On Friday, we'll figure out what makes this Biggerstaff punk tick. Girls, gambling, drugs, fags . . . whatever. We'll find the right bait to lure the son-of-a-bitch in on Saturday."

"I'm on it," Goldie blurted.

Franco downed the rest of his whiskey. "Let's get down to The Castilian to look things over. Goldie, you're driving. We'll take the limo."

"You got it, boss."

As Goldie marched out of the office and turned toward the garage, Papa Martini abruptly doubled over in a fit of coughing.

"Jesus, Pop, if you want to live to see us clean this mess up, you've got to cut back on the coffin nails!"

Papa nodded his agreement as he reached for his smokes.

An Associated Press entertainment writer had been following Dixie Houston on tour, and had written a piece about Luster's comeback. It came out in the Sunday edition of newspapers all over the country, particularly in cities across the South, and as far west as the *Austin American-Statesman*.

In the article, the writer made the assumption that Luster had intentionally acquired an antique bus to make a statement:

"... *even the 1961 Silver Eagle bus that transports Luster Burnett and
The Pounders to their shows speaks to their mission of taking country-
western music back to a more honest and humble time when the songs were
written and performed by men and women who had actually pushed a plow
or busted a bronc.*"

"I like that," Luster said to Creed over coffee, pointing out the photo of
the old bus in the paper. "That bus is part of our image now. We've got to
drive that thing to Vegas." He looked at Creed as he tossed the newspaper
aside on the kitchen counter. "Do you think it will make it?"

"I'll make it make it," Creed promised.

So now, two days later, motoring through El Paso on Interstate 10, Luster asked Creed to turn south on U.S. 85.

"Get on Stanton Street and we can cross the river into Ciudad Juarez.
There's a good restaurant over there called El Herradero de Soto. And this
way, we can claim we're international."

"You want me to *drive* across?"

"Sure, I do it all the time."

"In a bus?"

"It's only ninety-six inches wide!"

"Where are we gonna park?"

"At the motel where I always stay. They know me there."

"What brings you to Juarez on such a regular basis, Boss?" Creed shot
a knowing glance at Luster.

"Poker."

"That's what I thought." Creed looked into the mirror aimed back at the
bus interior. "Anybody got any contraband in here?" he shouted. "They're
liable to search us coming back into the States."

"Metro and I smoked the last of ours in Austin," Tump said.

"Where is Metro?" Luster demanded.

"Asleep in his bunk. Don't worry about him. He's clean as a fifth grader."

"These days you don't even know about the fifth graders," Luster complained. "Exit here, Hoss, and that'll take us to the Stanton Street Bridge."

Creed motored across the Rio Grande and followed Luster's directions
down the narrow streets to the parking lot of the motel where he said he
liked to stay.

Tump woke Metro.

"Where are we?" the drummer said, rubbing his eyes as he stepped off the bus.

"Ciudad Juarez," Luster announced, coming back from the motel office with permission to park there.

"*Chingado!*" Metro hissed. "Nobody told me we were going to Mexico! I'm wanted in Mexico, man!"

"For what?" Creed demanded.

"You don't want to know, dude. Anyway, how am I supposed to get back across the border? I don't have a U.S. ID!"

"Wait a minute," Creed said. "The day we hired you, I asked you if you were a citizen."

"I *am* a citizen. Of *Mexico!*"

"Oh, great," Kathy said.

Tump began to laugh. "Y'all figure this one out. I'm going to get a beer at The Kentucky Bar." He sauntered toward a line of taxis waiting at the edge of Chamizal Park.

"Good idea. Maybe we can drink you legal, son." Luster followed Tump up the dirty street, past stores painted in sundry pastel shades. "A tough problem is always easier to solve after a couple of cold ones."

Two hours later, after beers and steaks, the band decided to hide Metro in his own kick drum case in the luggage compartment in the belly of the bus. He could just curl up inside it. They took the drum itself aboard the bus and hid it in one of the bunks under some pillows and blankets.

Luckily, the ranking Border Patrol guard at the bridge turned out to be a Luster Burnett fan, and called off a search of the bus in exchange for an autograph. A few miles outside of El Paso, Creed pulled over at a Stuckey's where they could sneak Metro out of the drum case, out of sight in a corner of the parking lot. Metro cussed them all up and down, but none of them minded much, since they didn't understand most of the Spanish cuss words anyway.

Back on the road, Creed and Trusty Joe took turns driving, while the rest of the guys in the band drank beer and napped. Kathy and Lindsay spent some quality girl time together, becoming quite chummy. Creed worried about Tump, who had acquired a bottle of whiskey somewhere. He hadn't seen the bass player stay this intoxicated this long since the band formed. On the other hand, he stopped worrying over Trusty Joe, who seemed to have found some peace, as if he had come to an epiphany of some kind. No more sobbing or vomiting. His voice sounded calm, and he proved a good hand behind the wheel of the bus. Maybe he had learned to think of himself astraddle of ol' Baldy when his nerves got rattled.

The old bus drank a lot of diesel fuel, and the band fund quickly diminished. Still, it looked as if they might have just enough cash to get to Vegas. Most of the musicians had long since spent their Houston wages on past-due bills, drinking binges, loans to other broke musicians, pawnshop settlements, overdue car repairs, drum sticks and guitar strings. Now that Metro's nationality had been established, he bragged that he had sent almost all his money to his family in Mexico. Trusty Joe lamented that he had had to send most of his to his divorce lawyer.

Then, while driving north on I-25, Creed felt an odd shudder in the bus. Instinctively, he eased his foot off the accelerator. His eye caught movement in the passing lane to his left. He looked and saw his own wheel roll past him, and knew that wasn't good. The wheel, rubber tire and all, sailed across the median into the oncoming lane, where luckily no vehicle traveled to meet it head-on.

"What was that?" Kathy said.

"Part of our bus," he admitted. He noticed a mile marker on the right. "Remember mile one ninety-seven. We'll come back and find that wheel. The tire is still good."

Since the Silver Eagle was still pushing up a slight incline, he reasoned that the wheel had flown off the tag axle instead of the drive axle. "I guess I should have repacked those bearings," he muttered.

He limped along for several miles, then saw a truck stop up ahead with a repair shop. He coasted into the parking lot and found a mechanic named Gus.

"You're gonna need a new tag axle," Gus said, staring at the missing wheel. "Lucky for you, I know where one is."

"Where's that?"

"My brother-in-law's junkyard, up the road. There's an old Model Oh-One been there for years."

"How old?"

"Old. But not ancient, like this one. I can fix it in about four hours. Cost you about two hundred dollars."

"I'm not sure we have two hundred. What if I help you?" Creed offered.

"Then it'll cost three hundred. I like to work alone."

Creed kept after the mechanic, reciting his mechanic's credentials as if applying for a job, and explaining that the bus belonged to his band, and they had to get to Vegas for a big show.

"Band?" Gus said. "Country?"

"Damn straight. Luster Burnett."

"Thought he was dead."

"No, he's making a comeback. That's him over there in the phone booth." Creed pointed, wondering to whom Luster was speaking.

Gus squinted through the bright desert sunlight as he wiped grimy hands on his overalls. "Be damned. Reckon he'll sign me an autograph?"

"I guarantee he will. You come to the show in Vegas and he'll sign a copy of his new record and give you front-row seats."

"Vegas?"

"The Castilian. Biggest casino in town."

The mechanic mulled the deal over for a few seconds. "All right, then. Half price if you help."

"Let's get after it."

Luster strolled up then and Creed told him the deal he had worked out. The country legend shook the mechanic's greasy hand.

"I appreciate the special deal. Fuel prices are eatin' us up." He glanced up at the two-foot-tall digits advertising the price of diesel at the truck stop pumps. "Thirty-nine cents a gallon! Did you ever imagine diesel going that high?"

"Nope. I'll get the jacks." The mechanic ambled into the shop.

"Y'all reckon you'll be done by nine or so?" Luster asked.

"Yeah, probably," Creed answered. "Why?"

"I got us a gig tonight for some road money."

"Kind of short notice for a gig."

"Hoss, me and Bob Wills are still big stars out here in the wild west. We'll draw a crowd."

"How are you gonna get the word out in the next few hours?"

"There's an AM radio station in Albuquerque where I once did a live show. I already called them. I'm gonna stop in for an interview and they're gonna play my old records all afternoon long. They're even gonna play me on their FM sister station."

"Where's the gig?"

"A bar up in the Manzanos called The Blarney Stone." He gestured toward the mountains to the east. "I played there back in 'fifty-five. Or maybe it was 'fifty-seven. Anyway, I called them, too. We can play for the door and tips, plus grub and an unlimited bar tab."

Creed grinned. "They're gonna take a bath on the bar tab."

Luster chuckled. "Yeah. They got their own sound system, so we don't have to lug ours in."

"Great," Creed groaned, imagining some antiquated PA.

About then the mechanic came back out of the shop wheeling a heavy-duty hydraulic jack.

"You wouldn't have a loaner I could borrow, would you?" Luster asked.

Gus fished some keys out of his pocket. "You can take the shop truck," he pointed to a Ford pickup parked nearby.

While Creed helped position the first jack under the drive axle, Luster and the band moved the instruments from the bus to the pickup. On his back under the Silver Eagle, he smirked at the band members' prattle:

"You ride in back, kid," said Tump to Metro. "That way everything will look natural."

"*Besa mi cula,* Tump."

"Was that a racial stereotype?" Lindsay demanded. "It was, wasn't it?"

"I was just kiddin'," Tump said. "I'll ride in back."

"All us guys should ride in the back," Trusty Joe offered, "so the ladies can ride in the front seat with Luster."

"Shotgun!" Kathy sang.

"I gotta ride bitch?" Lindsay complained.

"I called shotgun!"

"What's so bad about ridin' next to me?" Luster demanded. "Come on, get in. It ain't that far, anyway."

Creed spent an hour helping Gus remove the tag axle from the Silver Eagle. Meanwhile, up the road, Gus's brother-in-law cannibalized the tag axle from the bus in his junkyard and hauled it to Gus's shop on a flatbed trailer. Gus's brother-in-law then drove Creed back to mile marker one ninety-seven to find the old wheel and retrieve it for the good tire. They repacked the wheel bearings on the replacement axle and muscled it into place under the bus with some shop dollies. With the new tag axle jacked and bolted in place, they reinstalled the wheels and let the bus down off the jacks about the time the crimson sun dipped down to smooch the desert skyline.

Creed shed his greasy T-shirt at the shop sink, and with a clean dipstick rag and some lava soap, scrubbed the black grease from his hands and face as best he could. He splashed some water in his armpits and around his neck, and scurried into the bus where he changed into some clean clothes. Then he opened a beer and headed for the venue in the mountains. Luster had left directions.

He was tired from the work on the bus, not to mention hours of driving prior to that. Now he was staring a four-hour gig in the face. Oh, well . . . He wanted to go on the road. He smiled wryly. Nobody could say he hadn't paid some dues.

CHAPTER

Creed found the Blarney Stone surrounded by pickups and motorcycles, ponderosa pine trees standing beyond the edge of the potholed gravel parking lot. The bar itself seemed to lean a little, but the old wood frame structure pulsed with life, laughter, shouts, and the bass line from the jukebox. Creed stepped out of the bus and smelled tobacco smoke and pine trees as he tucked his forty-five into the back of his pants.

As soon as he walked into The Blarney Stone, Kathy handed him a beer with a smile, and pointed to the stage. The band was waiting, waving him over. Creed waded through a rowdy crowd, stepped up onto the small stage, strapped on his guitar, and kicked the first song with the band. "Wow," he said, listening to the mix over the sound system. Somebody had spent some money on the PA. The whole bar rang like the inside of a vintage Martin guitar.

From the tiny stage, Creed enjoyed a vantage point from which to get a feel for the joint, which was already Saturday-packed though this was only Wednesday. If anything in the bar had ever been painted, it had long since worn off. With all the cigarette ashes being flicked around, Creed thought it was a miracle the tinder-dry ramshackle tavern had not yet burned down. The old wooden floors were so uneven that crushed beer cans had been shoved under the legs of the single pool table in an attempt to level it out. Here and there, an old car license plate had been nailed to the floor to cover a hole. Scrap lumber had been nailed over the glass windows, with the slots between the boards too narrow to let a fist or a bottle pass, though a few panes had been busted out, presumable with cue sticks. An old woodstove dropped burning coals into the box of sand in which it stood on all fours, for the mountain evening had grown quite cool.

It was one of those places where hundreds of people had nailed, stapled, tied, or otherwise affixed their cheap, gimme ball caps to the rafters to collect cobwebs and mounds of dust. Creed had always detested the practice. It was an insult to the carpenters who had crafted the rafters generations ago. The stuffed heads of deer, elk, and bighorn rams jutting from the walls sported an equal supply of allergens.

The bar patrons represented quite a smattering from the human gene pool. Creed smiled at an ancient Mexican man dancing with a little girl who must have been his great-granddaughter. There were loggers, mountain men, Navaho and Pueblo Indians, cowboys and cowgirls, businessmen in Polo shirts, bikers, a few frat boys with sorority girls hanging on them, two hippie dudes with their hippie chicks huddled fearfully in the corner, several crew cuts from Kirtland Air Force Base, a bunch of retirees wearing T-shirts from the Delaware Airstream Club, and some forest-fire fighters who had just that day put out a stubborn high-country blaze.

The situation had brawl written all over it.

In the middle of the third set, Creed saw the door open, and glanced to judge what form of humanity might be entering now. What the hell? He swore he recognized the guy from Bud's Place, not so long ago. At Bud's, the guy had had his arm in a sling, making Creed suspect him as the masked robber he had shot that night at the Manchaca poker game. There was no sling now, but the guy still carried his arm funny. The Blarney Stone was a long way from Bud's Place.

As Trusty Joe took his fiddle lead on "Dear John Note," Creed stepped up next to Luster and spoke in his ear.

"You remember that guy I shot at the poker game?"

Luster nodded.

"You remember the guy in the arm sling at Bud's?"

"Yeah. Why?"

"He just walked in."

Luster's glare shifted to the front door. "Oh, shit," he said. "Are you carrying?"

"I put my piece in my guitar case."

"I'd stand near that case if I was you."

"Roger that."

As the night went on, the place got rowdier. A couple of shoving matches erupted but were broken up. Creed witnessed something he had never seen from a stage before: two, simultaneous, unrelated hair-pullings, each caused by some jealous jerk suspecting his girl of flirting with some other guy. All the while, he kept his eye on the poker game robber who prowled The Blarney Stone as if seeking some vantage point from which to execute some nefarious deed. Peculiar. At Bud's the guy had constantly drilled Creed with a glare. Now, he seemed to spread his attention out to the other guys in the band, as well. That guy was up to something dastardly.

Finally, in the middle of the fourth set, the hard liquor in some cowboy's veins swelled beyond his small mind's ability to hold it. The cowboy in question poured a full pitcher of beer over a hippie's head in the corner. A skinny little hippie chick then broke a pool cue across the cowboy's jaw. Watching, as he played the lead break for "Chuck Will's Widow," Creed caught himself thinking that the hippie chick must have played softball in school, because she took a grand slam swing at the redneck, laying him out cold.

What happened next, Creed had witnessed a few times before from el-evated stages. It was quite the study in physics. Every action has an equal, opposite reaction. The cowboy whom the hippie chick struck with the pool cue fell over onto a biker who stumbled into a frat boy who turned and shoved back at the biker who then punched the frat boy who then fell back into a fireman who bumped into an airman who turned and shoved back, and so on, until a pitcher of beer poured on a hippie's head had spread across the tavern like ripples from a rock tossed into the corner of a pool of nitroglycerin.

"Just keep playing!" Luster shouted. "Trusty, take another lead!" Then, as two brawlers stumbled toward Lindsay's pedal steel, he stepped in the way to shove the two head-locked goons aside with his boot before they barreled into Lindsay.

"Thank you, LusTAIR, honey."

"That's my job, LindSAY!" As he continued to strum the rhythm, he eased over toward Creed, a wry grin on his face, as if having the time of his life. "Where's that guy from Bud's?"

Creed pointed with his chin. "Over there getting the shit beat out of him by some logger." As he watched, he saw the one-armed poker game robber reach under his shirt for what looked like a pistol butt. About the same time, the fight began to spill uncontrollably onto the stage. "Uh-oh," he said.

Against Luster's order, Creed quit playing and scrambled to his guitar case for his automatic. He flipped the safety off and sent a bullet through several dusty gimme caps, and into the rafters. He knew this was chancy. It could either end the fight, or escalate the violence into a shootout.

Still holding the pistol high for all to see, he watched the fighting come to an abrupt end, and wondered what would happen next. In that moment of silence, Lindsay's gorgeous voice began to sing:

"Amazing grace, how sweet the sound . . ."

Trusty Joe added a harmony line below the melody. Creed, easing the hammer down to the safety position, took the higher harmony. The tension drained from the crowd. Luster sang melody on the second verse *". . . when we've been gone ten thousand years, bright shining as the sun . . ."* and Lindsay found a soprano harmony line that brought forth tears.

". . . was blind but now I see."

"Let us set our differences aside now," Luster said, like a preacher on a pulpit. "We are all Americans here. All music lovers. Lovers of life. Lovers of freedom. Children of God. Sing with me, children. I think you know the song . . ."

He strummed a chord and began to sing his most powerful romantic ballad, "Love of All Loves." And the crowd did know the song, and the erstwhile pugilists eschewed further violence for the sake of the lyrics, and by the end of the top-ten hit, every man who had been knocked down had been lifted up and dusted off, and the show went on.

Later, after the gig, while loading equipment into the bus baggage compartment, Creed noticed a pickup truck with Texas plates idling across the gravel parking lot. It was the same make and model of truck he had seen leave the Manchaca poker game in a cloud of dust after the foiled robbery attempt. He went in for another load, entering the back door of The Blarney Stone just after Trusty Joe and Tump carried out a heavy speaker cabinet, each man lifting a handle on the side of the plywood box.

"You think we'll have roadies some day?" Trusty said.

Tump answered. "I hope we get groupies first, then roadies."

Inside, Lindsay was meticulously cleaning and stowing her equipment, pausing often to sip a whiskey sour or to take a drag from her Virginia Slim cigarette. She was always the last to load her equipment out and Creed knew she intentionally made slow progress so she wouldn't have to carry any of the equipment other than her own stuff, and even that she usually sweet-talked one of the guys into lugging for her.

Smirking at the prima donna tactics, Creed began wrapping a speaker chord around his palm and elbow, when he heard Trusty shouting at someone out in the parking lot.

"Huh? Can't hear you, man!" In a smaller voice, he asked Tump, "What'd he say?"

"Damned if I know," Tump replied. "I'm damn near deaf as a post."

"Hang on," Trusty shouted.

Creed heard the speaker cabinet settle into the gravel. Growing suspicious, he dropped the chord he had been rolling and stepped out of the back door. He saw Trusty and Tump walking toward the truck with Texas plates.

"Wait, guys!" he shouted, trotting toward his bandmates. As Trusty and Tump turned to face him, the truck's wheels spun gravel across the parking lot and the vehicle shot out of sight down the blacktop road.

"What was all that about?"

Trusty shrugged. "I think he was asking where we played next. Is that what you heard, Tump?"

Tump shrugged.

"Are you really deaf?"

"Huh?"

"No, really?"

"What? Speak up."

"I said are you deaf!"

"Don't yell at me, man!"

Creed shook his head and walked back into The Blarney Stone. Something smelled fishy, but he couldn't quite put his finger on it. He could feel his hackles rising, like a wolf scenting a rival. Just then, Kathy stormed out of the back door of the tavern and stomped toward the bus.

"What's she pissed about?" Creed asked Luster, who stepped out behind her with a wad of cash in his hand.

"Oh, the son-of-a-bitch owner shorted us a hundred dollars."

Creed cringed. "What for? That hole I put in the roof?"

"No. He said we exceeded our unlimited bar tab. Anyway, we got enough cash to get to Vegas. Let's load up, Hoss."

"Forty-Roger on that, Boss."

CHAPTER

"You what?" Franco growled, feeling the surge of anger. He glared at Sling, who was sitting across from him in the plush chairs of Papa Martini's office at The Castilian.

"I almost had him," Sling claimed. "He was walking up to my truck when that guitar player came out and screwed the whole thing up."

Franco jumped from his chair and pounced on Sling, grabbing him by the throat, knocking him out of his chair with a rugby field body block, pinning him to the floor. As the empty chair slammed against the floor, Franco drew his fist back, ready to punch.

"Don't hit me in the face," the underling wheezed. "Not in the face!"

Franco complied by thumping Sling on his broken collarbone, inducing a howl that he quickly choked by clamping the breath out of Sling's trachea. He glared as the idiot gangster wannabe gripped his wrists helplessly, tears streaming from his eyes.

"Your job was to keep an eye on them from a distance. Not to try to do the job yourself. You don't get paid to think. Understand?"

Sling nodded his blue face as best he could with the killer mitts clamped on his throat. Franco turned him loose, got up, and straightened his silk suit as Sling wheezed and coughed on the floor.

"Get up, you bum! Pick up that chair!"

Sling dragged himself to his knees, righted the chair, and used it to pull himself to his feet.

"What did you just learn?"

"I don't get paid to think," Sling said hoarsely. "Only . . ."

"Only what?"

"Only, I haven't been paid in a while."

Franco turned to his father, who had sat and watched the whole confrontation with pride. "You believe this puke, Pop?" He turned back to
Sling. "You've got a room in The Castilian, don't you? A meal card, a bar
tab?"

Sling nodded as he wiped the tears from his eyes. "And I thank you
both for all that. It's just that I need a little cash. I didn't have time to pack
when I left Austin. All I've got is the clothes on my back."

Franco sighed. "Jesus!" He reached into his pocket for his money clip.
"Here," he said, handing his henchman a hundred. "Get out of here. Wait
by the phone in your hotel room. And tell Goldie to come in."

"Yes, sir." Sling strutted out of the office as if nothing out of the ordi-
nary had happened.

"Hard to find good help," Papa said.

"No shit, Pop." He sat back down.

Josh Gold entered the office, lumbering as he grinned. "Morning, sirs!"
he sang.

"Morning, Goldie," Papa said.

"Sit down." Franco waited for Goldie to settle. "Everything ready?"

"Yeah, sure."

"Elaborate," Franco ordered.

"Huh?"

"Give me the details!"

"Sure, boss. I landed two TV news crews from Vegas and one from LA.
A half dozen newspaper hacks—you know, entertainment writers. And I
called in the paparazzi. They're all waiting for the bus to get here. But they
ain't here just for the bus or the old country guy. They want Dixie."

"You let me worry about Dixie."

"Yeah, sure, Franco."

"Did you get the tree?" Papa asked.

Goldie looked at his watch. "They should be putting it on the forklift
right now at the tree store."

"What about the girls?"

Goldie grinned. "Five of the finest top-dollar hookers." He leaned forward with a leer. "These girls are nasty. They'll do anything. And they
look like showgirls! Two of 'em are twins. Blondes."

"These girls, they know the score, right? They've got to disappear after
tomorrow night, right? They know that."

"Their flights are already booked. They're going five different ways."

"All right, good," Franco said. "Now, listen. This is important. If you screw this next part up, *you're* screwed."

Goldie leaned forward in his chair, his palms on his knees. "I'm listening."

"Once we get the Luster Burnett Band in the hotel, I don't want any calls getting through to them from the outside. Keep them busy inside the casino with booze, cards, hookers, food, whatever. I want them happy. And no calls from the outside to their hotel rooms. None. If somebody calls the hotel from the outside looking for them, have the operators tell them they're not here. No contact from the outside, *capice*?"

"I got it," Goldie said.

"I want the theater packed tonight. Give away tickets if you have to. I want this to be the best show that band ever played. Tonight, everything goes smooth. Everyone is happy. Nobody is suspicious. Then, tomorrow night, we grab Junior."

"I hear you loud and clear. I'm on it!"

"All right, get out of here," Franco ordered. "The bus should be here in half an hour. I want this press conference to come off without a hitch."

"You got it, boss." Goldie hoisted himself up on the stuffed leather armrests and trudged out.

"Don't swear on camera!"

"No swearin'! I promise!" Goldie clicked the door closed behind him.

Franco looked at his father. "The tree store?"

"Goldie has a limited vocabulary."

He noted a faint look of concern on Papa's face.

"What is it, Pop?"

"You're sure about all this? Why don't you just off Junior and be done with it?"

"Because there's too much money to be made from this. When this weekend is done, Junior will be dead and our worries over whatever he saw on that boat will be over. But we'll also have a piece of Dixie, and a piece of the old guy, Luster."

"How do you plan to do all that?"

"Luster likes to gamble. My dealers will see that he wins big for a day, then loses everything. We still own his markers. He'll have to sign over his royalties to pay off. Plus, I'm going to record his shows both nights. Dixie's, too. The bootleg money overseas is huge."

"And a legit piece of Dixie? How are you gonna get that?"

"Hey, I already got a piece of Dixie, Pop." He grinned.

"Yeah?" Papa's eyes lit up. "How was that?"

Franco shrugged. "Disappointing."

"Too bad. Anyway, you know what I meant. A piece of the action."

"She's a cokehead. By tomorrow she'll be so wasted she'll sign anything I put in front of her."

Papa grimaced. "It's complicated."

"I can handle it, Pop. Hey, didn't you always tell me that the mark of a real pro was in his ability to turn a negative situation into a positive? That's what I'm doing! Christ, don't worry!"

"All right, all right . . ." He reached for his cigarettes on the desk.

"Pop, are you gonna smoke yourself to death?"

"I'm down to a pack a day. Don't bust my balls!"

48

CHAPTER

Creed glanced in the rearview mirror and smirked at the band members lined up along the bus windows, ogling the fabled city of Las Vegas through the glass.

"Look!" Metro sang. "There's a pirate ship!"

"Complete with grog and wenches, no doubt," Trusty Joe added.

"Grog." Tump echoed in a privateer's voice. "Wenches. *Argh.*"

"Wow," Kathy said, riding in the chair nearest the driver's seat as they passed a casino that looked like an Egyptian pyramid, then another that looked like a medieval castle. "Wow . . . Wow . . ."

"Save a few wows for The Castilian," Creed recommended.

He had played Vegas once before, touring with Dixie Creed. They had filled a smaller casino downtown, and had put on a pretty good show. After the gig, Dixie had dragged him down to The Strip, to see The Castilian, as it was the largest casino in town, with the biggest theater and the hottest stars. From that visit to Sin City, Creed remembered the location of The Castilian, and was able to drive right to it.

He motored up The Strip and turned into the main entrance of The Castilian. A horse and mounted horseman greeted them with a wave, the rider and horse both bedecked in something that passed for authentic Spanish accoutrement. The facade of The Castilian itself was a bad copy of The Alhambra—the famous Moorish fort in Granada, Spain. Flanking the driveway on both sides was a replica of a Spanish olive grove, but Creed knew for a fact that the trees were made of aluminum and plastic, as real olive trees couldn't survive Nevada winters.

"Wow," Kathy said, having saved one. "Pull up to the front, and I'll go in to get the rooms."

"What the hell?" Creed muttered, as he coasted up to the lobby entrance. "Hey, Luster! There's a TV crew out there!"

"Oh, cool!" Kathy blurted. "Free publicity!"

"Oh, no!" Lindsay complained, reaching for her mirror and makeup bag.

Creed soon realized that there was more than one TV crew outside, and they were rushing the bus. This was an unexpected welcome. He killed the motor and followed Kathy out through the bus door, anxious to stretch his limbs after the long drive, even if he had to endure a bunch of reporters.

"Where's Luster?" asked some hair-sprayed talking head with a microphone.

Creed jutted his thumb toward the bus. He turned to see Metro, Tump, and Trusty filing from the Silver Eagle, all of them a bit overwhelmed by the press attention. Finally Luster appeared on the steps where he stood, flashbulbs popping all around him, reporters begging for interviews.

A burly, middle-aged man in a designer leisure suit came shoving his way toward the bus. About the time Luster stepped down to the concrete, the man threw an arm around Luster's shoulder.

"Luster, you old gunslinger!"

"Goldie? Josh Gold? You old so-and-so!" The two of them traded false punches, instinctively hamming it up for the cameras. "Last time I saw you, you were bleeding in the emergency room in Fort Worth."

"No thanks to you. I still got a scar on my cheek, and I ain't talkin' about the one I press against my girl when I'm dancing!"

Bemused, Creed shook his head. "Let's go get the rooms," he suggested to Kathy. "I'd like to lay down on a bunk that ain't movin'."

She agreed and they entered the casino, the smoky wave of air-conditioning hitting Creed in the face as he passed through the automatic door. As Kathy stood in a short line at the reception desk, he looked around at the casino, listened to the endless chiming of bells and rolling slot machine wheels, watched the sad people with cigarettes hanging from their lips, each with a drink in one hand and a handle in the other.

The lobby entrance itself was actually pretty impressive. It was modeled after the gardens of The Alhambra, complete with hanging plants and trickling water sluices running every which way. Creed wondered what it would be like to go to Spain and see the real Alhambra someday.

He wondered if this cheesy Vegas casino lobby even did the real thing justice. He suspected not.

"They actually had all our rooms ready. One for each member of the band. And the bell boys are going to bring all our things up."

"We all get our own rooms?"

"Yeah, and they're all suites."

"Suites? Sweet!"

She gave him one of the room keys, and they walked back outside to round up the band members. Luster had moved into the shade of the porte cochere away from the bus door. Creed saw Lindsay make her grand exit from the bus, wearing fresh makeup and a change of clothes. She seemed disappointed that no one noticed her. She got off the bus and trudged over to join Trusty, Metro, and Tump, who were standing just beyond the media frenzy, smoking cigarettes, and watching Luster entertain reporters with his country charisma.

Kathy passed out the keys. "We all get our own rooms!" she announced, triumphantly.

"I have to sleep alone?" Trusty complained.

"It's Vegas," Tump said. "I'm sure you can hire somebody to sleep with you."

Trusty took the key handed to him. "You sure this is my room?"

"It doesn't matter. They're all the same."

"But it's seven thirty-three," Trusty said.

"So?"

"The numbers add up to thirteen."

"I'll trade with you, Slick," Tump said. "Thirteen's my lucky number."

"I don't know about this gig," Trusty said.

Oh, no, Creed thought. The old Trusty Joe was back, obsessing over some invented worry.

"What do you mean?" Kathy snipped. "This is a great gig. Look at the TV cameras, the luxury rooms."

"Yeah, but how did we get this gig? Does anybody know how we got this gig?"

"Luster got us this gig," Creed said.

"But how?"

"By losing at poker."

"I know who *really* got us this gig," Lindsay said. "And here she comes."

Lindsay's perfectly manicured index finger gracefully pointed a long scarlet-painted nail at the automatic sliding doors as they parted like stage curtains to reveal Dixie Houston stumbling and giggling over the threshold on the arm of some well-dressed guy built like a bodyguard.

"Oh, my God," Kathy groaned. "I can see her pupils from here."

"Uh-huh," Lindsay agreed. "They're like black holes in outer space."

"*Mamacita,* she looks good to me," Metro said. "Oh, no offense, Creed."

Creed ignored the kid. "I've seen her high, but this is a new low in highs." He shifted his eyes to the guy escorting her toward the TV cameras. Who was that guy? He looked familiar. He nudged Kathy with an elbow. "Do you recognize that guy she's with?"

She shook her head. "One of her bodyguards, I guess."

"A bodyguard in a thousand-dollar suit? I know that guy from somewhere." He raced through the memories in his brain, but there were so many shows, so many crowds, so many faces . . .

"This is no time to get jealous," Kathy scolded.

"It's not that. I just know that guy from somewhere."

Dixie stopped and let out a loud, "Hi, y'all!" in her East Texas twang. The cameras shifted from Luster and Goldie to her and the silk sleeve she was clutching.

"Luster, come over here with me and Franco," Dixie slurred. "I want to show you off."

"Franco?" Creed muttered.

Lindsay stood on her tiptoes to get closer to Creed's ear. "That's Franco Martini, the mob hit man. His daddy owns half of Vegas."

"Oh, great," Trusty said. "I'm going to my room."

"How do you know these things?" Creed asked Lindsay.

"I saw him on the news at Bud's Place. His cousin—that mob girl—was killed on Lake L.B.J."

Creed nodded, the memory of the news story coming back to him. "He doesn't look too tore up about it right now."

"Come on, kid," Tump said to Metro. "Let's go to the bar."

"Sound check at six!" Kathy warned.

"Perfect," Tump replied. "We got three hours to get drunk, and three hours to sober up."

"I'm coming, too," Lindsay said. "I didn't get all dressed up for nothing. I see a Long Island Iced Tea in my future."

As the band filed into the casino, Creed shifted his attention back to-

A SONG TO DIE FOR

ward the impromptu press conference. Dixie had introduced Franco Martini as the new primary stockholder in Cornerstone Records, but one of the local news reporters knew Franco's mob rep too well to pass up this opportunity.

"Mr. Martini, with condolences for the death of your cousin, Rosabella, have there been any new developments in the investigation of her murder in Texas?"

Franco frowned and looked at the pavement for a moment. "My cousin was killed by a jealous lover who committed suicide. End of story. That's not why I'm here today."

"But Franco, I understand from F.B.I. sources that a sunken boat was found in that lake in Texas, with a bullet hole in the windshield, and the boat has no known connection to the late Lieutenant Jake Harbaugh, the suspected murderer."

Franco chuckled. "A bullet hole in Texas? Imagine that. Their lakes are full of poisonous snakes, so of course their boats are full of bullet holes." He looked directly into a camera, lowering his shades to reveal his slate-blue eyes. "Stay away from Texas and come to Vegas, folks. It's safer."

The reporters laughed.

"Hey, what about *me*?" Dixie said, only half pretending to feel left out. "This is supposed to be about *me*! Ask *me* a question!" She gyrated her slinky body a little too much for the camera.

"Where'd you find Luster Burnett after all these years?" an LA writer asked.

Dixie draped herself on Luster. "I discovered Luster hiding in Texas and talked him into making a comeback, starting at my show in Houston."

Franco chimed in: "Cornerstone Records recorded Luster and his new band at that concert, and we're going to release it as a live album."

The reporters fired an excited bunch of questions about the new album, the Houston show, the new band . . .

"Well, now," Luster said, "it was actually me who arranged the recording, not Cornerstone. I haven't received any offers from Cornerstone or anybody else for the record just yet. But what better place to do some horse tradin' than Las Vegas? Friends, it's been a long ride here from Texas, and I've got a show tonight, so you'll just have to let me go for now, and I'll see you in The Castilian Theater tonight!"

"Good boy, Luster," Kathy said under her breath. "Oh, that snake, Dixie! I could just ring her little neck! Come on, Creed."

Creed let Kathy pull him forward to join Luster as they entered the casino. What the hell was going on here in Sin City? Dixie and Franco Martini? Franco Martini and Cornerstone Records? Cornerstone Records and Luster Burnett? Then there was the thought he couldn't shake—that he knew Franco from somewhere. He had seen that guy somewhere—in person, too; not just on the boob tube. The realization came to him as Kathy was chattering away at Luster about Dixie and her manipulations. Creed caught her by the arm and stopped.

"I remember where I saw that guy now."

"What guy?"

"That guy with Dixie. Franco."

"Are you still hung up on her?"

"Not her. *Him*! He took our picture after the Houston gig. He said he was a newspaper reporter."

"You sure?" Luster said. "That guy's the second-richest man in Vegas, after his daddy."

"He posed as a newspaper guy and took our picture. You remember? He came around late, and dragged us all off the bus. Kat, you asked him what paper he worked for, and he said he was freelance. He took the picture and wrote down all our names."

Kathy threw her hands up, exasperated. "Creed! Maybe that guy just looked like this guy. What does it matter? We've got a problem here. They're trying to steal our record! Wait . . . Did you just call me Kat?"

Creed smirked. "I guess I did."

"I like that. I always wanted to be called that. Anyway . . ."

As she dragged Luster toward the elevators, Creed heard her invoke the term *lawyer*, and felt a pang of dread sink into his stomach. This is not what he had had in mind for the Vegas gig. Suddenly, he missed The Blarney Stone, Bud's, and even The Red Rooster. Then he changed his mind about missing the Red Rooster. He glanced toward the bar and happened to see the band sitting there. Even Trusty Joe had apparently been dragged in for a drink. He thought about what Tump had said. Three hours to get drunk, and three hours to sober up. Sounded like a pretty good plan.

49

CHAPTER

Creed had found a sweet spot onstage among the amps, where the music enveloped him in a swirling shower of stardust. As he played his guitar parts, he closed his eyes, his head swimming with colors in layered, translucent textures. He felt himself levitating, more like a meditating yogi than a Vegas magician, free from worry and pain, high on a drug only available to the gifted.

The sound system in The Castilian Theater was among the best in the world, and the soundman, who worked nowhere other than this room, knew every speaker, every cable, every corner, and every theater seat. Monitors and side fills gushed a perfect torrent of instrumentation and vocals that twisted into a whirlpool above Creed's sweet spot onstage and bathed him in vibrations all mathematically calculated to interlock and bundle him up in living satin.

The theater sat eight hundred, but over a thousand fans had crammed in, standing three deep along the back walls. The local fire marshal could have shut the show down had he not been sitting in the front row with a showgirl for his date. As Creed's eyes opened, they happened to fall on that long-limbed showgirl, who was smiling at him alluringly. He smiled back, remembering having met the girl and the fire marshal backstage at the meet-and-greet before the show.

Creed could hear Luster's voice echoing off the balcony, sounding as pure and natural as if singing in a room devoid of electronics, as he belted out the final lyrics of the fourth and final encore. The crowd sprang to its fourth standing ovation, roaring with lingering applause, cheers, and whistles as the band bowed and waved and shuffled, finally, offstage.

"Thank you, Vegas! Thank you, America!" Luster said above the din of adulation as the theater curtain dropped. "We are L.B. and The Pounders! Stick around for Dixie after the intermission!"

Backstage, the buzz of the near perfect show continued to resonate. The theater sported a lavish green room, albeit painted blue. Creed swirled into it with his band, ignoring the jealous sneers and halfhearted compliments of Dixie's band members, who were not looking forward to following the performance of The Pounders.

The green room included not one, but two full bars, and a buffet heavy with hors d'oeuvres. Five of the sexiest women Creed had ever seen in his life were working as barmaids, supplying drinks to The Pounders, and Dixie's band members. They were dressed in low-cut and short-skirted cocktail waitress dresses, nylons, and high heels, and they smelled of enough sweet perfume to cut through the backstage tobacco smoke. Two of them were identical twins—perfectly gorgeous blondes named Clarice and Sharice.

Dixie's band members reluctantly filed out, heading for the stage to tune up. Creed spent some time huddled with Luster and the band, all of them reveling in their performance as they slammed drinks, and laughed idiotically with pure, delirious joy. Eventually, the boys in the band became distracted with the barmaids. Tump and Trusty Joe gravitated toward the friendly blond twins who became their own personal, one-on-one barmaids. Creed politely rejected a thinly veiled offer from a redhead to join him later in his room.

"You must have it bad for Kathy Music," Lindsay said, stepping up close to Creed. "You just shot down the hottest redhead in Nevada."

Creed shrugged. "Not my type."

"That girl is anybody's type."

"Even yours?" he hinted with a sly grin.

"Miss Lindsay don't swing that way. But if I did . . ."

He laughed. Everything seemed funny right now in the giddiness following the show.

"You'd think that with all this eye candy they provided for you boys in the band, that they would have arranged for just one African prince to serve Miss Lindsay." She propped her hand on her hip and snaked her neck as she spoke, seething with sexy attitude.

"Clearly they could see that you don't need any help. What prince could possibly resist you?"

Her smile seemed to fill the whole room. "Oh, Creed, you sweet-talking Romeo. You better hush your mouth."

He grinned and wondered where Kathy was, then remembered she had arranged to set up a booth in the lobby to sell the new live album, a thousand copies of which had been flown in from Nashville and had arrived this afternoon. He took another drink from the redhead, who didn't seem the least bit discouraged that he had shrugged off her advances. *Can you just imagine?* he thought. Luster was entertaining two brunettes at the bar with rustic palaver. Metro had been willingly cornered by an unusually tall Asian girl who leaned all over him at the other bar.

Just when he started thinking this was all too good to be true, he remembered that he wasn't getting paid, as the band had taken the gig to pay off Luster's gambling debts, which had been bought up by Josh Gold, who was supposedly the casino manager and part owner. About the time reality started to sink back in, the door to the green room opened to admit Dixie and that guy, Franco. Dixie was wiping something away from her nose, wobbling a bit on her platform show shoes. Her outfit rivaled one of Elvis's costumes for pure ostentatious flare—a pink jumpsuit adorned with hundreds of sequins. Maybe thousands.

"Not bad, boys!" she blurted, her voice a harsh intrusion.

"Boys?" Lindsay replied.

"You, too, sugar plum." She waved the back of her hand at Lindsay.

Lindsay turned to Creed and mouthed *Sugar plum?*

Kathy came bursting into the green room suddenly. "I think everybody in the audience bought an album!" she sang.

"Then I'm sure you'll be sending the money to my manager, since I own the record!" Dixie demanded.

"Actually, we've conferred with our lawyers, Dixie, and since you don't own the sound system through which the album was recorded, you don't own the album. You contracted the sound company. They've already given us permission to release the record. So has the production company that booked you into Houston. This record is ours, not yours."

Dixie seemed unfazed. "We'll just see about that. My lawyers eat lawyers like yours for breakfast."

Franco raised a hand. "Now, ladies, this is no time to discuss business. Dixie, you have a show to put on."

"That's right. I have a *kick-ass* show to put on. Luster, I want you onstage, just like in Houston. Creed, you too, hotshot."

"No," Creed said, a bit surprised to hear his own voice.

"What do you mean *no*? You're turning Dixie Houston down?"

Right now he couldn't remember why he had ever fallen in love with her. He only knew that was a long-gone thing of the past. "I'm done for the night. It's your stage now."

Dixie tossed her head. "Luster?"

Luster turned on his bar stool. "I'll sing the song with you, Dixie. Now, go on out there and knock 'em dead."

"That's more like it," the starlet said, turning to weave her way out the door, through the wings, and onto the stage.

Franco chuckled when she exited the green room. "Whew!" he said. "Sassy." He took a step toward Creed and stuck out his hand. "I didn't get a chance to greet your band earlier, what with the media and all. Franco Martini."

Creed felt the man's heavy-handed grip. "Don't I know you from somewhere?"

"I get that all time. I've got one of those plain faces. I look like a lot of other dopes." Franco took Lindsay's hand next and kissed her knuckles, then continued to make the rounds, introducing himself. "I hope you all are enjoying the hospitality of The Castilian. If you need anything, just say so, and my girls will provide for you, right ladies?"

"Yes, sir, Mr. Martini," they all sang in unison.

Franco came to Tump. "Franco Martini. Pleased to make your acquaintance."

"Tump Taylor."

"Funny stage name. Tump." He went on to the fiddler. "Franco Martini, welcome to The Castilian."

"Thanks," Trusty Joe said, seemingly reluctant to shake Franco's hand, but doing so anyway.

"I didn't get your name."

"Trusty Joe Crooke."

"Another amusing stage name. Crooke? Is that your real name? I've known some crooks in my time." He laughed at his own lame pun.

"I was born Joe Crooke," the fiddler claimed. "The *Trusty* part is for the stage. Get it? It's an oxymoron."

"You calling me a moron?" Franco said.

"No, I said *oxy*-moron."

"I'm kidding. Relax, Joe." He slapped the fiddler on the shoulder with an open palm.

Trusty choked back a gag.

Creed could hear the band members testing their amps onstage. Dixie's set was about to start.

"So, Luster," Franco said. "May I call you Luster?"

"Sure."

"Dixie seems to think you should be touring with her for Cornerstone, opening her shows."

"Luster Burnett is not an opening act," Kathy said.

Franco shrugged innocently. "He was here tonight. And tomorrow, right?"

"Yes, but not after this weekend. Luster is a headliner."

"L.B. and The Pounders," Luster corrected.

Franco acquiesced with a nod. "I wish you luck with that. What do I know from headliners and opening acts? I run a casino, right? Speaking of . . . I've set up a friendly poker game with some high rollers in the private card room. I understand you two like to play." He pointed hand pistols at Luster and Creed.

"Sure," Luster said. "We'll be there as soon as I sing the one song with Dixie."

"Beautiful. I, myself, will be playing as well, so go easy on me. I know you boys from Texas don't mess around." Franco nodded good-bye and walked casually from the green room.

As soon as the door shut, Kathy began jumping up and down like a cheerleader. "We sold hundreds of records! I lost count!"

"Good," Tump said, one of the blond twins draped all over him. "I'm gonna need a draw."

50

CHAPTER

Creed tossed in his king-sized bed, his heart beating furiously. He tried to wake himself from the dream, a recurring one. He was back at Fire Base Bronco. Flames engulfed the hooch and he knew the enemy was waiting to shoot him down when he bolted out through the only door. Then that face appeared in the window. But this time it wasn't the old, familiar face of some farmer's son sent into battle. It was Franco.

He blinked hard and shook his head as he woke, gasping and sweating. He had to pee something fierce. The room was dark, but he could see daylight around the edges of the opaque curtains, designed for night owls who like to sleep all day. He glanced at the clock. Almost noon.

Nightmares at noon, he thought. *Not a good omen.*

He got up and cracked the curtains, smiled as he thought about the show last night. He trudged to the bathroom, fumbled for the light switch. His smile grew as he thought about the poker game with Franco, Goldie, Luster, and a couple of other high rollers who claimed they were from Brazil and Canada, respectively. He had won several thousand dollars last night. Luster had won even bigger. The game was supposed to resume at two o'clock this afternoon.

He flushed and yawned as he went back to the curtains and opened them wider, letting in the glaring Nevada sunshine. He sighed as he remembered walking Kathy to her room last night. He recalled almost kissing her at about three o'clock in the morning. His lips had been heading straight for hers, but he swerved at the last instant, and wrapped his arms around her in a lingering hug instead. Her hair was softer than he had imagined. She smelled like an actual woman, as opposed to a bottle of perfume, and he had liked that. He shivered and rolled his eyes back in his head, recalling how her body had felt in his arms. Soft, yet firm.

He had run his palm down her arm to her wrist. He remembered her skin so perfectly smooth that he was reminded of a sanded and varnished rosewood guitar neck somehow warm and alive in his grasp. And there, he had left it. Was he crazy? He could have invited himself in. She would not have refused him at that point.

He rubbed his eyes. No, it was better this way. By three in the morning they were both exhausted and more than a little tipsy on free casino drinks. And then there was the band and the unwritten rule about relationships therein. For now, it was better that he had woken up alone. But there was something waiting in the future. He couldn't shake that feeling. He was not going to let Kathy Music slip away on account of a band—even one as special as The Pounders. He could feel a change in the wind. It sort of spooked him, but he was ready for it.

Showered and dressed, he headed out of his room for a late breakfast. He heard a door open, and looked up to see that tall Asian girl from backstage exiting the room next door—Metro's room. Metro, all misty-eyed, said good-bye to the girl, then noticed Creed. The girl left, and Metro smiled at Creed.

"I love my life," he said.

Creed glanced at the girl walking away. "I wouldn't get used to it."

"I love rock and roll."

"We're a country band, Metro."

"I love you, too, man."

"Right."

"No, really. I love you, man."

"All right, little brother. Get some rest."

After an extravagant brunch in The Castilian's gourmet restaurant, Creed went to the bar for the best bloody mary he had ever tasted. When Kathy surprised him by sitting on the bar stool beside him, he felt his heart double-shuffle. She looked fresh as a dewy rose and smelled of lavender bath soap.

"Thanks for walking me to my room last night," she said, staring into a tequila sunrise. "That was very sweet."

Other than that, she didn't speak of their personal relationship, or lack thereof. Creed had to wonder what she had meant by *"sweet."* Sweet as in touchingly intimate, or sweet as in wimpy, or maybe even gay. Was she wondering if he liked guys instead of girls? Or maybe she thought he was impotent or something.

One-by-one, the rest of the band gathered in the bar by early afternoon, Lindsay rolling her eyes at the thinly veiled boasts the guys made of their recent overnight conquests.

"I hope you boys protected yourselves," she said, shaking her head. "Those girls were not fresh off the farm."

"You make a damn fine bloody mary," Tump said to the bartender, ignoring Lindsay's belated admonition.

"No shit!" Metro agreed. "This is the best bloody mary I ever had in my whole mouth!"

Tump shook his head. "It's life, kid. My whole *life*."

Metro raised his glass. "Life is good. I love my life!"

They all toasted life.

"I'm gonna go win some more money," Creed said, throwing a twenty in the bartender's tip jar.

"Can I go?" Kathy asked.

He shrugged. "You're my good-luck charm, aren't you?"

"Oh, well, my-my!" Lindsay said.

"Ooooh!" sang the boys in the band.

"It's just poker," Creed drawled, wincing inwardly even as he uttered the word.

"Poke her?" Trusty Joe blurted. "You barely know her!"

"Grow up," Kathy groaned. "Anyway, what about blondie last night? You barely knew her."

"Her name was Clarice," Trusty Joe bragged.

"No, I had Clarice," Tump corrected. "You had Sharice."

"You sure?"

Tump shrugged. "Not really. What difference does it make?"

"None. You go to screw in a lightbulb, the sockets are all the same, aren't they?"

"Not a left-handed thread in the bunch."

"I think I'm gonna throw up," Lindsay said.

Metro pointed. "Hey, that's Trusty's job!"

———

Creed met Luster at the poker table, along with the gents from Brazil and Canada. Neither Franco nor Goldie were on hand to play, but one might assume they had a casino to run.

"You want me to deal you in?" the casino dealer asked Kathy.

"Okay!" she giddily agreed.

As they played the first dozen hands, Creed was impressed with the way Kathy handled a poker hand. She was full of surprises.

From where he sat, Creed could look out through the large glass window that isolated the poker table from the general commotion of the casino. As he folded a crappy hand, he happened to look out through that glass to see a familiar face pass by the blackjack tables. He only got a glimpse, but he was sure it was the poker game bandit he had shot.

"I'm gonna take a break," he told the dealer. "I'll be back later."

He left his chips on the table and strolled casually out of the private card room until he knew he was out of sight, and then walked as fast as he could in the direction he had seen the bandit disappear. He searched fruitlessly until he thought he had lost the guy. Then he caught sight of him near the front of the casino. He was standing at the lobby door, apparently listening to instructions from none other than Franco Martini.

What in the world? A poker game bandit from Texas was now working for Franco Martini?

Creed stepped behind a nickel slot so he wouldn't be noticed. He saw Franco wave the bandit off. Franco walked away through the casino as Bandit stepped outside through the lobby doors. A shiny black Chevy pickup with a lift package and big mud grips coasted up to the front door. Bandit opened the passenger door to get in. To his surprise, Creed recognized Goldie in the driver's seat.

As the Chevy pulled forward, the pickup truck bed came into view. Protruding from it was a spruce tree, it's slender trunk leaning on the top of the tailgate. A big burlap-wrapped root ball was just visible over the top of the bed. What in the hell was going on?

He tried to make sense of it, then remembered his winning streak back in the private poker room. He trudged back to the game.

"Where have you been?" Kathy demanded, back at the poker table. "You missed it! I've been winning my ass off! Luster, too!"

"I went to spruce up a little. Deal me in."

51

CHAPTER

It was Saturday, and a rare day off for Hooley. He should have gone fishing, but he was sitting at home alone, watching a basketball game on TV. He didn't even know who was playing, much less who was winning. He felt like the loser.

The facts in the Rosa Martini/Celinda Morales/Jake Harbaugh murders would not let him be. He realized that he was obsessed with the case to the point of near insanity. With the discovery of the sporting goods store videotape of Franco buying clothes near Celinda's apartment, he had thought that he had made a breakthrough in the case. But word had come back from F.B.I. Special Agent Mel Doolittle on the decision of the federal judge who had the authority to issue an arrest warrant. Mel had faxed the judge's memo to Hooley's office at D.P.S.

"There is no crime in buying a jogging suit three blocks away from a murder scene." The judge was probably on the mob payroll, Hooley had thought. Meanwhile, Franco Martini was getting away with murder, and was probably stalking his next victim. Hooley couldn't sleep at night for thinking of it. Some poor sap who drove a vintage Correct Craft to The Crew's Inn one night on Lake L.B.J., just to have a few beers, listen to country music, and flirt with some girls, had somehow ended up giving a boat ride to Rosa Martini, a doomed young woman adopted into the wrong family.

The only other scenarios Hooley could concoct was that the boat driver was in on the murder and was hiding out, or had already been murdered by Franco or some other mob hit man. He hoped that wasn't the case, because if it was, he would probably never know, and would go to his grave wondering. He hoped and even prayed that there was someone left in this case to save, more for his own selfish purposes than for the would-be victim. He had let three murders go unsolved on his beat, and his feeling of failure over that fact was eating away at him inside.

He had never felt worse over a case in his career. He had promised those two young women that he would bring their killer to justice. He knew very well who their killer was, but couldn't touch him. At least not legally. He couldn't deny that the thought had occurred: Hit the hit man. It was a shameful thing to consider. Hooley had upheld the law and worked within the system for decades. He didn't believe in vigilantism, and in fact had busted a few self-proclaimed vigilantes. To go that route would destroy a distinguished career.

He had even thought once or twice—though he would never admit it to anyone and would never follow through on it—about picking up his autoloader and going out the way Jake Harbaugh supposedly went. That's how bad it had gotten, and he had no idea what to do about it.

He kicked back in his La-Z-Boy recliner, wishing he could go to sleep and forget about all this for a while. But he could only stare at the sparkled and textured ceiling and mull over the evidence one more time. The thoughts went round and round in a bloody, hazy spiral that looped back on itself and blocked out thoughts of everything else.

When the phone rang, Hooley almost didn't even hear it for the first two rings. Then he fought through his depression, laboriously pulled himself out of the recliner and answered the call.

"Johnson."

"*This is Charles Biggerstaff. Thank God I got ahold of you.*"

Hooley felt a spark ignite in the back of his troubled brain. "What have you got for me, Mr. Biggerstaff?"

"*I've made a huge mistake. My son is in danger. I trusted the guy when he said he was a lawyer for my insurance company.*"

"Slow down. You're not making sense." Hooley grabbed a piece of paper and started scribbling notes. Biggerstaff was almost blubbering with guilt. He told how he had gotten a call from a man who claimed to be a lawyer working for his insurance company on the boat wreck claim. The lawyer had told him not to talk to anyone in order to protect himself from the claimants—the mobsters related to the victim.

"*Then I didn't hear anything, so I called my insurance agent. He said no claim had even been filed. There was no lawyer working for me. I realized I was tricked by the guy on the phone who said he was the lawyer assigned to my case. I realized maybe he was a Mafia guy.*"

"I need to know what all you told the guy on the phone—the guy who said he was a lawyer." Hooley demanded.

"I told him I thought maybe my son had been driving the boat that night. He had a key to the lake house."

"What's your son's name?"

"Charles Biggerstaff Jr., but . . ."

"Address?"

"I don't know."

"You don't know your son's address?"

"We had a falling out a long time ago. We haven't spoken in years."

"We need to find your son!" Hooley said.

"I know! He changed his name."

"To what?" Hooley made a note of the peculiar name.

"He's a musician. It's his stage name. I had forgotten it, but my wife dug it out of some old newspaper clippings. We called some musicians Charles used to know in Austin, and finally somebody told us that he's now playing in a band with Luster Burnett."

"I'll be damned," Hooley said, recalling that Luster was making a comeback.

"We tracked down the booking agent for the band. The agent said they're in Vegas. They're in Las Vegas right now, playing at The Castilian!"

"Shit!" Hooley said. "Did you call the hotel? Did you try to reach your son?"

"They said he wasn't there. They said the band wasn't there. But the booking agent insisted they played last night, and will again tonight."

"Don't call the hotel again," Hooley said. "We don't want them to know that we know."

"Should I call the Vegas police?"

"No! The mob runs everything in Vegas."

"Then I'm going out there myself."

Hooley looked up at the clock. It was late afternoon. "Can you get a flight this late?"

"I have my own company jet. I'm calling from Houston Hobby Airport. I'll be taking off as soon as they gas up my jet."

"Do you fly into the Horseshoe Bay airport when you go to your lake house?"

"Yes."

"I'll be waiting for you there. You don't want to mess with these bastards on your own."

"Okay. I'll pick you up. I'll be there in less than an hour."

"I'll be waiting." Hooley hung up the phone. "Please, God," he said. "Help me save this poor dumbass." He dialed in the numbers for Mel's spy phone. After some clicks and pops, and some static, the thing actually started to ring.

"Doolittle."

"This is Hooley. Where the hell are you right now?"

"Bored shitless. Stakeout in Reno."

"Get your ass to Vegas. Now! Pick me up at the airport. Private jet. Biggerstaff came clean. You copy?"

"Vegas? Now?"

"Yes! Wait at the airport!" He was shouting into the phone, as if that would help force the transmission through. "Biggerstaff's son is Franco's next victim!"

"I'll meet you at the Vegas airport. I'll be there by . . ."

The connection went dead, but Hooley had heard what he wanted to hear. He grabbed his holster and gun belt, his hat, wallet, and keys, and stormed out the door. As he left, he heard the crowd erupt in cheers over some basketball shot on the television.

52

CHAPTER

Creed's sweet spot onstage had shifted a little since last night. Funny how that could happen. Same stage, same speakers. What had changed? Maybe some stagehand had repositioned an amp, or some door was open in the back of the theater. For whatever reason, the best sound mix was a step closer to the edge of the stage tonight, which was even better, as far as he was concerned.

Likewise, Luster was better. He had put on a career performance last night, but tonight his voice was even stronger, his control of the notes sharper, his tone as smooth as an aged whiskey. Luster had also taken charge of the band the last two nights. In the beginning, he had relied on Creed to lead the group, but he had gradually assumed command, calling his own shots, announcing well-thought-out changes, challenging the band members to stray from the rehearsed versions of the songs, shorten a tune, lengthen a solo, heighten the dynamics. Creed saw the brilliance in this, for it kept the players on their toes and interested. The improvisation was fun and challenging.

Now they began the fourth and final encore. Last night, they had gone out with a big production number—a great choice with which to end. But tonight, in a set list change, Luster had told the band before the show that he would set aside "Fair Thee Well" as the final encore. Though Creed wondered about ending with their lilting ballad, he could not argue. It was a huge compliment to him that Luster would close the show with this co-written tune. This was the song, and the sentiment, he would leave to the audience.

Fair thee well
May your good times never end

May you always find a friend
At every crossroad and bend
And may the sun
Shine warm upon your trail
May a fair wind fill your sail
Fair Thee Well

As Creed closed his eyes and plunged into the vortex of vibes he had located onstage, a thought came over him. For some stupid reason, this had not occurred to him before. This song was Luster's good-bye to his fans. Not just for this show or this night, but for all time. This was his wish to his fans and to all of humanity, and his last good-bye. He had them charmed with this wish right now. At this moment, Creed could not shake the feeling that this was Luster's last show.

As if reading his mind, Luster turned his misty eyes to Creed as he sang the last verse.

May your heart
Lead you down the path you follow
May your trail soon and often cross my own
And in the end
When your wandering days are over
May the road you travel safely lead you home

And, then, with the graceful gestures of an orchestra conductor's hands, he bade the band to slow the tempo,
. . . May the sun shine on your trail . . .
so he could sing it alone,
. . . May your good luck never fail . . .
save for the sustaining notes of the guitars and the bass, the shimmering of a splash symbol that Metro tickled with the brushes, and a long low note that Trusty Joe bowed from the strings of the violin.
. . . May a fair wind fill your sail . . . And fair thee well . . .
Now Creed took control of the band, leading them back into the chord progression as Luster spread his arms in a huge embrace to the audience. He bowed, and the fans sprang to their feet, stunned and gratified. Creed kept the band going, for the applause lingered, and lingered longer.

"Fair thee well," Luster said. "May God watch over you and shower you with blessings. I wish you all health and prosperity. And mostly, I wish you love. Thank you, and good-bye!"

With the eyes of all the musicians on him, Creed brought the progression around one last time in a perfectly orchestrated ending. The curtain dropped, muffling a final roar of approval from the theater.

Luster turned. "And to you all . . ." His eyes were glistening. "You don't know how much I love you. I *love* my band." He spread his arms and beckoned his players near.

Lindsay and Metro rose from their seats. Creed, Tump, and Trusty Joe racked their instruments. They all came together in a huddle onstage like a six-man football team, and then locked together, arm-in-arm.

"Thank you for the best show of my life," Luster said. "Now . . . Who wants a cold beer?"

Later, in the green room, Trusty Joe pried himself away from the blond bombshell, Clarice—or was it Sharice—for a private word with Luster and Creed.

"I've been meaning to talk to you both," he began.

"'Bout what?" Luster said.

"Yeah, what is it, Trusty?" Creed said.

Trusty Joe looked back at the beauty waiting for him at the bar. "Not tonight. I'll tell you tomorrow. I need to get something off my chest."

"Sounds serious," Creed said, suspiciously.

"I'll explain it all tomorrow." He turned back to his groupie.

"I hope he didn't go and marry that bimbo in some Vegas chapel," Creed said.

"I don't think that's it. Why would he want her off his chest?"

"Good point."

"You know what really worries me, Hoss?"

Creed played along. "No, Boss. What really worries you?"

"Not a cotton-pickin' thing!" they yelled together.

As if to give them something about which to worry, Dixie burst into the green room at that moment, leaving the door open behind her. Franco stepped in next, as cool as ever. Dixie, not quite as stoned as the night before, but in a much feistier mood, stormed over to Luster and Creed and dragged them both by the arm out of earshot of the others.

"I had a talk with *my* lawyers today, boys, and they assured me that you can't release your live album without my permission. I control what hap-pens on my tour. So, Luster, if you want me to give you my blessing, your country ass had better be on my stage on the third song."

"Now, hold up," Creed warned.

Dixie turned on him. "Hotshot, I'm giving you one last chance to take up where we left off, and take country music by storm. If you ever want a piece of sweet Dixie again—and what red-blooded American man wouldn't—then you had better start playing my tune." She punctuated her demand with an obnoxious finger snap in Creed's face.

"Dixie," Creed said, loud enough for everyone in the room to hear. "I've seen my red American blood ooze between my fingers, and it wasn't for you. I wouldn't stoop low enough to play a note with you onstage. And as for offstage, I wouldn't touch you with a ten-foot pole."

"You don't have a freakin' ten-foot pole!" she hissed.

"After all the coke you've snorted up your nose, how would you even remember?"

"Oh, Dixie never forgets, hotshot! You'll see! You will ruin the day!"

"That's *rue* the day," Luster said.

"It is not!" And she stormed out of the green room, flinging the door open to reveal a wide-eyed Kathy Music, whom she shoved aside as she stormed toward the stage.

"Kat," Creed said, surprised to see her.

Kathy gave the men a thumbs-up and a big smile. "It's about time you two knocked her down a peg or two!" She slipped past Franco, into the green room, and proceeded to the bar for a long-awaited drink, but not before raising her eyebrows seductively at Creed, presumably for the way he had brushed off Dixie.

Tonight's the night, Creed thought. Band or not. It was time. Now he trained his eyes on Franco. He knew he was looking at a reputed killer, but Creed reminded himself that he was a killer, too. "Have you had somebody following us around?" he demanded. "A guy in a pickup truck. He had his arm in a sling a while back."

Franco didn't falter. "I've been keeping tabs on your progress. I'm a businessman. I look for good investments."

"You bought into Cornerstone Records," Luster said. "Are you trying to get a piece of our live album, too?"

Franco chuckled. "That must have been some show in Houston."

"You ought to know. You were there. You took our picture by the bus."

Franco smiled. "You've got a good eye for detail. Like I said, I've been checking you out. I like what I see, and what I hear. I don't want a piece of the Houston album, though. In fact, I can offer a way around it."

"Dixie's not gonna like that," Luster said.

"Dixie hasn't been playing ball," Franco said. "I mean, she's been playing with my balls, but she won't play ball, if you know what I mean? No offense, sport." He slapped Creed on the shoulder.

Creed was neither offended nor surprised.

"How is there a way around the Dixie problem?" Luster demanded.

"I like to listen to good music in the comfort of my own home. So, when somebody plays here at the theater who I like, I record them."

Creed narrowed his eyes at the mobster. "Did you get tonight?"

Franco nodded. "Last night, too. This room is designed by acoustic engineers. Our recording equipment is better than most studios use. The tapes from The Castilian will beat the hell out of your Houston recording. I guarantee you that."

"It's nice to have options," Luster said, forever the diplomat. "But I don't want to jump into anything right now."

"Of course not," Franco replied. "What's the hurry? Tonight, enjoy my hospitality. We can talk tomorrow. But, let me ask you something. That last encore tonight . . . Is that song on your Houston tapes?"

"No," Luster said.

"You're going to want that song on your record. That's a song to die for." Franco smiled and turned away.

Creed could hear Dixie introducing Luster Burnett onstage. "What do you want to do about Dixie?"

"Here's what I want to do right now," Luster suggested. "I want to get a beer, and watch from the wings while Dixie makes an ass out of herself when I don't walk out on that stage to sing with her. Then, I want to play some poker."

"That sounds like a plan to me," Creed agreed.

53

CHAPTER

The cabin door to Charles Biggerstaff's jet, a Cessna Citation 500, swung open. Hooley rushed down the steps, his boots hitting the tarmac together. He saw Mel waving from an unmarked car, the red and blue lights blinking behind the grill to attract Hooley's attention. Hooley trotted to the car.

"We may be able to save somebody's life, after all," Hooley said, buckling on his gun belt. "I'll brief you on the way to The Castilian." He turned back to the jet. "Biggerstaff! Hurry up!"

Charles Biggerstaff Sr. scrambled down the steps and trotted to the F.B.I. sedan. Hooley and Biggerstaff explained the situation to Mel on the way.

"Maybe we're in time," Mel said, racing through traffic for the short drive to The Strip. "I haven't heard any chatter on the radio about missing persons, or kidnappings, or murders."

Biggerstaff buried his face in his hands, and started to sob in the backseat.

Hooley turned around in the front passenger seat, grabbed him by the shoulder, and shook him roughly. "Pull yourself together. We're gonna need you to ID your son."

Biggerstaff straightened up in the backseat, nodded, and wiped tears away from his face.

"Listen," Mel said, changing lanes, weaving among cars. "We can't just burst in there and start asking questions and flashing badges. If this is what we fear it is—if your son has been lured here by the Martinis—then they're bound to have somebody watching his every move until they can grab him and spirit him off. If we go in there causing a commotion, we're likely to rush them into what they had planned all along."

"We should check the theater first," Hooley said. "This time of night, the show should still be going on."

When Mel neared The Castilian, he switched off his flashing lights and pulled into the parking lot.

"Look!" Biggerstaff said. "The marquee!"

Hooley saw the bill: Appearing Tonight. "Dixie Houston" in big letters. "Luster Burnett and The Pounders" in smaller type below.

"He's here," Biggerstaff said.

"Let's hope."

They parked the car in the lot and ran to the front lobby door.

"Theater's this way," Mel said. He led the way in a brisk walk, Biggerstaff on his heels, Hooley bringing up the rear.

Hooley took in the surroundings as they hurried to the theater. Slot machines, blackjack tables, roulette wheels . . . Behind a big glass wall some high rollers were playing poker. He saw a young guy with a pretty girl leaning on his shoulder, an older guy smiling at the hand he had just won, raking in an armload of chips.

"Mel!" Hooley shouted, having stopped in his tracks.

Mel turned back to look at him, exasperated. "What?"

Hooley beckoned him closer. When Mel approached, Hooley tossed his head toward the poker game behind the glass. "That older feller in the poker game is Luster Burnett."

"You're sure?" Mel said.

"I saw him on TV in Austin just last week. That's him!"

Mel turned to Biggerstaff. "That wouldn't happen to be your son playing poker with the old guy, would it?"

Biggerstaff shook his head. "That's not Charlie."

Hooley led the charge into the private, glassed-in poker room.

Creed was shaking his head over losing the hand to Luster. "This is just your night, Boss. Only you could turn a pair of deuces showing into four-of-a-kind." In an instant, Creed's mood changed as he caught sight of movement at the glass door. His eyes focused on three men rushing the door—a tall white man in a cowboy hat, a young black man, and another white guy bringing up the rear. Instinctively, he stood so his body would protect Kat, who had been watching him play.

The tall older guy, wearing a cowboy hat, burst into the room.

"Hey!" the dealer said. "This is a private game!"

"This is a public badge!" the young black man said, flashing a shield.

"Luster Burnett?" The cowboy hat asked.

"Who's asking?"

"Hooley Johnson, Texas Rangers. This is Mel Doolittle, F.B.I. This guy is Charles Biggerstaff from Conroe, Texas. You got a band member in your outfit named Charles Biggerstaff Jr.?"

"No," Luster said.

"Trusty Joe Crooke."

"Well, yeah," Luster said. "Trusty Joe's our fiddler. Is he in some sort of trouble?"

"The worst sort. Where is he?"

"He was backstage about forty-five minutes ago."

"Oh, no," said Charles Biggerstaff Sr. "Forty-five minutes!"

The Ranger waved Luster out of the room. "Lead the way. Quick!"

Luster jumped up and stormed out of the glass room, followed by the Ranger and Charles Biggerstaff Sr.

The F.B.I. agent grabbed the dealer. "You come with us. I don't want you blowing the whistle."

"I don't even own a whistle," the dealer complained.

"It's a figure of speech. Come on."

"What the hell's going on?" Kathy said.

"I don't know, but I better go along," Creed replied.

Kathy went with him as they followed the men out of the glass room. Creed thought to look back at that room before he got too far away. He saw the other poker players—from Brazil and Canada, respectively—heading for the front desk. Heading for hotel security? Mob backup? He remembered Trusty Joe wanting to come clean about something. What the hell was going on?

Luster led the way through a door marked "Employees Only" to the backstage area. Trotting now, down a long hallway, they crossed paths with the hired barmaids who had bedded certain band members last night.

"Where are you girls going?" Creed demanded.

"To powder our noses," said the tall Asian chick.

"Is the band still backstage?"

"Yeah, sure," said one of the blond twins. Creed couldn't help noticing that the other blond twin was not in the bunch. As they rushed by the wings of the theater stage, Creed heard Dixie wailing off-key. She always sang a little sharp when she was high.

When he piled into the green room behind Luster and the lawmen, Creed's heart sank. He saw Trusty Joe nowhere.

"Where's Trusty?" Luster demanded.

Lindsay was making herself a drink behind the bar. Metro and Tump were sitting on stools across the bar from her.

"He was just here," Lindsay said.

"How long ago?" Mel asked.

She shrugged, smiled at Mel, and fluffed her Afro. "I don't know—a minute?"

"Where'd he go, boys?" said the Texas Ranger. "We have to find him, now! For his own protection."

Tump swiveled on his stool. "That girl, Clarice. Or maybe it was Sharice. Anyway, she said she wanted to take Trusty over to her place tonight. They just left."

Over the music coming from the stage, Creed's trained ears heard the rattle and rumble of an overhead metal door slamming against a concrete floor. "The loading dock!" he said. "I just heard the door close."

Now *he* led the way. It was a short distance to the loading dock door where he had watched as the stagehands loaded in the band's amps and instruments yesterday. He got there first, and in the dim light filtering through the wings from the stage, he grabbed the door to lift it.

"Wait!" the F.B.I. agent ordered, drawing his gun. He took his place at the side of the door, along with the Texas Ranger, who was also drawing a weapon. Creed lifted the back of his shirt, put his own pistol in his hand, and noticed that Luster had produced his revolver from somewhere. Creed shoved Kathy behind him and the F.B.I. agent pushed Charles Biggerstaff Sr. to the other side of the door, behind the wall.

"Now!" F.B.I. ordered.

Creed lifted the door in one sudden swoop, ducking under it as it rose, stepping out onto the loading dock. He met the guy he knew as Bandit stepping toward him, lifting an automatic forty-five. He grabbed Bandit's wrist and slammed it against the corner of the cinder-block wall, dislodging the handgun. He followed by striking Bandit on the bridge of the nose with the butt of his own forty-five, rendering him instantly unconscious.

Now he looked down off the loading dock, and everything seemed to slow to a crawl, though he knew it was going to happen lightning-fast.

Surprised faces were looking up at him and the others on the loading dock. One of the faces belonged to Franco, who had a pistol drawn, and was trying to shove Trusty Joe into the backseat of a Lincoln Continental where the blond twin waited. Goldie was there, too, also armed, also pushing Trusty Joe in the car. It seemed that Trusty had been putting up something of a fight. On the other side of the car, an older man in a sharp business suit was waiting at the driver's side door, apparently ready to drive Trusty Joe away.

Creed took all this in within a fraction of a second. Then the F.B.I. agent spoke:

"F.B.I. You're all under arrest. Drop your weapons."

Creed was looking over his pistol sights at Franco, for Franco had his weapon aimed at Trusty Joe's head. Yet Creed knew he couldn't fire, for Trusty and the girl were both in his line of fire. Then the girl in the car screamed.

"Screw you!" said the driver, who had the car between him and the lawmen. He reached into his jacket where a shoulder holster might await.

Trusty Joe took advantage of the fact that Franco was looking away from him, and grabbed Franco's gun hand, sending a bullet through the top of the car and forcing the blonde's scream into another octave.

The driver started blasting away over the top of the car and bedlam broke loose at the loading dock. The lawmen and Luster were ducking bullets and firing back toward the would-be driver of the Lincoln. Glass from the car windows shattered as muzzle blasts lit the dock area. Creed couldn't shoot at Franco or Goldie, as Trusty and the girl were still right behind them.

Franco grabbed Trusty Joe by the shirt, pulled him out of the car, got a choke hold on him, and used him for a shield as he and Goldie began firing at the lawmen, moving toward the back of the car, seeking cover.

Luster and the lawmen were still shooting at the driver, who hid behind the car. Now Luster saw an angle on Goldie, and hit him with a bullet in the stomach, taking him down to his knees.

"Damn it, Goldie!" Luster said, as if pissed off at the man for needing to be shot once again, after all these years.

Bullets from Franco and the driver were flying all around him, some ricocheting around inside the concrete dock area, yet Creed stood his ground and awaited a clean shot at Franco. He saw the F.B.I. agent jump down off the dock and scramble toward the front of the car to get a shot at the driver. Franco was gaining the rear of the car now, which he would use as cover, so Creed followed the example of the F.B.I. man and jumped off the dock to take the fight down to ground level. He landed on his stomach on the oily concrete deck. He saw Trusty Joe's footwear: lizard boots. Franco wore shiny patent leather shoes. Creed took aim and ruined the shine on the left shoe, inducing a scream from Franco, and taking him to the ground as the impact from the forty-five slug yanked his foot out from under him. When he got hit, he lost his hold on Trusty Joe Crooke.

Trusty, free now, sprang to his feet and ran toward the loading dock door, in the process becoming the number one target of the hit men. But the mob gunmen, all under heavy fire now, let bullets fly wild, only clipping Trusty Joe's flesh a time or two as Trusty ran for the safety of the open loading dock door. Goldie fired at close range from the ground, until Luster's revolver finished him off for good.

Charles Biggerstaff Sr. stepped into view. "Run, Charlie!" he screamed.

Creed heard the mob driver swear violently, and knew the F.B.I. man had wounded him. The wounded driver dove onto the front seat of the car, crawled all the way through to the passenger side, firing the last rounds in his handgun at Trusty. The F.B.I. agent scrambled to the open car door, slamming it on the gunman's hand, disarming him.

Now only Franco was still putting up a fight. He drew another autoloader, grabbed the blonde by the hair and pulled her in front of him as his new shield. Her screaming rivaled the gunfire, curdling the blood. The Texas Ranger, having descended somehow from the loading dock, passed Creed, looking for a way to get a shot at Franco.

Trusty was running toward the steps that led up to the loading dock, when a bullet from Franco finally hit him, taking both legs out from under him at the bottom of the steps. Charles Biggerstaff Sr. screamed, "Charlie!" and ran into the line of fire to help his wounded son.

The blonde bit Franco on the wrist, causing him to release her.

Creed heard Kathy scream. He turned to see that she had picked up the gun dropped by Bandit, who had recovered consciousness, and was wrestling with Kathy for the weapon. The struggle took them both to the loading dock surface, where they rolled down the loading dock steps, onto the Biggerstaffs.

Creed scrambled toward them all, pinned Bandit's handgun to the oily concrete, put his own gun against Bandit's head, and pulled the trigger, killing the gangster in a splatter of blood and brains. He realized now that the two cops were closing in on Franco from both ends of the car, so he pulled Kat behind him to protect her. Franco continued to fire everywhere, wildly. Creed clicked his autoloader, realizing he was out of ammunition. Suddenly, Luster was in front of him, shielding him, Kathy, and Trusty.

In his last living act, Franco sent his last thirty-two-caliber bullet through Luster's right lung, and through Creed's, where it lodged against the inside of Creed's rib, short of doing any damage to Kathy. An instant later, Texas Ranger Hooley Johnson succeeded in blowing Franco away with a bullet sent through the back windshield of the Lincoln Continental.

The gunfire ended. Luster fell forward, and rolled over, holding his chest. Creed toppled over to the side. He felt no pain, but knew he was hit. The shock would take over soon, but for now, he heard and saw everything clearly. He could see Luster's eyes blinking. He saw Trusty Joe pick up Bandit's pistol from the loading ramp, and put it to his own head.

"Charlie!" yelled Biggerstaff Sr. "No!"

Great sobs burst from Trusty Joe's chest. "This is all my fault!" he blubbered.

Creed felt Kathy hovering over him, felt her hands pressed against the bullet hole in his chest. Then he saw Luster reach a hand toward Trusty Joe.

"Put the gun down, son," Luster said, in a quiet voice. He coughed and spewed blood, but continued. "This is not your fault. Things are never quite as bad as they seem. Put the gun down."

Trusty lay the gun down on the grimy concrete, and wept, falling into his father's arms.

54
CHAPTER

About sunrise, Hooley looked out through the emergency room windows at the gathering of press hounds who had been ordered to wait at the end of the driveway so they wouldn't interfere with ambulances. In his head, he rehearsed what he would say to them until he felt a hand on his shoulder, and looked back to see Mel smiling wearily at him.

"You sure you want to go out there?" Mel said.

"I can face one last press conference before I retire," Hooley said. They had already talked this over for quite some time, so there was nothing more left to say on that issue. "You performed well under fire, Agent Doolittle."

Mel shrugged. "I'm gonna miss you, Hooley."

"Likewise, sport. Now go home and get some sleep."

They shook, and Mel slapped him on the shoulder before turning away. Hooley doubted he would see the young man again. He pushed the door open and walked toward the cameras. Anxious reporters fired questions about the shootout, the mob figures, the famous country singer. He raised his hands and waited for them to quiet down. He heard Lucille's voice telling him to stand up straight.

"I'm Texas Ranger Hooley Johnson. I have a brief statement to make." He coughed.

"Yesterday, in Texas, I received a tip on a kidnapping and murder plot that was about to take place at The Castilian Casino and Hotel here in Las Vegas. The intended victim was a musician who played in a band with the legendary country music singer Luster Burnett. In cooperation with an agent from the Federal Bureau of Investigation, I attempted to intervene. We arrived as the intended victim was being kidnapped by Mafia members, which led to a shootout. There were a number of casualties." He paused to wait for the camera flashes to settle down.

"Wounded was a guitar player in the Luster Burnett band. His name is Creed Mason. He is in stable condition and expected to make a full recovery from a gunshot wound to the chest. Also wounded was another band member—the intended victim—who suffered a bullet wound in the leg, and is expected to make a full recovery. His identity is being withheld to protect him from future mob attacks.

"The dead, on the side of the Mafia gunmen, are one Joshua Gold, a.k.a. 'Goldie,' a longtime associate of the Martini family crime ring.

"Also dead, the two leaders of the Martini crime ring: Paulo Martini, a.k.a. "Papa" Martini; and his son, Franco Martini. A forth mob associate was also killed. He is still unidentified."

Now Hooley removed his hat and bit his lip. "Also, unfortunately, hit by a bullet while using his body as a shield to protect his band members, was the great country-western music singer-songwriter, musician, band leader, and entertainer, the legendary Luster Burnett. He's gone."

CHAPTER

Creed banked his new Harley into the gravel driveway through the open gate, rattling over the cattle guard as he accelerated toward the pecan orchard and the ranch house that had once belonged to Luster, and was now the home of Mr. and Mrs. Creed Mason. Creed had explained to Kat that Luster had left him the ranch in his will.

The dog days of summer had passed with band rehearsals and studio sessions. The Pounders had recorded the kind of album Creed had always dreamed of making. Even now, he was returning from a final marketing meeting with the record company executives. His bride, Kat Mason, had brokered an enormously sweet deal for the band. The lead single, a Luster Burnett composition called "You Don't Know How Much I Love You," was already up to number ten on the charts, after just three weeks, and the nationwide tour was going to start in New York City next week.

Trusty Joe Crooke had tried to quit the band, but The Pounders had talked him out of it. The record company was providing tight security, and the F.B.I. had deemed the Martini family crime ring now defunct, as all the Martinis were dead, their underlings and flunkies having found nefarious employment elsewhere.

Life had taken on the characteristics of one big blur since the announcement of Luster's death. Creed had been hounded by reporters to the point that he just had to go into hiding, with Kat by his side, of course. Luster would be known ever more as the man who took a bullet for his band, and Creed was honored as the war veteran who took the same bullet to protect the same band. Grassroots tributes to Luster had sprung up nationwide. *Life* magazine had photographed the spreading of Luster's ashes along Onion Creek on his ranch.

All this was accompanied by the fallout over Dixie losing her record deal due to her association with the late Franco Martini, which didn't sit well with country music fans. The live album—*Luster Burnet and The Pounders—Raw*—had gone double platinum faster than any country album in history.

Then there was the wedding, and the secret honeymoon in Hawaii. Then, back to work in the studio, photo shoots, meetings, preparations for the twelve-week-long tour. Given the big-money nature of the deal, Sid Larue had convinced the I.R.S. to settle for a reasonable cut of future royalties, so Luster's estate—which basically amounted to the ranch—was safe. Creed was looking forward to a weekend off with his beloved bride before flying to the East Coast to kick off the tour.

As he approached his ranch home, he caught sight of Luster's new grave marker next to Virginia's headstone. He grinned as he motored into the garage. He looked at his watch. Perfect timing.

"Honey!" he said, entering through the kitchen door. "Kat?"

"I'm on the patio!" she said.

Stepping out, he found Kat catching some rays in her bikini on a chaise lounge. She smiled as she got up to kiss him. "Last chance to tan before the tour."

Damn, she looked good. He thought back to their first kiss, in the I.C.U. Their first night together, after two weeks of healing in the hospital. She was the perfect blend of everything he had ever desired in a woman—looks, smarts, energy, sweetness, and just enough hardheadedness to keep his sorry ass in line. He slid his hand around her naked, slightly sweaty back and pressed his lips on hers.

"How'd it go?" she asked, reaching into the icebox for a cold Schlitz, which she handed to Creed.

"Great. The marketing department is going all out. Shows are selling out. It'll be great." He sat in a patio chair and smiled at her as he opened the beer. "But you know what worries me. I mean, what *really* worries me."

"Not a cotton-pickin' thing," she replied.

He chuckled.

"Hey, I know you just got home, and you've been busy . . . but you promised me you'd find someone to look after the ranch while we were gone on the tour."

"I know." He felt his smile widen.

"What are you grinning at?" she said.

"Your gorgeous body."

"You saw me naked just this morning."

He leaned forward in his chair. "I need to talk to you about something."

She shot a puzzled look at him, lowering her shades to meet him eye-to-eye. "Everything okay?"

"Oh, yeah. I just need to talk to you about that night. That night that Luster . . . died." He couldn't hold back a smile.

"What is it, Creed, you're creeping me out."

"What I'm about to tell you, only a handful of people know, so I've got to swear you to secrecy."

"Do I *want* to know?"

"Yes. Trust me. You're going to want to know this. I've actually been itchin' to tell you this all along, but I was ordered to wait until now—until things settled down in the aftermath of Luster's . . . passing."

"Okay. I promise. I'll never tell. What is it?"

Creed faintly heard the crunch of tires out front and saw that Kat apparently hadn't noticed, as she was intent on what he had to say, and a breeze was blowing in the treetops. "So, I come to in I.C.U., and I look over, and Luster's in the bed next to me."

"Yeah. Tell me something I don't know."

"I'm gettin' there. Luster says, 'Hey, Hoss, pick up that pen and that notepad. I want you to write down my last words.'"

"Yeah. I know that part. So . . ."

"I'm a little groggy from the pain medicine, but I pick it up and say, 'Go ahead, Boss.' Luster says, 'I played my best show ever tonight. This is a good time to die. My final verse is sung.'"

"I know. That's so sweet, but . . ."

"Just be patient, Kat! So, I'm scribbling for a while, and he says, 'Did you get that?' And I say, 'Well, yeah, but now, *did you get that,* will be your last words.

"He says, 'No, I want that other quote I said to be my last words!'

"I say, 'Well, then, say it again, then shut up and die!'

"He says, 'No, Hoss, I ain't really dyin'!'"

"Aw," Kathy moaned. "He fought it right up to the very end, didn't he, baby?"

"No, he didn't die."

She sat on his lap and embraced him. "He lives on in his music, Creed. He always will. But you've got to let him go."

"Actually, he doesn't," Luster's voice said, coming from the living room door.

Creed felt Kathy's body jolt as if shot full of electricity. Then she screamed as if she had seen a ghost and sprang to her feet.

"Good Lord, Boss, I was trying to break it to her gently!" Creed scolded.

"Sorry. I got thirsty." He pointed at Creed's beer. "Do those come one to a box, like a dead man, or do you have one with my name on it."

"If you're name is Luster Schlitz," Creed replied, getting up from the patio chair to reach into the icebox.

"What in the hell is going on!" Kat screamed.

"I ain't dead."

"I can see that!"

"We faked it," Creed admitted.

"Who's *we*?"

Creed started counting on his fingers. "Me and Luster . . . the Texas Ranger . . . The F.B.I. agent . . ."

Luster opened the beer Creed had tossed to him. "We figured it would be better this way, Kat. The I.R.S. doesn't get a kick out of hassling dead people. But they'll be making plenty of revenue off my old tunes through Creed. In my will, I granted my royalties for the live album to my band members. Except for you and Creed, of course, and I wanted you to have the ranch."

"The only catch is, we have to share the ranch with the dead guy," Creed explained, jutting his thumb toward Luster, who took a huge swig of beer from his can.

"Oh, you piece of shit!" Kathy screamed. "I thought you were dead!"

She started to cry, then rushed him, beat him a few times on the un- wounded side of his chest with her fist, and then sobbed into his shirt, wrapping her arms around him, and hugging him so hard that Creed saw him wince.

Creed and Luster looked at each other for a while, a little nervous, until they realized that Kat's sobs were gradually evolving into laughter. She pulled away from Luster and glared at both of them, only now thinking to reach for her silk pool robe.

"You sons-of-bitches," she said, unable to hold back her grin, as she wiped the tears from her eyes. "You are two rotten peas in a pod."

Creed shrugged. "I told you I'd find somebody to look after the ranch while we were on tour."

"But why?" She turned to Luster. "Why did you have to die? Why not continue with the comeback?"

"I gave it everything I had that last night in Vegas. Man, what a show we put on! After that, I couldn't disappoint my band with anything less. I knew I could never top that show. Especially not after that bullet I took in the lung. Here is where I belong. On this ranch. With my wife." He looked out at Virginia's grave site, and his fake headstone beside hers.

"Me, too. On this ranch, with *my* wife," Creed echoed.

Luster grabbed a spare beer out of the cooler. "I'm goin' for a walk," he announced, turning away.

"This is so weird," Kat said.

"Welcome to our life," Creed replied.

A breeze whipped through the cypress tops as a mockingbird scolded Luster for staying away so long. Onion Creek sang an endless chantey over the limestone falls and a bobwhite quail called out in the pasture.

Creed took Kat under his arm and they watched the living legend stroll out to his own grave.